PRAISE

THE FORGER *of*

"Myers movingly conveys the traumas faced by her Jewish characters who flee Nazi Germany only to find themselves caught up in the turmoil of the 1940 Paris exodus and the early months of the occupation of France. Their involvement in Marseilles' growing resistance movement highlights the crucial work of Varian Fry and Donald Caskie who aided the escape of countless individuals pursued by the authorities. In this gripping story of a tumultuous period of history, Myers offers us a vivid and compelling read."

—HANNA DIAMOND, author of *Fleeing Hitler*, and professor of French History at Cardiff University

"*The Forger of Marseille* transports you to interwar Europe where you experience warmth, wine, and song in the cafés of Paris and also discover skills the forger must master to rescue Europe's victims. In her historical novel, Myers reveals important figures such as Varian Fry who saved thousands, and points an accusing finger at France as it capitulates to occupation and betrays its citizens. A lesson for nations of today and a call for peace through art."

—JUDITH BERLOWITZ, author of *Home So Far Away*

"This well-paced story of an artist-turned-forger in WWII-era France weaves fictional characters with real-life people in a novel of gripping authenticity."

—BARBARA STARK NEMON, author of *Even in Darkness* and *Hard Cider*

"In this carefully researched and crafted novel, *The Forger of Marseille*, Linda Joy Myers tells the story of resistance by those who risked their lives to save others—one of the few bright spots in the Holocaust. While accurately portraying what went on in France in 1940, Myers weaves elements of love, tension, art, music, and the gradual unfolding of her characters as they begin to trust one another. Myers draws the reader in with her descriptive prose and insight into what individuals endured during that horrific time."
—MERLE R. SAFERSTEIN, former Director of Educational Outreach, Holocaust Documentation & Education Center, South Florida

"*The Forger of Marseille* is a historical gem! Myers delivers an absolute page-turner with just the right amount of suspense and laced with a gripping love story. The historical detail, pitch-perfect prose, and realistic dialogue makes this one unputdownable. You'll be thinking about these characters long after the last page is finished. Highly recommend!"
—MICHELLE COX, author of the Henrietta and Inspector Howard series

THE FORGER
of MARSEILLE

THE FORGER
of MARSEILLE

A Novel

LINDA JOY MYERS

SHE WRITES PRESS

Published 2023
Printed in the United States of America
Print ISBN: 978-1-64742-231-8
E-ISBN: 978-1-64742-232-5
Library of Congress Control Number: 2022923893

For information, address:
She Writes Press
1569 Solano Ave #546
Berkeley, CA 94707

Interior Design by Tabitha Lahr

She Writes Press is a division of SparkPoint Studio, LLC.

This book is dedicated to democracy and to everyone who works, sacrifices, and fights for freedom.

$\mathcal{C}$ontents

$\mathcal{P}art$ 1

Those who cannot remember the past
are condemned to repeat it.
—George Santayana

The Reich

Berlin, 1938

Red and black swastika flags crack in the wind like gunshots. Fascists on streetcorners bark the glory of the Reich while the Schutzstaffel (SS) strut in black death's head caps and knee-high boots. Hitler Youth sport knives at their belts and harass Jews on the streets.

At any moment, the Gestapo could knock on the door.

The sun was low as Sarah rushed out of the store where she'd managed to buy a small piece of cheese and a potato for dinner. It would be a long walk home, but since the enactment of the Blood Laws, buses in Berlin were no longer safe. She'd just rounded a corner near the café where she and her mother used to enjoy hot chocolate on Sundays. Now a sign on the wall announced *No Jews allowed.*

She felt their eyes on her. The Hitler Youth. Boys who played war games, wearing uniforms that imitated the Sturmabteilung (SA), the thugs of the Reich. Now nineteen, she sometimes marveled that for so many years she'd avoided being the focus of their menacing attention. But on this day they surrounded her like wolves on a hunt, growling from deep in their throats.

1

"Ah, young lady, you got something for us in the bag? How about underneath your coat?"

They pushed her into an alley, then shoved her against a brick wall where they took turns grabbing and groping. Sarah pushed blindly at hands and arms, her cries of "*No! Stop!*" muffled by the leader's mouth pressed hard against hers as he thrust his hand up her dress. She struggled as he slid his rough fingers along the bare skin of her thigh.

A harsh male voice sliced the air. "*You! Get away—leave her alone!*" And as suddenly as it had started, the pack of young Nazis scrambled off, leaving her stunned and her clothes in disarray. Who had stopped them?

She smoothed her dress and wiped tears from her cheeks. When she felt she'd pulled herself together, she looked up and met the piercing eyes of a handsome young man in a Nazi uniform. Unlike the idealized Nazi with blond hair, his hair was black and his eyes were dark as a moonless night.

"It's all right, Miss. They're gone."

She tried to fix her mussed hair, not sure what to do next.

"I'm sorry for your troubles," he said, sounding genuinely regretful.

Sarah wanted desperately to run home, but she knew that this man was expecting gratitude. Trying to control the tremble in her voice, she looked up and said, "You are so kind. I don't know what might have happened if . . ." then her voice trailed off. What did he want?

His lips formed a smile, but his eyes were lifeless. He pressed a hand against her back and said, "I'm Captain Schmidt, and now you are safe. Come, please. Let me get you a drink. I'm sure you could use something after such a terrible ordeal." He gestured to the café across from the alley.

Sarah's heart raced, and she took quick, shallow breaths,

hoping to conceal her fear. "I must hurry home," she said. "I'm late, and my mother is expecting me."

He grasped her elbow and began to push her along the alley toward the street as if she hadn't said a word in protest. "We won't be long. Let's relax. Get to know each other."

His words sent a chill down her body, and her heart thumped at the sight of the café's *No Jews allowed* sign. He didn't care that she was Jewish? Or he didn't know?

Once inside, he gestured to the host, commanding a table in the corner, then pulled out a chair for her and murmured, "A fine young woman like you needs protection."

She would be polite. She would drink quickly, then insist that she must go home.

He ordered hot chocolate and sponge cake. She tasted the hot chocolate and nibbled at the cake, playing her part, smiling and nodding at his small talk about the neighborhood and how the great Reich was going to create an even better Berlin. She sipped the last of the hot chocolate, stood up, curtsied, and thanked him politely as she turned toward the door.

He grabbed her hand. "Why leave so soon?" he said, brushing a curly strand of hair from her forehead. "We're only beginning to become familiar."

Her muscles tensed, and she suppressed a gasp at the idea that he felt free to say such things and to touch her. This was the kind of man who did as he pleased. She tried to show no fear as she let go of his hand and smoothed the section of hair he'd touched. "I must help my mother. She's ill. It's pneumonia." She moved a few inches away, but he'd boxed her in.

"Your father can care for her." His face was so close she could see the pores of the evening beard that darkened his face, and his breath was heavy with tobacco. She turned away, but still he was so close.

"My father is no longer with us." She prayed he wouldn't ask questions.

"Ahh," he said with a sneering smile, "all the more reason I must keep a close eye on you. We shall visit the museums, you and I. We will . . ."

". . . My mother—please, she needs me." Sweat ran down her ribs. It was disgusting, his offer. *Art with a Nazi?*

His smile disappeared, and his cold eyes seemed to look right through her. He snatched her purse from the table, yanked out her identity papers and studied them. She held her breath.

"Ah, who have we here? *Sarah Rosen.*"

What did he have in mind now? Maybe she could disarm him with charm. Flashing a smile that she hoped didn't look forced, she asked, "Are you surprised?"

He looked her up and down. "I didn't guess, but I suppose I should have. The Hitler Youth seem to know who the Jews are, don't they?" He shook his head and grinned, as if proud of the young thugs for their powers of detection.

Sarah's heart was beating fast as she said, "I'm here with you in a café that doesn't accept Jews. What will happen to us?"

"*Us*, you say?" He closed the identity papers and clenched them in one hand. "Yes, you're illegally here with me, but don't worry, we can work something out. So 'Sarah' is your given name?"

"Yes," she replied quietly. She felt sorry—even a bit guilty— that Jewish women not named Sarah were forced by law to add *Sara* to their documents.

He smiled, this time in a way that made her shiver. An oily smile that brought a glint to his eye. "Please call me Kurt. About your identity documents—you're in luck to have just met me. Tomorrow, yes, it happens to be tomorrow that all Jews will have a red *J* stamped on their identity papers and passports. But you won't have to worry." He paused to look at her again and reached for her hand. "What shall we do about this, Sarah? Perhaps I could help you, if you let me."

Sarah guessed the cost of this "help." She lifted her head and smiled. She'd play along—what choice did she have? "Kurt," she said softly, practically wincing as she said his name, "you make me wonder what exactly you're suggesting."

He stood up. "I'm so pleased that you're in agreement. I'll see what I can do. We can meet tomorrow and discuss all this. Better yet, I'll send a car to your home," he said, opening her identity card and checking her address. "I can give your mother assurances that you will be well taken care of."

Sarah felt a surge of dread that now he knew where she lived, but she smiled and said, "All right. I'd be happy if I could go home, please. I really am late, and my mother will be worried."

She stood up abruptly and scooted away from the table. Then she stopped and turned to him. "I'll need my papers."

Kurt pursed his lips, no doubt working out what course of action would get him what he wanted. He handed her the papers, and in that moment Sarah decided she'd try to pacify him with feigned interest and figure the rest out later.

His driver was waiting by the car, a tall, uniformed man wearing a cap. He nodded at her and bowed slightly as he greeted the officer. Was that a smile on his face?

They settled in the back seat of the shiny black sedan, and right away it began—his hands, his lips, his indecent whispers in her ear. She held back as much as she could, hate sizzling in her chest as she allowed him to busy himself kissing her cheek and her neck. And then slowly, her lips.

Then she felt something alarming. She'd never been kissed like that, and against her will, her body began to respond in a way she didn't understand. She felt a warm sensation rise from her legs to her stomach, which made her lean toward him and kiss him deeply. Then her mind called her back, *What are you doing?* as her body trembled in response to his searching lips. This was so very wrong. She felt hot—was it shame? She got hold of herself and pulled away from him. What was happening? She'd never been kissed, not in the passionate way a man kisses a woman, and now she felt that something had been unleashed inside her.

Pretending to cough, she opened her purse to find her handkerchief, then blew her nose, trying to draw out the acts of dabbing her nose and smoothing her hair. She didn't want his lips on her again. Her own body had betrayed her.

He leaned back in the seat, smiling. "My, you're a live one, aren't you? I can see we're going to have a *very* good time. Let's say I'll come by tomorrow at seven in the evening. You can tell your mother to prepare to meet your new friend."

The car pulled up in front of her apartment. Sarah could feel her face burning from shame and confusion, and she said a fast goodbye, then tripped as she ran up the stairs. She pressed herself against the wall of the building as she watched the car pull away, disgusted and shocked. Disgusted with him, disgusted with herself. She would never speak of what happened—not fully—but she had to tell her mother something.

Sarah held onto her composure until she was inside her home with the door closed. Then came the explosion of tears. Through a flood of anguish, she dashed into the living room. "Mama! Help me! Please! *Mama!*" She collapsed on the sofa, her face buried in her hands as she cried.

Her mother sprinted down the stairs and threw her arms around her sobbing daughter. "Sarah! What is it? Tell me what happened! Are you hurt?"

Sarah sat enveloped in her mother's arms and cried deep wails that stole her breath. Then she grew quiet, pulled away, and looked into her mother's terrified eyes. In between gulps of breath she said, "Mama, I was attacked . . . I was . . . they, the Hitler Youth. They . . . pushed me into an alley and . . . and . . . they touched me."

"Oh no! Are you all right?"

"I'm . . . not hurt. I'm fine. But there's more." She could see in her mother's eyes a tortured combination of fear and confusion, so she let her story tumble out in a frenetic ramble. "A Nazi officer stopped them—he drove those horrible boys out of the alley but then he made me have coffee with him, and he grabbed my papers and saw that I'm Jewish. When he drove me home, he started kissing and grabbing me and said that he'll be back tomorrow night so we can get to know each other much better." When she pictured herself kissing the Nazi and remembered the surge she'd felt in her body, she began to cry again.

Her mother took Sarah's hand in hers and said, "Sarah, all that matters now is that you're not hurt. Mr. Lieb—he'll know what to do."

"But I can't tell him about this—it would be so humiliating."

"He's loved you all your life, Sarah. Nothing could ever make him ashamed of you. But we don't need to tell him all the details. We need to act quickly now—already he and I have been making some plans. We just hadn't completed all the details."

"A plan? What kind of . . ."

"We'll explain everything. You must be strong. Call Mr. Lieb—*right now*. You need to tell him about the Nazi—that he's coming back. Be as honest as you can, and then I'll speak to him. Right now I must find some papers and our hidden money. Hurry, Sarah!"

As her mother dashed off to another room, Sarah wiped her eyes and caught her breath. And as she picked up the phone, she knew in her bones that from that moment on her life would never be the same.

$\mathcal{D}$read

$\mathcal{O}$n the other side of the city, Joshua Lieb stood in his studio and stared into the German officer's icy eyes. Today he would not look down, he would not look away. Today he stood firm and tall, as if bolstered by the bone and muscle of his ancestors.

The two men stood in the middle of Joshua's studio, a small space overcrowded with the materials of a master luthier. On every surface, every shelf, every inch of wall space were violins, violas, and cellos in various stages of creation—some with open bellies, some with unfinished fingerboards and scrolls.

The stripes and medals on Werner's uniform were dull in the dark room, but his eyes were a piercing blue. "You know that your business can be seized," he said. "Tonight, if I wish."

Joshua didn't know why this time he chose not to cooperate with Werner. Several times before, he'd sold his handcrafted violins—priceless violins—to this sneering German for not even a quarter of their value. But suddenly, it all felt like a knife in his backbone, the idea of Nazis getting his instruments for almost nothing. He knew it was extremely dangerous to try to negotiate with Werner, but still he looked the man in the eye. "Your offer is not enough. These instruments are worth four times your sum. You know this."

As he spoke, he wondered where his bravado had come from. This man had been shortchanging him for months, and Joshua had acquiesced each time, but today something had snapped. The idea of Nazis owning, even touching the extraordinary instruments he crafted was demeaning and painful, but he was also being cheated, cheated by thieving members of the Reich.

"You try to change terms now, when I'm expecting ten violins, *tonight*?" Werner bellowed. "Or do you have a sudden taste for hard labor?" Then he went quiet and narrowed his eyes. He gestured to the luthier's hands. "Dachau would ruin a man like you. You think you would ever play the violin again?"

Joshua tried not to react, but the threat was chilling. He was a Jew in Hitler's Germany. This man was an officer in Hitler's army. An officer, an Aryan involved in commerce with a Jew, which happened to be against the law.

Werner leaned in close and almost whispered, "You seem to forget who you are, Herr Lieb. Perhaps your business could disappear tonight?"

Joshua was sure that standing so close Werner could hear the thundering of his heart, so he looked away from the man and tried to focus on the tools and instruments hanging on the walls of his studio. The aroma of linseed oil and raw wood in the room helped to calm him. Then he took a step backward. "All right," he said as calmly as he could, "you will have your violins tonight, those that are ready. There are two that need more work. They will be ready tomorrow night. They need another coat of varnish to shine like gold." Joshua was making things up as he went, hoping to buy time.

Werner rubbed his hands together gleefully. "The lorry is waiting."

Joshua tried to steel his fury as he gathered up the violins and gently set them in their cases, bidding them a silent farewell before laying them carefully on blankets in the lorry.

The sun had set as Werner slowly peeled away the bills for the violins. "Tomorrow night. Be here—or . . ." Werner grinned and tilted his head as if he'd interrupted himself mid-thought. "I must say, Lieb, for a Jew you're decent, an honest man. But you walk a thin line here in the Reich. It will pay to have a friend like me as things are changing here. We have a fine friendship, yes?" He didn't wait for an answer but headed to his black Mercedes Benz, then turned to face Joshua. "But if you cross me again . . ." He dragged his finger across his throat.

Joshua Lieb stood and watched the car go, his legs shaking. Then from inside his studio he heard the telephone ring. He gathered himself, rushed inside, and picked up the phone with a trembling hand. For a few seconds he listened to the breathless voice on the other end, then interrupted, "*Sarah*? Are you all right? Sarah, slow down. Tell me what happened . . ."

In a tiny studio hidden high in an attic on a back street in Berlin, the forger adjusts his lamps to shine light directly on the documents. He'll work through the night on these papers—the situation is urgent. More and more such urgencies have crossed his table in recent weeks as so many people are rushing to leave.

His colored inks, along with an array of pens, official stamps, and brushes are lined up neatly across his desk. He peers through the magnifying glass at the clerk's signatures on the original documents—he must replicate them with complete precision and accuracy. He must also choose new names for these people. "Joshua" will be first to change—the name is too Jewish. "Lieb" is a solid German name—that can remain. Joshua will now be Josef Lieb. Same initials, this should be a help to him. Sarah Rosen— she will need an entirely new name. Rosemarie—that name would allow her to keep some of her original identity. Rosemarie

Bern—perhaps as Rosemarie, she can distract officials with talk of her English origins.

Erasing old documents and filling in new information is easy enough for a chemist who has formulas, but the signatures require the skill of an artist. The forger's work is the most dangerous underground activity in Hitler's Germany. If he were to be found out, he'd be lucky to end up in a camp. They might just shoot him on the spot.

His name is passed around in the shadows and back alleys through word of mouth. He knows it can be only a matter of time until it's passed to the Gestapo. Still, he works through the night, almost every night now. He wipes the sweat on his brow with an ink-stained handkerchief.

He fills in the documents and affixes the photos. Next, he alters the name on the letter that will admit this new Rosemarie to art school in Paris. He fills out everything carefully, then picks up his magnifying glass and checks his work again and again, then drops the papers on the floor and scuffs them. He looks one more time at his work and then rests the documents on the top of the most urgent stack.

He takes a long breath, sits back, and observes the tower of papers on his worktable. The documents of escape, the documents of hope. Documents that will be examined, scrutinized. Even seized. The horrors to follow such a seizure, he would not witness, but the images that blaze through his mind make him shudder.

$\mathcal{E}$scape

$\mathcal{J}$oshua Lieb jumped at the sound of the knock. He cracked open the door and took the package, keeping his eyes averted as he placed the envelope of cash in the open hand. It was his savings, nearly everything he had. He closed the door and turned back to packing his small satchel. A few pieces of clothing and his carefully wrapped violins. The small picture of his dear wife Lili and the cross she wore around her neck. Then he thought about how dangerous it was to try to smuggle the two instruments out of the country, even though he would be posing as an Aryan—a masquerade he hoped his blue eyes would make plausible. He scurried into his kitchen and returned with several lumps of pungent limburger cheese, which he tucked around the clothing that surrounded his violins. Then he closed his satchel and hoped.

At eight the next morning, blouses, skirts, and sweaters were strewn all over their bedrooms as Sarah and her mother packed, unpacked, and repacked their suitcases. Eva tenderly folded Sarah's favorite sweater in tissue paper and tucked it into her suitcase

12

along with two skirts and a pair of shoes. "This is all we can fit in one suitcase. But you'll be able to shop for Paris fashions!"

Sarah knew that Eva was trying to be brave, to redefine this departure as the start of an adventure, but Sarah's heart ached. Within the hour, she and Mr. Lieb would leave for Paris, but her mother wouldn't be going with them, and this reality was grueling for her. She and her mother had clung to each other since the death of Sarah's father when Sarah was just eight years old, and Mr. Lieb had been like a father to her through the years.

Eva promised that she too would leave Berlin before the morning was over. She would go to the home of her elderly parents, Sarah's Oma and Opa, who lived just outside of Berlin. She promised she'd stay there.

Sarah sorted through the rings and other jewelry treasures laid out on her dressing table, then chose a necklace her grandmother had given her when she was ten years old to celebrate Sarah's first art exhibit. It was a lovely gold heart pendant that had been handed down to her grandmother from Sarah's great-grandmother. She put the necklace on, clasped it, then tucked it under her blouse. Scarcely twelve hours after the attack in the alley, Sarah was operating automatically, as if in a trance. It was all too much, so she was trying to pretend that none of it was really happening, as if this was all just an exercise in theater.

Sarah looked into her mother's dark eyes. "Promise you're going to Oma and Opa's house as soon as we leave, that you won't wait, not even a few hours. Promise you'll be out of here by late morning? Please, I need you to swear you'll do this." Her own words surprised her. Pressing her mother to make promises?

Eva pulled her daughter into her arms. "I will be gone by late morning, I promise on my life. Now I don't want you to . . ."

A loud knock at the door made them both jump. Sarah's heart quickened as she heard a key turn in the lock on the front door.

13

Mr. Lieb burst breathlessly into the house. "I'm so sorry to barge in. I hate to interrupt your goodbyes, but we must go—now." He opened his satchel. "I have everything we need." He pulled out the papers and showed them to Sarah. "From now on," he said, "you are Rosemarie Bern."

She stared at him. "What? Rosemarie? Bern?"

Joshua said, "Rosemarie has a hint of English. It's a good name."

Eva said brightly, "Rosemarie? Lovely name. Back in school, my dearest friend was an English girl named Rosemarie. This is a positive omen, my dear. My sweet Rosemarie."

The sound of her mother calling her this strange new name caused Sarah's heart to wrench.

Mr. Lieb tucked the new papers back into his satchel.

Eva faced her daughter and rested a hand on each of Sarah's shoulders. "My beautiful Sarah," she said, and the words caused their tears to flow again, "only nineteen. So talented. Go and become the artist you've dreamed of becoming. You'll stay with the Rosenbergs, a lovely family, an established family. Don't worry about me—I'll be fine. I'll write to you at the Rosenbergs', and you'll write to tell me all your wonderful stories, *ma belle fille*."

Sarah couldn't bear it. She could barely speak as she threw her arms around her mother. Then she stood back for a long look at her mother's face, taking a memory photograph to cherish.

Eva and Mr. Lieb embraced, made many promises to write, and reminded each other to be careful.

The wipers of the waiting taxi flapped back and forth in the autumn rain. Sarah followed closely behind Mr. Lieb as he dashed to the car and loaded her suitcase next to his. Then they slid into the back seat, and the car pulled away from the curb. She looked back at her mother, standing up straight as she waved, a bright smile fixed on her face. As Eva became a smaller and smaller image in the distance, Sarah strained to keep her mother in view, to hold onto every last glimpse of her. Then the car turned a corner, and she was gone.

Through the rain-spattered car windows, Sarah watched her childhood go by—the park she'd played in but was no longer allowed to stroll, its lush tree branches now spidery and bare of their leaves. The café where she and her mother had spent countless wonderful afternoons but were no longer allowed to frequent. The art school she'd been turned away from. All of it disappearing behind her.

She blew her nose and noticed that the taxi smelled of wet wool and Mr. Lieb's tobacco. The familiar scent of him comforted her as she took deep breaths and willed herself not to cry. They were headed for the station, and she would do her best to look like a respectable young lady on her way to France.

Mr. Lieb turned to face her, making sure the driver couldn't see as he slipped the papers along the back seat beneath his long wool scarf. "Practice," he said and pointed to her new name. *Rosemarie Bern.* He slipped open his own documents and silently mouthed *Josef Lieb, Josef Lieb, Josef Lieb.*

Announcements blared over the loudspeaker—train numbers and destinations, track numbers, the names of people being summoned to the main desk. Sarah tried to stay calm through the cacophony, but her nerves were seared by the sight of the menacing SS in their black uniforms and death's head caps and the Gestapo whose eyes always looked like daggers. The power these men held over everyone drove fear into the hearts of both the innocent and the guilty. Uniformed men swarmed all levels of the station. The travelers appeared pale—how many were Jews trying to escape? How many were ordinary Germans simply traveling? Sarah tried to steady her shaking hands as she clenched her papers and repeated to herself, *Rosemarie, Rosemarie, Rosemarie.*

Mr. Lieb glanced at her, his blue eyes soft with concern. Oh, the risks he must have taken to ensure her safety, to whisk her into a new life in France. Maybe someday he'd tell her how he happened to know a forger in Berlin, how he managed to secure train tickets to Paris.

Her legs trembled under her coat as she approached the steely-eyed officials. At the front of every queue, the hard eyes of men in uniform swept over the crowd, then peered at each face when they inspected the papers as if they could detect illegals with only a glance. Two queues over, a woman fainted and fell to the floor. Farther down, an old man begged to be let through, but the Gestapo punched him in the gut and dragged him away. The crowd went silent at the sight of it, and then seconds later the station exploded again with the sounds of harried, tearful passengers and icy officials who barked instructions over the huffing of the steam trains.

Sarah was next in line.

"Papers, young lady," the official said, sticking out his hand. He asked Mr. Lieb, "Are you together?"

"Yes, I'm her guardian. Off we go to get her enrolled in art school in Paris."

"Ah, Paris." Then he looked back at Sarah. "You don't like the art schools here in Berlin?" A frown appeared between his eyes.

She almost began to tell her story about no longer being allowed to attend art schools in Berlin, but she quickly remembered it was Sarah, a Jew, who could not attend. Rosemarie Bern as an Aryan was free to attend school anywhere. "I, it's that I love French art so much, and I thought . . ."

Mr. Lieb handed a letter to the official and added, "She's been officially welcomed to the school."

Sarah, *Rosemarie*, could hardly breathe, and her face grew warm.

The official glanced at the paper. "All right."

The new Rosemarie let out the breath she'd been holding and thanked the official while flashing a big smile and flipping a curl of her hair out of her eyes—she knew a thing or two about the ways of men.

"Let me see your bag," another official demanded of Joshua. *Josef.*

He hesitated, looking left and right. Rosemarie knew this was a critical moment to see if they'd be allowed to pass. If Mr. Lieb could keep his violins. She tried to convey an expression of nonchalance, as if this was just another step for two frequent travelers making their way back to France. Mr. Lieb opened his bag, and a whiff of air caused the official to gag. He stepped back holding one hand over his nose and snapped, "*What* do you have in there, a dead cat?"

Mr. Lieb opened the bag wider and sweetly asked, "Would you care for some delicious limburger cheese?" He reached for the cheese, but the official stepped back, almost tripping on the platform.

"No!" the man coughed. "Just give me your papers." He quickly opened and closed the documents, then thrust them back at Mr. Lieb. "Next," he huffed, backing up even farther.

As she and Mr. Lieb hustled toward the train, Mr. Lieb murmured, "Well done." Rosemarie felt numb, but she was walking, moving toward freedom for the first time in her life.

The farther from the officials they walked, the easier her breathing became until she took one long, luxurious breath and whispered, "Paris."

The Border

It was invisible, the border, Rosemarie thought, gazing out the window as the train steamed through Germany in a blur of gray and mist. On the other side of the border she would cross, a symbolic marker of her life at that moment, was Paris and a life without the Gestapo. *How wonderful that will be.* She imagined Paris to be a world of gold, pink, and azure blue. But here, as she sat next to Mr. Lieb on the train, the dust and ash of her Berlin life felt like a film on her skin. And her body burned with shame at the way she'd responded to that Captain Schmidt.

Mr. Lieb was humming, perhaps to cheer himself up or to soothe her despite it drawing stern glances from their serious and likely frightened carriage companions. He hummed his favorite tunes: Bach's "Ave Maria" and the first bars of Beethoven's "Moonlight Sonata." Her world appeared in colors; his was filtered through music.

As if sensing her attention, he turned his blue-eyed gaze to her, looking every bit as excited and afraid as she felt. She managed a wan smile and rested her arm on his, enjoying the nubby fabric of his wool jacket. "How long do you think it will take?"

"To cross?"

The woman sitting across from them spoke up. "Hours. They're combing the train for Jews."

Fear stabbed Rosemarie in the stomach. The word *Jew* was lanced with a thousand disturbing images—neighbors fleeing the city, men beaten in the streets and sent to camps. Jewish children who'd been taunted and grabbed and beaten by the Hitler Youth and SS.

The woman across from them in the carriage wore a fawn-colored suit that matched her hair. She sat with her eyes cast down as she gripped her pocketbook. Was she one of the Jews they were looking for? Rosemarie silently repeated, *Rosemarie. Rosemarie.*

She thought of the papers Mr. Lieb had secured so mysteriously. Created in such haste, would they stand up under scrutiny? What clues of counterfeit did the officials look for when they examined identity documents and passports? She didn't know, and not knowing drove the fear deeper.

The brakes of the train groaned, and industrial looking buildings replaced the landscape of trees and fields. Fear rustled through the carriage as people dug through purses and coats to locate their documents.

Mr. Lieb leaned past her to peer out the windows. "Now, the endless red tape." He squeezed her hand. "Just look them in the eye, Rosemarie Bern."

"Monsieur Lieb, I will."

The tall, imposing men in their gray uniforms loomed over the passengers. Outside the window on the platform, a man was on his knees, hands clasped as he begged one of the gray-uniformed men for mercy, but the officials tucked his papers into their file and took him away. A woman with a young child gestured toward an officer who smirked down at her. She cried, "Please, we are French. We are just returning to our home," but two officers dragged her and the child aside to stand with other miserable-looking people on the platform. Rosemarie looked away and focused on her gloved hands. *Rosemarie. Rosemarie. I am Rosemarie Bern.* She opened her purse and pulled out her documents, their leather covers worn and the pages dirty, weathered. Clever forger.

Mr. Lieb smiled, but she could see the truth in his eyes. They were usually a shade of calm blue, but now the sea of his mind was roiling. The two of them linked glances in solidarity. Whatever happened to one would happen to the other—together in this extraordinary venture. Together as they had been all her life.

Mutti. Mother. Was she secure now with Opa and Oma outside of Berlin? They'd agreed to write, but would their mail be tracked?

"Papers, please." A voice cut through the tense silence in the carriage.

The beige woman handed over her papers without looking up. The official frowned, and Rosemarie held her breath. He shook his head, then asked his superior officer to come over. They conferred over the papers as the woman and her husband stared straight ahead. Finally, the official said, "Come with us."

The woman gasped. "But why? We are perfectly legal. We . . ."

"Now. We need to check something."

Rosemarie's panic erupted in her chest. *What were those people suspected of? They looked completely normal. A nice married couple. What would these men think of Mr. Lieb and her? He was listed as her guardian—what if the officials challenged that?*

What if what if what if stoked the out-of-control chemicals in her body until she was shaking again. It would not be good for the officials to see her frightened. She had to get hold of herself. Mr. Lieb started humming again, a light French folk tune, just a few bars. She took a breath and rearranged her thoughts. Rosemarie thought of the academy in Paris where she would soon study art, distracting herself by imagining the beautiful colors of Paris, the art she'd see at the Jeu de Paume, the Louvre. She pictured the lovely trees along . . . "Your papers, please." The official held out his hand.

Mr. Lieb handed over his papers, and the official nodded at Rosemarie. "Yours too, young lady. You're together?"

"Yes, I'm her guardian," said Mr. Lieb.

"Why?"

"Her father died serving his country." Did Mr. Lieb's voice have an edge?

"Purpose for this trip?"

"Rosemarie here is going to art school." Mr. Lieb smiled proudly.

"And you?"

"I've had a business in Paris for years."

"With whom? What is the business?"

"His name is Lucien Fournier, of the Paris Viol Company. We make violins, and as you can see, I've made several trips over the years."

The official's forefinger combed through the lines on each page. He lifted up the documents and peered at each of their faces to compare them to the small image on the passports. Rosemarie tilted her head up and tried to appear cheerful even though just outside the train she could hear someone crying. She tried to ignore everything except her mission of presenting herself as a fine citizen of Germany: Rosemarie Bern, soon to be an art student in Paris. Mr. Lieb handed him the letter accepting her into the academy. The official glanced at it and handed it back.

Rosemarie opened her purse and pulled out a packet of mints. She offered a mint to the official and then to Mr. Lieb. The official's eyes crinkled at the edges, as if he was somewhat charmed. She had no idea what she was doing. Just trying to make it through each moment.

He slapped the papers against his palm, and the impact sounded like a gunshot. Rosemarie jumped.

"The French are right behind me," said the official. "You will present papers to them next."

Rosemarie's spirits sank. Now they had to face the French? She'd heard they weren't very welcoming now that so many refugees had flooded their country to escape Hitler.

"Bonjour, *papiers* s'il vous plaît."

The carriage rustled with the emergence of French officials in navy blue, and when each one greeted them, Mr. Lieb replied in French. Rosemarie nodded and smiled. She'd studied the language for a year in school, but that was two years ago—when she'd still been allowed to attend school. She'd forgotten most of the vocabulary, and her accent was abysmal. She hoped that some of it would come back to her now that she'd be immersed in French every day.

Mr. Lieb handed the official the letter from the academy. "Ah, *oui*, an excellent school. And your purpose, monsieur?"

"My business in Paris."

"What business is that?" He looked down his generous French nose at Mr. Lieb.

"I'm a luthier. I make violins."

"The violin, excellent profession. I see you are a frequent visitor, but not so for you, young lady. Your first visit to France?"

"*Oui.*" Rosemarie flashed him a smile.

"As soon as you arrive, be sure to sign up with the prefect in Paris to register your address."

With a quick nod, he handed back the papers and went on to the next carriage.

She sank back in her seat, clutching Mr. Lieb's arm, exhausted from the tension of the past two hours. *How strange*, she thought. *I'm no longer Jewish.* From here on, she would be just an ordinary German student.

To her relief the beige couple returned to their seats, their eyes the only clue that they'd endured something they'd rather forget.

The train finally lurched forward, stopped and started, squeaked and rumbled. Then the steam flowed in billowy clouds past the windows as the rhythm of the train picked up and began to rock them gently through the French countryside.

Cheers rose up in the car. Someone softly sang "La Marseillaise."

"Now we taste France," said Mr. Lieb. "The promise of *liberté, fraternité, egalité.*"

Rosemarie folded her arm into the crook of his elbow and closed her eyes. She breathed in a long, deep pull of air and let it out, calming her heart rate.

Then her eyes flew open wide. That Captain Schmidt couldn't find her now, could he? Could he follow her trail? He would have been utterly furious upon arriving at their home and finding that she had rejected him with such courage and cunning. To him it would be as if she'd laughed in his face, and that could be enough of an ignition to set a man like that into a fiery rage. How many times would he return to her home? Knock on the door? Interrogate the residents?

But maybe he hadn't told anyone. Maybe to avoid public humiliation, he'd kept the entire incident to himself. But his driver knew. And Captain Schmidt knew. Would that be enough for him to vow revenge? She shook at the thought of what that revenge might look like.

She had to calm down. She had a new name. She was no longer Jewish. She'd be hundreds of miles from him and across an international border. But *what ifs* crept back into her mind, and they were all horrifying.

No, she must stop this. It made no sense that an important Nazi would give her another thought after he vented his anger. It made no sense that a soldier like him would cross into France. She was just a Jewish girl who got away.

City of Light

The taxi driver's cigarette bobbed between his lips as he gave a running commentary on the stupidity of Germany's invasion of the Sudetenland in September and how Paris was now one big traffic jam, thanks to the influx of immigrants.

Rosemarie wondered if the driver resented her and Mr. Lieb as well, but he seemed pleasant enough, calling out monuments and sharing facts about the city as they passed the Notre-Dame de Paris Cathedral, Our Lady of Paris, and the arched bridges over the Seine. She gasped at the graceful way the Seine reflected buildings and clouds and the azure sky. Mr. Lieb laughed at her wide-eyed awe.

As she was growing up, Mr. Lieb would return from his luthier trips to Paris with postcards featuring the Eiffel Tower, trees in springtime bloom, Notre-Dame, and bustling cafés with bright awnings. Sometimes she'd open her box of treasured postcards and imagine being there, standing in front of the Arc de Triomph, settling on a café chair with a book and cup of café crème before her. She could barely believe that here she was, right in the middle of what must surely be the most thrilling city in all the world.

Mr. Lieb interrupted her daydream. "The Rosenbergs are very excited to receive us—I've told them all about you. And of course, you'll join Celeste at the academy."

"I can't wait! Look—the Eiffel Tower! I can't believe it!"

The taxi pulled up in front of an ornate home on a street lined by graceful trees dressed in autumn colors.

"Are you sure about me living here?" Rosemarie asked, suddenly uncomfortable about being introduced to new people. How could she become this new person, no longer Sarah, the girl she'd been all her life?

Mr. Lieb nodded, collected their luggage, paid the driver, and then gently tapped the doorknocker. As they waited on the doorstep, Rosemarie, still very much on the alert, glanced up and down the street. No soldiers. No Nazis.

A slim, vivacious woman with a jaunty red and gold scarf knotted at her neck flung open the door. "Bonjour, Joshua! Welcome back to Paris!" she called out, standing on her tiptoes to kiss him on both cheeks. A middle-aged man with kind eyes and a white streak in his hair and a young woman about Rosemarie's age appeared, beaming with warm smiles. The young woman's face was framed by waves of auburn hair, and she looked chic in her wool sweater and skirt.

The young woman spoke first. "Welcome! Very pleased to meet you. I'm Celeste." Celeste enveloped her in an unexpected hug and kissed her cheeks. Rosemarie didn't know what to do and ended up kissing one of Celeste's cheeks before awkwardly stepping backward.

"Bonjour, bonjour," Mr. Lieb chuckled. "Rosemarie, this is Madame and Claude Rosenberg, and Celeste."

"Joshua, you know to call me Nicole!" Celeste's mother said.

Mr. Rosenberg nodded with a big smile but didn't kiss Rosemarie. He seemed to notice her reserve, and she appreciated it.

She would have to work to become less reserved. Would she ever feel natural kissing people on both cheeks?

Celeste's dark eyes sparkled as she spoke. "Mr. Lieb told us all about you! I can't wait to take you to the Louvre and Café Angelique, where you can get the best hot chocolate in the world. The galleries, the shops! We'll have lots of good times."

"Thank you," Rosemarie replied. "My greatest wish is to visit the Louvre and the Jeu de Paume." It would be a dream come true to finally visit the galleries of the best museums in the world.

Celeste smiled and said, "Of course! Those will be first on our list!"

The family guided Rosemarie and Mr. Lieb into the house. The rooms were decorated with casual French chic, wallpapers in moss green and white. Gauzy curtains billowed to the floor.

Nicole welcomed them to taste the exotic-looking pastries arranged on china plates and offered to pour them coffee from a lovely pale blue enamelware pot. A vase of pink roses crowned the centerpiece on a white tablecloth. This beautiful setting made Rosemarie feel as if she'd walked into a Bonnard painting—sunlight streaming through a window, roses in a vase. Was she dreaming?

After chatting about the weather—the days were cooling now—everyone expressed relief that the treaty Hitler had signed with Britain and France had averted the possible outbreak of war a couple of weeks ago, but would Hitler stop his territorial greed?

Mr. Lieb said, "We must believe, hope, that Chamberlain's 'Peace in our Time' treaty they all signed will hold. Is it possible Hitler will keep the agreement and not invade any other countries?"

Claude shook his head. "The celebrations of the Anschluss in Austria were sickening. The Jews kneeling and scrubbing the streets. The men marched off to camps."

Rosemarie thought of Berlin. The beatings, the attacks on Jewish men. Mr. Lieb looked at her. They both remembered the brutality there all too well.

For a moment, they all sat in silence. Europe and the rest of the world hoped the invasion of Austria and Hitler's acquisition of the German-speaking part of Czechoslovakia would satisfy his greed for territory. But if he pushed for more, the world would teeter on the edge of war.

Mr. Lieb folded his serviette and said, "My friends, I must tell you about a recent change I had to make. For reasons I'll explain at another time, I've had a bit of an identity change. On my papers, I'm *Josef* Lieb. As I adjust to this, I ask my friends to call me by this new name, especially in public."

Mr. Lieb's friends were quiet for a moment. Claude and Nicole shot each other curious looks, and then Claude raised his coffee cup. "Here's to the arrival of our new friend, Rosemarie, and our old friend, Josef!"

Mr. Lieb nodded in appreciation, then stood and said, "And now I must make my way to Lucien's studio. Many thanks for hosting my dear Rosemarie. Her mother asked me to convey her deep gratitude."

Rosemarie stood with him, trying to hide the wrench of him leaving her.

"Art school!" he exclaimed, his blue eyes full of light and love. "Finally, you are here!"

She hugged him close and whispered, "I'll miss you." Then she quickly stood back from him and made sure he didn't see her teary eyes.

He gathered his case and violins and shuffled toward the door, clearly very tired. What an ordeal the last few days had been. Everyone wished him well and told him to visit soon.

"Au revoir." He smiled, turning to salute Rosemarie. She saluted back, not trusting her voice.

She watched him hail a taxi and felt a lump forming in her throat. Mrs. Rosenberg rested a soft hand on Rosemarie's shoulder. "You'll see him soon. We'll have him over for dinner every week."

As Mr. Lieb's taxi drove away, Celeste said, "He's such a lovely man. Now, why don't I take you to your room?"

Rosemarie was touched by the understanding kindness of the two women and felt her sorrow lift just a little.

Nicole and Claude bid her goodnight, then Celeste picked up her suitcase and started up the stairs with Rosemarie right behind. Once in Rosemarie's room, Celeste said, "How about tomorrow we see the Louvre and have coffee at Les Deux Magots!"

"The café of the famous writers and artists?"

"The very one. We'll soak up the genius just by being there."

Rosemarie looked into Celeste's affectionate eyes and experienced what felt like a beautiful moment of understanding between Parisienne adventuresses. Then Celeste set Rosemarie's bag in a corner of her room and said goodnight.

Linseed Oil and Sawdust

Josef Lieb rode in a taxi in the direction of his friend Lucien's studio but asked the driver to let him out at the Notre-Dame Cathedral. For several moments, he stood silently in front of the magnificent building, watching as the setting sun bathed the cathedral in a magical amber light. When he entered the great medieval structure, he marveled at the peace that filled the enormous space under its soaring Gothic arches. The very air in the cathedral seemed to ease his soul. He lit a candle, then sat on a pew and remembered the comfort he'd found here after his wife Lili's death. It was difficult to believe that it had already been more than twenty years. He raised his eyes to the cathedral's magnificent rose window.

How strange it was to return to Paris, as a man in exile from his homeland, the land that held his heart but where he was no longer safe. *No longer safe in my own homeland.* He folded his hands together, his chest heavy with grief that he'd left behind the graves of Lili and their stillborn child resting in a quiet place in the woods. Would he ever be near them again?

For now, he wanted to sit here at the heart of Notre-Dame, in this sacred space where he felt protected from the fractured world, a place that seemed to welcome all. He closed his eyes and returned to the forests of his childhood where he'd walked beside his grandfather, the master luthier who taught him to respect the spruce and maple trees his family harvested to make violins. To respect all the trees and all living things. Josef had grown up in awe of his father and grandfather, men who would craft a violin from raw seasoned wood, men whose deft finger movements on small gouges and masterful varnishes created exquisite instruments. Lieb violins were judged to be some of the best in Europe.

Aching for all that had been lost, Josef opened his violin case and took out one of his grandfather's prized instruments, the very violin he'd rescued from a book burning in Berlin back in '33. He turned it over in his hands and marveled at the grand history and power it represented, crafted from five-hundred-year-old wood harvested by his grandfather, wood whose very cells remembered centuries of being buffeted by winter's cutting winds and summer's scorching heat.

He got up and stood near one of the cathedral's immense pillars and nestled the violin under his chin, then began to play Bruch's "Kol Nidrei," a song of longing and mourning that poured out his feelings in the language he knew best. He played for everyone lost in exile. He played for everyone taken from those they loved. He played for everyone whose life had ever been torn apart by a tyrant.

As the music rose high into the air, all around the cathedral people listened. Some wrapped their arms around those beside them. Josef closed his eyes and played.

When the last notes faded away, people bowed their heads respectfully and many wiped away tears. A priest in his cassock offered a gentle smile. Then Josef carefully laid the instrument in its case and locked it. For now, his anguish melted away.

His footsteps echoed on the old stones as he emerged into the pearl-blue light of evening.

Josef stood in the courtyard at Lucien's studio and peered through the windows into the workshop. He'd given his friend little warning of his arrival, and he hoped the standing invitation to stay was still open. This friendly association between a French and a German luthier had begun back when their fathers had traveled between Paris and Berlin to share luthier designs, varnish formulas, and other details of the business, and the friendship continued on with the sons.

Josef looked up to see Lucien at the window of his studio, waving. A minute later, Lucien ran outside and embraced his old friend. "You've arrived at the violin hotel," he said, then kissed his friend's cheeks.

He was pleased to see that Lucien was enthusiastic about his arrival despite the last-minute notice. Josef greeted the apprentices he'd last seen two years earlier. How different life was now. In Germany. In the world. Whispers of war had increased since the Sudetenland crisis in September, and no one knew what would happen next.

"Welcome back, Mr. Lieb," the young men called out before they returned to sculpting, sanding, and varnishing.

Josef breathed in deeply the aroma of wood, linseed oil, and varnish—these meant home to him. He set his violins on the floor littered with the usual luthier debris, wood curls and sawdust. "Smells like where I belong. Ah, it's good to be here." Overwhelmed by relief and exhaustion, he grabbed a stool and perched on the seat, then tugged his handkerchief from his coat pocket to wipe his forehead.

Lucien peered at him through his thick glasses as he poured coffee beans into a grinder. "You all right? Georges, get him some water. You must be run off your feet. I wasn't sure what to make of that telegram. Sarah is here too, I presume?"

Josef drank the water quickly and asked for more. "Yes, Sarah, now called Rosemarie. I'll explain that after I catch my breath, but she's doing well and staying with the Rosenbergs. Celeste will show her around the city tomorrow."

Lucien poured water over the ground beans, filling the room with the scent of rich coffee. He filled cups for the apprentices first, then said, "Let's get you up to the flat. Boys, it's time we close the shop for the day." The young men said goodnight, and Josef followed Lucien up the stairs.

They sat at the dining table in the compact apartment above the studio. It was plain but practical, with two small bedrooms, one not much larger than a closet, but it was his favorite room because it looked out at a grand chestnut tree, at least three hundred years old, from what he could tell. Now illuminated by the streetlights, the remaining leaves were shimmering amber.

"What's going on?" Lucien asked, looking at Josef as if expecting a confession.

Josef cleared his throat. "My friend, it's like this—I'm Josef now, not Joshua, and Sarah is Rosemarie. Both Sarah and I had very disturbing encounters with Nazis, and we had to leave quickly. Fortunately, her mother and I had been planning it for some time. It's strange, I know, these different names, but we're getting used to them." He sipped his coffee, its warm richness and the comfort of Lucien's company a balm for his soul. Josef let the coffee brighten his senses as he contemplated how much more to tell his friend.

"Was it that Nazi, Werner?" asked Lucien. "He was hounding you years ago."

"I put a stop to the hounding," said Josef, "and now I'm here." He set down his cup. "Now that I'm here, I want to make a new violin. May I take up my old spot in the studio?"

Lucien stood up. "Consider this place yours, Monsieur Josef of Paris. We're partners in crime."

Josef smiled and said, "That's very true, my old friend." Silently, he thought, *perhaps soon I'll tell him of my other crimes.* Josef bid Lucien goodnight, settled into his room, and began to unpack. Then he sat on the bed and drew back the curtains to look at the chestnut tree just outside the bedroom window. The tree sent his thoughts back to his studio in Berlin with all those carefully crafted violins. Precious, exquisite works of art now in the hands of Nazis. Such beauty now owned by monsters—it was agonizing. But there was one gleam of light in that dark scenario, and he smiled at the thought of his secret crime, which at this very moment was like a bountiful flower spreading its seeds across Germany.

Winged Victory

*P*aris. *Am I really here?* From her seat on the bus next to Celeste, Rosemarie watched the city flow by in her new City of Light. The perfect name for Paris. At nighttime, bright neon lights flashed at clubs and cafés, and in the late afternoon, the descending sun illuminated the facades of buildings, painting the stones in an amber glow.

Celeste laughed. "Your mouth is hanging open!"

"I'm just so amazed by it all." An electric thrill ran up Rosemarie's spine.

"Prepare yourself to be amazed even more. I'm going to show you my favorite sculpture, and after that you'll never be the same."

A cold breeze ruffled the golden leaves of the plane trees. Rosemarie loved the geometric layout of the Tuileries Garden, the Grande Allée of trees framing the Egyptian obelisk rising from the Place de la Concorde. *I'm really here, I'm in Paris.*

They entered the exalted halls of the Louvre, with its great arches and inlaid marble floors. It felt more like a place of worship than a museum, and Rosemarie tried to absorb the grandiose space and vaulted ceilings, but it was all more wonderful than she could have imagined.

Celeste tugged her arm. "You have to see this."

They stood at the foot of a long staircase that climbed toward a domed ceiling bathed in light. On the plinth at the top stood a statue of a woman with gossamer wings, and at that moment, she seemed to be rising into the air. The sense of life emanating from the sculpture was breathtaking.

"That's the *Winged Victory of Samothrace*. Isn't it magnificent!"

"It seems magical," Rosemarie said, examining the finely detailed sculpture of a woman with wings and a gown that looked like a web of lace.

Celeste said, "It's two thousand years old. Can you believe how the gown looks so delicate? The grace of the wings . . ."

Rosemarie felt as if she'd just travelled through time. The Louvre, with its sculptures from hundreds and thousands of years ago, its paintings that told the stories of civilizations and mythology through the ages—it all launched her into an irresistible trance.

They explored the galleries of Greek and Roman sculpture and the art of the Renaissance period. They stopped to admire the *Venus de Milo* and another famous lady in the Louvre, the *Mona Lisa* with her enigmatic smile. The way her eyes seemed to follow the viewer—how did da Vinci do that?

La Grande Galerie seemed to extend into infinity with its skylights and walls covered with Italian artworks from several centuries, their colors still as lush as if they'd just been painted. By the time they'd visited several of the galleries, Rosemarie felt inspired by the riches of the art, but Celeste told her they'd seen barely a quarter of what the Louvre had to offer. They vowed to go every week until they'd seen everything.

As they left the museum and entered the brilliant light and life that was Paris, Rosemarie sensed it was possible to turn the page on her past and free herself from the fear she'd felt in Berlin. With Celeste as her guide, she had the freedom to walk and wander and even dance if she wanted to. But whenever she let herself get swept up in the gaiety of Paris, she was stabbed by guilt. Where was the fairness in her being able to enjoy the luster and light of Paris, free to spend her time sipping coffee and taking in art, while her mother and grandparents and friends lived every day in fear within the dark and dangerous confines of Hitler's Germany?

Laughing girls ran past them, their dresses swirling as they leaped and twirled. Women dressed as if they were on a fashion show runway walked little white dogs. Every day, Paris wrapped its arms around Rosemarie, but it couldn't ease the pull of what she'd left behind. The loved ones she'd left in Germany were with her every moment, always on her mind, even showing up in her dreams. She would simply have to keep sending them her thoughts, hoping that they were well and safe. Sobered by more thoughts of fear and injustice and longing and loss, she hooked her arm into Celeste's, and they quietly strolled between the flower beds of Paris.

In the Fields of War

By the winter of 1938, Franco's forces had pushed ever east toward Barcelona, vowing to defeat the elected Republican government by any means necessary. German stukas had introduced a new kind of warfare, blitz bombing. The 1937 bombing of the town of Guernica, soon immortalized by Picasso, came to symbolize the tragedy of the war: the death of innocents, women and children; a town in tatters; the indescribable grief of a nation.

Tomás emerged from the shelter of rocks and breathed bitter air. He wiped blood on his pants, lit a cigarette, and inhaled deeply. Three amputations in one morning—it was a ghastly new record. Dirt and sand blown by the wind bit into his neck and arms, but what right did he have to complain? Wounded and dying men lay on pallets inside the tent. The tent's canvas flapped and struggled like an injured bird as gusts off the mountain tore at it mercilessly and exposed the bodies of the soldiers to the frigid air. Their cries were lost in the keening wind. He pulled his thin coat close to his body and blew warm air into his hands. Gunfire ratcheted in the distance.

Ricardo, the other doctor on duty, called to a patient, "Lie down, it's all right." They did everything they could to save the soldiers in this makeshift hospital clinging to the side of a hill, and the doctors suffered over how little they could help, barely easing the dying men's passage to the next world. Their ineffectuality was their own kind of war wound. For two years, doctors, nurses, and volunteers had been doing their best to care for the men who had signed up to fight Franco's soldiers, who were slaughtering innocent people on behalf of rebels intent on ending the country's elected democracy. But nothing they did could bring men back to life or stop Franco's forces from taking possession of the whole country.

The clip of hooves made Tomás look up. Horses and donkeys, their heads hanging low, pulled carts that spilled over with injured men. Ribs showed through the patchy fur of the animals' winter coats. He grabbed a piece of canvas and spread it on the ground where the injured would be laid to be triaged, exposed to the cold and wind. He mashed out his cigarette and entered the tent where soldiers were sprawled next to each other, their cries for their mothers piercing the thin air. Tomás heard prayers, even from the lips of those who despised religion.

He softly rested his hand on a wounded man's shoulder and whispered words of comfort. There wasn't much talking in such a place, but he asked the man—barely more than a boy— about his family. Where he was from. If he liked to fish. Tomás looked into the soldier's eyes, eyes that would reveal life or death. He detected a flicker of future in those eyes and murmured a promise to help him as he readied the instruments to stitch up his wounds.

Next, he set a shattered bone for a man who had to suffer the grueling pain without morphine, his staccato breath and anguished cries filling the tent. Ricardo unraveled a rubber tube to create a direct transfusion from a dying man into one who still had a chance. A desperate thing to do, but when blood supplies were scarce, they took the chance and prayed for a match. Without more blood, the badly wounded were dead anyway.

In rare, quiet moments when patients were settled, Tomás's mind would turn to the nature of war—asking himself if all these principles were worth fighting and dying for. He'd always landed on the side of righteousness, but on some nights as war pressed them farther toward Barcelona, he knew in his bones how this would all end. Would he even live to see the world on the other side of the war? Where were his mother and little sister now? It comforted him that many of his countrymen were already on the road to the Pyrenees, escaping with their neighbors. For them, there was hope.

Kristallnacht

*I*t was a cold November night in Paris as Josef made his way through the narrow passageways of the Left Bank. He carried a baguette, a hunk of cheese, and some chicken to share with Lucien at the flat. In the distance, he heard the shouts and calls of a crowd. There were always demonstrations and gatherings in Paris about some political thing or another, so he didn't investigate. His feet were numb with cold, and he wanted to get home.

As he walked, he could feel the city on edge. Police cars whizzed by with sirens screeching, their *wah-wah* bringing back memories of Berlin and the menacing SS and Gestapo on the hunt for Jews. He tucked his neck down into his collar and hurried to the studio.

Lucien and the apprentices were gathered by the wireless radio, grim expressions on their faces. Lucien glanced up and shook his head. "It's very good that you escaped Germany."

Michael, one of the apprentices, nodded in agreement. "Just in time. I wonder how my Aunt Ester is, if she's safe."

"What is it? What happened?" Josef felt a familiar ice in his bones.

"Remember that guy who killed the German ambassador vom Rath a few days ago here in Paris? He was arrested, and there are riots all over Germany. The assassin was a young Jewish man—from Poland, I think. Grynszpan," said Lucien.

"They're burning synagogues, smashing up the Jewish shops," Michael added.

Georges let out a heavy breath. "Arresting hundreds, thousands of Jewish men."

The baguette Josef was holding fell to the floor. *Burning synagogues?* He remembered the flames from the book burning he'd witnessed in 1933.

Lucien touched his shoulder sympathetically, then picked up the baguette and brushed off the sawdust. "Sit, my friend. You look pale. Antonio, get him some water."

The next thing Josef knew, he was sinking into a chair. Static from the radio filled the room as the announcer's breathless voice spoke of broken glass and fires in cities throughout Germany. Shop windows were smashed, and synagogues and Jewish businesses burned while firemen stood and watched.

Three of the apprentices were also Jewish refugees. They patted his shoulder, broke off bread for him to eat, and cut him slices of cheese. The aroma of fresh coffee filled the room, and a steaming hot cup appeared in front of him. He drank it and burned his lips.

Lucien set the needle on the phonograph and filled the room with Mozart. They turned back to their work, but as it grew late, they moved from coffee to whiskey. More news flowed in, more arrests across more cities, and Jewish men were quickly hauled off to camps. Finally, the whiskey, the companionship, and the shock of the terrible news wore Josef out, and Lucien suggested they go to bed. "Try to sleep," he said.

Lucien shut off the lights in the studio and helped Josef up the stairs. He seated him on the sofa and tucked a blanket around him, then poured another drink and sat in a chair across from him. "What is it?" Lucien asked. "Tell me about it." He crossed his legs and pulled a blanket around himself. Josef's good friend was going nowhere.

"It was May 1933," Josef began, and just like that he returned to the horrible night in Berlin, back when he was still Joshua Lieb, a Jew in Hitler's Germany.

Evening light flickered gold and green on the trees on the Unter den Linden. It was a spring evening in May, but the night tasted like autumn, the air heavy with the scent of burning leaves. Clouds molded into seething shapes backlit by a rising moon.

Joshua hummed Beethoven as he stood on the sidewalk adjusting the straps of the violin cases that hung from his shoulders. One held his grandfather's creation—a very special violin Joshua protected as if it were a child. The other held a beautiful violin he himself had crafted after years of learning luthier secrets from his father and grandfather.

Polished black cars festooned with swastikas glided between taxis and buses, and the avenue swarmed with Berliners eager to taste the city's culture—museums, theatre, the symphony, and the opera. Suddenly, lorries full of books swerved past him into the Opernplatz across the street. SA men, "Brownshirts," piled out of the truck and threw armloads of books into bonfires. Men marching down the avenue carried flaming torches and sang "Deutschland über Alles."

Hitler had it right: Patriotic music never failed to stir the blood of the German people. The looks on their faces were crazed, as if they were all in a trance. Joshua hefted the straps of his violin cases over his shoulders and crossed the street to get a better look. The noise and crowd built to a frenzy as trucks screeched and more books came tumbling out. Something very big was happening. Hitler Youth, their faces gleaming and their eyes wild, shouted, "Heil Hitler!" and lobbed books into the flaming pile. Sparks soared high in the air, rising and floating like fireflies.

Students and businessmen threw books into the fire, shouting "Heil Hitler!"

They were burning books.

Goebbels stepped up to a podium with a raised fist, Goebbels with his devil eyes. Joshua shivered despite the intense heat and pulled his violins close. The hatred of the crowd grew hysterical as they chanted *"Juden Raus!"* and "Death to Communists!" The scene reminded him of fourteenth-century paintings of the Inquisition.

He felt the heat from the pyres and watched the flames devour books by Sigmund Freud, Jack London, Thomas Mann, and countless other influential writers. He took a breath against the wall of heat and knelt to save scorched copies of *Civilization and its Discontents* and *Call of the Wild*. He'd just rescued a music manuscript by Mendelssohn when he felt a clap on his shoulder. "Stop! Put that back," a rough voice commanded.

A boy in a Hitler Youth uniform glared at him from only inches away. Joshua's hands throbbed, but he could not, would not let go of the music. Burning music? A sacrilege.

The boy's breath was foul, and when he smiled, his lips parted to reveal blackened teeth. "Put it down," he sneered, and before Joshua could respond, the boy shoved him toward the flames. The shoulder straps of Joshua's violins slipped from his shoulders, and the cases fell at the edge of the fire where scorched papers burned. "No!" he screamed, lunging for his precious violins, then forced by the searing heat to leap back. A scream caught in his throat and he watched in horror as the boy picked up his violin cases and dangled them over the flames. Joshua reached to grab them, but the youth shoved him back, knocking him to the ground.

The boy's eyes were slits. "Throw all of it in the flames or I'll burn your violins!"

"Please, give them to me. My grandfather made one, and I . . ."

"Now!" Flames licked and crackled.

He could barely see through the smoke as he crawled to the edge of the flames and shoved books into the fire. The boy stood there, cackling. His buddies grabbed the straps of the violin cases and took turns dangling them over the fire, lowering them closer and closer to the flames. "Burn, burn, burn!"

Fire crawled up one of the violin cases, and Joshua felt sick with rage. Then came a surge of panic. *Which* violin was in that case? Within seconds, the fire began to scorch the other case. One of the instruments released a pinging sound as a string snapped in the heat.

Suddenly, Goebbels's voice boomed, and the crowd went wild shouting and saluting. In that second, the boys whipped around to face the podium, letting the violins fall into the fire. Joshua grabbed the strap of one and yanked it from the blaze, then watched in agony as the other one began to burn into ashes.

Dizzy, he stumbled to the edge of the crowd. His hands throbbed, and his mind spun with a desperate craziness as he agonized over whether he'd rescued his precious grandfather's instrument or his own. The city all around was a blur as he staggered the two miles to his workshop. He opened the door to his flat and inspected his face in the mirror, black with soot. He sank to the floor and examined the charred case. What would he find inside? Had his grandfather's precious creation been destroyed? What had they done? His heart thudded as he clicked open the case and sobbed at the sight before him—it was his grandfather's violin!

The heat had softened the varnish and the bow was broken, horsehair hanging in loose arcs. On one side, the instrument's belly was cracked into pieces around the f-hole, and the bridge was snapped in two, but he could fix all that. The ribs on one side were charred, but the other side remained relatively untouched, which he found miraculous. He lifted the instrument and held it gently to his chest, rocking back and forth as he wept. It would take a long time, but he could repair it.

In his trance, something powerful began to happen in his mind, and he sat at his worktable, paper and pencil in hand. He wasn't sure what he wanted to draw, but something seemed to beckon him, as if by whispered invitation. His pencil moved on its own as he sketched and sketched and lost all sense of time. After the drawing was complete, he selected his sharpest carving tool and a piece of scrap wood and began to practice etching the new design into the wood.

He worked at it until morning light began to peek through the windows, and then there it was—the design that had all but forced its way from inside his psyche and onto the page, then into the wood: a tiny, thinly etched swastika entirely enveloped by a thick edged, deeply engraved Star of David, the Jewish star bold as it engulfed the Nazi symbol.

The aroma of wood and linseed oil wafting up from the workshop below brought Josef back to the present. He looked at Lucien, who'd listened without a word. Lucien shook his head, "My God, it's a nightmare you've described. They're animals. Far lower than animals." Both men were silent for a moment, and then Lucien asked, "My friend, why did you endanger your hands that way?"

46

Josef knitted his fingers together as in prayer. "I couldn't bear what they were doing."

Lucien nodded solemnly, then his dark eyes began to twinkle behind his round glasses. "And what a secret symbol you've created."

"For the past five years, I've carved that symbol into every one of my violins. It's hidden in the dark where the fingerboard joins the body."

Lucien laughed and slapped the table. "And you sold these violins to the Nazis?"

Josef nodded and grinned. "I sold hundreds. They'll never know."

Lucien tapped his pipe on the table. "Until someone opens the instrument for repair."

Lucien poured wine into their glasses.

Josef drank down his wine and poured another. "It's not my country anymore," he said.

"It's tragic, what's happened."

"I have so much guilt for having left others behind," Josef said, rubbing his stomach as an ache spread through his body. "It's torture."

"You needed to offer Rosemarie a life here. You've done a good thing." Lucien raised his glass. "To Rosemarie." He downed his drink, stood, turned off the light, and bid his friend goodnight.

Tomás

Tomás's muscles burned from the climb up the steep roads to the Pyrenees and to the border of France and Spain. Clouds on the shoulders of the great mountains drifted toward the Mediterranean Sea, gray with January light.

Desperate to find his family, he asked everyone he encountered, "Have you seen Maria and Carla Vidal? *Please* tell them I will find them." People shook their heads and tended to their own troubles, crawling and shivering as winds sliced through blankets that barely clung to their bodies. The road was steep and wet and rocky, slippery from the rain and sleet.

In the dark of night, the stars witnessed the silent suffering in the eyes of mothers. Children. Old men. Tomás watched the frail, ragged people struggle their way up the mountain and reminded himself of his vow to never become numb to suffering. It seemed that his heart could bear no more, yet he had no choice. He would have to find a way to absorb it all. There seemed no end to the agony everywhere he looked.

People trudged all the way from Madrid to Valencia and then on to Barcelona, trying to escape the army that had overtaken their homeland. They headed toward the border of France with terrified hope that they'd find safety there. They camped on the rocks along the way and shared whatever bread they had. Women gave birth on the side of the road, their anguished screams lashing the air. And up in the sky, *stukas* continued to screech, their machine-gun fire raining down on the innocents and tearing through flesh. The frozen ground couldn't accept the dead, so their bodies were carefully laid in small indentations in the rocks near the road.

Mothers were draped in long wool capes that flapped like birds' wings in the wind, children sheltered underneath. Onward they all pressed with desperate determination to escape Franco's forces and cross to safety on the French side. "The border! The border!" hopeful voices called out. But once they crossed, they were met by French guards who harbored anti-communist beliefs and distrust of Spanish Republicans. The exhausted people were herded into barbed wire camps that had been slapped together along the beaches in the fishing villages of Argelès-sur-Mer, Collioure, Cerbère, and Banyuls-sur-Mer. People were forced to camp on the narrow beaches in wet sand.

Within the barbed confines of the camp at Argelès-sur-Mer, Tomás stood freezing, his belly empty. Grief punctuated his every breath. He'd seen unthinkable suffering along the road and now could barely believe he was witnessing even worse. Children were lying on the beach with no escape from the icy water that washed over them. The milk of new mothers dried up, leaving their babies to die.

Someone handed Tomás a cigarette and he took a drag. It was harsh on his throat, but he welcomed the burn. He studied his hands, hands that had once healed and soothed but that now seemed useless. Hands he no longer recognized.

$\mathcal{A}$rt and $\mathcal{W}$ar

Prague: March 15, 1939

Europe held its breath hoping Hitler would keep the promise for peace set out in the Munich agreement in September 1938, but six months later, he threatened to bomb Prague if the Czechs didn't surrender. On a grim snowy evening, Hitler's tanks overtook the city and arrived at Prague Castle.

$\mathcal{O}$n a wintery afternoon in March, Rosemarie and Celeste rushed to an opening at Gallery J on the Left Bank. The wind tore at Rosemarie's coat as they wandered through narrow passageways, getting lost three times before they found the tiny closet of an art space.

A smoky haze filled the gallery. It was cozy and colorful and crammed with bohemian artists, art students, and people dressed for an evening out. All of them were drinking wine and chatting enthusiastically. Candles burned on makeshift altars, and Greek statues were outfitted in French soldiers' uniforms and adorned with flowers.

The young women squeezed between sweaty bodies gathered in front of various works. There were modernist sculptures, experimental paintings, and surreal creations—manikins with green leaves snaking out of eyes and mouths. Rosemarie and Celeste grabbed two glasses of wine from a passing tray, and Rosemarie stared at one of the Greek statues. "What do you think is the meaning of the soldiers?" she asked.

Celeste laughed, "Who knows—it's art! It must be a protest statement about the war. The news from Czechoslovakia is on everyone's mind."

Shivering at the thought of war and from the sting of the March wind on her legs, Rosemarie took two long sips of wine and welcomed the burn of the alcohol. With Hitler poised to invade Czechoslovakia, everyone, the whole world, was nervous. If he invaded, it would mean certain war. The buzz in the room was as much about the expected invasion as it was about art.

"Poland is next."

"We can't have war—we're still rebuilding from the last one."

"It won't affect us. France won the first war, remember?"

Celeste said, "You hear what they're saying? My parents and I just didn't believe it would go this far. If only Hitler would keep the treaty."

Rosemarie looked at Celeste through the eyes of Sarah, a girl who knew exactly what the Nazis were capable of, and her stomach pinched at every comment. Though she'd been in France for five months, her body vividly remembered those years in Berlin, what it felt like to hear the thrum of thousands shouting "Heil Hitler" as they thrust their arms into the air. Trucks mounted with loudspeakers roared through the city proclaiming the glory of the Reich. *What if they decided to exercise their power over all of Europe?* The thought made her grab another glass of wine. Here she was, in Paris at an art gallery. It was something she'd dreamed of, being that kind of Parisienne, hobnobbing with artists. But in the middle of a possible breakout of war?

Rosemarie gave Celeste a look that said *please, don't be so naïve.* "Everyone predicts that if Hitler breaks the peace treaty, Poland will be next. You prefer to be optimistic, don't you?"

Celeste smiled and patted her on the shoulder. "I know, I know. I'm chronically cheerful. But it feels better than always seeing the worst. You just need to experience a few years of happiness in Paris, and you'll see life like I do!"

Was such a shift possible? Rosemarie had spent the winter looking over her shoulder—would that Captain Schmidt appear? It was unlikely he'd know what happened to her, but the fear lingered. What if she encountered another Nazi just like him? And Kristallnacht had launched her into a whole new level of worry and guilt. Every day, she fretted more over not hearing from her mother for so long. A few weeks earlier, a letter had arrived at the Rosenbergs' addressed to *Josef Lieb* and written in a strange code: Her mother spoke of Christmas presents and wished him well, writing that she hoped he'd enjoy the art in Paris. It was written as if the family weren't Jewish and with no mention of Sarah or Rosemarie, no doubt to protect her daughter. Rosemarie knew that Jews in Germany had been forced to move from their residences. Had her mother ended up in a camp? Rosemarie spent the day weeping. The mystery of the letter was almost worse than not hearing anything.

To attempt to lift herself from such dark moods, she tried to focus on beauty. There in the bustle of the gallery's art and energy, she looked into Celeste's bright eyes and said, "Thanks to you, my wonderful tour guide—let's see—we've seen the Louvre, the Jeu de Paume, and we think we saw Picasso at les Deux Magots." But then the weight of the war made her pause. "What will happen to all that beauty if there's a war?"

Celeste shook her head. "They just can't allow war to break out. Not again."

Rosemarie chose to let the subject drop. What could she know for sure in this moment? What could she solve here, today?

Celeste and Rosemarie milled about the gallery in an atmosphere thick with smoke, tense voices talking about war, and free-flowing alcohol. "What do you think?" asked Celeste, gesturing toward the whole gallery.

Rosemarie laughed. "I think you can create whatever kind of art you want, and if you know someone, you can get your work into a gallery."

"Our dear professor would give you a bad mark for saying that," Celeste joked.

"That's because he's so biased." As they proceeded through the crowded gallery, Rosemarie thought about the professor and her own progress. He wasn't a fan of her art—encouraging her to brighten her palette, to paint with more verve and movement. To open up and be less tight. She could see his point, but she'd spent years learning classical techniques, slow drawing with pencil and sketching with pen, hatching, and creating dark and light in subtle ways. She thought painting would be her focus because she so loved the intense colors of the Impressionists and the German Expressionists. Van Gogh. But what she loved to look at was very different from the kinds of art she created. She was drawn to black and white ink sketches and etchings.

She stood in front of a captivating painting, an image of a woman wearing a veil, her eyes looking far away. Something mysterious seemed to emanate from the unusual piece made of gauze and layers of paint, ink, and cloth with a silver overlay that created a magical illusion, as if the subject were a woman from another time.

"What do you think of this one?" asked a woman standing next to her. Rosemarie turned to look at her. She had a classic beauty—a flawless complexion and the face of an art model. Rosemarie admired the woman's red lipstick and classic black dress set off with a scarf in abstract patterns of blues.

"I don't know," Rosemarie answered. "It makes me think of another world. I'm not sure it's on this earth."

"Perhaps a dream world," the woman said.

"She wants to be somewhere else. She's missing someone," Rosemarie improvised.

"I like how you're translating the vision. But I suppose it shouldn't matter what people think."

Was this woman the artist? Rosemarie began to stumble over her words. "Oh, I hope I . . . I had no idea." Her face grew hot.

"My name is Sophia Bauer." The woman smiled. Her hat was decorated with the same blue fabric used in the painting.

"Ah, very nice to meet you. I'm, I'm Rosemarie Bern. I'm here with my friend Celeste from the art academy. I do admire . . ." She noticed the initials SB in the corner of the painting.

"So you're a fellow artist," Sophia said, fitting a cigarette into a silver holder, then flicking the flame from a gold lighter to the end of her cigarette. The tobacco snapped and crackled as she drew in a breath. Rosemarie watched with fascination as Sophia blew smoke in circles.

"A mere student," Rosemarie confessed.

Just then the gallery buzz grew louder. One of the artists began weeping, dabbing at her eyes with her scarf. "I was supposed to be in Prague tomorrow. This is terrible!"

People draped their arms around her, offered her a glass of wine. Everyone in the gallery gathered into groups, talking, crying, swearing. Looking subdued, Celeste joined Rosemarie and Sophia. "You heard? Hitler marched into Prague an hour ago."

Sophia looked distressed. "Oh, I know too well what those people are going through."

Rosemarie noticed a slight accent. "What do you mean, Sophia?"

"I was in Vienna last year." Her previously animated voice was now flat, her eyes dark with memories.

Rosemarie felt a stab in her belly. She knew Hitler's invasion of Austria was brutal. Manic joy for pro-Nazis. In only one day, thousands of Jews had been paraded in disgrace down the streets and sent off to camps. She'd seen the newsreels.

Hazy smoke from Sophia's cigarette circled her hat. "One day, we lived a normal life, parties and gallery openings and work, and the next we were scrubbing anti-Nazi slogans off the streets."

"How awful. You were hit all at once. In Berlin, the breakdown was slow, so we, I mean the Jewish people, adjusted and adjusted, and . . ." Rosemarie stopped mid-sentence after realizing she'd forgotten who she was—and who she wasn't.

Celeste touched Rosemarie's shoulder. "I think I should apologize. You were right about Hitler. He's determined to . . ."

". . . conquer Europe. This is just the beginning," a male voice broke in, a young man with dark hair and fiery eyes. "Hello, I'm Max. I'm, I'm no one, but I help artists show their work when I can. I heard you talking about Vienna and Berlin. Hello, Sophia."

Rosemarie found her voice again, "This is Celeste and I'm Rosemarie."

"I'm pleased to meet you, Rosemarie, and you too, Celeste. It's interesting how war can bring people together as well as tear them apart."

Sophia asked, "You think Britain and France are going to keep the treaty with Poland?"

Max shook his head. "Everyone says Poland is next—more living space for the Germans."

Rosemarie knew too well the excuse—lebensraum, living space to expand the Reich. The usually cheerful Celeste looked distressed, her innocence rapidly being challenged by the invasion. It was painful to watch.

Sophia blew a circle of smoke in the air. "My dears—get ready. The war everyone is talking about begins today."

"France is safe, don't you think?" asked Max. "The best army in Europe."

Sophia looked at him askance. "You presume everything you've heard about France is true. You're young. You'll see—you can't count on the government. In a pinch, you must look out for yourself." Then she looked at Rosemarie. "And keep creating art that speaks to the times."

Rosemarie asked, "Have any of you seen Picasso's *Guernica*?"

Celeste nodded. "My father made sure we saw the exposition in Paris in '37. The painting is enormous. And you feel like you're walking right through the carnage—the broken bodies of horses and mothers and children. It stopped our hearts."

Sophia's face looked drawn and tired. She put away her cigarette holder. "Yes, but that's why we must keep trying. Art speaks louder than the newsreels. But alas, I must go. Here's my card. Let us meet again, Rosemarie. Celeste. Goodnight, Max."

Rosemarie and Celeste watched her leave, her hips swaying as she made her way through the crowd. Rosemarie tucked the card in her purse, and they said goodbye to Max. They left the gallery and found the streets thronged with excited people, the air filled with the conflicting voices of alarm and confidence:

"War is here!"

"No, it can't be!"

"Will Hitler really start another war?"

"This will all blow over."

As the young women walked down the streets of the Left Bank, dread crept through Rosemarie's body. If war broke out, what would happen to immigrants like her and Sophia?

Celeste must have had the same kinds of thoughts. "My father says the Maginot Line will stop a German invasion."

"The Maginot Line?" Rosemarie asked.

"It's a tunnel made of concrete with guns and cannons. It goes all the way to Belgium. We're safe because of it."

Rosemarie looked at Celeste. *Safe?* Celeste knew nothing of the dead look in the eyes of the SS, the Gestapo. The Nazis. Their brutality. And she hoped her friend never would.

The Catalans

Tomás knew he'd have to save himself from this camp the French were surrounding with barbed wire. He had to get out. He'd heard rumors that fierce Senegalese guards would soon arrive to patrol the perimeter of the camp, to more tightly imprison his countrymen who now barely survived in a living hell of filth and cold and starvation. Some of the women and children had been carted off in lorries—were his mother and sister in that group?

He waited until dusk to slip through a gap in the wire, then practically crawled to the road where he came upon some men, Catalans who'd fought for Spain and later found their way to this part of France. They fashioned new lives as vignerons, working in the vineyards in the Pyrenees foothills. They were heading home with their tools slung over their shoulders, and when they saw a dirty, ragged man with blood on his clothes, they spoke to him in Catalan and took him to a hut nearby. Over roast rabbit and wine, they asked him to tell them his story.

The men looked like him, they were built like him. The poetry of their language was his own. They were men who'd watched the blood of their compatriots soak into the ground during the civil war. Tomás learned that these men had escaped in the first flood of refugees from Spain. They understood. These men fed him, though they had little food, and gave him a place to sleep. In turn, he cared for their injuries and went with them to work the vines that produced a sweet wine from the grapes that grew on the mountain.

During the weeks he stayed with them, he learned they possessed the secret to living free in a country that would imprison them: the power of the pen. Letters and words, they explained, could reshape the world, and soon his fingers became stained with ink as they taught him about the skill of forging. They showed him the magic of a new name. A new birthdate.

He was reborn French, César Garcia, from Catalonian France. He learned how to be invisible and how to hide his past. These men took the time to teach him the secrets of forgery, and every day with the focus of a medical student, he practiced his calligraphy and the other fine elements of the craft.

A network of Spanish Republicans hid throughout the towns and villages of Catalonian France. Wanted men. If caught, the French government would send them to forced-labor camps. They needed help. They needed someone with skills in shape-shifting.

Tomás heard about refugees forming networks in Paris, and he believed that his new skills would be very useful to them. He needed to be a soldier in the battle against the Fascist chokehold, so he thanked his Catalan friends for changing his life and made his way to the city.

Conjunctions

May of 1939 delivered Paris a bloom of glory. Everywhere Rosemarie looked, beautiful flowers were sprawling across gardens and cascading from window boxes. Vivacious Parisians strolled by the Seine and packed the outdoor cafés. A breeze rustled the plane trees, and birdsong filled the air. This was the Paris Rosemarie had dreamed of.

At Café de Flore, her café crème steamed as she soaked up the pleasure of sitting at her own table with a coffee, a sketchbook, and all the time in the world. For the last six months, she'd enjoyed this iconic Parisian café just off Boulevard Saint-Germain. Every morning, she'd sketch the café patrons who sat drinking coffee and watching the world go by. Across the street stood a perfectly Parisian Haussmann-style apartment building, and she lined up her pens neatly as she prepared to replicate its stone facades and wrought-iron railings.

After sketching the apartment building, she watched an older couple, regulars, toddle into the warm area inside the café. The man wore a wool cap, his gray hair fluffed below his ears. The woman wore a long black coat, red scarf, and black shoes in the latest style. The man and woman always came in at the same time of day, and they were always together. Rumors said she had once been a great beauty and a dancer and that he'd been a soldier who'd wooed her for years. The story was that she'd refused his offers of marriage but then twenty years ago accepted, just after the war. They always sat with their heads together, whispering. Rosemarie would try not to stare and would often sigh at their devotion to each other.

She sketched a portrait of the couple in quick lines, capturing how they leaned toward each other, their fingertips touching on the tabletop. After a while, she looked up from her drawing and noticed an attractive, dark-eyed young man wearing a red beret. He met her eyes, nodded and smiled, then turned his gaze away as if respecting her privacy. When the waiter arrived, he ordered an espresso. She continued to sketch, and the next time she looked up, he was looking at her again. She flushed and looked away, but not before she'd taken note of the way his dark hair curled along his neck and that he had beautiful hands, strong with veins and muscles, like a Greek statue. *Who was he? Why was he looking at her?* she wondered.

The man softly cleared his throat and smiled. "Excellent portrayal."

"Merci. I just, well, they seem so . . . devoted." She couldn't bring herself to say, "in love." *What did she know of love? Would she ever be able to feel that sensation? To trust someone?*

The man leaned back in his chair and touched his fingertips together, nodding thoughtfully. "Devotion. You know you can count on that person."

Rosemarie wasn't sure how to respond. She wasn't even sure it called for a response. He spoke with a strong accent—Spanish?—and his dark looks and burnished skin suggested he was from the south.

"Have you been in Paris long?" She stirred the frothy cream on her coffee.

"Ah, Paris," he said. "I imagine we are both guests of this fine city. Of France."

Rosemarie's face grew warm. *My German accent must be stronger than I imagine.* "I'm here with my father. From Berlin."

The man leaned forward, pushing a lock of hair under his red beret. "I'm César Garcia. I come from a place that no longer exists." He shook his head, giving the sense that he was still coming to terms with that loss. "Catalonia. The Spain where I grew up is no more."

"It must be heartbreaking, losing everything." Rosemarie laid down her pen and looked at him. He was older than her by at least a few years. Solid, not a big man, but he looked strong. *What was his story?*

There was a soft sorrow in his dark eyes, but he managed to smile. "I must sound so serious, but the times, they are serious. There are many wanderers now in Paris, in France." He waved his hand for the waiter to bring another coffee. "May I get you one?"

She shook her head. "No, thank you. I'm going to finish this sketch and go to my etching class."

Buses roared by, spewing exhaust. Taxis whirled to the curb, and passengers jumped out. Waiters bustled by. The late morning arrivals at Café de Flore had taken up residence in the cane chairs around small round tables under the awning that faced the street. Rosemarie wanted to talk with him but was at a loss for how to proceed. He broke the silence.

"I see you are a serious artist, perhaps a fellow seeker," he said, rolling a cigarette, his tongue licking the paper.

"What are we seeking?"

He leaned back and looked at her with those soulful eyes. "Justice. Peace. The hope that mankind won't destroy each other, though there are times when conflict is necessary." He flicked the lighter, and tendrils of silver smoke curled up from his cigarette.

"How long have you been in France?"

He laughed and leaned forward in his chair. "Long enough to see that she is a country in trouble."

"Why?" She gestured at the trees, the avenue, the café. "It's beautiful. Especially after Germany. France is famous for opening her arms to people in flight."

"Welcome to France, mademoiselle. I would like to see her treat you well, but I fear that her ideals have grown tarnished."

Rosemarie squinted as she regarded this interesting man. "Tarnished, how?"

Smoke streamed from the corner of his mouth. He spoke in soft, flowing words, "I apologize. My cynicism will ruin this beautiful morning."

She picked up her pen and began to draw the dark-eyed stranger. Hair and eyes, a shoulder, his hand cradling a cigarette folded inward—Mr. Lieb had told her that soldiers held cigarettes that way to hide the orange glow when in the field. Moisture gathered on her forehead. She felt both impelled to draw him and shy.

He moved his chair closer. "May I?" he said, looking at the sketch. "You're talented. Excellent likeness."

He was so close now. He smelled like tobacco and sweat. She drew in a deep, involuntary breath. With a flick of the pen, she added his beret.

"You're easy to sketch." She set down her pen and looked at him, noticing a couple of gray hairs in his moustache. "When did you arrive from Spain? I know something of that struggle, but . . ."

"Mine is the story of an unlikely tourist. It was snowing, and the border guards wouldn't let us in. But it's too grim to discuss on a lovely day like this." He gestured to the waiter for another coffee.

"We have something in common," Rosemarie said. "We both escaped tyranny, and here we are in this great city."

"There are many lost people in Paris," he said. "But you, the artist. You have found your métier." From a corner of the café, an accordion played an offbeat rendition of "La Marseillaise."

"Ah, La France! 'La Marseillaise.'" César leaned back in his chair with an amused look. "France believes herself immune to war."

The bells rang from the Saint-Germain church nearby, the sound floating across the azure sky. Rosemarie looked into César's eyes. "You believe there will be war?"

His shoulders heaved a big sigh. "Like I said, I don't want to ruin your morning."

"But I need to know." Before she realized it, she'd grasped his arm, her words tumbling out. "You're right—I don't want to think about it. I hate the thought of it. But everyone is talking about war as if it's inevitable. The French boys I know are very casual. 'Ah, we have the greatest army in the world. The Maginot Line will protect us from Germany,' they say."

She noticed then the pressure of her fingers on his skin and quickly withdrew her hand. "I'm so sorry. I don't know what's wrong with me. I'm sorry." The shame of losing control and touching a strange man like that warmed her face and neck. *What did she know of him? What would he think of her?*

She looked away toward the taxis barreling down the street, the pedestrians rushing by on the sidewalk in front of them. He hadn't said a word, so she stumbled on. "Berlin was chaotic, all that marching and so many people leaving. My father and I decided I'd apply to the art school here and would stay with family friends. I adore Paris. Am I selfish? I just want things to stay beautiful. Peaceful. To do art and hope Hitler will . . ." She stopped and saw a bemused expression on his face. "I know, Hitler has already shown his intentions for Europe."

She realized she was late to class and quickly stuffed her pens and sketchbook in her satchel. Once she was packed up, she sat back and pretended to finish her coffee just for something to do. It was difficult to leave this interesting man. He seemed to tune into more than just her words.

He sipped his coffee and smoked his cigarette, seemingly not perturbed by her bumbling conversation. He said, "These are troubling times, and no one knows what is coming. But it's coming."

Silence fell upon the table although the sounds of the city were all around them—accordion music, the buzz of conversation in the café, the groans and squeals of buses and automobiles. But strangely the silence wasn't awkward. He looked at her, and she held his gaze. Something passed between them—perhaps a sort of recognition.

He said, "Your eyes are lovely and your spirit, well . . . optimistic. Despite being shy, you express your outrage well. I know you must go, but may I suggest something?"

Rosemarie nodded, a frisson of electricity running up her spine. *Why did she just think of kissing him?* In a rush of confusion, she stood up, knocking the table with her purse. It was strange, the effect he was having on her, making her awkward and silly.

He stood in front of her, looking amused in a kind way, his arms folded across his chest. He seemed so manly with a day's growth of dark beard. "May I escort you to dinner? Are you free tonight?" His smile filled his eyes as he paused. "Or perhaps another time."

Suddenly breathless, she wasn't sure what to say. It wasn't proper to get picked up at a café and then go to dinner. Against all the rules for young ladies, and indeed, it could be dangerous. After all, she had no idea who he really was. He could be anybody. *He could be a German*, she thought, then she laughed to herself. He was the furthest thing from any German she'd ever met.

"I suppose. I'd . . . well, where would we meet? I need to speak to my father."

"Feel free to bring your father with you if you wish. I suggest Café Mozart, just off the Luxembourg Gardens. How about seven? The light is beautiful that time in the evening, and the music there is perfect for a pleasant conversation."

Rosemarie couldn't think of the right words to say. In public, she'd be safe on her own with him. She agreed and restrained a giggle as he bowed and leaned down to kiss her hand. His moustache tickled her skin, and more electric flashes went through her body.

"Â bientôt," he said, as she bumped into a chair on her way out. She turned to wave. "Yes, soon!"

Oh dear, I'm such an idiot, so clumsy. She rushed to the bus, her satchel of pens and her sketchbook bouncing against her ribs. She was feeling that sensation again, the rush of blood and excitement. The last time she'd felt it . . . Captain Schmidt. That was something she didn't want to think about. *But what was this feeling?* She climbed on the bus and sat back, her heart pounding. Café Mozart—it was a public place. She would meet him; she would not ask permission from her Mr. Lieb.

At the Rosenberg's that night, Rosemarie put on and took off three dresses and two pairs of shoes—all the clothes she had, mixing and matching the options. Nothing seemed right. Celeste stood in the doorway, laughing and offering her yet another choice—a pale green silk dress with bell sleeves and a V-neck. "It's not too low, is it?" asked Celeste, smoothing the fabric on Rosemarie's shoulders.

Rosemarie looked in the mirror at her figure and the waves of shiny brown hair falling around her face. She pinned her hair into a roll at her neck in the current fashion, then fastened her gold filigree heart necklace around her neck, the only treasure she'd brought from Berlin.

"Do you think the heart is too . . . too much?" Rosemarie asked, covering it with her hand.

Celeste smiled. "I think it's just right," she said as she smoothed Rosemarie's full silk skirt.

"I think you're more excited than I am," Rosemarie teased.

"Well, you did agree to go out the same day you met him! It's exciting. But don't seem too excited!"

Rosemarie had met a few men in Paris, but so many of them seemed immature and arrogant. One man in her art class had repeatedly sat in front of her to talk about the latest classroom gossip. Another went on and on about his visions for his art, which soon became boring. But César, he was fascinating. As she thought about the dark-eyed stranger, Rosemarie felt off-balance. She fanned herself with a newspaper. Yes, she'd find a way to manage this evening. If only she would stop feeling so fluttery.

Arm in arm she and Celeste rushed down the stairs to the front door.

"Don't forget your shawl!" Celeste wrapped it around her shoulders.

"Merci, bonsoir, uh . . ." She laughed and added, "Oh forget it!" and headed out the door and down the street.

The café was on one of the narrow medieval streets that wound through the Left Bank amid stylish boutiques and cafés that promised an intimate French meal. As Rosemarie entered the café, César stood and bowed. He'd shaved, leaving a trimmed moustache, and his black hair was neatly combed. He wore a casual suit with a cravat instead of a tie, and his stylishness made him seem like even more of a mature man. She wondered how old he was. Clearly, he'd had some life experience.

"Bonsoir, Mademoiselle. Would this seating be acceptable, or would you prefer inside?" He gestured to a cozy table under the canopy. A red candle flickered on the tabletop.

"This is lovely," she said, hoping she seemed grown up enough for him.

César asked her dinner selection and chose a wine. Then he leaned back in his chair and fixed his gaze on her. After a few minutes, her shoulders relaxed as they talked about the café, the beauty of handmade garments in the shops nearby, and the flowers blooming in the Jardin du Luxembourg. Why didn't he seem nervous? She felt that frisson of electric shock again, and her face grew warm.

The waiter poured wine into their glasses. César lifted his. "To peace," he said.

"To peace," she said, raising her glass. "I hope it's the best solution to everything."

"Paris," she waved her hand to indicate the gentle music, sophisticated setting, and the beauty of it all. "I love it. My friend, Celeste, has been taking me all around to the museums and art galleries. The shops." She sipped her wine, feeling Paris embrace her even more sweetly on this summer evening.

He leaned forward. "But to know what is best—that is the problem. And I agree, we must appreciate Paris while she is still free."

Rosemarie stared at him, sobered by his question. "You really think Germany would attack France?"

"Eventually, yes. The war is coming. Can't you feel it in the air?"

"I don't want to think of war. All I know is—war killed my father."

"But I thought your father was here in Paris," he said, lighting a cigarette and blowing the smoke discreetly away from the table.

"It's my second father who's here in Paris. My real father fought in the war, but he finally died of his injuries when I was eight. The war destroyed so many. And now, again?" She recalled the image of her father sitting up in his bed covered by a green coverlet, a weak smile on his face.

"I'm very sorry to hear that. Tell me about the father who is here in Paris."

"That's Mr. Lieb—my parents' best friend. He's been like a father to me all my life."

"Ah, fathers. I too lost mine. It was his heart. But it would have been broken even more tragically if he'd lived long enough to see what Franco did to Spain. He very much believed in freedom and rights for everyone, including women."

"So you must have fought in the civil war."

"I fought in the way that I could, working in field hospitals to save lives. But . . ." He shook his head sadly. "Too often I couldn't save them—we needed everything—water, food, bandages, blood. Time. It tears your soul to see your country eaten by vultures who destroy everything. Men in power who care nothing of rights or freedom."

"You're a doctor?"

"Almost—just short of it, officially. The war began before I'd finished my training, but the Republican side needed everyone they could get for the cause, so I joined up. I have a lot of experience if you ever need medical care," he joked.

"It must have been . . . terrible." She paused, imagining the bullets flying while he tried to stitch wounds. She couldn't imagine living through something like that, each day getting up to face that kind of danger. "Were you scared?"

He looked away, as if remembering. "I suppose you can get used to anything. You just stay focused on what you *can* do. But it's never enough."

"I know," Rosemarie softly responded. She had her own memories of what people had to adjust to, and a sense of the helplessness. As he lit another cigarette, she noticed that his fingers were ink-stained. She asked, "What are you doing in Paris?"

"I help people here as I can, but I'm unable to practice medicine in France. So many refugees, especially Jewish, are trying to get into France, but France is not so keen to allow that or to allow people to become naturalized citizens."

Rosemarie felt like a fraud, having this conversation while pretending not to be Jewish, but how could she confess right now? She'd just met him. She'd learned that many people in Paris were anti-Jewish, and although she didn't think this man was capable of such injustice, she'd have to get to know him better.

"What we do to our fellow man." He grimaced, a sorrowful look passing across his face. "You must have had Jewish friends in Berlin?"

"You've heard about the Blood Laws. No intermingling." That was a truthful response, at least.

Just in time, the waiter arrived with steak and frites, which gave Rosemarie a moment to think. They cut their steaks and began to eat, but Rosemarie had lost her appetite. Pretending not to be Jewish was going to be more and more difficult if she hoped to have a genuine friendship with this man.

"Tell me about your family. Are they here in Paris?"

He sat back, his eyes darkening as he lit a cigarette. "My mother and sister—the last time I saw them was in the Pyrenees. It was snowing, and people were freezing on the road as everyone tried to escape Franco's soldiers."

Rosemarie startled at the edge in his voice. The anger. The grief. "Oh, my goodness. I'm so sorry. What happened?"

"Those of us who were loyal to our government and democracy—as you know Franco won the war—were forced to flee for our lives. We dared to believe in freedom. Our people climbed the Pyrenees in the winter, trying to get over the border." He shook his head, his eyes soft with grief. "Too many didn't make it. So many. I was lucky, but sometimes those who survive may be cursed as well. We're guilty for living."

She didn't know how to respond, so she simply looked at him, her heart aching for this man. Now she felt ashamed for having pressed to learn more about him. There were reasons people didn't speak easily about themselves. She touched his hand and said simply, "These times must be so difficult for you."

Her fingers tingled as she withdrew her hand. This was the second time in a day she'd reached out and touched him. *What is going on with me?* She hoped he didn't find her too forward.

"There are many tragedies during this time. Ours is one—but if you multiply it by the hundreds and thousands of other displaced people, the Spanish, the Jews of Austria, and recently Czechoslovakia . . . well, it's clear we're all in trouble. And did you hear—the Germans have just made a pact with Italy. The possibility of war grows ever closer."

Rosemarie sat in a miserable puddle of thoughts, aware that she was talking with someone who'd both suffered greatly for freedom and also cared about the suffering of other people. And she—who was she? She'd betrayed herself and her mother. She was a liar with layers of secrets. She didn't deserve to know someone like César. She munched on a couple of frites, not trusting her voice. He gave her a look that said, please don't feel sorry for me, then refilled their wine glasses.

An awkward silence followed as classical guitar music, clean and refreshing, filtered through the café. Did the music remind him of Spain? She sipped her wine, thinking of the easy manner in which they'd met earlier that day, that simple bridging of the gap.

He moved close to her, his face so near she could see the new growth of his evening beard and the fine lines beginning around his eyes. His scent of tobacco and wine made her feel lightheaded.

"Mademoiselle, we are here to celebrate life, n'est-ce pas? All the dead will stay dead, but life, she is here in Paris, in the music, in the food. The lights. Please don't be sad for my story. We all have a story, and I hope to know yours if you wish to tell me."

Rosemarie felt the two parts of herself knit together again. In her heart, she was still Sarah, but she had begun to feel like this new Rosemarie. An artist. Free in a way she never had been in Berlin as a Jewish girl. *A Jewish girl.* She would have to tell this man who she really was. But when?

She found herself laughing in appreciation of his poetic invitation, his understanding of life, his deep throaty chuckle joined hers as they reached for each other's hands, this time with intent. His hands were warm, his fingers strong and well cared for. Hands that healed, fingers that were stained with ink. She caressed his fingertips and looked at him with a questioning glance.

He nodded, looking chagrined. "I do a lot of writing, and the ink never comes out." He wiggled his fingers at her.

People looked over at them smiling, and the waiter arrived. "Are you ready for dessert? We have a lovely concoction of cherries, chocolate gelato, and whipped cream."

César ordered the dessert and coffee, then turned to her. "If you're willing Mademoiselle, may we continue our conversations at another time?"

Rosemarie nodded, half-smiling. "I'd like that."

The waiter rushed over with the ornate gelato and whipped cream topped with nuts. They clinked spoons and began to dig in.

Warmth filled his face and eyes. "Can you believe we met just this morning? I think there are reasons people meet each other in certain moments in life. We can't know what it is about now, but . . . well, I hope we can find out, if you are willing."

Rosemarie knew her face was growing red as she took another bite of her dessert, trying not to act like the ingenue she was. She smiled over her spoon, then said, "Yes, I also believe that things happen for a reason."

They finished their dessert, and César asked for the bill. Café lights illuminated the cobblestone street as they left the café and slowly strolled in silence. Rosemarie felt somewhat dizzy and off-balance after such intensity with the man in the red beret.

They walked toward the Seine and then stood looking at the city. In the distance, the Eiffel Tower blinked its magical lights. He turned to her, and they held each other's gaze as he reached for her hand. "Mademoiselle Rosemarie, it would please me very much if I could see you again. Soon."

Her voice shook, "It would, that would please me also. What are you . . . I mean, when?"

"Ah, the lady is saying yes. Let's say on Sunday?"

"Sunday—in three days, yes," she said, trying to control the tremble in her voice.

"At Café de Flore again?"

Rosemarie agreed, and César leaned close, his scent tugging at her senses. He placed a scratchy kiss on each of her cheeks. "Â bientôt," he said as he pulled away. She gently kissed his cheeks, her lips feeling the prickle of his beard. They let go of each other's hands.

He hailed the taxi and helped her in, giving her a last slow glance with those dark eyes of his. "May the moon follow you. *Bonne nuit.*"

She sat back, exhilarated and confused, looking up for the moon. *Oh my*, she thought as the taxi pulled away from the curb, *is he a poet, too*?

Jeu de Paume

It was a perfect, clear June day in Paris, and with nervous anticipation César awaited the arrival of beautiful Rosemarie. They'd met a couple of times for coffee in addition to their dinner dates, and each time he'd been fascinated by her intelligence and charm. His attraction to her made him feel slightly crazy—she was so beautiful with her dark hair and eyes and a kind of beauty that seemed to emanate from within.

There she was, weaving toward him through the trees of the Grande Allée promenade in the Tuileries. Her lovely green dress swayed around her shapely legs, and her hair flashed in the sunlight.

"You look like a painting yourself," César said, feeling his face warm. He laughed, realizing he sounded excessively romantic.

Rosemarie smiled. "I'm not sure which school of painting I'd put you in. You're too handsome to be a Picasso."

César laughed. He couldn't remember how long it had been since he'd felt this content and happy.

They strolled into the galleries of the Jeu de Paume, entering a world of beauty and light. The joy on her face revealed how much she loved the art, that and the way she stood close to the paintings to study the brushwork, then stepping back for a different view.

Standing before a Monet, he asked, "What do you like about this one?"

She lifted her head and met his eyes, sending a thrill down his spine. "It's the light. The Impressionists made light their subject. Look at how many different colors create the impression of light in the painting. They were rebels, you know."

Rebel. Strange to hear that word coming from Rosemarie. "Tell me about that," he asked.

"They rebelled against the traditional styles of painting and therefore weren't accepted into the academies. So they went ahead and created their own salons. They believed in their work and made sure they shared it widely with the public."

"I know a bit about rebels, as you might guess."

Rosemarie looked at him quizzically at first, then nodded. "Ah, because you wouldn't accept Franco and his rebellion against your elected government?"

He said, "It's all in the point of view, who is rebelling against whom or what. Sometimes rebels have a vision that is intuitive, but other times it can be destructive."

"Are you a rebel?" she asked him, a slight smile on her face as they approached the paintings by Van Gogh. "Like him?" she asked, gesturing to a painting of a wheat field and sky. "He only sold one painting during his lifetime, traded others. But look how he offers us a window beyond an ordinary view of the world."

"Is this what your paintings are like—full of light?"

Her face clouded over. "No, not at all. But my professor is trying to get me to use color. I tend toward the moody and mysterious, and he doesn't understand that."

He leaned toward her. She smelled like vanilla. "Mysterious? Can I see your paintings sometime?"

She swished by him, avoiding the gentle brush of shoulders he'd hoped for. "I don't show my work to anyone."

"Well now you have me curious," he said as they approached a wall of Paul Gauguin, lush tropical landscapes and curvaceous, beautiful women.

Rosemarie announced as they passed into a different gallery, "As you can see, we've entered a new era here, the Post-Impressionists."

She'd skillfully avoided his questions. "I didn't know you were going to be my private docent."

She stopped and turned to him. "I suppose you think I'm showing off?" There was an edge to her voice.

Oh, he was messing this up. "No, not at all. I just—I guess I just wanted to know more about you and your own work. Why you paint. More about you."

She gestured to a bench, and they sat down. "The truth is, today I'm just trying to stay cheerful. I hear more and more predictions of war from the news, but so many people in this city don't want to talk about it. And when they do, I hear, 'We have a great army and we defeated Germany last time, so let's have more champagne.'"

"I suppose the predictions of war with Poland have made it all more real to you."

She looked at him and nodded. "The art helps relieve my worries. The light in the paintings, I let it burn into me."

Together they sat quietly, and César let his hand rest ever so lightly against hers. *Was she feeling the electricity between them as he was?* After several minutes, he couldn't sit still anymore, so he stood and said, "Let's go across the way and have a chocolate at Café Angelina."

Her eyes widened. "Oh, yes. I love that place."

They crossed Rue de Rivoli and joined the queue at the café known for its decadent chocolate drinks and desserts.

Sitting across from each other in a booth, they shared desserts that were artworks in themselves—whipped cream piled high on chocolate mousse—and laughed about chocolate mustaches and the whipped cream on Rosemarie's nose. She touched his hand when they talked about how she and her mother would share special hot chocolates in Berlin.

He decided to take a leap. "Did you have someone you cared about in Berlin?"

She pursed her lips. "You shouldn't ask."

"Why is that?"

"It's a forward question to ask a young woman, but the answer is no!"

César shook his head. He kept saying the wrong thing. He took a breath and reached for her hand. He stroked her fingers, and she allowed it, squirming a little in her seat. Then she took her hand away and looked up at him.

"I like you, César. I'm just not—" She smiled shyly. "I'm new at this." She focused again on stirring her chocolate.

"Rosemarie, listen. I know I'm a bit older than you, but I like you very much. When we first met, we talked seriously about war, about our pasts. We have a lot in common, I think. We're both here because of war. Fascists. Injustice. But there's more to both of us than that." Rosemarie seemed to relax and met his eyes. He smiled and said, "I'm twenty-six, in case you're curious."

She let out a quiet giggle and as they gazed at each other, more electricity seemed to pass between them. Then she hung her head. "While we're confessing things—" She looked away for a moment and took a deep breath. "I'm not just Rosemarie . . ."

He felt relief that she was finally revealing herself to him. "Go on. I'm listening."

"I told you about Berlin—but I didn't tell you . . ."

"That you're Jewish and you had to get away."

She nodded. "My name was . . ." She whispered it. "Sarah."

He leaned forward and took her hand in his. "I'm pleased to meet you, Sarah, and from now on, it will be our secret. Did you really think that would matter to me?"

She sighed. "Being who you really are can be dangerous."

"Our secret. And yes, these are dangerous times." He lifted her hand and brushed his lips across her wrist. "Rosemarie is a lovely name. And whatever your name is, it's the inner music that matters."

Her face flushed, and he felt himself relax. Perhaps from now on, they could find their way to friendship. He rested his hand on hers and reassured her with a smile.

The waitress came to gather their dishes, and César paid the check. Leaving the café, they walked past the lovely murals on the walls—an idyllic Fragonard French world, a soft-focus landscape. Rosemarie tucked her arm in the crook of his elbow. He tried to stay calm, but he felt that electricity again. Did *she*?

They walked back to the Tuileries and strolled under rustling trees in the Grande Allée. People walked by, and children laughed and chased balls. The air was scented with flowers. He turned to her and lifted her chin. He could feel her trembling, but she met his eyes. Then he bent forward and kissed her lips tenderly, softly, and she stayed with him. There were more kisses, slow ones and then deep ones. He lost track of what was around them. Her next kiss asked for more, and then they were kissing with a passion that surprised him. Finally, he held her, and she circled his waist with her arms.

When they stepped back from each other, he could see that her face was flushed. She looked down and smoothed her dress. César brushed a loose strand from her face and said, "Thursday at the café?"

"*Oui*, â bientôt," she answered, leaning in to kiss his cheek. Then she smiled and with a spin of her dress turned to head toward the Rosenbergs'. Her green dress blended with the greens in the garden as she walked away, her hips swaying. He stood and watched as she went and in spite of himself pressed his hand to his heart.

$\mathcal{P}recipices$

In the summer of 1939, Hitler made it clear that his goal was to conquer more and more land, and the world held its breath. In 1936, it had been the Rhineland. In 1938, his troops invaded Austria, and he annexed the Sudetenland. The last war had so devasted France and England that they signed the Munich agreement to secure peace. Then Nazi troops marched into Prague, and the allies saw that Hitler would not stop. In May 1940, the Pact of Steel between Germany and Italy put Europe on even higher alert. Poland was next—the only question was when Hitler would attack, and despite their desire to avoid war, France and England were committed to defend Poland. All across continents, people wondered, was the world headed for another massive war?

Also in the summer of 1939, Rosemarie was falling in love. The heavy talk of war was everywhere, in cafés, at school, and in the news, but she tried to ignore it. She'd come to Paris to escape the Reich. She'd come to Paris to start a new life, to lose herself in her art, and that dream was coming true. Every day, she painted, and throughout the week she explored museums and cafés with Celeste and César, experiencing all the delights of the city. Despite the dark rumors that rumbled around her, life was marvelous. She decided it was time for the two men in her life to meet.

One afternoon in late June, Rosemarie secured a table at La Belle Aurore, one of her favorite cafés on the Left Bank, not far from the Sorbonne. As she waited for César and Mr. Lieb to arrive, she sketched the Paris shops across the street.

What would her papa think of this mysterious man who'd so captured her heart and mind? César had been cagey about what he did for work—something about a workshop and helping refugees was all he'd told her. He'd been a doctor, but he wasn't practicing in France. How did he earn money? He seemed like the most trustworthy person she'd ever met, but who was he, really?

The enticing strains of violin music danced in the wind. Where was it coming from? She thought someone must be playing on the other side of the café around the corner. It was a kicky tune that made her feel like waltzing. Unable to recognize the composer, she left her table to investigate, and there was Mr. Lieb, serenading the café patrons. What joy he expressed when he played, swaying and grinning to the rhythm as he played the jubilant music. People clapped, and a young couple did a little dance. Rosemarie tapped her foot in time to the music.

César rode up on his bicycle. He was easy to spot thanks to that red beret and those smoldering eyes. He stood beside her on the sidewalk as Mr. Lieb continued a medley of tunes, some French café music, a few classical clips.

"What a great idea, a violinist at the café." César gave her a quick hug, then held her hand as they listened.

"He's good, isn't he?" Rosemarie laughed.

She watched Mr. Lieb's face carefully, but she saw no reaction to her standing there with a man in a red beret, holding his hand.

When Mr. Lieb finished, he bowed to gracious applause and wiped the rosin off his violin. He shook people's hands and made his way toward Rosemarie and César.

"Papa, what a surprise!" she said, laughing as she lifted a wood curl from his hair. "This is César, my Spanish friend I told you about."

Mr. Lieb's blue eyes were serious, but he was smiling as he grasped César by the shoulders and kissed both cheeks. "You're the doctor I've heard about."

César had to look up slightly to meet Mr. Lieb's eyes. "Well, not much of one these days. And you're the famous luthier Rosemarie brags about."

Rosemarie watched her two men look each other over for a moment, and then she led them to her table. They politely sat down and ordered coffee. She drew doodles in her sketchbook as they chatted about the weather in Paris in June. But she sensed that unspoken sentences hovered over the table. Were those unformed words about the rumors of war or the fact that it was obvious Rosemarie and César had become more than friends? She waited for it—she was sure César would bring up politics and that Mr. Lieb would ask César what kind of work he did.

She was wrong. Right away, César said he was doing various jobs around the city.

"What kind?" Rosemarie asked.

He looked at her and played with his mustache. She focused on his lips and for a moment lost herself in the memory of their passionate kisses a few days earlier. "I'm with an organization that helps refugees," he said. "We find food, clothing, and, well, there are other things refugees need, especially now."

Mr. Lieb looked impressed. "That's a fine thing to do. I hear they're flooding into the city."

Rosemarie asked, "Because of the possible war?"

César answered, "When, not if the war starts, the Jewish people who need to get away won't be able to escape the Reich. It's almost impossible to emigrate out of Germany now. And there will be trouble in France, too."

Loud voices interrupted their conversation as several young men sat down a couple of tables away. "It will never happen," one of them said, throwing down a newspaper with tall black headlines.

"We're not going to go to war for a bunch of filthy Jews," another added.

Rosemarie felt César tense. She rested her hand on his leg, hoping to convey that he should stay calm. Mr. Lieb looked at the men and shook his head as if to say, "Stupid young men." Then he whispered, "Many who are anti-war are also anti-Jewish."

César growled, "Don't they see—they'll just become cannon fodder if there's a war."

The men went on boasting, "Even if Hitler tries it on, we've got the Maginot Line. The French army is the strongest in Europe."

"Yeah, my cousin is stationed there already. It's a fortress!"

Rosemarie said to César, "You don't think there's any way to stop it?"

Mr. Lieb took out his pipe and started to fill it with tobacco. "War is the only way to stop Hitler. He's ignored all attempts to negotiate."

One of the men shouted out toward them, "Hey, it's not worth a war to save a few Jews, old man!"

Another shouted, "We can't save a bunch of foreigners. They should go back to their own country!"

Rosemarie saw how small their eyes were, pig eyes. She glared at them, then looked away from their daggers of hostility.

César started to stand up, and she jerked his arm down. "Don't fight, please."

Mr. Lieb shook his head and murmured, "I can take care of myself, César."

César said, "We're all refugees at this table. I can't abide that type. They're cowards." César said the last sentence loud enough to be heard.

Rosemarie sucked in her breath, sweat breaking out on her forehead.

"Hey—you're all foreigners, aren't you?" the leader shouted with a sneer.

The temperature at their table rose several degrees. César was taking deep breaths, trying to control himself.

"And that girl, she's a Jew?"

Rosemarie cringed, and César launched out of his chair and grabbed the guy by the collar. They screamed at each other as Mr. Lieb quickly pulled her away from the table. Three other men raised their fists and began to chant, "No Jew war! No Jew war!" A few people raised their fists, looked at each other sheepishly, and then lowered their hands. Other patrons picked up their belongings and rushed away.

César and two of the men shoved each other, their curses filling the air. They looked like fighting bulls, snorting and spitting insults. Just then, the café manager rushed up with a couple of waiters and pulled César away from the other two. Shocked, Rosemarie started trembling. Mr. Lieb stretched his arm around her and pulled her close. *How did those men know she was Jewish?*

Mr. Lieb rushed over to the table and grabbed his violin and Rosemarie's sketchbook. The men César had stood up to were now standing side by side, all puffed up and glaring at him. The waiter told the men to stop harassing the customers and threatened to shut down the café for the day. Then the owner marched out, a tall, strongly built businessman in an expensive suit, a thunderous look on his face.

"What did you say about my café?" he said to the three troublemakers as he rested a hand on César's shoulder.

The young men threw their coffee cups to the ground, shattering them to pieces. The owner grabbed the one with the loudest mouth and twirled him around. "Fifty francs now, or I call the police."

Café patrons cheered as the men tossed money on the ground and stalked off. The owner shook César's hand, swept up the money, and rushed back into the café.

Looking sheepish, César smoothed back his hair and joined Rosemarie and Mr. Lieb. "I'm sorry, I know I'm too . . . I don't know, but I can't—"

Mr. Lieb patted César's shoulder. "You defended my Rosemarie. And all desperate foreigners!"

César was breathing hard. He stopped, sucked in a few breaths, and met Rosemarie's eyes. "Sorry to have scared you."

After the broken coffee cups were cleaned up, they sat back down, and César ordered a carafe of wine. When the waiter set it down, César poured, saying, "This is my apology." He raised his glass. "To peace with honor."

Rosemarie tipped her head in acknowledgment and sipped the wine, feeling the warmth spread through her body. "I just can't believe it," she said. "They were so hateful."

She was proud of César for standing up for justice and for her, but he'd get hurt someday with that temper.

Mr. Lieb softly said, "I gather that I can expect this kind of protection for my daughter if you're out walking with her?"

César nodded his head. "I defend all my friends. I would dedicate myself to you, if it was necessary. We're all survivors of our own wars. And the big ones. There are more coming."

For a few moments they rested in the near silence, the café punctuated only by the sounds of cars, the clink of dishes, and murmurs of quiet conversation. But Rosemarie could feel the eyes of other patrons on them. She'd glance over, and they'd quickly look away. *Was it because César had fought them or because it was clear they were foreign? Jewish?*

Under the table her hand sneaked over to César's thigh, her fingers pressing his flesh to let him know he hadn't scared her away. Wondering if she'd been sneaky enough about it, she glanced up at Mr. Lieb. He grinned and winked.

Winds of War

As the summer progressed into late August of '39, signs of impending war swept across the world. In the United States, Roosevelt tried to loosen the anti-war sentiment in Congress, but the US remained staunchly isolationist. In Great Britain, the pro-Fascist Mosely and his followers demonstrated against war, declaring it wasn't worth British lives to save Jews.

As Hitler continued to threaten Poland, war preparations were underway in Paris. Workmen tunneled *abri*—bomb shelters—throughout the city, and signs pointing to the nearest shelter appeared everywhere. Fear pressed its cold fingers on mothers who packed bags and pinned name tags on their young children who were to be evacuated to the south, as far from the Germans as their families could send them. Parents crushed into train stations giving their little ones a last kiss before the children tearfully boarded the trains.

The government ordered every café, restaurant, hotel, and home to adopt blackout protocols. All over Paris, people worked together to try to hide their city of light from the enemy overhead, hoping to avoid the kind of destruction of the previous war that had left many of their precious churches and other buildings in rubble. Blackout cloth was used for curtains and was also nailed to wooden partitions that would quickly fit over windows. And terrified Parisians carried gas masks in cases slung over their shoulders, armed against a toxic gas attack. The memories of the last war hung over the city.

Josef knew all too well what impending war meant and what war did to a city, a country—to people. It covered entire countries with a dusty, bitter taste, looming over everything and everyone and bringing with it a never-ending tug of grief. At the café where he was meeting Rosemarie and César that August day, he watched soldiers in stiff uniforms having last drinks before heading to the train station for mobilization to their units. Conversations buzzed like hordes of bees. Everyone talked about the news—the threat of the war, the call up of soldiers. Sitting back with his coffee and pipe, Josef shuddered from the sense of déjà vu.

Across the street, students waved banners in the name of peace. On the opposite street corner, banners fluttered in the breeze—*Fight the Fascists.*

Conflicting shouts echoed in the wind. "No war!"

"Stop Hitler!"

"Peace lovers are Jew lovers! No Jew war!"

So there it was again—the slur against peace and Jews. What these people didn't grasp was that Hitler was after world domination and would stop at nothing to get it. Josef's dread of that possibility infused his entire body.

"Papa!" He saw Rosemarie and César approaching the café, their hands swinging in rhythm to their steps. With his black hair and warm dark eyes, her young man cut a striking figure. The two of them were obviously falling in love.

He stood to greet them, and Rosemarie held him in a lingering hug. She smelled like fresh air. César kissed him on both cheeks. "Bonjour, Monsieur Lieb."

The couple settled at the table, their cheeks flushed. They shared not-so-secret glances. *Had she spent the night with him yet*, Josef wondered, internally blushing. It was difficult to see his little girl so grown up. This man was her first love, this Spaniard with the red beret and the trigger temper that was sparked by injustice. César was fiery, but he seemed to be a very good man.

The waiter brought their coffees, and Rosemarie said, "Hundreds of children were gathering outside the train station with tickets hanging from their necks."

César added, "And so many soldiers were rushing around. Something must have happened?"

A man at the next table looked up and announced, "Didn't you hear—Stalin and Hitler signed a non-aggression pact. Germany and Russia are allies."

The sharp voices of other people at the café joined in the chorus of questions.

"When? What?"

"That's impossible."

"Oh no—communists will all be arrested."

"War!"

"No!" Rosemarie's eyes darkened. "How could they?"

César slapped the table, his face flushed with anger. "That means it's all over—war will start at any time now."

"Why is it so inevitable?" Rosemarie asked.

Josef said, "That pact means that Hitler can freely attack Poland without interference from Russia. They'll simply divide Poland between them as two superpowers."

"I really hoped it wouldn't happen—this war," César said, his eyes filling with sorrow.

Arguments and discussions filled the café. Waiters frantically rushed back and forth with orders, stunned looks on their faces. An announcer on the wireless radio droned on about troop positions, numbers of units, and an order to carry gas masks at all times.

César folded his hands together, leaned forward on his elbows, and spoke in low tones. "Look, I have been wanting— well, I had to wait for the right time to tell you something. We need to talk."

Josef sensed an urgency in César's voice, his face. Rosemarie raised her eyebrows as if saying, *what is it you haven't told me?*

Glancing around the café, César shook his head. "No. Not here. We must speak in private. It's important."

"Your flat?" Rosemarie said. Josef glanced at her and noticed how quickly she blushed. So she'd been spending time with him at his flat? That was news. He wasn't sure what to think about it. His little girl?

César shook his head. "The Tuileries Garden—it's not far from here. There are benches by the flower beds where no one will hear us."

A sense of barely contained chaos reigned in Paris as people scampered to buses and ran to the new shelters, looking up to the sky for planes. With panic in their eyes, they hustled along carrying gas masks. Josef found it so strange that at the same time, other Parisians strolled along walking their dogs as if nothing sinister was going on in the world.

César led Rosemarie and Josef toward the garden, but Rosemarie stopped when the Louvre was in view. Lorries had drawn up in the courtyard where workmen were loading boxes and large paintings wrapped in canvas.

Rosemarie cried out, "Oh, no! They're taking the art out of the Louvre. They can't—"

"They're saving the art." César spat on the ground. "The Nazis will loot and steal everything."

Josef slid his arm around her, and they stood transfixed, watching the workmen gingerly roll a huge statue that towered well over the height of the lorry. It was covered in canvas, and workers led it carefully down a ramp, guiding it with ropes.

"That must be the *Winged Victory*! How can they move her—she's so fragile!" Rosemarie cried out.

"They'll take good care of her," said Josef, pulling her close. "She's survived thousands of years."

Tears filled Rosemarie's eyes. "The Louvre . . . all the priceless art . . ."

César was getting impatient. "Probably kept safe in caves. Listen, we need to get moving. There are things we must discuss. Today. Now."

Josef couldn't imagine what was so urgent. They'd been talking about war, but there was nothing any of them could do about it.

The sun beat down as if to warm the chill that gripped the soul of Paris. At the Place de la Concorde, scaffolding and sandbags were being put in place to protect the iconic Egyptian obelisk. Lorries rumbled by full of soldiers shouting, "Vive la France!"

Once they'd reached the park, César gestured to a bench, then pulled up a chair and faced the two of them.

He looked like someone who was going to deliver bad news. César met their eyes and spoke carefully. "We need to talk about some choices you need to make—decisions about how you can be safe when the war starts."

"Safe? No one will be safe," Rosemarie said, turning away to pat her eyes with her handkerchief. "But at least we're not Jewish on our passports."

"There is more danger than you know," César replied.

All around them horns were honking, and in the distance, people were singing "La Marseillaise."

Josef tried to contain his panic and waved at César to continue. "Go on. Tell us." He took out his pipe and tamped down the tobacco.

"It is difficult to tell you this, but you need to know that at this moment the French are rounding up refugees from Russia and Germany. Austria. 'Enemy aliens,' they call them. They're being sent to internment camps."

Rosemarie's face twisted. "Camps?! *France* has concentration camps? And not just for Jews?"

César nodded solemnly. "Yes. When I first came to France, I was a prisoner in one of their camps."

Josef nodded for him to go on. César had something on his mind he had to say.

César gritted his teeth, his eyes flashing. "The French are *no* one's saviors. They wouldn't let desperate people into this country. Starved and broken women and children trying to escape Franco were stopped at the border. They died of exposure and lack of medical attention. Wounds from the *stukas* that fired on them. When France finally let some of us in, they set up camps on the beaches, but there were no shelters of any kind, so we were exposed to deathly freezing air and water. They threw loaves of bread over the barbed wire. No medical care, no blankets, nothing."

"They won't do that to just ordinary civilians, people like us here in Paris, will they?" Rosemarie's voice was barely audible.

César gave her a look that Joshua interpreted to say, *you must wake up.* He ripped off his beret, lit a cigarette, and spewed smoke into the air. "Ordinary? No one and everyone is an ordinary person."

Rosemarie looked away, her cheeks flushed.

César sat up straight, his dark eyes aglow. "You must listen to me. There is only one way for you to be safe—remember, the minute war starts, *you* become the enemy—both of you. But there is a way to protect you: You become French. New names, new papers, and voilà, you're no longer Jewish or German. You must take me seriously on this."

Josef said, "Again? Another new identity?" He reflected while what César had said came together in his mind. "We thought we were safe here—no longer being Jews." The words were bitter in his mouth. The knife edge of a headache burrowed into his head as he thought about life in a camp—filth, lice, rats . . . vicious guards.

César said softly, "I can help you with this. I know a great deal about forging papers."

Rosemarie got up from the bench and stood beside Josef, as if he might be able shield her from what she was hearing. She quietly said, "You're a *forger*?"

"Yes. I've been helping refugees for a few months. That's why I'm so busy." He wiggled his ink-stained fingers.

"You've been keeping this from me?" He could feel that Rosemarie was trying to absorb this news. César was a man living on the edges of society, exactly the kind of man she'd been raised to avoid. Josef stayed still, trying to understand what César wanted them to do.

César looked apologetic. "How could I not? The underground life is highly secret. And I'm telling you now."

Josef tried to take all this in. "Let me understand, you want us to go underground here in France?"

César used his cigarette to light another one. "That's right. Look, you did it to leave Germany. This is not so different."

Lieb stood up, his legs unsteady. "But we escaped. We didn't stay there with our illegal papers." His voice trembled.

"I know that these arrests are happening now for German aliens, 'enemy aliens,' and unfortunately, that's how your papers define you now." César stopped talking and sat back in his chair.

Josef sat in quiet fear and indecision. A few moments of silence passed between them. Rosemarie paced, her shoes swishing the grass. This man was telling them they needed to cross the line again, take a terrifying chance.

"Oh, Papa." Rosemarie threw her arms around him. "We must do this. There's no other way."

"I know. I know, Rosemarie." Then he looked at César. "All right, César. Show us. We need to see how this works. Where do you have this operation? I want to see your papers. See for myself."

César shook Josef's hand and put his arm around Rosemarie. Setting her jaw, she looked defiant. Once again, if they did what César suggested, they'd be criminals with false papers.

Rosemarie held Mr. Lieb's arm as they stumbled along cobblestones on the Left Bank a few blocks from César's flat. She was still in shock from César's revelation and tried to keep her balance as César led them down a narrow pathway and up an old wooden staircase. She hesitated at the doorway, and César motioned them in. Two men working at desks looked up and greeted César. Pinned along the dingy yellow walls were sketches of people sitting in cafés and strolling the Luxembourg flower gardens. They looked like the work of a beginning art student. This place had been decorated to look like an art studio.

Several people with dusty clothing and desperate looks in their eyes were hunched in chairs along a wall. The place smelled of ink, paper, and glue—and what else was that in the air? Maybe photographic chemicals.

"This way—Daniel and Raoul, this is Rosemarie and Mr. Lieb."

The men stood up from their desks and nodded, then quickly sat again and returned to their desks, pens in hand. The desks were stacked with blank documents and lined with pots of ink and pens. A cardboard box held an array of official-looking stamps.

César motioned for them to follow him. "Here in the back is the photo setup and a darkroom. We do everything ourselves so we can guarantee privacy and security."

He led them to a desk and took out a set of newly forged identity papers and set them beside legal versions. Rosemarie and Mr. Lieb ran their fingers over them. She saw no difference between the originals and the forgeries. She looked at César. *This* is what he'd been doing when he said he was working to help refugees?

Mr. Lieb examined the papers, then followed César to a workstation and watched Daniel fill in the stamps and signatures on a document.

César grabbed a box of round, square, and rectangular stamps and pointed out the bottles of red, blue, and black inks. "These are the tools Daniel uses." He patted him on the shoulder.

"We make copies of original stamps as we collect them— they need to match the city, town, and *département* of France—for a new identity. We choose new identities from remote parts of the country where officials likely can't check the records."

Fascinated, Rosemarie asked, "How do you copy stamps?"

"Several ways: carve into rubber. Make clay impressions. Even a potato can be carved to hold a design, but not for long. There's also photoetching, but we don't have that kind of equipment. Too expensive."

"A potato!" Rosemarie exclaimed.

"Most of the time, it's rubber." César smiled. "Daniel, please copy the signature from this document." He presented a blank French identity card.

Daniel drew circles on a piece of scratch paper, then letters.

"That's how he warms up after looking at the signatures. It must look natural."

Daniel looked at the official signature on the original and then shaped the letters carefully on the new document. His skill was obvious to Rosemarie as he created the flourishes used in the original clerk's signature. He dabbed a stamp on an ink pad and tested it, then slowly and precisely pressed it onto the document. With a small brush, he tidied the edges of the new mark and used a magnifying glass to compare the original to the forgery. Then he handed the document to César who held it up for Mr. Lieb and Rosemarie's examination. She could see that the quality of Daniel's work was remarkable.

César excused himself, saying he had to check something in the darkroom.

Mr. Lieb whispered to Rosemarie, "I'm nervous about doing this. My business for one thing—LiebViol—my real name is part of the business."

It was clear to her now, what they had to do. "We must do this. A camp is a very bad place to be, especially for someone your age."

"*My* age?" Mr. Lieb raised an eyebrow.

Rosemarie slipped into an empty chair next to Daniel and rested her head in her hands. There was so much about César she didn't know. Could they trust him? She sat up and wiped her eyes. She liked him, she might even love him, and now he was trying to save them. But now everything about their lives seemed unstable again, unpredictable. To calm herself, she asked Daniel if she could use a pen. He smiled and nodded, so she picked up a pen and ink and started drawing. She chose black ink and fell into the spell of drawing a forest, thickets of trees, a way to escape the pounding of her heart for a few minutes. She sketched autumn leaves and sweeping grasses, which led to drawing letters in graceful calligraphy, a skill she'd developed as a girl. Curious, she wanted to see if she could copy an official signature. She saw one of the documents stacked on the desk, and while Mr. Lieb was talking to Daniel, she copied a few. Soon César appeared and glanced at her paper. "I knew you were talented with the pen."

Her face warmed at his praise.

"Mr. Lieb, did you know about this talent of hers with copying?" César asked.

Mr. Lieb nodded his head. "She's been using pen and ink all her life. Playing with signatures. Once she forged a note to the school office so she could leave early."

Rosemarie laughed. "You knew about that?"

César returned to the business at hand. "Let's discuss the names you might use on your papers. Mr. Lieb, you registered your address when you came into the country?"

"Yes, at Lucien's. I registered us both there."

César frowned. "You'll need to move to a new place. They will come for you at the address listed. I'm sorry."

Rosemarie said, "Mr. Lieb, I have the perfect solution. You can live with me, at the Rosenbergs'. They have extra rooms."

César looked serious. "If you decide to do this, we need to take your photos and decide on your names. These papers need to be ready quickly." He paused to look at them both. "I've been thinking—in fact thinking about this for a few days. I suggest DuBois for your surname, in honor of our luthier here. You know, *bois*, wood."

Mr. Lieb nodded, a tight-lipped expression of approval on his face.

César said, "Rosemarie, we need to change your name too. There are a few names I can think of for you. French women's names are lovely—Marguerite, Chantal, Simone."

Rosemarie murmured, "I like Simone. You know, I like the actress Simone Signoret."

Rosemarie whispered it to herself. Simone. Simone. It made her feel . . . what was it? She blushed as she realized she felt more voluptuous. More attuned to her body somehow. Luckily, César was busy writing lists and didn't see how her posture changed. She folded her arms over her chest. She was Sarah, really. But Sarah wasn't like this, comfortable in her body. She wasn't quite sure who Rosemarie was—an artist? But this Simone—she seemed more mature. A woman of substance.

César finally looked up and said, "So we are agreed? Simone DuBois? Now you—Josef. How about a very French name? How do you like the name Mathieu?"

Mr. Lieb nodded, looking thoughtful, even sad.

"Papa, what do you think of being called Mathieu?"

He looked up as if he was lost somewhere in time. "Someone I knew in the last war was named Mathieu. I suppose in this way I could honor him. It's a good name."

Rosemarie patted his arm. "I like it. Mathieu. Very French."

César placed paper and pen in front of them. "You must become familiar with these new names, as you had to do before. When your new papers are ready, you'll sign them as 'Mathieu and Simone DuBois.'"

They were assigned Alsace as their birthplace, so their slight German accents would be unremarkable. While César went off to set up the camera, Rosemarie, now Simone, and Josef, now Mathieu, signed their names a few times to practice. Rosemarie thought Mr. Lieb had a new tilt to his head as he tried on Mathieu. Perhaps a new name brought out personality traits they'd never felt before. Truly new identities.

César told Rosemarie not to smile as he snapped the picture, but that was impossible. With him as the photographer, smiling at her in his beguiling way, a smile came to her lips. With him behind the camera giving her instructions, "move your arm, sit looking this way, now that way," she started laughing and couldn't stop. Despite being scared or perhaps because she was so nervous, everything seemed funny. Finally, on the third take, she managed to shape her face into a properly serious expression. Her own face looked back at her. But who was she? Suddenly transformed into Simone DuBois with the flick of a pen? Now she had to leave both Sarah and Rosemarie behind. Extraordinary, the power of paper and ink.

She paused to think, a rush of emotion as she realized what she'd have to give up. "You realize this is not going to work at the art school—me with a new identity."

César frowned, and Mr. Lieb shook his head. He said, "You can still paint at the Rosenbergs'. You and Celeste have your little studio, don't you?"

Rosemarie felt a pang in her heart as she considered giving up her dream of art school in Paris. But now, the world had changed, and there were more important choices to be made.

She patted Mr. Lieb on the arm. "Yes, of course I'm still free to paint whatever I want. In some ways it's better—no more struggling with the teacher about my dark palette!"

César patted her on the shoulder and got up to talk to his team about their new papers.

Three hours later, Rosemarie—no, it was Simone—held her new papers in her hands. Now she was Simone DuBois. She felt a little dizzy as she whispered the name over and over, "Simone DuBois. I'm Simone." The best part was that she would be officially Mathieu DuBois's daughter.

Sitting beside her, Mathieu, *her* Mr. Lieb, cradled the new documents in his hands, French identification documents, birth certificates, and passports. She would think of him as Mr. Lieb no matter what she had to start saying in front of other people, no matter what any papers stated.

"I like DuBois," she said. "Woods. Simone of the Woods. I like Simone DuBois."

"Father and daughter," repeated Mr. Lieb. Mathieu. She would have to concentrate. He was Mathieu now. She felt a pang in her heart. Yes, he had been her father for years. And now they'd be in the same house again—with the Rosenbergs. She glanced at Mr. Lieb. He met her eyes. She took his hand and squeezed.

"All right, Monsieur DuBois. We will be all right with all this. We should be safe." She would make herself believe it was true.

It Begins

The Sunday the world changed forever was balmy and beautiful. At 11:15 a.m. on September 3, 1939, Prime Minister Chamberlain announced that Hitler had failed to respond to British demands to leave Poland. In a grim, serious voice, he announced to his people, "This country is at war with Germany."

The Seine meandered through Paris, curling and curving through the city, under arched bridges packed with sandbags, flowing by Notre-Dame. She was ready for war with her rose window boarded up and scaffolding protecting her heart.

At 5 p.m., France officially declared war. Bells rang. Sirens screamed. Parisians looked to the sky for planes. Most people stayed home, trying to adjust to a war footing in the City of Light, but thousands scurried to shelters. The city was locked down. Shutters slammed shut on theaters and restaurants.

Red placards were pasted up all over town ordering enemy aliens to report for internment.

The night the announcement of war was to be broadcast, Rosemarie and the Rosenbergs invited Mr. Lieb and César over to listen to the wireless radio together. Candles flickered in the shadowy dining room darkened by heavy blackout curtains.

Celeste clutched one of Rosemarie's hands and César squeezed the other tight as they all huddled together, faces reflecting sorrow as they listened to the announcement of war. Rosemarie took comfort that she was with her Paris family. The war was now upon them.

"Can you believe it—this is the third war with Germany in seventy years," Claude said, turning down the radio and lighting a cigarette.

César clicked his tongue. "But the first involving a demagogue like Hitler."

"Mr. Lieb, I hope you're comfortable in your room," Nicole said, counting out silverware to set the table.

Mr. Lieb stood up. "We have something we need to tell you. César helped us, well, I suppose you'd say he helped us avoid the danger of being picked up as enemy aliens. We have new papers now. New names."

Rosemarie nodded. "Now I'm Simone DuBois, and Mr. Lieb is going by the name of Mathieu DuBois."

Nicole's eyes widened, and Claude looked serious. "You don't say. We'll need to be very careful then if we have company or meet outside the house. Here I can only imagine you being Joshua Lieb. Well, Josef too, but . . . It's okay. I'll learn. We'll adjust quickly."

"Rosemarie, that is, Simone, always calls you Mr. Lieb," Celeste said.

He smiled. "You all may call me that when we're together. It's my name to those who know me best. But do try to get used to Mathieu. All of you."

César said, "If our Simone and Mathieu have proper papers and aren't found at the original address where Josef Lieb registered when coming into the country, it's more likely they'll be safe."

Claude said, "Of course, you'll stay here with us, Josh . . . um . . . Monsieur DuBois."

Mathieu filled his pipe, and the welcome aroma of his walnut tobacco floated through the room. "I am very grateful to you for your hospitality, my friends. And for your understanding. My blue room upstairs, as you call it, is quite lovely."

Celeste said, "Hey, we're alive. I suggest we play dance music tonight and hope that there are no air raid sirens or bombs. This is still *our* Paris. Mama made a special dessert. She's calling it 'The Paris Victory cake.'"

Everyone applauded, and a glowing Nicole took a bow as she delivered the cake to the table, decorated in red, white, and pale blue frosting. Simone helped Celeste and Nicole set the dessert plates on the table as the Rosenbergs tried to turn the solemn gathering into an evening of music fit for dancing. They lifted glasses of bubbly champagne as Claude called out, "Who knows how long we'll have champagne? Let's drink it now!"

Simone tried to lift herself into the spirit by reasoning that as long as they were alive, they should live fully. As usual, the Rosenbergs had an uplifting effect on her, and for now her dark thoughts of war would be tucked behind a closed door.

Simone joined the chorus and lifted her glass. The bubbles tickled her throat. Perhaps the hope for victory would ease her heartache. Germany was her homeland, where she'd spent her childhood, where she'd been happy for fourteen years before Hitler turned the country into the Reich. How strange to imagine Germany and France at war. And what about her mother still in Germany? The rumors said that Jews had been forced to move from their homes. Where were her mother and grandparents? Now Germany could face attacks by the Allies. If only she could learn where her mother was and whether she and her grandparents were all right. She tried to swallow a lump in her throat with the next sip of champagne.

Simone distracted herself from her worried thoughts by swaying to the music as the Victrola played "Summertime." César too seemed to have surrendered to the pleasant atmosphere the Rosenbergs created. Looking at her with his ardent Spanish gaze, he took Simone in his arms and pressed her close to him. She felt his breath in her ear and inhaled his rustic scent as they swayed to the next song, "Begin the Beguine." *Why did the two men in her life always smell like a forest?* she wondered. And now, she and Mathieu were *DuBois*. A strange coincidence.

"Mon amour," César murmured, pressing her closer, his hands warm on her back. She could feel the muscles of his thighs, his desire for her, and hers flared in response. It was a desire she'd tried to push away, cautious about letting their love advance to the next stage.

"What do you say we go out tonight? See what's happening in Paris." He grinned, twirling her around.

She whispered, "Do you think M . . . Mr. Lieb will mind? The Rosenbergs?"

"Let's bid them goodbye. Have a drink on our own. If we can find a bar open."

Simone felt the thrill of breaking the rules. She announced to everyone, "We're going out for a drink."

"Nothing will be open," Mathieu said, a frown appearing between his eyebrows.

Claude said, "In Paris, even during war, the bars are open. Have a cocktail. Report back to us about the state of the city."

Celeste chimed in, "The bars will create new cocktails for tonight! You know, a rebellious response to the lockdown."

Simone embraced her Mr. Lieb. He kissed her forehead and told her to take care and to come home soon. He said he trusted César to take good care of her, and they assured him they'd be careful. Celeste kissed her cheeks and winked.

César held her hand as they skipped out the door, the streetlights with their flickering pale blue lights like necklaces twinkling in the dark.

They stumbled along, looking for a bar on the mostly darkened Left Bank. Only by the sound of loud music could they tell when they were near an open bar. People were drinking and toasting to victory. Simone heard the same phrases she'd heard repeated in cafés for the past month, "The Maginot Line will stop them!"

"We'll win again!"

"It will be over by Christmas."

They found a corner table, and César ordered a cocktail made of something she'd never heard of and later couldn't remember. The music was loud, American jazz with blaring saxophones and trombones. César sat close to her, nibbling her ear, his hand on her thigh making its way up her leg under her skirt. He kissed her softly, his eyes asking for more. The lights in the bar flickered, and then the room went black. There was a howl of protest, then voices, "Should we go to the shelters now? What are we supposed to do?"

A few seconds later, the lights flickered back on, and everyone cheered.

César said, "Let's go. Come with me. Please." There was something in his voice, an urgency.

Simone's stomach twisted. They'd kissed and touched each other passionately three or four times when she'd gone with him to his room, but when César grew more fervent, she would stop him. She'd apologize, and he would kiss her and tell her not to worry. There was no hurry. But she knew she'd been holding back from something that was natural. She was drawn to him, and he excited her, but she just hadn't been ready for the next big step. Was it because she'd been taught that marriage should come first or because she'd grown afraid of men as the boys she'd known turned into Hitler Youth who looked at her and other girls like objects to conquer? And tucked in the back of her mind, there was the Nazi.

Giggling, they stumbled up the stairs to César's flat, arms around each other, pausing to kiss on the stairway. They stopped kissing and laughing long enough to look out at the city through his skylight. The last time they'd been in his room, the lights on the Eiffel Tower had blinked and danced, but now all the way to the horizon there was nothing but black.

They could hardly see each other, but their bodies yearned to be close, her fingers outlining his ribs, tugging the hairs on his chest. *Was it the cocktail that made her feel free?* she wondered as they pulled at each other's clothes and collapsed giggling on his bed. She told him to lead, to show her. It was time for her to understand.

His skin tasted like sweat and tobacco. She ran her fingers over a scar on his shoulder, asked him what happened. He shook his head and kissed her, laugh-kissing. He rolled her over, his lips all over her body. She sank into his kisses and the places they took her. She'd never been able to imagine how it would be, making love, but words and doubts disappeared as he touched her in places that no one had ever touched. Her body rose to him, as if it had a mind of its own. His lips on her breast lit a fire in her belly, and she told him, "Now. Please now."

"Yes. *Mi amor*," he whispered and pressed himself against her. She'd heard about expecting it to hurt the first time, but she felt only a stab of pain, then a rush of desire and her body surging toward him until she lost track of where he ended and she began.

As they rested in each other's arms afterward, she knew something had forever changed. Now they were lovers. They were *together*. They were part of each other. In the middle of a war.

The Artist's Touch

That October, autumn transformed Paris into a lush painting of warm colors. The trees didn't know of war, and their leaves turned magical yellow, red, and golden amber. Six weeks after war was declared, the people of the City of Light continued to dance and eat and sing in the streets, wearing optimism and cheer like a newly designed garment. Paris reopened after the lockdown when war was declared early in September. Except for bomb shelters spread through the city and uniformed soldiers on leave sitting in cafés, Paris looked as it had before the war, its people going to work and enjoying the theater and cabarets, their gas mask cases cast aside as they determined not to be dour simply because there was a war raging in Poland, far, far away.

For Simone and Celeste, the most painful reminders of the war were the shuttered museums, empty of the art that made up the very soul of Paris. Without her friends Van Gogh and Matisse, Monet and Renoir, and the art that spoke of culture and vision and history, Simone felt bereft. And of course, the *Winged Victory,*

Nike. She'd flown off to safety somewhere deep in the countryside where she'd be safe along with her sister, the *Venus de Milo*. But when would the world see them again?

As she walked to the café to meet César, Simone's feet shuffled through fallen leaves, and she inhaled fresh air tinged with the aroma of earth. She'd come to Paris eager to immerse herself in art, but now that the war had started, it was clear that art couldn't be her focus. César had his secret work, and it meant something. It had a purpose. *He* had a purpose. For the last few weeks, she'd been developing a project of her own, and now she wanted to show it to César. To make him say yes.

When she arrived at Café de Flore, César was leaning back in his chair, slowly smoking his cigarette, notepad and pen beside him on the table. His jet-black hair and dark eyes made her heart pound more every day. Not only did he sweep her off her feet with his charms, she was smitten by his kind nature. She admired the toughness of someone who'd survived terrible things paired with a mind that always had an idea of how to make things better. She tried to appear calm, but her body always surged whenever he was near.

"Bonjour," Simone greeted him. "My name is Simone DuBois. What is yours?" She held out her hand and flipped her hair back.

Grinning, César leaned over and whispered, "Names. What do they mean, really?"

She smiled. How could one ever know for sure who another is? Names and family lineage had once been the way people established trust. Ancestry was a way to vet lineage and reputation, but the Nazis had made that dangerous for millions of Jews. And now the French were doing the same.

"You and I have a great deal in common." He leaned back and sipped his coffee.

"We do?"

"We're survivors. And we're magical, like chameleons." He called the waiter and ordered wine. "We change our colors as necessary."

Simone sat and spoke softly. "How do we ever know who people are?"

César tapped his cigarette ash and looked at her. Waiters bustled by. Sirens screamed. His eyes were dark and mysterious, and an amused smile played on his lips. "I suppose you'll need to decide if you can trust me."

She smiled and opened her satchel. "Actually, I want to know if you will trust *me*, whoever you are." She took out the work she'd been practicing at home.

"Oh?" he leaned forward to look at the pages she laid on the table, placing sugar cubes, spoon, cups, and saucers on each page to keep them from blowing away.

"I've been practicing."

She was nervous. She wanted to become a forger, and her plan was to persuade him to let her in. Whenever she visited the workshop, she'd practiced copying the signatures of clerks in the documents she saw stacked on the desk. But she'd gone even further than that. Using small brushes, she copied a couple of the stamps she'd found in Daniel's box.

Making sure no one could overhear, she leaned close and whispered, "I know you need more people to do your special work. You can't keep up with the flood of refugees coming into Paris—the Russians and Romanians, Spaniards, the Czechs, and all the others. And it's getting so heated now. I need to help."

She slid the papers toward him to examine, knowing that what was happening in Paris mattered to him. And that he needed more help trying to save people. Paris had become a city of lost souls. César knew that the gendarmes were combing the city, plucking refugees from alleyways and empty buildings, from refugee centers and apartments. The police carried rifles and marched them to lorries and forced them to climb inside for a one-way journey to the camps. All that made César's work even more important. He needed her for his cause.

César examined the papers, each line, each letter, and the details of the stamps she'd drawn. He looked up, a slight smile playing on his lips. "It's, well, it's more than excellent. You're very talented, but let me understand something—you want to be part of this? You're not worried about being caught? About it being illegal?"

She straightened her shoulders. "*You're* doing it. And the men at the studio. My work is better than some of theirs. You know that."

"Well, it's not that. It's—"

"It's what? That I'm a girl—" she huffed.

"No! It's *very* dangerous, and you're young. You have a whole life ahead of you. Do you have any idea what might happen should you be caught? I'm used to living with this kind of danger. But you have your art and your friends. Gallery openings and literary discussions."

"So I'm just a frivolous young girl who tinkers with art!" Her neck felt hot. She gathered and tucked the papers in her satchel and stood up. "I still think art is important even if the world is burning!" She grabbed her jacket. The heat of anger flushed her face.

"Wait, Simone. Please." He touched her shoulder.

She shook him off and glared at him.

"Please, come closer so I can tell you something." His voice was soft, inviting.

"I feel the same way you do about this war," she said. "I need to do something to help here." She crossed her arms over her chest.

"I want to tell you something." He rested his hand on her shoulder again and tried to pull her toward him, but she didn't give.

His scent was intoxicating, musky, with a hint of spice, and the game they were playing gave her a thrill. He lifted her chin with his forefinger, his breath on her cheek. His eyes caught hers, those dark eyes. He pressed his lips to her ear and whispered. "Tomás Vidal."

She pulled back and gave him a curious look.

César said, "He is Spanish. A Catalonian in exile. He has chosen to live as a Frenchman. Until he can go home."

"He was born Tomás Vidal?" she whispered, trying to align that name with César's face.

"*Oui.*" He gave her a wink. "And that César, he's very conservative and careful. But Tomás, he thinks you should have a chance to use your talent."

Simone wrapped her arms around this complicated man with the two names. "Thank Tomás for me and tell César that I will be at his studio in the morning."

Smiling, he nuzzled her neck. "My new forger." Then he softly kissed her on the lips. "*Mi amor.*"

"*Je t'aime,*" Simone whispered.

La Drôle de Guerre

That spring morning on her way to the workshop, Simone tried to keep her balance on frozen sidewalks, thinking back to the beginning of the war in September. Panic had filled Paris, and it seemed that no one could go longer than a minute without looking to the sky. Everyone was on edge, waiting for an attack. People had been hauled off to camps, and those who'd thus far avoided being picked up lived in constant terror. The French government was reluctant to press toward a new war after losing millions of its people only twenty years earlier, so the military developed a *wait and see* attitude. As in the previous fall when the war began, Parisians still carried rubber gas masks, and the frequent air raid sirens jolted Parisians out of bed. Again and again, Simone rushed to the shelter, but to her relief, no bombs fell. Within a few weeks, almost everyone in Paris had adjusted to the routine and would simply ignore the sound of a siren.

The period of war between September 1939 and April 1940 was free of anything resembling war. The French called it "*drôle de guerre*," the Brits called it "the phony war," and the Germans called it "sitzkrieg." Paris returned to its gaiety and unique style—theaters and cafés were full to bursting, the ballet and nightclubs were at full throttle. By November, Simone, like so many other Parisiennes, found the gas mask cases useful as a chic purse. In the middle of that winter, she had a birthday but hadn't felt like celebrating. She spent the day working with César, and he surprised her in the evening with a dinner of roasted potatoes sprinkled with cheese. Nicole and Celeste invited them to come over for cake, simple but delicious. Rationing had dramatically limited butter, eggs, and flour, and Simone was deeply touched by all their efforts to make her birthday special.

Shivering, Simone pulled her coat close around her. The wind flicked at her skirt and bit into her legs. It had been the coldest winter on record. As she scurried along, she heard noises behind her. Whipping around, she checked to see if someone was following her, but she saw only a vast white world and the wind blowing crisp leaves into frantic circles as stark tree branches etched the sky. She always startled at unexpected noises. Was she truly safe in Paris? What about Captain Schmidt—could he come to Paris and find her? Pulling her coat tight around her, she hurried on, trying to rid herself of the image of his face, those lifeless eyes.

Simone reached the workshop, unlocked the door, and entered the cold dark workspace. Four desks faced each other, and along the wall, chairs awaited their new clients. In the back were the darkroom and photo setup with camera and lights.

Her first task was to light the stove. Refugees would arrive soon for new papers, and she wanted to warm them with coffee and hospitality. The cups were tiny, but she could tell the coffee warmed their hands and their hearts. As she got to know César's business, she learned about a network of people who were trying to help refugees stay out of the camps. Some were communists who'd gone underground when Germany and Russia announced their pact in August. France judged all communists a national threat, arresting many thousands and sending them to internment camps. César told her about the Gurs camp in southern France with its rickety shelters that had no walls. During winter rains, the prisoners trudged through ankle-deep mud. The food was a thin soup of garbanzo beans, rotten potatoes, and maggot-ridden meat if they were lucky. Lice, typhus, cholera, dysentery. No medical care.

The idea of being sent to any of the French camps terrified even the most stalwart and gave fuel to the idea that one must risk everything to live free. That's where César and the forgers became necessary.

The flame caught, crackling and snapping, and Simone scooped coffee into the pot. Today it was real coffee; on odd days it was roasted barley. When the "real war" did begin, rationing would curtail food supplies even more.

The room began to warm, and the delicious aroma of coffee offered some comfort to Simone. Then the door flew open, and César rushed in, his hair flying all over the place as it escaped his beret. She lifted her face to kiss him, despite his face stubbled with three days of beard.

He leaned down, his hair tickling her skin, and when they kissed, it was prickly, sweet, and too brief. He pulled away, a troubled look on his face. Something was on his mind. "Listen, I just heard a rumor that gendarmes are combing Paris for illegal refugees, so we must be even more careful. I asked Georges to stand guard at the opening to the cul-de-sac that leads to our building. He'll whistle if someone who looks suspicious shows up, and we'll have to quickly hide the documents in the cabinets and spread the art that we have ready all over the tables."

Simone's breath caught in her throat. He kissed her gently again and assured her it was just a matter of caution. She needed to hear it even though she knew it wasn't true. She pressed close for his touch, the strength of his body against hers as he kissed her slowly, melting her tension.

"More of that later tonight," he said with a wink. The aroma of coffee and his kisses were only a temporary comfort. The lingering worry about their safety in Paris stabbed her stomach. There was no getting away from it. She couldn't bear to think about what might happen if they were caught.

She poured the steaming coffee into cups, and they sat together briefly at one of the workstations that was neatly set up with ink, pens, and documents. César gulped his coffee and squeezed her hand as he got up to welcome a new set of clients.

Men and women, young, old, and from different nationalities, shuffled into the room behind Daniel, César's right-hand man. He glanced at Simone and César, his brown eyes magnified behind his thick glasses. He smiled as he helped people find chairs along the wall where they'd wait to be processed: A photograph would be taken, and then they'd learn their new identities and professions. Tomorrow they'd return to sign their new papers. Daniel gave each person a small cup of coffee, and they replied with wan smiles. Every day, Simone thought about the significance of what they were doing here—giving people hope, giving fellow Jews and "enemy aliens" a chance for safety. They were actually *saving* some people from torture and death. She couldn't imagine any pursuit in all the world that could make her feel more useful, more satisfied. This was where she belonged.

Daniel was an excellent forger, and they were lucky to have him. Most of the young men in Paris had been mobilized, but he'd had rheumatic fever as a child which left him with a heart murmur, so the army had refused him. He was a gentle, polite young man and also a very good teacher. Simone observed his forging techniques and admired how diligently and carefully he worked.

Since she'd begun this work in October, Simone had learned something new every day about the fine details of the craft, from choosing the correct ink and pen nib to the many subtleties of calligraphy techniques. Most important, Daniel had patiently taught her how to manage the official stamps that authenticated the documents. If they had already carved stamps from the *département* of the village or town of their client's place of birth, the work went quickly. But if they had to copy from an old document, that's when Simone's skill as an artist became extremely valuable. She'd draw details of the stamp with a brush and the proper color of ink until she could produce a stamp that was a perfect match for the original. For the first time, she felt she was where she belonged using her art skills. She was making a difference.

This morning César was going over how to create documents that were less likely to be questioned. Simone listened—she was always looking for ways to hone her skills.

"For each person, we create an identity that can't be traced. Try to fit the new identity to their demeanor, personality, and physique. Find places on the map of France for potential birthplaces distant from major cities so the names can't be checked. Give people professions that seem to fit them physically—their size, their age—don't give someone with smooth hands the occupation of farmer. Ask them what they know, which profession they know something about and will be able to speak of convincingly. We can assign men jobs from a range of professions, but of course it's best they have some basic knowledge of the trade, though we've seen that people can be very good at improvising when their life depends on it. Married women can be listed as housewives and single women as secretaries or waitresses. If someone has a talent—like a singer or dancer—or if they have a legitimate profession, we can use that. A woman could be listed as a nurse even if she's only good at first aid. There needs to be variety."

Once the lesson was over, Simone returned to her workstation. She chose a brush to copy a stamp that was too complex to carve. To her, it was a challenge to see if she could copy something that would appear to be engraved—a challenge she relished. She settled in and concentrated on forming the proper letters and designs.

An attack from Germany was imminent, so she worked at least eight hours a day, while outside the workshop, she painted at home when she had time and enjoyed her gallery outings with Celeste. They mourned the loss of the art in the museums they loved so much, but they told themselves that those priceless pieces would one day be returned to the museums where they belonged. And they reminded themselves that they were still artists, that one day when the world was ready, their art would find its way into the world. They believed that completely.

After a day of hard work together, César and Simone would stroll by the Seine to visit the gardens, shops, and cafés of the Left Bank and watch the world go by—the French soldiers on leave in Paris, families enjoying the beautiful spring weather.

Then in early May, the news came that the Germans had attacked the Low Countries, bringing *la drôle de guerre* to an abrupt end. Parisians hoped the French military would beat back the Germans before they could threaten Paris. César and Simone, and all of Paris, held their breath.

Blitzkrieg

*I*n the spring of 1940, the blitzkrieg, the lightning war, exploded in Norway and Denmark, and on May 10, the German army burst through borders and crossed rivers at lightning speed, overrunning the Low Countries and France. Engines of the dive-bombing *stukas* screamed as the planes dove low for precision hits, terrifying the people below. Rotterdam burst into an inferno, attacked even after the Netherlands had already surrendered. At the last moment, barely escaping capture, Queen Wilhelmina, her government, and her family went into exile in England.

By 1939, the French army had stationed thousands of men on the famous Maginot Line fortification built between Germany and France, but the line ended at Belgium, leaving a gap at the Ardennes Forest. The German forces smashed through the Ardennes with their powerful tanks and swung around and pressed them toward the English Channel, leaving the road to Paris open and undefended.

To offer the illusion of normal life and to prevent panic, the French government kept Parisians in the dark about the assault, but the first clue to ordinary citizens that something was terribly wrong occurred on May 10.

At five in the morning that day, Parisian were awakened by screaming anti-aircraft sirens. Simone sat up in bed, dizzy and disoriented. She opened her door to find Celeste wiping her eyes and asking if they should really go to the shelters. Mr. Lieb came out of his room trying to tuck in his shirt, his gray hair mussed from sleep.

"It might just be another drill," he said, "but it's safer to go to the shelter."

"I have to find César," Simone said, disappearing back into her room. She grabbed her clothes, her heart pounding. *What if, what if,* peppered her mind, as she buttoned her blouse and then pulled on her shoes. *What if it's a real attack on Paris? What if he didn't go into the shelter? What if something happens to César or Mr. Lieb?* She flung open her bedroom door and found a severe-looking Mr. Lieb waiting in the hall, inches away. He clasped her shoulders with his strong hands and peered into her eyes.

In his authoritarian father voice, he commanded, "Simone, you will come with us now. You're not running around Paris on your own!" He rarely spoke in that voice, and she knew it signaled that she didn't dare go against his wishes.

Claude and Celeste met Nicole at the door, holding a torch to light their way through the dim, uneven streets. Mr. Lieb wrapped his arm around Simone as if to keep her from running away as they all slipped out the door. Neighbors joined them on the trek to the shelter three blocks away, footsteps clacking on the cobblestones.

The family had dashed to this shelter several times since the start of the war. Simone was also familiar with the shelter near César's apartment—dark, dank, and miserable. Over the months of these warnings, nothing serious had happened after the sounding of the sirens—no bombs, no attacks. A relief, so why bother to get out of bed? *La drôle de guerre* seemed to be just that, a funny idea of war that never began, so the common thinking was that perhaps it never would. Like most Parisians, the family would return to bed and grab another few hours of fitful sleep. But bombs or no bombs, after the start of the war in September, no one ever got enough sleep. In the unconscious, the body's deep wisdom was set to keep an ear open for clues of danger.

Airplanes buzzed overhead as everyone's feet tap-tapped on the sidewalk. Finally, they reached the shelter. They ducked inside, and in the shadows, they could see people perched on benches and pressed up against the moist walls. Cigarette smoke created a haze that made everything even murkier. The children who'd avoided evacuation whined, but for the most part the citizens of Paris were accustomed to the routine. The shelter was only half-full, so Simone and the Rosenbergs found seats away from fussing babies and old men who smelled as if they'd been sleeping in the alleys. Claude and Mathieu provided a barrier between the women and other men who might try to sit close by—there was always some fellow whose hands wandered.

Nicole took out her knitting, and Celeste and Simone drew on their sketch pads to pass the time. Simone's attention wandered to an old woman wearing a long gypsy scarf and multiple layers of beads, and she enjoyed sketching such an unusual character. A man several feet away murmured over and over, "They're coming, they're coming," and covered his eyes with his hands. A young French soldier wearing his uniform bounced a baby on his knee while the woman next to him played games with another child. He must have been home on leave. The owner of the boulangerie passed out pastries from a basket and reminded them all that because it was Friday there would be no pastries for sale that day—these were day-old. The air raid warden kept checking for the sound of the all-clear, and finally, at ten in the morning, the doors opened.

No bombs fell, but the ack-ack guns pounded away toward aircraft over Paris, their thundering booms reverberating in Simone's chest. The air was laced with the portent of more to come.

Later that day, Simone tried to keep her mind on her work at César's studio, and even tried to get herself to paint something— perhaps a dark painting was in order given what was going on in the world, but her worries about Nazis getting closer—possibly all the way to Paris?—made her feel the horrible tightening in her shoulders and chest she'd known so well in Berlin. In the afternoon, she forced herself to focus on making perfectly formed letters at César's workshop, but she had to throw away one document and start over.

It didn't help that César made cynical comments about the war. "The Germans could be upon us before the government would know it. My friends are listening to the German station Radio Stuttgart. They say we're in deep trouble."

Simone, always the optimist, tried to envision the French simply wiping out the Nazis. All around her on the streets and in cafés, she heard the French people declaring their confidence in their military.

A few days later, the idea that the French army was invincible began to unravel. The French ramparts at Sedan on the Meuse River—only two-hundred kilometers from Paris—collapsed in mid-May. A government official announced to his compatriots, "The road to Paris is open!" But this information was carefully hidden from the French people.

The government kept tight control on what its citizens knew. News about the invasion was excised from the newspapers, leaving blank white columns. The main sources of the information that circulated within the cafés of Paris were rumors and Radio Stuttgart, the German station that accurately, as it turned out, warned the French people correctly about the progress of the war.

As the news rolled out, fiery debates broke out at cafés, in government meetings, and among the elite of the French government.

"The Germans couldn't possibly defeat the French!"

"But the Germans and their blitzkrieg have created extreme danger."

"Paris in danger? Never."

"You can't trust the government. Who can we trust?"

Some Parisians preferred to cast their eyes only to what they wanted to see, so they walked their little white dogs as they always had and took their apéritifs at the usual time. They made certain to enjoy a fine dinner, as fine as could be had under rationing, and they pretended there was no war. In their minds, the Third Republic was well protected, and of course, fully defended. Soon, they believed, the dangers would pass.

But for those in Paris who were wide awake, it was impossible not to see the disasters already unfolding. Thousands of refugees had fled Belgium and northern France with their families, farm animals, and a cart or bicycle piled with possessions. Most fled with nothing but the clothes on their back. All over Paris, soup kitchens were set up under canopies to offer food, shoes and clothing, and kind words to thousands of starving people from the north of France who'd been traumatized by the blitzkrieg. They'd run for their lives as bombs exploded and the deadly German *stukas* machine gunned them as they ran down the road. The German tanks rolled over ancient grapevines planted three hundred years earlier and destroyed vineyards that produced some of the finest wines in the world.

Simone, Celeste, and Nicole volunteered at the soup kitchens. They sliced bread, filled bowls with soup, and distributed much needed items—plasters for cuts, jugs of water, clothes, and shoes. Simone could see the despair and grief in the dull eyes of people who had lost everything. They'd walked from Belgium and arrived with shredded shoes and bloody feet. What hope did they have now?

On May 14, the French government ordered German nationals to be interned. They were rounded up, loaded onto buses, and sent to internment camps. Simone and César were in the workshop when Daniel passed the word about the roundup, and César's eyebrows flew up as he cursed, "Bloody French!"

Simone panicked. Were her false papers going to keep her safe? And Mr. Lieb? They were German. *Jewish.* Would the Nazis recognize people from their own country?

She clasped César in her arms, needing to feel his solid comfort. "I'd be on one of those buses . . . if you hadn't . . ."

He stroked her hair and whispered, "We're safe. We're still safe."

"But what about the Nazis? They're less than seventy miles from Paris—they can be here in a day or two. People are already packing to leave."

Nazis in Paris?

Unthinkable.

Every day more refugees wound their way through the streets of the Left Bank on Boulevard Saint-Michel toward Route Nationale 6 that led to the south and, they believed, to safety beyond the reach of the Germans. Old women pushed prams of children sleeping nestled next to cats and chickens, their suitcases strapped on for the ride. In Paris, shop owners pulled down their gray shutters, closing for good, and by the last two weeks of May, streets began to look deserted as more and more Parisians left for the south. The well-to-do filled their Rolls Royces with lamps, jewelry, clothing, and as much of the wine cellar they could fit in. Dogs who'd been left behind searched for food. As people headed out of the city, they clung to rumors that the French would hold at the Loire River, almost three hundred kilometers south of Paris. Surely the Germans would not be able to invade farther into France.

All over the city were sights that Parisians had never seen before: gendarmes carrying rifles; schools, barracks, and hospitals overflowing with desperate homeless people; horses and oxen pulling carts through the streets; cooking fires burning in parks and alleys. Yet throughout most of May, the "official" news remained upbeat.

What the population of France didn't know was that on May 18, Reynaud, the head of the government, had told Churchill and the ministers of government, "The war is lost." The closest French officials came to sharing that truth with the French people came on May 21 when Reynaud announced on the radio, "*La patrie est en danger.*"

As May went by, rumors made their way through Paris about the devastation of the lightning war—how quickly towns were falling in northern France, how depleted the army. The Allied forces were trapped on the beaches at Dunkirk.

The population of Paris ran the gamut from complete denial to a gut-wrenching awareness that they might truly need to escape. The train stations filled with people desperate to leave, forced to camp out for days in a queue to get tickets.

Brave fighting by the French army couldn't keep the Germans from pressing toward Paris, but many Parisians knew nothing of their country's military failures. Because of their government's continued censorship, millions of people carried on their lives in ignorance and were left without guidance about whether to stay in Paris or to leave.

By the end of May, Churchill ordered "Operation Dynamo," a rescue by destroyers, merchant ships, and the "little ships" that belonged to fishermen and ordinary people who sailed all the way to Dunkirk under war conditions to rescue the soldiers—all that was left of the British fighting force. Three hundred thousand men were saved despite the *stukas* strafing men on the beach and sinking some rescue ships.

Parisians received no information about the collapse of the British army at Dunkirk while Radio Stuttgart touted the success of the Germans.

Simone and César clung to each other, grasping for hope despite the bad news and rumors. But one evening in the first week of June, they visited their favorite cafés, only to find all of them shuttered. Simone looked at César, and he looked back as they stood on a deserted street, the only sound the rumble of tires as refugees escaped the city. In that glance, Simone knew it was the beginning of the end of their time in Paris.

She buried her face in his shoulder, the tears she'd been holding back finally released. She sensed it was not if, but when, they would have to leave. *But would César give up his work? Would he stubbornly cling to his workshop and the operation he'd so carefully set up in Paris?* she wondered. She kissed him on the cheek. She had to talk to him about leaving the city—and soon.

Bombs in Paris?

The house creaked as everyone got up, and soon the aroma of ersatz coffee filtered into Mathieu's room. The low murmurs between Nicole and Claude as they prepared the breakfast table and the youthful voices of Simone and Celeste, chatting as they nibbled croissants in the dining room, brought a smile to his face. The home offered a semblance of normalcy in a world where everything was in question.

He wasn't ready to face the world yet. He needed to calm the growl at the base of his throat. No wonder his neck hurt. So did his stomach. His tense shoulders were trying to tell him something. *Get out,* they said. *It's not safe in Paris.* But go where? How? The feeling of entrapment he thought he'd left behind in Germany squeezed his chest. Doom was about to descend on everyone.

His bones objected as he got up from his seat at the work-table, his whole body aching with worry for the future. For Simone. He'd promised to look after her. What choice should he make now? For her. For both of them. If they chose to leave Paris, would César come too? Simone had said he was strongly against leaving the city, but would she leave without him? Was leaving the best choice? It had to be—there was no way they could stay in

Paris with the Nazis getting closer every day. It was the first week of June, and danger loomed with every day that passed.

He finally made his way to the dining room. Simone sipped her coffee and looked at him. "Something is on your mind, Mr. Lieb . . . Mathieu."

"Radio Stuttgart broadcasts dire warnings. They say the war is lost, the French army defeated. How do we know if it's just Nazi propaganda?"

Claude set down his cup. "I can tell you this, the truth of the situation is not being made public."

Simone sucked in her breath, then stood up quickly, knocking over her coffee cup. Brown liquid pooled on the white tablecloth and soaked into the table. She quickly grabbed the cup and tried to mop up the liquid with her napkin. "Oh, I'm so sorry, Nicole. I'm . . . I don't know what's wrong with me."

Nicole sighed through a wan smile and told her not to worry. They all carried off the dishes while Celeste got another cloth and smoothed it onto the table. Nicole swept the stained tablecloth off to the sink and began to soak it.

"I feel so bad. I'm so sorry." Tears pooled in the corner of Simone's eyes.

Celeste touched her hand as everyone sat down. "Stop apologizing. We know you're worried."

Simone nodded. "Yes, but what about you? You're Jews living in Paris, and the Nazis will be here soon—that's what all the rumors say. Won't you be in danger?"

Claude said, "Do you mean, are we planning to leave? No. I have my work. I—"

Celeste cut in. "But Papa, if the Germans take power, that will be the end of the government you work for."

Claude threw his shoulders back. "My family has been Jewish for hundreds of years. I believe we'll be safe. But we have made plans for alternate work—I could get my old position back at the bank."

Mathieu nodded acknowledgment but winced at the idea of the Rosenbergs staying in Paris. And what to say to Simone—she looked miserable.

She pushed her chair back and grabbed her bag. "I'll see you tomorrow, Celeste. I have something I need to do."

"Wait!" Mathieu called out, as she rushed toward the door. "I'll see you later!"

In the early afternoon, Mathieu looked out at the beautiful blue skies and decided to walk to a store in hopes of finding chocolate— a search he knew would likely be in vain, but he wanted to keep up the pretense that such comforts could still be found. He found only gray shutters closed tight, bits of paper blowing down the deserted sidewalk.

He decided to settle for coffee at a café across from Notre-Dame to distract himself from the endless loop of *what ifs*. After he ordered the bitter brew, he thought of Werner's steel gray eyes and that other Nazi, Schmidt. Ah, how naïve he'd been to think they could escape the Reich. He and Simone had had two years of freedom, and she had found César and her place in the world here in Paris. But now, everything was in flux, for everyone.

At the café, people gathered around radios talking and gesturing. Mathieu heard bombs and the wail of sirens. Even more alarming, the ack-ack guns boomed in the distance. He stood up quickly, knocking over his coffee.

"They finally did it! They bombed Paris!" People were shouting and running for phones.

They were coming. Mathieu had to do something. An idea had been tugging at him, a way to protect Simone, but he didn't want to use Claude's phone to make the private call, so he headed toward the public phones at the post office. On the door was a large handwritten sign: *No telephone service.* What was going on? People were weeping and chatting madly as they rushed into the post office, saw the sign, and ran out, moaning about the end of the world. Had the Germans cut the lines? How close were they?

It might be a risk, but Mathieu took the Métro to Lucien's and from there placed a call to Jules, his old luthier friend in Marseille. Surely, they could find safety there. The call was cut off after a minute but by then he had the information he needed, so he rushed back to the Rosenbergs' house.

He found Nicole in the kitchen and she told him that Claude would be home late. "Late-night discussions with the city staff," she said as she chopped vegetables. Celeste sliced the baguettes, and in the dining room, Simone set the table. Suddenly Mathieu heard the sounds of silverware clattering to the floor, so he rushed into the dining room where Simone held her face in her hands. Her shoulders were shaking as she quietly cried.

"What's wrong?" he asked softly.

She shook her head and wrapped her arms tighter around her body. Mathieu slowly approached her—not wanting to startle her. She'd never liked being touched when she was upset. She wiped her eyes, then turned to look at him. "César told me that he won't even think about leaving Paris, but I know it's not safe to stay here. The Nazis, what if . . ." She twisted the end of her handkerchief. "I know we all have false papers, but what if we can't just get on a train. And . . ." She stopped to blow her nose. "I love Paris. We thought . . ." Her dark eyes pooled with tears. "We thought we'd escaped the Nazis—but they're a two-hour car drive away, Mr. . . . Mathieu . . ."

He stood close, gently resting his hand on her shoulder. "Don't worry. I know where we can go and be safe."

"What?" Her face brightened.

"I called my friend Jules in Marseille. You might not remember him. He's another luthier, but he's also an attorney and knows what's going on."

Simone looked at him with hope in her eyes.

He went on, "His wife Émilie is an artist. He said we can stay there until things blow over." He remembered how everyone thought the first war would last only three months. Four years later the Armistice was signed in Versailles.

Turning to face him, Simone said, "Marseille—that's very far south. So different from Paris."

"It's a port city on the Mediterranean Sea and beautiful. I worked with Jules there a few years ago. They have an old house on the edge of the city, big enough for all of us if César comes. Jules said we should leave Paris soon. He's heard from his political friends that Paris will be occupied within a few days."

Celeste and Nicole rushed into the room. "A few days?!"

Simone grew pale. "Oh, no! But people wait for days at the train station. We can't wait three or four days for tickets."

Nicole said, "I can't believe this."

Celeste wrapped her arms around Simone. Frown lines deepened between Nicole's eyes. "We have a Citroën," she said. "We keep it in a garage—we hardly ever use it, but we can ask Claude."

"Drive?" The roads were overflowing but yes, he could manage it somehow. Better than the train. "Thank you for offering, Nicole."

Simone clasped her arms around him tight. "Please, talk to Claude, Papa—he knows what's happening with the war and what roads we could take. And I'll ask César to talk to you about the plan. Maybe you can persuade him. We just can't leave him here—they'd arrest him first thing!"

Mathieu said he would speak to César. He poured a glass of wine. They would escape with everyone else on the road—that's all there was to it.

Crossroads

"*The Germans are thirty miles from Paris and closing.*"

—Radio Stuttgart

Simone burst into the workshop, determined to convince César to leave Paris with her and Mathieu. She'd waited to talk to him until Claude and Mathieu had discussed the Citroën. It needed repairs, and for two days Claude had searched for a mechanic. After the bombing, more people were escaping the Nazis, closing businesses all over the city. But finally, the Citroën was with a mechanic who would get it ready for a long journey.

The workshop was nearly deserted. She saw only César, Daniel, and two clients. "Where is everyone?" she asked. César's head shot up, his eyes like daggers.

"Don't you know what's going on? What they're doing?"

He seemed so angry. What did he mean?

"Just tell her," Daniel said softly.

"Tell me what?" Fear shot through her body. "Are you all right? What happened?"

César's face was flushed, and his heels slammed into the floor as he paced. "The French, we still have to worry about *THE FRENCH*! They had a huge roundup last night and grabbed people without papers who were sitting in the cafés on Boulevard Saint-Michel. They threw them into trucks and drove off."

Frown lines deepening between his eyes, Daniel said, "César was there, about to meet clients who needed papers and bring them here. He arrived late, saw what was happening. There was nothing he could do about it. César's papers are good—but still, you don't want to get dragged into a roundup. Some people are never released even if they're legal."

Simone couldn't speak. If César was arrested, she . . . she couldn't imagine what she'd do. The thought of it made her lightheaded.

César puffed on his cigarette and kept pacing. "Stupid bureaucratic system. That's why people are trapped." He slapped a ruler down on the desk, then crushed the end of his cigarette and lit another. Smoke spewed into the air. He stomped around for a few minutes and finally slowed his pace. Abashed, he glanced at her. "I am sorry. I'm . . . you know . . . my temper. But we must work harder. We have to find more people to save before it's too late."

Daniel stood in front of César and set his chin. "César, the truth is, we need to shut down the operation and save ourselves. I'll help you pack up."

Simone felt the urge to agree, but César needed to be persuaded by someone other than her. She could see from César's face that just about anything could set him off again. Armed with good news about the Citroën and Marseille, she wanted a yes from him about going south, not another argument like they'd had the other day, glaring at each other, arms folded across their chests because he refused to consider leaving. She found it hard to believe he'd choose to stay in Paris if the Nazis were tramping down the avenues. But he was one of the most stubborn people she'd ever known. She couldn't bear to think of leaving without him, but if Mathieu was going to Marseille, she was going with him.

César raised his voice. "I can *not* give up all we have here that will help people survive. The refugees are desperate. They need us. So today, we're going to help these fine people here." He gestured to the man and woman making themselves look small curled up on the chairs by the wall. They looked like scared rabbits, ready to run out the door. "And then we'll . . . I don't know. We can look for . . ."

Daniel met him nose to nose. They stood facing each other, puffed up to full height, chests out. "Absolutely not. César. No!" He raised his voice and enunciated each word. "We will not, *not*, look for refugees and drag them here. It's over, don't you get it? The Boche are pounding on the gates. People are leaving, and you should too with your fine lady here!"

The couple glanced at Simone, a strained look on their faces. Her heart felt sick for how terrified she knew they must be. She gave a slight nod toward the door, and they hurried out. Their footsteps clattered down the stairs.

"What have you done?" César challenged her. "They'll be in more danger now. They . . ."

Simone stood her ground and glared at him.

Daniel softened his tone and rested a hand on César's shoulder. "I'm your friend, César, and I'm telling you it's over. The Germans are too close to Paris—they could march in at any time, a day or two away at the most. You two don't belong here. Yes, you have great papers, but these are Nazis we're talking about. You know what they're like. And if they catch you, they'll get the truth out of you—one way or another."

César shook his head. "But we can't camp at the train station—it's overrun. Or start walking down the road with all those people. That's crazy."

Simone spoke up, "Mathieu has a plan. A really good plan. Will you listen?"

She told him about Mathieu's friend, Jules, in Marseille and about Claude's Citroën. "The automobile is being fixed now. It's been in a garage for a long time, but it will be ready to go tomorrow."

César shook his head as Daniel filled boxes with stamps, pens, and ink and then began to rip drawings off the wall.

Grabbing one of the boxes, César shouted, "Stop that! Some of these items are irreplaceable."

Simone approached him gently and rubbed his back, stroking his muscles from his waist to his shoulders. He hung his head, heaving deep sighs, letting his shoulders drop. He had to be exhausted, having worked through the night. The creases between his eyebrows and the sag of the skin around his eyes told the story.

She leaned close to him and whispered, her lips caressing his ear, "Let's go to the apartment. We can talk it over quietly."

He shivered in response. She curled a lock of his hair over her finger and pulled him toward her for a kiss.

César wrapped his arm around her and called out to Daniel to lock up when he left. He squeezed her close—these were desperate times. But Simone was with him—they could find comfort in each other. They clattered down the stairs, and she squeezed his hand as they ran down the nearly deserted passages on the Left Bank.

As they burst into his apartment, he tugged at her dress and kicked the door closed, not taking his hands or lips off her body. Simone pulled back slightly and looked into his dark eyes as he slipped her dress off her shoulders. Then he reached for her and pressed her hard against him, kissing her face, her neck, his breath coming fast, tears in his eyes. He seemed desperate, as if losing himself in a tangle of sorrow and desire, exhaustion, and adrenaline. She'd never seen him like this, ripping and tugging at the fabric that served as the only barrier between their two hungry, naked bodies.

His lips moved down to her breast, and his kisses were hard, then feathery soft. She pulled off his shirt and massaged his skin, tracing his back, his spine. He shivered and guided her back onto the bed, lifting her dress, his lips tracing her hip bones and then finding the soft places that welcomed him. They'd always had passion, but this was hotter and more intense than ever, and her eyes pooled with tears as she met him in a wordless union of bodies and souls when he entered her and they rocked together. They were lost in time, both desperate for release and for the sweetness of love to counteract the bone-deep fear that united them. And haunted them. Her fingers clutched his back, his head buried in her shoulder as he cried out, then collapsed, sweaty, panting, clutching her in his arms.

He rolled away and propped himself on his elbow, then looked intently into her eyes. The hint of a smile tugged at his lips, his eyes dark but peaceful. "I can't let you leave . . ."

Simone caught her breath. What did he mean?

A low chuckle rumbled from his throat. "Without me."

"Don't tease me. Do you mean it?"

He nodded, and she kissed his face and neck and lips, nearly crying in relief.

With his lips, he traced the curve of her breast, her chin, then kissed her. "You have me in your spell, but sometimes I wish . . ." He paused and looked into her eyes. "I'm too old for you. I'm bossy, and . . ." He was silent then and lay his head on her breasts.

She loved the heavy feeling of his body on hers, the intimacy of feeling his skin, his breath on her face. Did they have to face the world outside the room again? She kissed his shoulders and pressed her fingers over his lips. "Yes, you're a man who likes to be in charge. But I can pull my own weight. I know we can get to Marseille with the Citroën and our dear Mathieu. But . . ." She sat up and made him look at her. "We need to leave now, as soon as the car is ready."

"First, we have to retrieve our forging materials. We can't leave them here."

Simone sighed in relief and pressed the seal of a kiss on his lips. They lay in silence for a while, then got up and peered out the attic window at Paris under blackout conditions. The sounds of war pierced the thick velvet dark. Air-raid sirens. The boom of cannon.

Darkness in the City of Light

We are in the greatest battle of history.
The trials which await us are heavy . . . We are
ready for them . . . France cannot die.

—Paul Reynaud

June 11, 1940. A smoky yellow light enveloped Paris and dimmed the sun. Government documents crackled and disappeared in small bonfires as officials prepared to leave the city. Ash and clouds of smoke folded into a dirty fog that hovered over the city, rendering even the obelisk at Place de la Concorde invisible. The Eiffel Tower was nowhere to be seen. An ill wind burnished the cobblestones, the sandbagged buildings, the marble monuments, statues, and the beautiful Sacré-Coeur. Ack-ack guns positioned on the Arc de Triomph took aim at German planes overflying the city.

Schools were closed, children evacuated. Cafés and hotels sat empty. The caravan inching out of the city rumbled with horse-drawn carts filled with children, chicken coops, and old people. Automobiles crawled along with mattresses piled on top. The roads were engorged, traffic at a standstill. The Germans were a half-hour away by car.

Claude's head peeked out from under the hood of the idling Citroën. Simone listened to him tell César about the water pump, the oil, and the brakes. She tried to push back her tears as she wrapped her arms around Celeste. Lingering in the embrace, she remembered how shy she'd been when they arrived in shock from Germany, when affectionate cheek kisses seemed like a strange custom. Now she could think only of the good things: their thrilling visits to the museums, hot chocolates at Café Angelina, sketching from the top of Montmartre, the entire beautiful city spread out before them.

"We'll both write. Or call," Celeste whispered, wiping her eyes. "I want to know all about your journey."

Simone nodded and swiped a tear. "It will take days, more than a week, to get there. But let's promise to write and sketch, and then we can mail everything all at once, like a diary." A surge of panic shot through her. What would happen to this wonderful family in a Paris occupied by Nazis? She clutched Celeste's shoulders. "Please be careful. Don't ever let them know you're Jewish."

Celeste waved her hand. "Oh, we've already registered as Jews. But I'm not worried. I refuse to let them make me ashamed. After all, we've been French for generations, and we don't practice a religion."

None of that mattered to the Reich. Simone did her best to smile at her friend, despite the wrenching fear she felt for the Rosenbergs, knowing what she knew about the Nazis. She would hope for a miracle, a near impossibility given that French soldiers were already surrendering in the suburbs beyond the city.

Holding hands, they joined Mathieu, who was checking the map with César. Thank goodness her beloved had changed his mind and was really coming with them. The dire news about the approaching Germans, her determination to leave with him, and the fact that they'd have a car had won him over.

With his finger on the map, Mathieu traced the spiderwebs of roads heading south. Until this moment, Simone hadn't realized how large the country was. Marseille was a small dot perched at the very bottom, on the Mediterranean Sea between Spain and Italy—two seething bastions of Fascism.

Nicole passed Mathieu a large basket covered with a red and white checkered cloth. "You'll need nourishment. There are baguettes, ham, cheese, and fruit. Wine and water. You must keep up your strength. I hope this will hold you."

Mathieu thanked her and embraced her, then tucked the basket next to one of his violins. They were limited to one small suitcase each for clothing, and alongside those they'd tucked forging supplies, art materials, and Mathieu's luthier tools. The boot was packed full and the back seat piled with pillows, blankets, and rucksacks with just enough space left for a passenger.

"Claude said we can't take anything else or the Citroën won't be able to go up the hills." Mathieu winked at Simone.

"We're leaving so much behind. Memories. People. Celeste, thank you for storing my art portfolio. I'll come back to Paris and get it. When everything is over."

A tear slipped from Celeste's eyes. Simone embraced her again, this wonderful friend who had filled so many empty places in her soul.

A brief silence followed as everyone looked at each other and the weight of the unknown pressed upon them. Simone kissed Celeste on the cheek again and looked in at Claude's tinkering. He stood up and slammed down the hood. "She's in good shape now. I'm sorry it took so long to get her repaired. Rosey here," he patted the car fender, "is ready for you. But you must treat her nicely. Take care of her water and oil and tires. And don't wait until the last moment to get gas. She likes to be at least half full."

"Rosey?" Simone whispered to Celeste.

"She was a dog who died when we got the Citroën. Also, it's for the pink seat covers!"

The smattering of laughter that followed felt hollow. Everyone was trying to stay cheerful, but the dark cloud of war couldn't be ignored. Their chests vibrated with the sound of the ack-ack guns and cannon fire that boomed in the distance. Closer today. Very close.

"Well," Mathieu said, bending to kiss Claude then Nicole on both cheeks. Tears streaked Nicole's face. César shook Claude's hand and thanked him for Rosey. "We'll bring her back one day. Promise."

Simone didn't know if César really believed that. Everyone there knew that no such promise could be made, but they all smiled. Would they return? Under what conditions? What was going to happen to all of them? What would become of Paris?

Simone's throat was tight. She squeezed Celeste again, running her fingers through strands of her lovely hair. "What a friend you've been. Be careful."

César kissed the Rosenbergs in the French way, his eyes clouded with worry, a forced smile on his face. She knew he didn't want this family to remain in Paris. He even suggested they take the car instead, but they'd refused.

Mathieu and César flipped a coin, which decided that César would be the first driver. Simone crawled into the back seat amidst boxes and bags and gave César an encouraging pat on the shoulder. "You're the pilot."

Folding himself into the passenger seat, map in hand, Mathieu said, "Navigator here."

César shifted the car into gear and slowly moved forward.

Simone cried out, "How can we leave them? What are we doing?"

"I told Claude to try to get a train south," Mathieu said. "If they choose to come to Marseille, they can join us at Jules's house. They'd be more than welcome."

Her spirits lifted. The family stood on the curb and waved. As the Citroën pulled away, she kept her eyes fixed on her dear friends, the lovely family of three standing on the curb, still waving as they grew smaller and then were out of sight.

Rosey threaded its way through deserted streets before joining the traffic that clogged the main road. Simone turned in all directions as she took in the sight of hundreds of carts and horses, prams, and bicycles inching south to escape the Germans. People were covered with a gritty yellow dust. Despair dulled their eyes.

Soot fell from the heavy gray air onto the car and coated the roads. The air smelled of oil. By noon a dark pall covered the city. Drivers flipped on their blue headlights, and the Citroën followed a necklace of lights into the unknown.

$\mathcal{P}art\ 2$

*The French people who had abandoned their homes
had become refugees in their own country.*
—HANNA DIAMOND

Exodus

Thousands of desperate refugees swarmed roads to the south as the Germans marched into Paris. People tied mattresses to the tops of their cars, hoping that it would protect them from falling bombs. Some families had walked with their livestock from Belgium to Paris and now continued toward the Loire where it was rumored that French ramparts would stop the Germans. Refugees drove cars riddled with bullet holes, their windshields shattered. Horse-drawn carts, bicycles piled with belongings, and baby prams filled the roads. Those without vehicles walked. Millions of scuffed shoes kicked up dust as they trudged toward the promise of safety. Surely the Germans wouldn't advance farther than the Loire valley.

For eight long, slow days under the scorching sun, Rosey had chugged along in a tangle of cars, people, and animals. The sun flashed off the metal and glass of vehicles, its glare aggravating the thundering ache in César's head. He lifted his hands from the steering wheel to rub his forehead, then quickly grabbed the wheel again as the vehicle bucked through the ruts in the road.

Ragged streams of refugees struggled on foot pushing carts piled with their children, pets, and clothes. Cars that had broken down lined the ditch like dead animals, wheels up. Discarded belongings—suitcases, candlesticks, furs—all abandoned. Every object left behind represented bigger losses: home, family, history, tradition, and of course, sons who left to fight for France. It was a sprawling vision of heartbreak.

César glanced at his passengers, Mathieu in the back seat nestled between suitcases, napping. In the navigator's seat, Simone kept a vigilant eye on everything happening in all directions. Every day, they'd watched the war get closer with its orange flashes of fire and planes like angry bees buzzing, circling lower and lower in the sky.

A plane suddenly roared overhead. Simone screamed, then apologized.

Mathieu snapped awake. "It's all right, it will be fine."

"But look how close they are!" she cried.

César knew, all of them knew, that at any moment, they might be hit. Everyone on the road knew. Some of those who were walking wept and screamed in anger at the Boche, but most were sullenly silent as they slogged along. César calculated that at this rate it would take them six weeks to reach Marseille, but they knew of no other routes and were forced to resign to this dull march. Perhaps there was a blockage at the Loire causing the backup.

In the rearview mirror, César saw orange flames flash in the sky and black smoke billow as the German army steadily advanced behind them. When a bomb fell close enough to vibrate the Citroën, Simone clapped her hand over her mouth to stifle another scream. He knew she was loathe to be seen as a girl who screamed, preferring to appear tough enough to endure anything, so he pretended not to hear her outburst.

As the line of cars passed farms, César yearned for a loaf of freshly baked bread slathered with butter. He'd known hunger during his own war in Spain—back then they could go days, sometimes weeks with little more than a hunk of stale bread and a piece of cheese. The same conditions prevailed here. Few shops in the villages had any supplies left now.

People on the road told stories of the "early" days of this escape, like back in May—just three weeks ago—when farmers offered strawberries and water to everyone who stopped. For some Parisians, the early days had been less like an escape and more like an outing to the countryside. But now, refugees scrounged for any lifesaving supplies they could get and were often turned away with nothing.

Though Mathieu was the eldest, César knew he needed to be the leader on this journey. He knew war. He knew all too much about the way it sweeps a man from all he knows and from everything he'd once counted on. Mathieu had been through war twenty years ago, but it had been only a year since César had been a soldier. He'd worn his uniform until it began to fall off him in tatters because he'd had to cut into it for patches of cloth to use for bandages.

But here César counted his blessings. He had Simone, dear Simone, at his side and Mathieu, who treated him like a son and managed to keep both a watchful eye and a respectful distance as César and Simone grew closer. A man who had no children of his own was now a father to both of them. Quietly. His language was music, and sometimes just an expression in his eyes said everything. A knowing smile, an arm draped across a shoulder, a kiss on Simone's forehead.

As they lumbered along, Simone delivered a running monologue: "A big bomb went off behind us—big orange flames. Planes are circling." An hour later, another update: "They're fighting east of us. I think they're coming this way. More smoke and flames!"

"You have a very watchful eye," César said, knowing she was trying her best to manage her anxiety.

"I don't like the look of this," Mathieu murmured.

His concern ignited Simone's. "We're hardly moving. How can we outrun them?"

Hearing the shrill fear in her voice, César quietly said, "This is the fastest we've moved since we started. It's a good sign."

Mathieu frowned. "We're unprotected, out in the open like this—the glare of the sun on these vehicles . . . they're like bullseyes."

Why wasn't Mathieu trying to sound more optimistic? This wasn't like him.

Simone sighed and said, "If only it would rain."

The sky rumbled again. Was it thunder? Or bombs?

César drove on through the cool night while Mathieu and Simone napped. A couple of days earlier, she'd bargained her way into taking a driving shift, reasoning that Mathieu was becoming exhausted. Simone had never learned to drive, but after good-natured arguments among the three of them, the two men agreed that the slow traffic offered a good opportunity for her to practice. She caught on quickly, and by the end of that day, her driving was smooth and steady, and she spent a few hours a day behind the wheel.

On most nights, they'd pull off to the side of the road to sleep, but now that the traffic was moving more quickly, César didn't want to lose their place in the queue. On this night, the round orb of moon hung in the star-filled sky, bathing the fields below in a silver sheen. For miles ahead, a necklace of dim blue headlights stretched and snaked south. It was almost beautiful.

The next morning César pulled into a queue at a petrol station where dozens of people were waiting to fill the tanks of their dust-covered automobiles. Claude had put two cans of petrol in the boot, but now they were down to fumes.

People paced and smoked, and a few argued over which roads to take south. No one knew exactly how far they had to go to be safely beyond the German lines, only that they had to keep going.

German planes soared in the air not far from the gas station, swooping and circling, then dropped bombs that reverberated in the ground. Simone took César's hand and laid her head on his shoulder. His anger was growing—for France, for Spain, for the countries already swallowed up by Hitler. His hunger for revenge grew by the day.

A radio sitting on a table outside the petrol station broadcast a crackling version of "La Marseillaise." Refugees gathered by the radio and sang along lustily, pumping their fists.

Then a broadcaster said, "Philippe Pétain has an announcement."

All around the petrol station, people broke out in cheers and applause. People shook hands and kissed each other on the cheeks. "Pétain! Vive Pétain!"

Pétain had fought in the first war and led his soldiers to victory at Verdun, one of the bloodiest battles of the war. César could tell from the hopeful chattering all around him that this crowd expected Pétain to declare victory now.

César pushed through sweaty bodies and stood near the radio.

The store owner, a gray-bearded man wearing a black beret, held up his hands. "Silence! Our leader is about to speak."

"Vive la France!"

Pétain's voice, tinny and distant, whooshed through the wireless.

During these painful hours, I have in mind the unhappy refugees who are crossing the country in a state of utter destitution. I offer them my compassion and my concern. With a heavy heart I tell you today the fighting must stop.

I contacted the adversary during the night to ask him if he is prepared to work toward finding the means to bring hostilities to an end in an honorable agreement between soldiers.

The crowd exploded in a confused swirl of cheers and questions.

"What?! It's over?" A woman exclaimed, clapping her hands.

"An armistice! We can go home!"

"He didn't say there was an armistice, you idiot!" growled a man wearing a linen coat, sweat streaming down his face. "He said *the fighting* stops today."

Mopping his eyes with a handkerchief, another man said, "My son. Now he can come home."

"Bloody Boche in France! *Never!*"

"It's the fault of the Brits!"

The pain in the back of César's head began to throb.

Weeping, Simone threw herself in his arms. "This can't be true. They gave in to the Germans *already*? But I thought we . . ." Her fingers dug into César's back.

How could he offer any comfort? He wanted to appear strong, but this news was the worst. France under Nazi control? It was unthinkable. He patted her back and murmured empty reassurances that they'd be all right.

This was agonizing news, and they had to keep moving.

Looking worried, Mathieu approached them carrying a baguette and something wrapped in paper. "The store had bread and cheese, not much of it. They're almost stripped clean. It's good we're this far south. Everyone still says we need to get across the Loire."

Just then, another bomb smashed into the earth. Planes circled ever closer, and refugees pointed to the sky as they scrambled into their vehicles. Those who had enough fuel squealed out of the station and into the traffic heading south. The rest had the look of trapped animals as they could only wait their turn. The attendants frantically tended to them, and after a long ten minutes César pulled the car up to the pump.

Simone tugged at César's sleeve. "But wait—will the Germans know to stop fighting? Did they hear Pétain's speech?"

César coughed. He didn't want to dim her spirit, but of course, the damned Fascists would keep fighting. Of course, there was no way the Germans a few miles away would know of the Armistice. But he wanted to offer hope. "I'm sure we'll see the courage of the French soldiers at the Loire! Onward!" He kept to himself his stark awareness that darkness awaited them, regardless of which road they chose.

An hour later, Simone wiped the sweat from her brow as she looked left and right and sometimes behind them. César's knuckles were white on the steering wheel as they continued their slow progress.

What terrible news, the worst: an armistice announced only a month after the start of the war in France. This sounded like pathetic appeasement to her. She agreed with the refugees who'd shouted to keep fighting against the Germans, harder, longer. It was disgraceful to think of France subjugated to the Nazis. What did this Pétain think he could do to appease the Germans?

Nazis taking over France. Her neck grew hot, and she could feel surges in her stomach. *Why* would any French people accept, let alone welcome, the occupation of their country? Why wouldn't they explode in fury at the idea of vile Germans holding any kind of power within their borders? What about their soldier sons, now prisoners of war? And *what about Paris*? How could proud Parisians feel anything but grief and rage? Nothing made sense anymore.

Simone wanted to be hopeful, but César's cynicism had usually proven to be an accurate predictor of events. His disgust for the Nazis and the French who went along with Nazis had no bounds. And Simone herself knew the realms of cruelty their kind were capable of.

The car halted with a jerk. Up ahead a vehicle that had broken down was blocking the road, and two other cars had crashed into it. Now they were all stuck while planes swarmed in the distance. Everyone got out of their cars and milled about while men using ropes and winches tried to pull apart the mess.

Suddenly the air erupted with the sounds of buzzing and screeching. César blurted, "*Stukas! Quick*, under the car!" But the car was too far away, so he pushed Simone into the ditch beside the road and flattened himself on top of her, pressing her into the dirt. She choked, her mouth full of earth and rocks. The *stukas* whined, and ear-splitting explosions and smoke filled the air in a scene that unraveled in slow motion. She heard a strange *ping, ping, ping* sound as bullets hit cars down the line. Where was Mathieu?

Another explosion, then a fountain of rocks and dirt rose and fell amid screams. Leaves tumbled from trees like confetti as planes roared overhead, circling and then shooting at innocent people who scattered and cowered by the road.

A few minutes after the attack, the roar grew distant as the planes streamed away, and all Simone could hear was César moaning. She tried to lift herself from the ditch, but César kept her pinned.

"César, get up," she said. Why wasn't he letting her go? His weight was crushing her. Simone gasped, "César, please. I can't ... breathe."

All around her, time seemed to have stopped. The air was gray, an eerie, swirling dust bowl. A strange silence settled over the entire scene. Then an eruption of screams from women and men who ran in all directions while searching for their people.

With a low moan, César rolled off her and growled words that Simone knew must be curses in Spanish. He was squeezing his right arm, and blood bubbled between his fingers as his face twisted in pain. "Rip . . . your skirt!" he demanded between gritted teeth. "Tie . . . around my arm . . . above wound."

"Oh no, you've been hit! Has Mathieu . . . where is . . .?" Then she shouted, "Mathieu!" César barked at her to hurry, to please stop the bleeding. She'd never heard this tone from him before—at once commanding and desperate, and she leapt into action, grabbing the knife strapped to his belt and slashing a long swath of material from her skirt.

He leaned on one elbow, gripping his other arm tight as blood continued to gush between his fingers. She'd never seen so much blood. Her hands shook, but she tried to do as he told her.

"Wrap it as tight as you can," he said between choppy, strained breaths. "*Tighter.*" She cut another strip of her skirt and wrapped it tight around his upper arm. *Is this what it's like to be a war doctor?*

When his arm was tightly wrapped, she asked, "Will you be okay? I need to find Mathieu!" But before he could answer, she crawled out of the ditch and stood, her head frantically whipping left and right. Where was he? She stumbled her way to their car, which didn't appear damaged other than a few holes in its roof. "Mathieu!" she shouted. "Are you all right? *Where* are you? Mr. Lieb!!"

Her heart boomed in her chest. He *had* to be all right. Then, to her horror, the planes rumbled toward them again, the menacing black dots growing larger and larger. She dropped to the ground and scrambled under the car, and there he was flat against the ground, covered in dirt and gravel, his face smudged. He clutched her hand and slid toward the edge of the car to give her room, and she belly crawled next to him.

"I'm okay," he gasped.

Bullets kicked up dirt again, and the rattle of machine guns showered the area all the way down the line. As soon as the planes passed over and into the distance, Simone crawled on her elbows through shards of glass toward where she'd left César. The man she loved was bleeding in a ditch!

When she reached him, his eyes were closed. *No!* Was his heart beating? She pressed her ear to his chest—yes, alive. Trembling, she kissed his face. Blood streamed from the gashes on her arms, but she felt no pain. "César, César, wake up," she pleaded. He was breathing. Wincing, he opened his eyes. "You're alive, you bastard. You scared me to death."

"You're bleeding," he said through staccato breaths.

"It's nothing, just glass." She cut another swath off the end of her skirt and wrapped it around her arms. "I'm fine. And Mr. Lieb, uh, Mathieu is all right."

Another explosion rocked the earth, but it was farther away. They could see the planes in the distance, circling some other cluster of terrorized innocents. Simone sat with César, catching her breath as they watched people crawl out of the ditches, pleading to God for help. People dashed around, checking each other for wounds, counting family members. Keening and wailing. A little boy with blood trickling down his arms stumbled along the road, calling for his mother. A man raised his fist to the sky. "You *murderers!*" He wept and cursed the Boche through anguished sobs as he rocked his dead child, a little girl who couldn't have been more than five years old.

César had gotten up and was sitting with his back against a tree, holding his arm above his head. Simone felt helpless at the sight of his face contorted with pain, but what could she do? In jagged whispers, he murmured, "My medical case . . . in the boot. Take out . . . bullet."

Simone stared at him in disbelief. "I don't know how. I can't remove a bullet."

"No choice," he insisted. "I'll guide. You must . . ." Then he winced through what must have been a horrible wave of pain. "It must . . . come out."

She'd try to do as he asked. *But how could she cut into someone's flesh? César's body?* She remembered the whiskey in the boot—that would dull the pain.

Mathieu, gray in the face, knelt beside César and mopped his face with a handkerchief. "Oh, no. Can I help?"

"You were . . . medic . . .?" César asked through gasping breaths. "Take . . . bullet out. Stitch . . ."

Mathieu began to suck in his breath, turned ashen, then turned away, his hands shaking. He sputtered, "Sorry, sorry, after the war . . . I just can't . . ."

"Medical bag . . ." César gritted his teeth.

Mathieu sat up, still looking sick, but he agreed to fetch the bag.

"Get the whiskey, too," Simone called after him.

The aftermath of the attack was all around them—people weeping, family members tending to wounds and moving the dead to the side of the road.

Simone prepared herself for what she had to do. Save César.

Mathieu handed César a bottle of whiskey, and he took two long swigs. César told Simone to use the whiskey to sterilize the forceps and needle and then pour alcohol into the wound. He told her she'd have to use the forceps to probe the bleeding hole in his arm and gently lift out the bullet. She looked at him—*did he really think she could do this?*

Mathieu still looked green, but at least he was by her side. "You'll do fine—you have a steady hand! I'll pass you the instruments and help to keep him calm."

She couldn't bear to see the oozing blood and César's torn flesh, but she focused on probing to find the object.

Mathieu helped César gulp down another shot of whiskey. He cradled César's head and wiped sweat from his brow.

"Go," César gasped.

After probing for a few minutes, she found something solid and looked at Mathieu. He nodded—that was it. "Gently tug it," he told her.

She tried not to lose her grip on the bullet as she slowly eased it out. César cried out, his face contorted in pain. Mathieu stroked his forehead and murmured soothing words. Simone felt sweat run down her back.

"It's out." She dropped the bullet onto the blanket.

César grunted. "Umm. Pour . . . alcohol. Sulfa powder. Press . . ." he gasped for air, "it tight. Needle and sutures. Sti . . . stich."

"How can I do that?" Simone mopped her brow with her sleeve. They were under the shade of a tree, but the air was sweltering.

"Please!" he hissed, sweat running down his face. With his good arm, he picked up the whiskey bottle. "Sulfa powder . . . sew it." He slurred his words and his arm flopped back down to the ground. "Bandage . . . tight." His voice faded to a whisper, "Please . . ."

She sprinkled in the sulfa powder, then Mathieu handed her the needle and suture. "I've threaded it. Here, just pull the skin together."

Simone steeled herself to do the most extraordinary thing she'd ever done. She pinched her forehead in concentration, blocking out all other thoughts as she poked and looped and pulled until the wound was closed.

An hour later, the sun began to drop behind the trees and paint the road with long shadows. They'd sleep alongside the road again. César slept in the back seat of the car, protected from the elements, while Simone sat in the front keeping watch over him. That evening, Mathieu walked through the encampment carrying his violin. At times during this journey, he'd played music for refugees as they cooked over their campfires. Tonight, he would play gentle music, folk tunes. He would play for everyone.

A satisfying sense of pride crept over Simone, pride that through it all she'd been able to muster a cold, clear focus in the face of terror and pain. She'd become a machine of efficiency. And right then, she vowed to herself that she would be brave and do her best to keep up César and Mathieu's spirits as much as her own. She understood that given their wartime histories, both men would experience these horrors in ways she couldn't understand. For them she would need to be strong.

She wrapped herself in a blanket and listened to violin music on the evening breeze. Mathieu was playing for the grieving families camped by the side of the road, their fires glowing orange in the night as his music soothed their hearts.

Tomás was there again, watching the darkness creep silently over the dry hills. The war, almost over. Franco is winning. Franco, evil, is winning, taking everything. But Tomás feels nothing, no sensation of any kind. Dull nothingness. The stars shine over the familiar hills, and then the ache grows in his chest. The men huddle around him—some dying, some murmuring prayers. Someone hums a lullaby. He remembers his youth. School awards. Birthdays. His sister, her missing tooth. Her shining dark eyes. His father, a learned man, reading poems.

Tomás sits up, gasping for breath. Where is he now? He hears the stukas, the terror of their screaming descent. The stukas fire as everyone struggles to climb the steep mountain. There's blood, and he can't get away. He tries to run, but his legs don't move. He calls out to his mother and sister. He shouts again and again and again.

A voice in his ear, a woman's voice: "César? It's all right, I'm here. It's a bad dream. Go back to sleep."

I'm Tomás. Where is my family?

Bridge over the Loire

The Citroën coughed and lurched like a car three times its age, but Mathieu was grateful that it kept going. They'd heard rumors that the French were bombing the bridges over the Loire to keep the Germans from crossing, so the situation was becoming dire—they *had* to get across that river before every last bridge was destroyed.

He'd chosen roads that led to bridges he hoped were still standing, and each time they made it to the water's edge, they found nothing but a tangle of cars trying to find their way to another bridge, winding through piles of boulders and rubble and dust. But just ahead of them was another chance, a bridge that was still standing—for now.

They inched their way forward along with countless other refugees desperate to make it to the arched stone bridge that stood between them and their best chance for survival. Bombs continued to splash into the water ahead, spurting massive fountains into the air, but for now the bridge remained intact.

"*Why* are we trying to cross here?" Simone shouted over the roar of planes and bombs and car engines. "We'll be blown up!"

"It looks like this is one of the only bridges left," said Mathieu. "We have to keep moving."

"Why is anything being bombed? What about the Armistice?" Simone said, looking enraged and terrified at once.

Mathieu shook his head. He didn't have answers. César was leaning against a piece of luggage in the back seat, apparently still in shock. He called out weakly, "Keep going."

Just down the river they could see another bridge being blown up before their eyes—by Germans or French, they'd never know. The entire scene was a swirl of screeching bombs, whining car engines, humming planes. The pace was excruciating, but after several minutes of pointless ducking and covering their heads at the sounds of bombs dropping nearby, they reached the beginning of the bridge.

Now they'd face the most terrifying part of the journey: moving so slowly they'd be sitting ducks on a bridge that might be the next target of bombers overhead.

For ten torturous minutes, they inched ahead, holding their breaths at the sound of every thunderous boom. Finally, the clot of vehicles began to thin as cars started to pick up speed. Now they had only a few feet left to reach the end of the bridge. The planes roared behind them, growing closer.

Then the car bumped and thumped over the end of the bridge. Simone clapped her hands to her mouth and cried out a squeal that sounded like something between fear and joy. They began to move faster—ten kilometers per hour, then fifteen. Now twenty. Rosey sputtered and rumbled but kept going.

Behind them the sounds of battle thundered on, but overhead they saw no signs of warfare—it was now all to the north of them. *Were they really leaving the war behind?*

For several miles they remained silent, each of them looking right and left and behind them, and up into the sky as Mathieu drove on.

Finally, Simone let out a delightful laugh. "Careful, driver, you might be stopped for speeding!"

For the first time in days—or was it weeks—the three of them laughed. Mathieu felt his eyes begin to burn with tears. Simone reached over to squeeze his arm. For a few seconds, he rested a hand on top of hers, then gripped the steering wheel with both hands and drove his precious cargo onward to the south of France.

A day after escaping the battle at the Loire, they were still only sixty kilometers out of Paris, while hundreds of kilometers still stood between them and Marseille. Simone enjoyed driving—it gave her a sense of accomplishment to learn a new skill and to be useful in this seemingly endless trek toward safety in Marseille. It was slow going, but at least they were moving, now about twenty-five kilometers per hour, though they still had to stop and start throughout the day. The windows were down, and the hot air whipped all around the inside the car.

The inns along the way were full, so at night they slept in the car. It was hot and each morning they awoke twisted and cramped, but people running for their lives could adjust to anything, so they grew used to this way of life on the road—driving for hours and hours and grabbing what food they could find in the villages, bread and cheese, sometimes onions and potatoes. They'd make a campfire and roast their food in pans they'd found discarded along the road. Every night with Mathieu's help, Simone changed César's dressings, and his wound continued to heal. They'd been lucky finding fuel, though some stations had run out. Of course, the Germans helped themselves, leaving the refugees stranded. Simone knew that eventually they too might be faced with walking the rest of the way to Marseille.

That June afternoon, Simone was driving along slowly when she heard the *clomp clomp* of boots. Germans were coming up from behind, marching alongside the queue of cars. Blond men in field-gray uniforms with silver buttons. Steel blue eyes. Shoulders like scalpels. Black boots. Thick gray helmets despite the scalding heat in the middle of the day.

Fear shot through her, an electric shock to her body.

"Merde," growled Mathieu. "They're this far down into France."

Simone glanced to the back seat to see César's reaction as rows and rows of soldiers passed them, rifles over their shoulders, eyes forward like machines.

César's eyes were open, black pinpricks glaring out the window at the Nazis. She caught sight of an object wrapped in cloth lying in his lap.

"César, what is that? *What* are you doing with that?" she hissed. *A knife?*

"Nothing."

"Where did you get that? Put it away!" she snapped.

Without taking his eyes off the soldiers, César spoke in a flat, deadened voice that rattled her. "Nazi killers. Look how they swagger. Filthy murderers. We must defend ourselves."

Simone watched his eyes in the rearview mirror and found this transformation of her lover alarming. It was as if César had taken on someone else's face, someone else's voice.

His injury had changed him. Since he'd been hit, he'd grown sullen. Gone was the sparkle in his eyes, the glow she'd known from so many long looks between them. She hardly knew this man who now sat in the back of the car. His arm was healing well, but it seemed his mind had gone to a very dark place. She couldn't help but think there was darkness all around him, and she could only wonder what seethed beneath the surface.

Mathieu looked back, then his voice cut through the hot, sticky air. "Put it away!" he barked at César, reaching for the knife. César didn't resist as Mathieu grabbed the weapon and slid it under his seat. "Are you out of your mind? Think straight. For Simone's sake, if not your own."

Simone held her breath.

Clomp clomp clomp. The steely-eyed men marched.

Hundreds of jeeps and lorries filled with these soldiers and supplies rolled past the Citroën heading south, kicking up dust and spewing exhaust fumes. Officers dressed in crisp uniforms and hats rode in fancy cars, lording their luxury over their new conquests.

Mathieu told her to pull to the side of the road—he needed a nature break, and then he would take the wheel.

Simone pulled the car over and parked beside other vehicles gathered under graceful leafy trees that offered the blessing of shade. César remained silent in the back seat.

"Let's get out," she suggested. They stood with Mathieu and watched the seemingly endless column of soldiers marching by.

Nearby, a gray-haired man wiped perspiration from his stubbled face. "You've heard, haven't you? The Boche occupy all of France, but a demarcation line divides France in two parts. The south will be the Free Zone. Not a full occupation."

Mathieu raised his eyebrows. "What? We've not heard about this."

César slammed his hand on the seat. "Mark my words, there will be total control one day. The slow method, so you hardly know you're burning to death."

The man added, "People say that Pétain will protect unoccupied France from German control, and we believe he will help us. We're grateful to have him on our side."

Wanting to avoid a debate, Simone quickly asked the couple, "Where are you heading now?"

"We have family near Aix-en-Provence. You?" The man lit a cigarette.

"Marseille," she answered. "My father has a friend there."

"Oh, that's very far away—hundreds of kilometers."

Simone sighed. "It seems to take forever when most of the time you're sitting still or going ten kilometers per hour."

The woman said, "Ah, Marseille. You must take care as a young woman. It's a dangerous city."

Another man sidled up to join them, tippling a bottle of wine. "Yes, we heard it's called the Chicago of France. You know, mafia—bang, bang," he said, pretending to shoot a gun.

The first man continued, "It's the only open port in France. We've met Brits who made it this far—all the way from Dunkirk. They're trying to get to Marseille and find a boat back to England. But if the Germans catch them, it's a POW camp for them."

"Or worse," muttered César.

Simone didn't ask him what he meant. Instead, she touched his arm. "How's the pain?"

"The last time you asked, only two hours ago, it was fine." His eyes looked dull. Detached. Or was it smoldering anger?

"What happened?" asked the woman, gesturing to César's arm.

César sounded angry again. "The *stukas* gunned us down. Just like in the Pyrenees in '39."

There was an awkward silence. Then the man ground his cigarette into the dirt.

Mathieu patted the hood of the Citroën. "We'll need petrol soon. Where's the next station?"

A woman answered, "The Germans have been confiscating fuel. I don't know about a station, but the demarcation line isn't far away. They're setting up checkpoints all around—that's what a farmer told us."

"Will they let us through?" Simone asked.

The man shrugged. "Who knows what the bloody Nazis will do?"

Finally, the pounding of the earth and the roar of military vehicles faded, the German army leaving dust in their wake as they proceeded deeper into France.

"They've passed us going south," César growled as they got back into the car. "France belongs to Germany now."

Mathieu settled at the wheel with Simone beside him studying the map. "Let's find a way to bypass the main road and go faster," she said. They needed to get into the unoccupied zone, but where was the dividing line?

Conquered

*I*n the distance, heavy gray clouds promised rain. Lightning flashed, and the billowing dark clouds looked like mountains. Mathieu pulled Rosey to a stop in a long queue of cars. The Germans had halted traffic, but no one knew why.

As they waited, lorries and jeeps sped by, and up ahead several German soldiers were gathering refugees in a circle, war-weary folks who'd probably been walking for weeks. Mathieu knew the ruthlessness of the Germans. It was evident in the angle of the jaw, the dead look in their eyes. Conquerors. Nazis weren't simply German. They were twisted versions of people who had once been German, raised on art and music, Goethe and Beethoven. Now, they were creatures of destruction.

Finally, they were allowed to move forward again amid the chaos. People held up signs: *Have you seen a blonde girl? Eight years old. Chantal. Green dress.*

As their car moved steadily forward, Mathieu saw refugees frantically waving down vehicles, pleading for a lift. They were wraiths, scarecrows—bony and ragged with hollow eyes. Perhaps they'd escaped from a camp. They begged rides on the back of bicycles, hung onto bumpers, and jumped onto running boards, clinging for life.

This scene looked very strange, very bad. Germans were everywhere. Now after weeks on the road, they were deep into France, surrounded by an idyllic landscape of amber fields and trees that glowed in the afternoon sun. Villagers offered water and sometimes food, but supplies were very low.

The unknowns were many: How long would petrol be available? Would the Citroën make it all the way to Provence? What would they do if confronted by Germans? He thought about all the horrible things they'd witnessed. They'd seen death and blood. *Stuka* attacks. Lost children. Thousands, millions even, of homeless and frightened people wandering France. Where would they land? What would become of all of them?

There'd been one brief oasis a few days earlier when they'd spent a luxurious night at an inn. Baths. Clean sheets. Simone's happy face, her freshly washed hair streaming down her back like a rich, dark river. César soaked away grit and blood. Mathieu shaved his beard. They'd been given a feeling of civility. But soon they were back to the reality of the road.

Thunder seemed to rumble above and below them as they continued their journey south. With the Citroën's dim blue headlights illuminating only a few feet ahead, Mathieu clutched the wheel with white knuckles and strained to see through the fogged windshield.

The Demarcation Line

The steering wheel rattled under Simone's hands as they hit rocks and ruts, but they were moving more quickly now that they'd left the main road, the July heat pressing down on them, the Citroën like an oven. Despite the fact that two weeks had passed since the signing of the Armistice in late June, many refugees still pressed south, wandering through France without maps, and every day Rosey had to pull over to allow German lorries and military vehicles to pass. The young men in their steel helmets laughed and pointed at the muddy cars and the pedestrians with their carts being pulled by exhausted horses and oxen. They grinned and thrust out their arms in the Nazi salute, whooping, "Heil Hitler" with all the bluster of young conquerors. She wanted to slap every smirk off their faces.

Was it only a month ago that the first bombs had fallen in Paris? According to César's estimate, they were still more than two hundred kilometers from Lyon and five hundred from Marseille. It was best not to count the kilometers. Just keep driving.

They found themselves alongside a group of French soldiers standing by a beat-up lorry. They appeared to be trying to pass for civilians in their non-military clothes, but they all wore military-style boots, which gave them away.

"Those boys better find different shoes," Mathieu said. "They'll be grabbed for sure." Rumors said that Germans were picking up French soldiers and shipping them to POW camps in Germany. They'd serve as free labor for as long as the Nazis could use them.

César called out the window, "Did you run out of petrol?"

One of the soldiers snuffed out his cigarette in the dirt. "We're trying to get to Switzerland." He patted the fender of the lorry. "But she's broken down."

Mathieu frowned. "My sympathies. Our Citroën has not been feeling well, either."

"If you see a tow truck, send her our way!" The soldiers all laughed at the joke.

"Bonne chance," everyone called out to each other.

Simone said, "They seem too cheerful."

"Just keeping up their spirits," Mathieu said. "Probably trying not to think about what will happen to them if Germans show up. They'll be arrested."

César grumbled. "Or shot."

"What?" Simone said, tightening her grip on the wheel. "That's against the rules of war."

César jumped on that. "Come on, Simone. You think the Nazis care about rules of war? Don't be naïve. I heard rumors about the Germans shooting French soldiers in a village. And what about the rapes—"

Mathieu interrupted, "César, there's no need to scare her."

"She's not a child, are you Simone? You know about Nazis."

Simone slammed her hand on the steering wheel. "Both of you stop it!" The journey had pushed all of them way too far, and it upset her to hear the two men sniping at each other. And she didn't want to be reminded of Berlin. She sighed and asked, "How far now?"

Mathieu unfolded a ragged map. "We're still many kilometers from Lyon, but if the traffic thins, I think we can be in Marseille in three or four days."

They all sat in silence as Simone drove on.

Two hours later, Simone pulled up behind a long queue of vehicles. German lorries and jeeps blocked the road, and soldiers with rifles patrolled the area.

César let out a sarcastic laugh. "Ah, Mathieu. So now we see our Germans."

Simone said, "Now they're examining papers. Lining people up." Fear rushed through her body.

Fields of amber grain stretched out on both sides of the road, topped by an azure sky dotted with white clouds. It could have been the scene of a painting, but Simone's stomach pinched at what else she saw. People were handcuffed and standing in a row in the wheat field.

César said, "Those poor bastards are headed to the camps."

"How do you know?" Simone asked, afraid of the answer.

"What do you think? They have dark skin. They're dirty and wearing torn clothes. Do you think the Germans are going to treat them like human beings?" Bitterness dripped from his lips.

Simone felt tears begin to burn her eyes—for the people in the field who'd apparently been arrested and for César's bitter turn. Since the *stuka* attack, he barely resembled the man she'd fallen in love with. Perhaps the injury had opened a secret door and released the demons of his past. That was something she could understand. German uniforms set off deep alarm bells that jangled through her body and mind and dreams. Nazis in their gray-green uniforms. Sarah had fled to Paris's welcoming arms, but she hadn't actually escaped anything.

Mathieu murmured, "Get your papers ready."

Simone felt a surge of panic as she dug into her purse. She trusted that César's work was meticulously executed, but that didn't stop the blast of adrenaline that continued to shoot through her abdomen.

A soldier appeared next to the driver's side window and said to Simone, "Pass your papers over."

She forced a pleasant smile and passed her documents to the soldier while Mathieu handed his to a soldier on his side of the vehicle. The man might have been an officer—his uniform bore some kind of insignia.

Simone folded her hands and looked straight ahead at the group of at least fifty uniformed men who seemed like an unknown species. They were blond and fit, and she marveled at how very young some of them looked. One had a deep dimple, like boys she'd known in Germany before they'd all been subjected to the divisions that tore neighbor from neighbor, friend from friend. Another soldier was dark-haired with a sharp jaw—he reminded her of Captain Schmidt.

Simone realized that César had said nothing in quite some time, and she glanced toward the back seat. He sat perfectly still, his hands folded. She started to speak to him, but he hissed for her to turn around. She faced forward again and heard the soldiers banter about the peasants in France, about their ignorance. They erupted in guttural laughs as they spoke of women in the south of France—"so ugly," they sneered.

It startled her to hear German spoken with such familiar accents, and the sound of it made her flush with shame. *She* was German. Would the soldiers in France detect her Jewish background? Or Mathieu's? And what about César? Like hers and Mathieu's, César's papers said he was French, but what if they questioned his accent?

The officer on Mathieu's side of the car examined his documents carefully, turning pages slowly. Then he slapped the papers shut and spat, "*Raus*. Out."

The soldier's harsh German accent jarred Simone, but she forced herself to appear calm. She bowed her head and folded her hands in her lap.

Mathieu asked why he was being told to get out of the car.

"Orders!" the soldier shouted in German.

Simone jumped when a different soldier approached the driver's side and slapped the roof of the car. It sounded like a gunshot, and she saw his satisfied grin—he'd frightened her, as intended. She struggled to open the door and finally emerged into the glaring sun.

"Mademoiselle," he said, handing back her papers. He pointed to César in the back seat. "Who is that man?"

"Ahh, he's my, he's my husband," she said, hoping that their being a married couple might offer César some protection. Then she remembered their different names on the papers and added, "*Soon* to be my husband."

The soldier tapped on the window, motioning for César to get out. He stumbled from the back seat and slid his arm around her. She kissed his cheek, and given how cold he'd been toward her recently, his affectionate gesture felt staged. Had it appeared convincing?

"Papers!" the soldier snapped. "This is not a party."

César clamped his jaws and thrust his papers toward the soldier. Simone touched his arm and nodded toward people gathered in the field already under guard.

On the other side of the vehicle, the soldier questioned Mathieu. "You are going where?"

"To Marseille."

"Ha, you are an optimist. That is a very long way in this old car. Purpose?"

"To visit a friend," Mathieu mumbled.

"You're on holiday? Your residence is in Paris. Go back to Paris. You will see many of us there!" The soldiers laughed, joking in German about how they would be posted in Paris next and what a great posting it would be—dinner at the Ritz, the Moulin Rouge, beautiful Parisienne women.

Simone watched Mathieu prepare his response, pretending not to understand the jokes. "Long ago we were invited to visit this friend."

"Why is that? Who is this friend?"

"He's a luthier, like me. We do business with each other."

"Luther—what is that?"

"*Luthier*," replied the soldier examining César's papers. "They make violins."

Mathieu's examiner leaned in closer to Mathieu and said, "So you make violins? You have violins? Show us." He winked at the other soldier and laughed.

"I have a violin, yes," he answered.

Several other soldiers eyed Simone and drifted around the car, poking each other in the ribs, commenting on her legs, her curves. Her face turned red, but to hide that she understood German, she turned to look down at the road behind them where more cars had pulled up in the queue.

A soldier with several insignia pinned on his coat walked up from the roadblock, stiff legged in his knee-high boots, swaggering and clearly of higher rank.

"What is all this noise? We need to move this line along. What's happening here?"

"This man, he says he makes violins. They should be seized, yes? They could be valuable to the Reich."

Simone heard Mathieu gasp. She knew it would break him to lose the only violins he had left, and to lose them to the Nazis.

"Ah—we will decide," said the officer. He towered over Mathieu, looking down on him with a sneer. "Where are they?" His eyes narrowed like a serpent's.

Mathieu gestured to the boot of the car. "I put it here to be safe." An officer opened it and told him to take out the violin. César had wisely hidden the other one in the back seat among the blankets and clothing piled in the back.

Simone could feel César's body vibrating. She kissed him and murmured in his ear. "Stay calm. We will get through this— they want people to be upset."

Several soldiers gathered around them, and the officer tossed the violin case to the ground. Simone watched Mathieu's face turn pale as he knelt protectively by the case.

"Open it." The officer kicked at the case with the toe of his shiny black boot.

Mathieu clicked open the case and lifted out the violin. Simone knew his violins well—they were like his children. The violin he was holding was one he'd made several years before, its auburn varnish gleaming in the sunlight. He'd carved a star on the tuning pegs. Simone recognized it by the ornate pear wood purfling inlaid along the top.

"Prove yourself," the officer ordered. "Play."

Simone felt César flinch next to her. She grabbed his hand and squeezed.

Mathieu turned the screw to tighten his bow and began to tune the violin. As she listened to that familiar sound of open fifths, Simone hoped the Germans wouldn't notice the LiebViol label just under the f-hole of the instrument. They might ask questions.

A soldier kicked at the case, dust puffing onto the blue velvet lining.

Mathieu hung his head and hesitated. What was he doing?

She tried to catch his eye. *Just play, Mathieu.* She knew how humiliating this spectacle was for him.

The officer mimicked sawing back and forth on his shoulder, laughing. "Go on and play something. Show what a virtuoso you are."

Mathieu seemed to move in slow motion, tightening the horsehair on the bow. His face softened into a look of concentration as he slung the violin under his chin. He lifted his arm, half circles of sweat on his shirt.

She expected him to play a few notes and chords to demonstrate his facility and then drop the instrument to his side. But he cradled the violin under his chin, then dipped his head, and with one long, slow stroke pulled the bow to play the first beautiful chord, the heavenly sound of it winging its way through the air, over the car, past the soldiers, and across the landscape—even to as far as the refugees who stood all around, looking confused about the scene happening before them. It was the famous Bach Partita in D Minor, one of the most heartrending solos ever written for violin. He used to play this selection in Berlin to comfort himself through his darkest moments. It was a slow, meditative deliberation of chords woven with a haunting melody that spun through layers of sound. The bow whispered as it revealed the delicate mysteries of emotion. Longing. Love.

Simone understood his choice. It was a wise nod to soldiers who knew something about music. German music. Most educated men would know Bach, this composition in particular. What they didn't know was that the man with the violin was a Jew, Joshua Lieb from Berlin. In Germany, the laws forbade Jews from playing German music. But here he was, a Jew playing Bach for Nazis on a dusty road in France.

The soldiers stopped pacing. One soldier removed his hat as if attending a religious service. Another's lip was trembling, his eyes welling with tears.

A bird cried out, and the cicadas offered a bass rhythm to violin notes that rose over the fields toward hills in the distance. For a few moments, Simone forgot where they were and sailed back to a life where violin music graced every day and night, to a time when she'd been proud to be a Berliner.

To her surprise, the German officer didn't tell Mathieu to stop playing. What felt like five minutes passed, and then even more as the violin wove its magic. Everyone listened to the hypnotic rendering of the chaconne, a moment of peace in a French wheat field.

After the final note, he lifted his bow from the strings and bowed, his ribs heaving as he caught his breath.

The gruff officer now spoke in a much gentler tone. He nodded at Mathieu, then at all of them, and spoke in rough French, "That's enough. You may pass."

A young blond soldier bowed his head to Mathieu. "Thank you, thank you, sir," he said. "That was quite beautiful."

Another one added, "*Oui*, excellent. My mother wanted me to study violin, but I never . . ."

"That's enough, move on, move on," the officer called out gruffly, ordering the soldiers to return to their stations. Mathieu laid his instrument tenderly in the blue velvet cloth, covered it, and closed the case.

The soldiers seemed disarmed by the music. Their attention and the emotion on their faces made them seem even human. Simone guessed that at home their families played Beethoven and Bach on the Victrola, and they viewed themselves as good German citizens.

César wiped tears from his eyes and rested his hand on Mathieu's shoulder. And for one peaceful moment, the three of them stood in beautiful quiet as birds sang over the field.

"All right," the officer broke in. "Move on. Vite, vite."

The German soldiers moved along to the next cars. Mathieu

looked pale and his hands were shaking, but he held his violin case to his chest. He slid into the passenger seat and sat for a moment. César cranked the engine, his jaw set from gritting his teeth in rage. Simone resumed her place at the wheel and turned to look at Mathieu who said with a tremble in his voice, "I was sure they were going to destroy my violin. Just like at the book burning." Simone knew better than to try to ease his pain with words, so she said nothing. César crawled into the back seat, and for a few moments the three of them sat in silence.

Clouds blew across the sky and covered the sun. Then down came the rain. Simone saw it as a sign, a washing. First it fell as a light sprinkling, then increased to a hammering rhythm. When the rain began to ease again, she lowered her window and took deep breaths of the fresh, earthy air. Finally, she was ready and pressed her foot on the accelerator.

They had driven only a few miles when Simone stopped the car in front of a handwritten sign: *La ligne de démarcation.*

César pursed his lips then said, "Look, we're entering the *free zone.*"

The irony wasn't lost on anyone. Simone shifted the car into gear and sped over the line.

⚬

A day later, fate caught up with them. Simone was driving when she felt the car hesitate and cough before it rolled to a shivering stop. They all exchanged glances and jumped out of the car.

Mathieu's face grew red as he cranked and cranked until he gave up in a frustrated sweat. César lifted the hood and fiddled with wires. Mathieu gave Simone a hopeless look. They would have to walk.

Claude's Rosey had gotten them through the belly of France; without this trusty little Citroën, they'd surely be dead by now.

But now she would sit in much deserved rest. With few words, they removed the instruments, bags of clothing and tools, and art supplies from the back of the car, then gathered around the car and bowed their heads. After a moment of proper mourning, they pushed Rosey into the ditch.

The sun pressed on Simone's head and shoulders as they trudged along the road, now almost empty of walking refugees. Cars whizzed by, and Simone tried to feel grateful that they'd made it so far without having to do this grueling slog in the heat, loaded with belongings. The wind lifted dust from the fields and swirled it up into funnel clouds. Grit and dirt from the road powdered their skin. Simone kept washing dust particles from her eyes. All this walking seemed impossible, but they did it, one step, then another, pausing to sip from the little bit of water they had left. According to the map, Lyon was the next large town that would have a train station. It might take a few days to get there.

Before long, the sky was scattered with stars. They pushed on.

A lorry roared up behind them—full of German or French—soldiers? It was a French lorry, but you couldn't know who anyone was any longer. The three of them dove toward the ditch. In French, someone called out, "Bonsoir! We're only going as far as Lyon, but there's room in the back."

Three young men in civilian clothes got out of the truck, but they looked like French soldiers with their mismatched boots and brown shirts that had once been uniforms. The insignia had been torn off, leaving loose threads. Two women peeked out from behind a drape of canvas, a gray-haired woman and a younger one holding her hand. They tilted their heads in greeting, no doubt also rescued by the men.

"Trying to get to Switzerland before the Germans get us. Get in."

Mathieu looked to Simone and César. "Okay?"

César nodded, and the three of them climbed in and squeezed next to each other on the floor. Everything was communicated with eyes—how exhausted they all were, how impossible and chaotic everything was—a world turned upside down.

Simone leaned against César and closed her eyes as the lorry swayed and rattled down the road. The next thing she knew the lorry had stopped. She'd fallen asleep, and now everyone was gathering their things in the dark.

The men opened the canvas and told everyone to get out. "This is the outskirts of Lyon. You'll need to take that main street to the train station. Bonne chance."

They all thanked the French soldiers, then hefted their bags over their shoulders and set off.

Here they were in France again, a France that belonged to the French, a new France. With no idea what was to come, they walked down the dark streets toward Lyon.

Part 3

*. . . it's a story of pains and sorrows, successes and
failures . . . the country, the people, the things they ate
and what they couldn't find to eat, the fear . . .*
—VARIAN FRY, SURRENDER ON DEMAND

Marseille

The Armistice signaled the end of fighting but the beginning of a war of words and beliefs. Article 19 of the Armistice called for the French to "surrender on demand" anyone the Germans wanted to arrest: anti-Nazis, stateless people, and influential figures in politics, the arts, and literature. Most of them Jews.

As refugees flooded south, Marseille remained France's last open port, so the city became a stew of humanity; in the mix were people without papers, British soldiers who'd been wounded at Dunkirk, and members of underground organizations dedicated to undermining the oppressions of the new Vichy France.

Simone was numb from exhaustion, packed into a train car with Mathieu, César, and at least three times as many people as the train should hold—all of them sweaty, exhausted, and miserable. Passengers were mashed together in the compartments, on the floor, and even in the toilets. They jostled with every bump as the train rode over bomb-damaged tracks that had been hastily patched. Wide-eyed children and old people swayed back and forth, trying to stay upright. Some passengers slept standing up. All of them were headed for the unknown, all headed for Marseille.

As the train slowed to a stop, Simone found herself thinking ahead. At Jules's, there would be food and wine. A proper shelter. Never again would she take for granted things like fresh water and clean clothes. A bed. But Marseille itself seemed like a blank slate. What would the three of them do there? The city had been bombed in June. How much had been destroyed? They'd heard the Free Zone was governed by a puppet government located in the spa town of Vichy. What did that mean?

She gazed at César, so clearly exhausted—his beard heavy and dark, his eyes dull. Simone gripped his hand and tucked her arm around Mathieu's elbow as they shuffled toward the door and made their way down the crowded pathway toward the authorities in blue uniforms and jaunty caps. She silently prayed that their papers would pass muster. France was known for its complicated, soul-killing bureaucracy, so one never knew what random decision an official might make.

The sound of weeping swept over the crowd. A young woman and her elderly parents were being held at bay by three officers. As she begged and cried that her parents had done nothing wrong, she flailed her fists at one of the tall, strong men. He forced her arms behind her back and led her away.

Finally, it was their turn to face the beak-nosed gendarme for inspection. In silent agreement, Mathieu went first. In a clear, confident voice, he declared they'd come to work with his friend who had a business as a luthier and cabinetmaker and had lived in Marseille for many years.

"So, your residence is in Paris? Why come to Marseille? What do you want from us?"

Mathieu smiled, "My friend Jules owns the L'ébéniste shop, and my colleagues and I work with him."

The official continued, "Excellent. You won't be standing around with your hand out. And you two—quickly, your papers."

Simone decided to take advantage of her dress and her curves. She flashed the official a smile and casually flipped her skirt.

He looked her up and down from her hair to her shoes and back up again. "Young lady, do you make cabinets too? Or do you sell them using those pretty legs of yours?"

César sucked in his breath and said, "She's an expert with varnish. One of the best in the business."

The gendarme ran his finger along their identity papers, slowing when he reached the information about birthplace and professions. Simone had claimed student status, and César had listed himself as a cabinetmaker.

"You must acquire residence papers immediately." He gave them their papers and waved for them to move on. "Next!"

They hurried toward the station waiting room where they gathered in limp relief.

Mathieu nudged César's arm. "Cabinetmakers. Varnish!"

César laughed as Simone gave him a big hug, enjoying the prickle of his beard against her face.

The St. Charles station was on top of a hill, and all the streets from the station led down to the brilliant blue Mediterranean Sea. Its door opened out to a terrace from which they could see Marseille spread out before them in a panorama of copper-colored tile roofs and amber buildings with ironwork balustrades. As they started down the long staircase to the street, hot air blew through Simone's damp dress.

Mathieu pointed toward a church tower situated on a hill. "See that basilica? It's a famous landmark, the Notre-Dame de la Garde. She overlooks the city and protects them."

"But Marseille was bombed by the Germans," César said.

Mathieu frowned. "We can only hope Our Lady of Paris watches over us now."

They made their way down the stairway past statues of graceful goddesses, art nouveau–style streetlights, and rustling palm trees. A crush of people, horses, and carts swarmed the long street that led down the hill to the port. The only car in sight was a taxi with a box-like attachment that belched smoke.

A voice called out from the taxi, "Joshua!"

A gray-bearded man wearing eyeglasses and a fedora waved and smiled as he emerged from the taxi.

"Jules!" Mathieu called out. "Oh, my goodness." He rushed toward the man, and they threw their arms around each other and patted each other's backs. Mathieu introduced César and Simone, and they all hurried to get into the vehicle.

Simone wondered when Mathieu would explain his name change to this old friend.

Just then a black Citroën made a U-turn near the foot of the stairs and pulled into the front of a hotel with a large neon sign on the roof that announced *Hôtel Splendide*. The three formidable-looking Germans who emerged from the car wearing gray-green uniforms with caps, long coats, and knee-high black boots stilled all motion on the street. Simone froze as she watched the officers rush past the doormen into the hotel and saw—or did she see?—a familiar silhouette. That officer from Berlin? It couldn't be. A brief glimpse—a carved jawline, the nose. Could it be *him*? *Here*?

Mathieu must have seen her reaction. He leaned toward her and said, "Those uniforms again. They haunt us still."

Jules scanned the scene. "Don't get me started about Nazis in the Free Zone."

Simone finally found her voice. "But I thought 'Free Zone' meant it was free of Germans."

Jules said, "Nothing is free in Vichy France."

Respite

Jules directed the taxi to the edge of town, and after a few minutes they arrived at a rambling château of patched stucco in colors of rustic tan and dove gray. A large blond dog barked and scampered toward the taxi. Flowers grew in pots by the door, and the air was rich with the scent of lavender.

A smiling middle-aged woman breezed out of the house. She wore a long blue dress and a white apron stained with food or paint, or both. Simone felt immediately drawn to her. Oh, how she missed her mother.

Jules helped Mathieu out of the taxi. "This is terribly exciting for Mozart," Jules said, petting his wiggling dog. "Émilie, our dear Joshua is back with us, and meet César and Simone." Before Émilie could greet the newcomers, Mathieu rushed into Émilie's arms. Simone was warmed by the intimacy of their old friendship. The dog, the openhearted welcome—the entire scene helped her release some of the tension in her body. Staying here, they might begin to remember normal life again.

Inside the house, a wide wooden staircase circled up to a second floor. The rambling home was decorated with brightly colored wall hangings, paintings of landscapes, and sensual portraits of women. Hand-wrought rugs were scattered around the floor. The delicious aroma of soup wafted through the air.

Jules's booming voice filled the house. "Welcome to our humble abode. First things: Émilie will show you to your rooms, and she has a bath already drawn."

Mathieu held up his hand to interrupt. "First, I need to tell you something. We've had to go through some name changes. We'll tell you more later, but I'm now Mathieu. So we're very carefully trying to adjust to these new identities."

Jules nodded. "Say no more. In Marseille, we all must be very careful. There are many here who are having what you might call 'identity crises.'"

Émilie said, "Please do bear with us if we slip and call you our dear Mr. Lieb in private."

"I haven't entirely let go of that name either," said Simone. Then she patted César's shoulder. "But we're trying to stick with the identities that César helped us assume in Paris. He predicted the arrest of enemy aliens and insisted we take on new identities and get forged papers."

"I escaped Spain in '39. I'm also French now." César smiled.

Everyone was silent for a moment, exchanging glances of camaraderie as all this news sank in. Finally, Émilie said, "Now how about that bath? Simone?"

Simone went limp with gratitude. "I'd give anything for a bath!"

"Enjoy!" Mathieu curved his arm around her and squeezed. César gave her a quick kiss on the cheek.

Émilie guided her up the stairs. "You men have a cigarette while I help Simone settle in."

Simone called out over her shoulder, "I'll try to be quick."

Jules said, "Take your time. We'll have a whiskey. At least we still have the right to imbibe."

"What does he mean?" Simone asked Émilie.

"The Germans are siphoning off everything as fast as they can."

Émilie guided Simone to the bathroom, a beautiful room with black and white checkered tiles and a huge porcelain tub filling with water. Bubbles floated on the surface.

"Bubbles! Oh, you are so kind!"

"It's nothing, my dear. What an ordeal you must have had on that road. I can't imagine. Now, you enjoy the bath."

Émilie turned off the water and told Simone that food would be waiting whenever she was ready. Then she left the room, quietly closing the door behind her.

Simone stripped off the dusty, ripped dress and underthings. They'd go straight to the bin. Naked, she took stock of her body—legs brown from sun and dirt, face and arms blotchy and red. Her breasts had almost disappeared, not that they'd been large to begin with. She did like the muscular firmness of her legs.

She slipped into the water and held the lavender-scented bar of soap to her face and inhaled. Oh, the luxury. She scrubbed every inch of her skin until she felt the last bit of the road had been washed away, and then she closed her eyes and sank into a world of peace and quiet.

After what felt like an hour, her stomach reminded her that food awaited, so she stepped out of the water, wrapped the thick terrycloth towel around her body, and nipped over to her room. She sorted through the lovely dresses, skirts, and blouses laid out for her and slipped into a yellow dress printed with daffodils. An inlaid pearl comb and brush sat on the dressing table, so she brushed her hair and then pinned the long bits into a roll at her neck, as was the style. And lipstick—there was lipstick! Simone looked in the mirror and thought she was beginning to recognize the young woman looking back.

After whiskey and baths, the golden afternoon light of Provence danced on the leaves of the plane trees. Gusts of wind kicked up dirt as everyone sat together at a wooden plank table.

"We did find a chicken that dedicated itself to the next few meals, but with rationing getting started, we're mostly eating vegetables now," Émilie said as she set down a bowl of thick stew.

"Vegetables! That's wonderful. We ate bread, cheese, and strawberries for a month," Mathieu said. "We're so grateful to be here with you. Thank you for welcoming us."

"We're lucky to be outside the city and have a large garden," Jules added.

The taste of the stew and the bread still warm from the oven melted into Simone's stomach and heart. It was like a dream eating at a table with friends again.

There was silence around the table as the three travelers enjoyed their first real meal in weeks. César looked handsome in his white shirt, his chin clean-shaven. Then Mathieu took out his violin, and at first his fingers fumbled the notes, but he soon swayed and smiled as his fingers began to find their way. Simone understood it would take a while for his craft to return to what it had been in Paris. The notes lifting into the air felt like a home-coming—food, friends, and music.

When Mathieu finished playing, he raised his wine glass and sang César's praises, telling the story of the *stuka* attack, how he'd talked Simone through the surgery between gritted teeth. Émilie and Jules poured more wine and lifted their glasses. "Congratulations on surviving that trek from Paris. We heard how terrible it was," Jules said.

"And tragic," Émilie added, wiping her eyes. "For so many."

Simone saw a wan smile pass across César's face, but even that little bit of expressiveness seemed to call for great effort. He was still restless, lighting too many cigarettes. She could practically see the images of the war imprinted on his mind.

"Good thing those aren't rationed yet," Jules joked, noting two cigarettes burning at once in the ash tray.

César murmured he was sorry and blew smoke into the evening air.

Simone turned to César and whispered in his ear, "Come to my room tonight." Under the table, she pressed her fingers against his thigh. He ground out the cigarette and nestled closer, slipping his fingers under her skirt.

Winds of Vichy

$\mathcal{E}$ stablished in the spa town of Vichy, not far from the demarcation line, the new government under Maréchal Pétain set out to mold its policies to mirror those of Nazi Germany. In July of 1940, a month after the fall of France, laws were passed that revoked the citizenships of naturalized citizens and restricted immigrants and Jews in the workforce and public life. The German Kundt Commission was sent to Vichy France to assert the terms of the Armistice, which meant examining the Vichy internment camps and hunting immigrants.

For the first week after they arrived, Simone, César, and Mathieu had been so exhausted, they'd been able to do little more than sleep and eat. They'd spent their days recovering—strolling around the garden, picking vegetables, and playing catch with Mozart. Now they were stronger, and tonight, with a serious air about him, Jules called them all to the table.

Émilie poured wine into all their glasses, and Jules's mouth was pursed as he set out cheese, bread, and olives from their own trees. Mathieu sat quietly and watched his friends with curiosity.

Jules stood up, ran his fingers through his generous beard, and began to speak like a statesman. "I apologize in advance for my lecturing. As you may know, I'm an attorney as well as a luthier. But because of the new laws recently passed by Vichy, I don't know if I'll be allowed to continue to practice law, which brings me to my point: The Vichy government is in full collaboration with Germany. Most people here support Pétain, believing he's the savior of France once again."

Mathieu shook his head. "At a petrol station we heard his speech. It was shocking to see so many French people thrilled with him. Cheering and weeping with joy."

Émilie snipped roses and began to make a bouquet of the crimson and ivory blooms. "The collaboration can only prove to be a disaster for Jews and refugees—for everyone who has sought freedom in France," she said. "People from Germany, Austria, Czechoslovakia, and so forth—the countries that have been absorbed by the Reich—many are stateless. Most were Jewish and were denied citizenship by Germany. And of course, any anti-Nazi is a target."

Jules took cigarette papers and tobacco from a pouch and rolled a cigarette. Mathieu fumbled with his pipe, fingering the smooth wooden bowl as he tried to hide his trembling hands. How strange to have to worry about Nazis wherever they went, no matter how far they ran. He tried to hide his nerves as he held the match to his pipe and inhaled the walnut flavor he so loved.

Lighting his cigarette, Jules went on, "Those who have spoken out against Hitler are in particular danger—politicians, writers, intellectuals. They'll be picked up and thrown into camps. Possibly be deported to Germany."

"Can these people go underground?" César asked.

Jules nodded, winked, and held a finger to his lips. Mathieu chuckled to himself. Jules had no idea about the talent these young people had.

"And they'd need false papers." César flashed Simone a knowing look.

"These young people are quite versed in the art of creating useful documents for those who need them." Mathieu puffed on his pipe. Surely, they'd realize that César and Simone could be useful here.

Émilie and Jules shared a glance, but Mathieu didn't know how to interpret it. He hoped he hadn't overstepped, but he knew Jules. He'd always been pro-democracy.

Jules looked at César. "Spanish Republicans are targets too. France is still rounding them up and signing them into the labor services to build the Atlantic wall, barricades, and fortresses for the German army. You need to be extremely caref—"

César interrupted, "But I want to find my mother and sister. I wonder if they were sent to Perpignan where I heard that many Catalans live."

Émilie shook her head. "There's a camp near there, but it's almost impossible to get a travel pass—and too dangerous for you as a Spanish man. To travel, you'd have to apply directly through the Vichy government. Then they'd have your address, and that would put you in danger of immediate arrest."

Narrowing his eyes, César said, "So most of us are prisoners here in Vichy France. Me. My family—if they're even alive."

Simone saw the hurt in his eyes. "It must be so painful, not knowing where they are, how they are. But Jules and Émilie, we appreciate all this information. We had no idea." She rested her hand on César's arm to try to comfort him. She understood all too well, being in a similar situation with her mother and grandparents.

César's face reddened. "I'm sorry. I don't mean to be rude. The last time I was in the south of France, I'd just escaped French guards at a camp and saw my mother and sister taken away in the back of a truck."

Mathieu saw César's pain. "It must be difficult for you to be in the south again, so close to Spain. Hoping to find your family. So far from home."

Looking at César with kind eyes, Émilie said, "Naturally, you want to find your family. People hear 'armistice,' and they think we're returning to life as we knew it before the war. But this is Vichy now."

"We and many others do not approve of this Vichy government, but most people do," Jules said. Mathieu saw the distress in his friend's eyes. Vichy France held Émilie and Jules in as much jeopardy as it held their guests.

Émilie shook her head. "They're our neighbors, so be careful what you say."

Peering over his glasses at César, Jules said, "We and a few others are starting to create some kind of resistance movement, an underground that works against the Fascists. Can you tell us more about the documents you created? Where was this?"

Simone and César exchanged looks.

"Tell them," Mathieu said.

César began, "We, I, set up a studio in Paris on the Left Bank, a workshop where we created false papers, excellent quality papers, for the refugees in danger there. Simone here, she learned fast. She's an artist and very talented with the pen."

Looking like a leader of their newly formed cadre, Jules stood up. "I believe your skills could be useful here. We will contact our people about this."

César said, "We want to help. As soon as possible."

Jules said, "First though, in order to move around in Marseille, you need to become legal residents. Tomorrow, we'll go into Marseille to get residence permits. It will take all day, but it must be done."

Mathieu asked, "What else do we need to know, Jules?"

"Ration books. Long lines. Restrictions on chocolate, wine, tobacco. Meat. No dancing in public!"

César said, "They want to cut out all the joy in the world."

Émilie gathered up the dishes. "But most of all, we must live with extreme caution. You never know who's listening. Informing."

Sighing, Mathieu said, "And here we are, hiding again from those who have no respect for the human soul. For freedom."

Simone and César went to him, and he leaned into their affectionate hugs and Simone's kisses on his cheek. Now they were all united by a purpose in this new place called Vichy France.

A few days later, César sat in Jules's courtyard with Simone and Mathieu and lifted his face to the sun. He welcomed the heat, a bone-deep intensity that bore down from the sky and heated the earth. He breathed it in, hoping the heat would calm his nervous need to do something, anything. Émilie was right, being here in the south reminded him of his life in Spain, a country of fragrant earth and flowers. Bougainvillea and lavender. The taste of paprika and garlic. Marseille shared Spain's hot and spicy flavors and aromas, and since arriving in the city a couple of weeks earlier, César's body had pulsed with memories of a home that was no longer his. His mother's loving face as she cared for his sick father, his little sister's dancing dark eyes when she played with the dog. How the four of them had been a family— all destroyed by Franco.

In his lap were the residence papers, which had been hard won. Before heading back to their new home in possession of official documentation, César, Simone, and Mathieu had spent seven hours in winding queues packed with agitated refugees who wilted in the heat.

"Now we're proud citizens of Vichy France," César announced

sarcastically as Jules and Émilie carried out bread and a steaming bowl of soup and placed them on the table.

"We don't belong anywhere, least of all here," Mathieu said, unfolding his napkin and smoothing it on his lap.

César thought he looked depleted. He imagined that all the political talk had made Mathieu remember Berlin all too well.

Simone turned to Émilie. "What will happen to those refugees we saw in the queues in Marseille? They looked like they'd given up."

Émilie said, "That's why rescue groups are forming. You'll go with me tomorrow to make the rounds—take food, find clothing, and bring it to residences where the refugees live. Let them know that someone cares."

"I'll introduce you all to friends who manage the underground network," Jules said, "but I warn you, I met with their leader this morning, and he trusts no one. He won't be an easy wall to scale. But for now, let's enjoy this lovely meal."

César raised his glass. "To the rebellion."

Émilie smiled and raised her glass, and the others followed. "To the fight for justice and freedom."

César smiled as he saw Mathieu's eyes light up.

The heat lay heavy on Simone's shoulders as she and Émilie hustled through the crowded streets of Marseille carrying bags of clothing and parcels of food. Simone marveled at the vast array of humanity she saw in every direction, crowds thick with Africans, French, and Eastern Europeans. The refugees were easy to spot— so many of them haggard and sweating, practically buried under layers of clothing they'd piled on themselves to lighten the load of their suitcases.

Simone and Emilie delivered clothes and food to the foreign women and children who'd found shelter in run-down, deserted buildings. Some had been allowed to crowd into hotel-like configurations, essentially like camps even though they were in town. Being illegals, they had to stay out of sight of the Vichy police.

Mothers still waited for word about children lost during what was referred to as "the exodus." *Have you seen this person?* posters were all over the city, nailed to poles and trees by desperate families looking for family members. The well-to-do people in the hills around Marseille donated clothing, as did the nuns, the YMCA, the Unitarians, and the Quakers. Dozens of relief groups had set up their services in Marseille to help the homeless children and mothers, all innocent victims of the war.

Simone and Émilie reached a shelter where they had to step over and around straw-filled pallets that lined the floors and hallways. The place smelled like urine and sweat. A little girl with big dark eyes clutched a tattered stuffed animal. She stared wide-eyed as Simone handed her a little doll in a flowered dress. She gently accepted the doll and hugged it to her chest. Her mother smiled and spoke to Simone in a foreign language—was it Polish? Émilie handed the woman a bag as other women and children gathered around them. "And here are potatoes, carrots, and tomatoes from our garden."

Émilie said it was time to leave, but Simone stood still and looked at the small children, smiling despite everything they were going through. Their resilience brought tears to her eyes. Touching her arm gently, Émilie said, "I know. It's hard to see, but just know that every small gesture of kindness helps."

Next, they climbed the steep Rue d'Athènes to donate their last bundles at a school. Struggling upstream against the hordes rushing down from the train station, they came upon a group of refugees gathered in front of the Hôtel Splendide. "Please, please, I must see Mr. Fry," a gray-haired man with a thick beard called out to a frantic young man who carried a clipboard and a pencil. The old man looked like Simone's grandfather who had been displaced and terrorized by the Reich in the mid-thirties—Jewish, intelligent, and without a country.

"Mr. Fry will see each of you in order from this list." The young man tapped his clipboard with the end of his pencil. "Give me your name and country."

An elderly man waved his hat. "Horowitz. I know I'm on your list. Please just let me see him."

"I will note your name, sir," the young man answered as people in the crowd threw questions and requests his way. He looked extremely harried but seemed to be doing his best to be patient and kind. "No Ma'am, we don't know if there are any boats." "If you don't have a passport, stand in this line." "I'm sorry, Sir, there are no French exit visas."

Another man rushed up, adjusting his hat. He and the woman clinging to his arm were wearing clothes of the latest style—Simone guessed they'd been professionals, perhaps attorneys or professors. "My wife and I, we've been waiting for three days! We keep coming back. We're desperate—if we're deported, well—" He shook his head.

"Sir, you must fill out an application. Tell me your name again."

The crowd surged forward, everyone waving papers, shouting questions. Simone was overwhelmed by the panic in their voices.

Émilie grabbed her elbow and moved along the sidewalk. "Ach, this is terrible. Those people—it's . . ." Her thoughts drifted off as she guided Simone farther down the street away from the hotel and the refugees.

"What is happening at that hotel, Émilie? Who is that Mr. Fry?"

"Fry is an American who arrived in Marseille a couple weeks ago with a list of refugees he's supposed to save. The rumor is that they're well-known people who will be deported to Germany for crimes against the Reich. Anti-Fascists of all stripes, like journalists, politicians, professors. Even artists. They came to France for asylum when France proudly offered such things." Her deep frown made clear what she thought of France now.

The story piqued Simone's interest. *An American helping in France?* "How does he find these famous people?"

Émilie shrugged. "I don't know. But someone in Toulouse was selling Fry's name for fifty francs to people desperate for a connection to someone who can get them money and papers. People have been flocking to him, more each day. They'd better be careful or the flics will sweep down that sidewalk and grab the lot."

"Grab them? Don't they need a reason to arrest people?"

"No," Émilie whispered, "they could just be standing in a queue, and the Vichy police could cordon them off and haul them away. It's called a *rafle*. Marseille is full of illegals, and Vichy wants to clean up the refugee mess. It doesn't matter if you're innocent. If you end up in a camp, you pray that someone will get you out. Many will never get out."

The aroma of sweat and sewage wafted through the hot wind. Simone's stomach turned and she swallowed bile. Gestapo lists. Vichy *rafles*. What kind of world was this?

René and Gabrielle

$\int$ imone knew it would be hot in the city and chose a light cotton dress that Émilie had in stock from her clothes-gathering missions, this one patterned in green and yellow flowers. She wanted to look nice when they met Jules's fellow compatriots.

Jules called upstairs, "I want to talk to you all about our expedition. Come down for breakfast."

César dashed out of his room, trying to button the collar on his shirt. Cursing in frustration, he unbuttoned it and let it hang open at the neck. "It's too hot to button up. I have a clean shirt, clean pants, and Émilie's haircut. I should be presentable enough to meet Jules's friends. What do you think?" He gave Simone a wink and a mischievous grin.

She sidled over to him and straightened his collar, then rubbed her cheek against his just-shaved face and felt a tingle through her body. "Mmmm, just the right amount of sandpaper there."

She pressed her lips against his skin, and his hand firmly cupped her hip. She smiled with pleasure and looked up at him, certain they were both thinking about the other night, their merging of souls and flesh. It still amazed Simone to discover the magical things that could happen between two people in love. He kissed her forehead, and they clattered down the stairs.

Mr. Lieb looked up at her, the expression on his face a mixture of adoration and caution. She realized it was difficult for him to see her this intimate with a man—sharing secrets with him, turning to him for support—given that Mr. Lieb had been the man in her life since she'd been a young girl. But he was wise and considerate, and he'd known since Paris that she was in love.

It was the journey from Paris to Marseille that had sealed their bond, the three of them. They'd not only survived together but had had to confront multiple terrors as they repeatedly came close to losing everything, including their lives.

Émilie welcomed them to a breakfast of bread and the hot brew they called coffee. Everything was laid out on beautiful plates, as always. Rationing may have been upon them, but for Émilie, it was important to maintain a proper style of living. As she sipped the warm brew, Simone tried not to lament the loss of the coffee ritual she so loved. No longer were they allowed to drink the rich, dark coffees so beautifully prepared throughout France. Instead, rationing had relegated them to drink ersatz coffee here too. It was slightly bitter, but she resolved to make believe it was a delicious brew worthy of the finest cafés.

Émilie seemed to derive great pleasure from Simone and César's presence. She'd been mentoring Simone on painting—demonstrating for her the bold use of color, characteristic of the expressionist style of painting. Simone still preferred her black and white worlds of mystery, but she felt free here to explore both as she wished. And César—was he like the son Émilie had never had? She'd give him treats, like a nibble from some concoction she was making from new ingredients like rice and potato flour and their own homegrown apples. She asked his advice about adding more vegetables to the garden. They were beginning to feel like a family.

César, Simone, Mathieu, and Jules boarded the bus and then the tram, which rolled down La Canebière and cut through streets packed with people from all over the world—Africans, Arabs, and Europeans. Simone had never seen so many colors of skin, from burnished gold to the darkest black. Though Berlin was an international city, it wasn't generally welcoming of dark-skinned people. Simone realized how sheltered she'd been, now that she was surrounded by such diversity of the world's people—so many different sizes and varieties of hair and skin. And so many types of clothing, from caftans to military uniforms to finely cut suits to the work clothes of the laborers. Some of the women were covered in billowing dresses, heads and faces hidden from view.

The tram took them all the way down to the Vieux Port, a shimmering blue U-shaped port, its entrance to the sea framed by the ancient Fort Saint-Jean and Fort Saint-Nicolas. They stood looking at the scene, the sun's rays brilliant on the sparkling water, and Simone marveled at the intricate iron filigree of the transporter bridge that hung over the port. It reminded her of the magnificent Eiffel Tower.

Jules gestured toward the forts. "British officers are imprisoned there, but as a nod to their status, they're allowed to walk the Vieux Port during the day—as long as they promise not to try to escape."

César said in his best sarcastic voice, "Don't tell me no one's trying to help them escape."

Jules smiled. "That information is beyond my official knowledge." He led them down a labyrinth of streets behind the Vieux Port where his friends René and Gabrielle lived.

The Forger of Marseille

What a different world this was, Simone thought as they made their way past bombed-out buildings where cats hunted amid the bricks, broken dishes, and other rubble. The city was a warren cast in shadows. As they passed through the streets near the port, a sliver of bright sunlight glimmered between the buildings for only a moment, and then they found themselves again in the shadowed world of old men playing chess at small tables set in front of doorways, laundry flapping on clotheslines strung between buildings, and scores of brown-skinned children at play, shouting and running. A strange mixture of odors permeated the neighborhood. Simone thought she detected garbage and sewage but also mouth-watering aromas of stews that must have been bubbling on stoves. She wondered how hard they'd all been hit by rationing, whether they had enough to eat.

Finally, Jules stopped at a weathered building with pale green numbers marking its address and opened the outer door. They climbed the stairs to the first floor, and Jules rapped a kind of code. A bearded giant of a man opened it. "Yes?" His lips tight in a grim smile, he held the door open for Jules to come in. Simone, César, and Mathieu hung back while Jules spoke to the man. After a moment, Jules gestured for them to enter. Simone followed the men into the dark, cramped apartment, wondering what kind of people they were meeting. A well-used sofa, chair, and worn rug filled the small parlor.

Jules said, "René, these are the guests from Paris that I told you about: Simone, César, and Mathieu."

A woman nearly as tall as René was wiping her hands on a dishcloth and rushed to René's side. "I'm Gabrielle. Welcome, please have some . . . well, coffee, of a sort."

René caught her eye and shook his head, but Gabrielle pulled him aside into the small kitchen just off the parlor. After a moment he returned. "We've an appointment soon, but yes, coffee coming up."

Jules said, "My friend, Josh—Mathieu is a luthier from Berlin. This is his daughter, Simone, and their dear friend, César."

It seemed to Simone that René's bulk filled the room, and she thought Gabrielle was attractive in a strong-featured way, with her prominent cheekbones, jet-black hair tied back and out of the way, and big brown eyes that gleamed from behind her glasses. She fluffed a pillow on the sofa and then hurried into the kitchen. Over her shoulder she said, "Jules mentioned he was having guests. Where are you from, César?"

César lifted his chin proudly. "I'm from a place that no longer exists."

René's voice boomed, "Well, that could be Austria, Czechoslovakia, or France. But let me guess—Spain?"

César nodded. "We're all from somewhere else. You're lucky to still have your home."

"Ha! *That's* what you think?" René slammed down a plate. All his gestures seemed oversized and explosive.

Mathieu jumped. Simone startled and reached for César's hand. Jules looked surprised. Simone saw a telltale twitch of César's mouth. René had gotten their attention, but why that way?

Gabrielle intervened. "This Vichy business has troubled many of us deeply, but we're in the minority. What René means is that we're not residents of the France we belonged to even two months ago. We live in the same flat we've occupied for many years, but we too are in exile from the government we once believed in."

René's eyes flashed with anger. César was simmering, and Simone felt adrenaline rush through her body from all the high emotion in the room.

Jules spoke, his voice steady but subdued. "These are very challenging times for people who think as we and you do. That's why we've come here today."

René mumbled something and went back into the kitchen. Simone and Mathieu perched awkwardly on the edge of the worn brown sofa while César stood, fingers gripping the back of a wooden chair.

Gabrielle cut bread into thin slices and placed them on a plate, then poured a small amount of coffee into five cups, taking none for herself. "I already had my coffee. Enjoy."

René carried the cups and handed one to each guest. He threw his head back and swallowed his in one gulp. "Jules, you're a long way from your farm."

"These people are, shall we say, quite experienced in matters of protecting refugees."

Gabrielle said, "We know of several excellent rescue groups—the Unitarians, the YMCA, and a Jewish group. I'm sure they'd appreciate help with food and clothing."

César said, "We have something else in mind, and I'd say we're prepared to help *the most* challenged here in Marseille."

"What can you possibly offer? You know nothing of Marseille." René waved his hand dismissively.

Jules gestured toward his guests. "My friends have survived the exodus from Paris, and they were deeply involved in saving refugees in that city, by any means necessary."

"Mmmm," René murmured, striking a match to light his cigarette. Smoke spewed into the air. César and Simone exchanged glances. Had they made a mistake coming here?

Jules said, "Some refugees, as you know, need very *specific* kinds of help."

René pinned them with his dark eyes while Gabrielle gazed at them with interest.

César said, "We know it's dangerous to get involved with refugees. We saw the red placards with nooses pinned on trees all over town." Just thinking about those posters made Simone shiver.

Jules went on, "You know me. And my friends, all of us here, believe in democracy. Vichy goes against basic principles of decency, and not enough people are standing up for what's right."

René's eyebrows furrowed. "You think I don't know that? What exactly is it you want?"

"To help the refugees," Jules said.

Simone clutched César's arm. If only René wasn't so fierce and blustery. She could tell he was on the right side, but he was a tough man.

René's eyes were fierce. He took a breath and seemed to try to control his impatience. "Again, why should I trust these people?"

Simone had had enough of this. "We forge papers, and we're very good at it." She stood up, her hands on her hips. "In Paris we forged identity papers and dozens of passports, every day. We helped hundreds of refugees who otherwise would have been arrested and put into camps. We even took the photographs."

Silence fell across the room, then Gabrielle said, "How old are you, eighteen?"

"Twenty-one." Simone glanced back and forth between Gabrielle and René, looking both of them in the eye.

Gabrielle and René glanced at each other, then Gabrielle started laughing. "But you're so young!"

René shot her a skeptical look. "Show us what you can do. Here." He shoved a passport and identity card toward them. "Copy these documents. And you." René looked at César. "What about you?"

César raised himself to his full height, still several inches shorter than René, his voice firm and deep. "We had a studio of six forgers hidden in plain sight in the heart of Paris, one of the busiest cities of the world. How's that for starters?"

"You weren't born a forger," said René, "and you're not French. Who are you?"

"I'm a Catalan, a Republican. A doctor. I worked in the fields during the war, and along with my countrymen and my mother and sister ran away from Franco's brutal soldiers. Up the Pyrenees, stuck on the French border because they wouldn't let us in. Shot at by *stukas*."

Mathieu spoke up, his eyes moist with tears. "A courageous man. He lost that family."

Simone saw that Gabrielle and René were finally listening.

César went on, "Some Catalans in a beach town in France taught me how to save myself and others who were in danger by learning to create forged papers. I want to use that knowledge here—it's really that simple."

For what felt like several very long minutes, the air in the room seemed suspended in tense silence. Simone watched Gabrielle's face change from curious to bearing a faint smile that Simone interpreted as admiration. René's arms flexed at his sides, but his face began to soften. Then they all heard a rustling in the hallway followed by a loud thump against the door. Nobody moved. René grew pale and said, "Oh, no."

A weak voice called out, "Help."

Everyone looked at each other, then at the door. Another bump. A scratching sound. Fingers clawing at wood. Someone was moaning.

René rushed to the door and César opened it to find a man facedown on the threshold. He wore a blood-splattered military uniform, and blood dampened his blond hair. Simone backed up all the way to the kitchen, her heart pounding.

César and René began to lift the man inside. "One of them found us," René hissed. "Quick, let's get him out of sight."

"How did he know where to come?" Jules whispered as he helped lift the barely conscious man into the parlor. Simone was impressed by how quickly César shifted into being a skilled doctor, checking the man's pulse and pulling away his clothes to check for wounds. Simone tried to be gentle as she slipped the sleeve of his shirt off his limp arm.

"The underground telegraph passes the word on. People sympathetic to the Allies try to protect the injured British soldiers, take them in and feed them and get a trustworthy doctor to tend to their wounds," René said, positioning the man with a pillow under his head.

Mathieu said, "He probably got those rough-woven pants from a farmer who sheltered him. When we were on the road, we heard about the British soldiers who'd been taken in by French farmers. If these guys don't find that kind of protection, they're rounded up and sent to German POW camps."

Simone watched the soldier's chest rise and fall slowly as he breathed. "What's wrong with him, César?"

"He was hit over the head, and the bullet wound in his arm might be infected—you can smell it. We need to get him into a bed. He's probably starving too. Look at the ribs."

The man waved his hand and murmured something, then his head fell to the side and he went silent. Simone followed the others into a bedroom where they laid the man carefully on a narrow bed. The room was piled with boxes; it seemed to be a storage room, but clearly it had been used as a guest room. Piles of towels and sheets were folded neatly on a box, and men's civilian clothes hung from hangers in front of the window.

The man's body was long and starkly thin, ribs and breastbone exposed, and he was covered with crimson insect bites, purple bruises, and dirt. Quickly, René covered him with a blanket. He looked at Simone. "Bring warm water and a cloth to wash him. We must make him drink water or at least open his mouth so we can drip it in."

Gabrielle rolled the clothes into a ball. "Off to the incinerator." René and César nodded to each other across the body of the man.

Simone rushed into the kitchen for water and a cloth and lit the fire for the teakettle. Mathieu stood next to her, his face creased with sorrow. "I feel helpless," he said. "What can I do?"

As Gabrielle rushed by, she said, "Quick, chop the carrots and swedes there on the cutting board. There are bones wrapped up on the counter. Start boiling them for broth."

By mid-afternoon they were all functioning as a team, exchanging few words. Gabrielle propped up the young man and spooned water in his mouth followed by warm broth. César had cleaned and wrapped his head wound and said that later he'd open the arm wound to check for a bullet, but that first the man needed to grow a little stronger and had to be able to drink whiskey for the pain.

Simone discovered that Gabrielle had a trove of bandages, alcohol, and aspirin in her bathroom. Needles and thread wrapped in gauze. To stitch wounds? No one commented on this, but it was clear that this was not the first wounded soldier they'd cared for. Questions hung in the air, but for now, everyone was busy.

Mathieu made himself useful by cooking, cleaning up, and even making bread, following Gabrielle's instructions to mix rice and corn flour in with what little wheat flour they had.

The young man whispered that his name was Barry, and he even managed a smile and a thank you in English and French, but nobody pressed him for information. Gabrielle acted motherly, sponging his face, adjusting his pillow, spooning broth. Simone got to work finding bandages and cleaning up the used medical supplies César dropped to the floor. Simone observed that René was gruff but carefully nurturing when he moved Barry as César directed. Watching César in action as a doctor seemed to shift his attitude or at least soften his tone of voice. Now René spoke to him with respect, and Gabrielle repeatedly thanked him.

A couple of hours after Barry had arrived in a heap, his rescue team gathered in the parlor to eat soup while he slept.

René furrowed his brows and waved his spoon. "So you see what we're doing. We all understand, do we, the risks of these kinds of operations? Clearly you have skills we can use. But about the other business—I need to see your work."

Simone and César exchanged glances of solidarity. Mathieu nodded.

René pushed a passport, an identity card, and a piece of paper toward Simone, along with pen and ink. She picked up the pen and looked up at him.

René said, "Just copy the signatures on these documents. I need to see your hand and how quickly you can work."

César looked directly at René and said, "I've done my share of forgeries. Would you like to see a sample of my work as well?"

René shrugged. "Sure." He pushed a sheet of paper and a pen toward César. For a few moments, César and Simone assessed the documents. Simone studied the end of the y and the curve of the s. To duplicate it would require a certain lift of the pen. The amount of pressure applied while writing was critical, so she practiced several times before doing the final signing. César also carefully scanned the documents as the four other people watched. A clock ticked in the parlor. Then Simone and César began to write.

Simone made quick work of the assignment, easily copying the signatures and the clerk's penmanship on the original documents. César finished just after she did, and they pushed the papers toward René.

René picked up the passport César had copied and ran his fingers along the lines, then Simone's papers, examining the lines and the letters with a magnifying glass. "I see. Very well done."

Gabrielle smiled at René and said, "I think they'll prove useful, don't you?"

"Mmm," is all René said as he stuck out his hand toward César and gave a quick smile to Simone. Then he and Gabrielle stood up. "We'll see you chez Jules soon."

"I'll stop back in tomorrow to check on Barry," César said.

René nodded, and Simone thought she saw a flash of approval in his eyes.

Gabrielle said to César, "In a couple of days we'll need to transfer Barry to you. We must make room here for other men." She tucked a chunk of cheese into a cloth and gave it to Jules. "Give our greetings to Émilie."

As they walked out onto the street, César draped his arm around Simone and whispered, "I think we've found our way in."

Safe Houses

*T*wo days later, René and Barry showed up at Jules and Émilie's home. René half-carried Barry, who seemed to be smiling. Or was he grimacing? René said his stay would be quick as he had to leave for "another rescue," so César helped Barry into the guest room. After settling him in, César began to examine his head wound and his arm where a bullet had grazed him. Simone noticed that the young man now had more sparkle in his eyes. He winked at her. "Bonsoir, Mademoiselle."

"You remember Simone?" César said as he helped guide Barry to the bed.

"Lovely," Barry said over his shoulder before the door closed.

After Barry was resting comfortably, Jules gathered everyone into the dining room. "Now you see what's happening here in the south—there's a system of rescues and safe houses in Vichy, and several are functioning here in Marseille."

Simone leaned forward, eager to hear more.

Émilie said, "When Barry gets well, his next stop will be Donald Caskie's Seaman's Mission where they'll get him ready to go to England."

Mathieu asked, "Tell us about this mission. And this Caskie fellow."

Jules explained, "Donald Caskie came here after the exodus from Paris and set up a mission for seamen and British citizens. He'd been the pastor for the Scotts Kirk in Paris where his strong preaching against the Fascists made it necessary for him to escape. He refused the last space left on the last ship to England, convinced he had to stay in France. Some say he's following the voice of God. A few weeks ago, he opened the Seaman's Mission, and he puts his life on the line to hide the British airmen and soldiers until they can escape over the Pyrenees. At six every morning the police search the Mission for a reason to arrest him but haven't found one."

"What extraordinary risks he takes," said Simone. Anxiety rushed through her body as she imagined the courage of recently wounded young men climbing the Pyrenees to escape France—how determined they were to get back into the fight. "They're all so brave."

Mathieu nodded, then asked, "Where does he hide them?"

"He has panels in cupboards, spaces under the floor. Places all over the Mission."

"How does he get the men out of the country?" Simone was fascinated.

More information about Caskie and Vichy seemed to tumble from Jules's mind. "*Passeurs,* guides. The vine workers in these small villages have trained guides who lead the refugees in the early mornings. And all these Englishmen—they need visas, which are almost impossible to get. The Germans on the Kundt Commission, they're running around making sure Vichy adheres to the Armistice. Those Germans have been seen in towns near the Pyrenees. Meanwhile, Caskie's people help the soldiers cross the Spanish border, and from there, they'll go to Lisbon and board a ship to England."

Émilie added, "They're desperate to fight again. England is in a roaring air battle between the RAF and the Luftwaffe."

"All the more reason to get those pilots back into the war. They all want to jump back into the fight. Crush the Nazis," César said.

"Well, England is the target now." Jules's face was red and he mopped his brow.

Mathieu rubbed his forehead. "Ahh, it's so terrible. Our LiebViol branch is in London—I hope they'll be all right."

"Who's that, Mathieu?" asked Jules.

"Remember Thomas Banks? They sell our instruments."

Everyone sat for a moment as the weight of the war hovered over the room.

"I understand about the safe houses," Simone said, "but what are *maisons de rendezvous*?"

"Brothels," said César with a smirk.

"Not quite," Jules hurried to say. "They're like a hotel that's unofficial. At a *maison de rendezvous* there's no official register, and the police won't bother the residents. The police have their own 'special friends' there too."

Émilie poured water in a pot for afternoon tea. "In Marseille, there are other ordinary people like us who help the British boys. One couple—he's an industrialist and she's from New Zealand—they take food to the soldiers at Fort Saint-Jean, food that no one else can get. And they help with money and network connections that are starting to develop in the south of France. A real underground railroad that operates by word of mouth."

Jules said, "There's a doctor in the Vieux Port who marks the British servicemen fit or unfit to fight. The unfit are sent home through official channels, saving their lives from arrest or a prisoner of war camp."

"That's not all," said Émilie. "There are even nanny networks—women who take care of the British children, part of the expatriate British community. They hide these guys upstairs in the nursery and no one is the wiser."

Simone looked at César and raised her eyebrows. "There are so many people involved already. That's good."

"Well, it is, but it's never enough. Too many soldiers are picked up, arrested. Too many are still dying." Émilie's face looked sad as she poured cups of weak tea for everyone.

Jules nodded toward César. "It's going to be your job to take Barry to Caskie, along with a basket of food. There will be a system if we keep doing this—Simone, you will do the forging for the Brit boys, but César we're going to need you as our doctor."

Simone shook Jules's hand. "Thank you again for inviting us, trusting us. César and I want to save people. We want to do what we can." She squeezed César's shoulder.

Mathieu, Émilie, and Jules surrounded her and César, encircling them in warmth. She could see in their eyes that they were welcome. That they belonged to this new network to try to make a difference.

Seaman's Mission

hree days later, Barry the Englishman was well enough to begin his next steps—the journey to Caskie's Mission. César looked forward to escorting him and seeing Caskie's operation. After hearing Jules speak of Caskie's underground efforts, César's heart began to beat faster. He couldn't wait to meet this pastor who so boldly stood up against Vichy and seemed to have God protecting him.

Barry turned out to be a cheery fellow, quick with a laugh. César and Barry did their best to communicate in French and English, but they often had humorous moments of misunderstanding. Despite that, César found Barry's lightheartedness and his colorful expressions delightful. The Englishman was always grinning and saying things like, "Let's have a chin wag." As he began to feel better, he gave a thumbs up and said, "Now everything is tickety-boo."

Émilie had found a suit that almost fit him, but the pants were too short, and the belt looped almost double around his thin frame. Laughing, César and Émilie managed to help him dress as he hobbled on one leg. They were relieved to see that the jacket hid the too-short shirt sleeves, though his wrist bones still poked out. Shoes, they were a bit tight, but they'd do once the swelling receded. As they stood together in front of the mirror looking at the suit, Barry smiled. "Say, this is the bee's knees!"

After Barry's fitting, Émilie gathered his clothes to clean and press them before his journey to Caskie's Mission in only a few days.

That same afternoon, César and Simone laid out their forging materials on the table to see what had survived the long journey of dirt and bullets. He brushed off the dust and grit and checked their supply to see if they needed new pen nibs, ink, or brushes. Fortunately, Émilie had plenty of art supplies for drawing the stamps by hand as needed. René was to come over soon with other forging materials—his forger had gotten arrested, which brought the reality of the danger into the house.

César looked at Simone. How proud he was of her. Now and then he thought he saw caution in her eyes, but he knew her determination to help was stronger than her fear. She gave him a big smile and told him to quit worrying.

Once they had the new supplies from Émilie and René, together they spread old newspapers on the walnut table and laid out the pens, a collection of nibs, and bottles of ink in black, red, blue, sepia, and green. They sat at the table side by side and began to practice their hand on large sheets of paper—big circles, loops, and then tiny cursive letters. The alphabet, large and small. Doodles to loosen them up. Simone said, "I'm so rusty now. My curved lines aren't graceful, and I'm shaky on the upward strokes."

César focused intently on his lettering. It was gratifying to return to the kind of work he'd done in Paris, but he shared Simone's sense of being out of practice. "We just need to keep at it," he said. It's like playing the violin."

Simone smiled. "Yes, exactly like that. We'll practice with the commitment of the greatest violinists in the world."

René's box of forging materials included several inks, pens, and the stamps his previous forger had made. "My forger was damned careless," he said. "Some of the papers were bad. We're lucky you two showed up—there are more Brits every day in desperate straits. Fifteen need to be readied for Caskie right away."

César smiled to himself at René's kind words. Then he said, "René, Barry needs a photograph for his papers."

René pursed his lips. "He was in so much pain when he came to us, we never got a photo." Just then Jules entered the room. René said, "Jules, we need your camera. César, take the photo here, and we'll develop it and bring it back tomorrow."

"That would mean using a whole roll of film. Isn't film hard to find?" Simone asked.

"Not a problem," René answered. "Go ahead and take a roll of photos of Barry and your gang here. Someday they'll be souvenirs. I must rush off, but I'll return later for it. And don't worry—we have sources for finding film." René said goodbye and rushed out the door.

Simone gave Jules a skeptical look. "Sources for film?"

Jules said, "He knows his way around Marseille, don't worry."

Fresh air blew into the room as Mathieu came in from the courtyard holding a violin. He smiled and said, "Any requests?"

Simone got up and stood on her tiptoes to kiss him on the cheek, camera in hand and a mischievous look on her face. "Yes, we want music, but first let's take pictures. Of all of us! We'll set up a photo station for Barry with a sheet for a background, and tomorrow I'll do his papers."

Émilie walked in from the kitchen and said, "I'll get the backdrop ready."

Jules smiled at her. "She has everything under control— thank you, my dear!"

Émilie said she'd be back after ironing a sheet. In a corner of the dining room, César and Jules busied themselves setting up a makeshift studio using a chair, lamp, and camera tripod.

Simone snapped photos—Mathieu and Jules grinning, arms around each other, Mozart barking and leaping in joy at all the activity. Jules and Émilie standing next to the lavender and sunflowers in the courtyard, their arms wound around each other.

"Now us!" Simone said to César. "Who will take our photo?" Simone handed the camera to Mathieu, then took César's hand and guided him toward a large fuchsia bougainvillea.

Simone squeezed him close, her body supple and warm, and he realized he missed her. He missed the world without war when they first fell in love. The warmth of the sun, the laughter, and the light mood reminded him of that other life. Pulling her close, he found her lips and kissed her. The kiss seemed to send them both to a quiet, soft place all their own. Vaguely he could hear laughter and the click of a camera, but all he wanted just then was Simone.

Breaking away breathless, she looked up at him, her eyes soft and full of desire. "*There* you are."

Mathieu, or was it Jules, cleared his throat. "Better get Barry's photo. There are only a few frames left."

Mathieu handed the camera to César. "Just my girl and me in this one!"

Simone wrapped both arms around Mathieu, then laid her head on his chest, and César snapped a photo of just the two of them—daughter and father. His heart warmed at these moments of ordinary happiness despite the danger they were all in. Barry limped out from his room and laughed at the photo scene as Émilie pushed his hair this way and that until she was satisfied.

Barry arranged himself on the chair, smiling broadly, then César directed him. "Sorry Barry, but you have to look serious for the official photo."

"Me serious—never!" He grinned even harder, his nose and ears flaming bright red. Then Barry looked into the camera, and for a second there was a fierce determination in his eyes. A few clicks later, César said, "Got it," and Barry burst into tears. César wrapped a strong arm around the soldier as Barry wiped his eyes and apologized. "I'm such a blubberer. Very sorry. It's just that, well, you people are so kind, and I'm finally going home."

César held him for a moment, feeling his own emotions rise to the surface. This guy was brave, and what a wonderful character. How lucky they were to know him.

That evening, René came by to pick up the film and found Simone working on the new documents by lamplight. They'd decided that Barry's name was to be André Gilles, and then René dashed off again to take care of more refugee business. César stayed by Simone's side as she carefully copied the official names and signatures from an original set of papers René had brought. She went through her usual warm-up, creating the large circles and doodles, then stopped, shook her hands loose, and drank some tea. She was like an athlete preparing for a race. It took her two hours to finish all of Barry's documents. Barry joined them at the table and practiced writing *André Gilles* several times and then signed his new official papers. He turned to César with a serious look on his face. "But my accent, it's bad. What if someone speaks to me?"

Émilie came into the room carrying a brown, slightly blood-stained scarf. "Wear this around your neck and show them this card. It says you were wounded in the war and can't speak."

The new André Gilles laughed. "I'm so relieved. I've been worrying about this all day."

"Good evening, André."

"Good night to you, César."

As César walked away, he thought about names, identities. He himself had once been *Tomás*. How far away *Tomás* seemed now.

As the two men made their way to the Mission, Barry walked slightly hunched and with his hands in his pockets so he wouldn't stand out as he ambled along beside César. With their heads down in the spitting rain, they walked from the bus to the port—an area known for its dark shadows and underground tunnels. César peered out from under his rain hat to check for suspicious people and officials, but so far local residents were all they saw along the narrow streets. They'd arrive at Caskie's as Marseille was waking up.

As they approached the Mission, César noticed two men loitering in the doorway of a nearby building. They wore long overcoats, and their hats were pulled down over their faces. César made a mental note to make sure no one followed him when he left the Mission. The stove pipe of a small café across the street from the Mission expelled curls of smoke that smelled of grease. He could see silhouettes of laborers hunched over the counter, and his heart beat faster as he wondered if some of those men were Vichy lookouts hoping to inform on Caskie's people in exchange for a reward. Barry was carrying the basket of vegetables Émilie had sent, their donation of food to the Mission.

As they arrived at 46 Rue Forbin, the low cream-colored building seemed to emerge out of the mist. Caskie's Mission appeared to be hunkering down, as if to protect itself from the force of the sea. Constant winds lashed at buildings along the port. Their peeling paint and weathered shutters told the story of storms and gales that had battered Marseille for centuries.

César tucked his arm in Barry's and pulled him close as he rapped out the prearranged signal: three knocks, then two. From inside, he could hear the deep rumble of men's voices, laughter, and the *thwock twock* of an energetic game of table tennis. The rain pelted harder, and César had to wipe water out of his eyes. Barry grinned and lifted his face toward the rain.

"*Oui*, who comes?" The voice had a lilt and a burr.

"*Le canard orange*," César replied, following René's instructions.

The door cracked open to reveal a short man with bright blue eyes.

César said, "Donald Duck? Je suis Mickey."

Caskie waved them in. "Bonjour! Vite, vite, the weather is foul."

César glanced around the large smoke-filled room where more than a dozen men were playing table tennis and games like cards, checkers, and chess on long tables. As they all called out greetings, the men's many accents rose and fell like music from other lands. All eyes fastened on the new guests, but as Caskie invited them in, the men returned to their games. Barry looked around the room, his eyes gleaming. César could see he was overjoyed to be among his people.

Several gray-haired ladies wearing long dresses with aprons rushed over to take the basket of food. Caskie said, "Thank you, sisters," and then turned to Barry. "Young man, welcome. Your Uncle René told me of your desire to visit your family. Do come over here and have some tea." Two men pulled out a chair for Barry. "Please, sit." Caskie looked Barry up and down, his face wreathed in a smile. "You have quite the suit, and you look ready for what comes next. Monsieur, the papers? Just put them in here," Caskie said as he passed César a large heavy copy of *Treasure Island*. César tucked the papers inside and closed the book as the ladies returned with a tea pot, small tea cakes, three mugs, and a pitcher of milk.

"We try to keep up the English traditions here," Caskie said. "Barry, where do you hail from?"

"A village in Yorkshire. My mother is still there, and she wonders, is my son alive or dead."

Caskie patted his arm. "We've set up a system through the church. Write your mother a letter, and we'll try to get it to her."

"Oh, blessings upon you. Thank you." Barry's eyes teared up, and so did César's—lost mothers and sons was his story too.

César wiped the tears away and looked into Caskie's clear blue eyes. "I'd be honored to help you and your men. I and another comrade can take care of the papers for you. She did Barry's here. I mean, she's the expert who prepared *André's* papers."

"Quite the lovely young lass, I have to say," Barry said, his mouth full of cake.

Caskie was simply a man, but when he spoke César could hear in him a kind of power that lifted him above ordinary men. César sensed that he listened deeply not only to words but to the subtle ways people communicated their very souls.

They finished their tea, and it was time for César to say goodbye to his English friend. César tapped Barry on the shoulder, and the Englishman looked at César, his bright blue eyes full of hope. The two men raised their cups of tea in a toast and then stood up and gazed warmly at each other for a silent moment. Barry leaned over and clapped his long arms around César and nearly squeezed the breath out of him.

At the door, Caskie looked into César's eyes and shook his hand. "Fare thee well, friend. We shall see you soon. There is a train each day that the men must catch."

César understood. The work went on daily to save these men.

After bidding them all goodbye, César stepped out onto the street, carefully looking to the right and left for the two men in trench coats, but they were gone. The rain had lightened up, and children played ball on the wet streets. Women called them to come in for breakfast. Men sat in doorways, slowly smoking cigarettes. The sea slapped the rocks and spray burst into the air. Walking the few blocks to the bus, César breathed in the welcome scents of sea air, paprika, and garlic, the aromas of home.

The Englishmen

The men kept finding their way to René and to Jules, the downed pilots and lost soldiers. Robert, William, Thomas, Ralph. Duncan, Colin, Bernard. Timothy, Hugh, Gavin. Simone met some of the men as they arrived at Jules's to be treated for their wounds while others found their way through the refugee telegraph to other safe houses. All of them needed papers. And all of them were hungry. Some had broken wrists, arms, legs. Sprained ankles and blisters from ill-fitting shoes or punctures from wearing no shoes at all on their long, dangerous trek from northern France. Head wounds. Infections. They hailed from different parts of Great Britain, and now that the Battle of Britain was raging, most of the Brits who showed up at their door were pilots who'd been shot down over France. Great Britain had become a fortress in preparation for an invasion, and all the Englishmen Simone had met were eager to get home and back into the RAF to protect England. During these encounters, she found herself improving her English and having fun adding quirky English expressions to her repertoire, like "tickety-boo" and "chuffed."

The Pétainists had been certain Great Britain would fall, but the Brits fought on. England was still an official enemy of France, but in Marseille the English who had money and lived in the hills weren't harassed by officials. There was a live-and-let-live attitude for the English who'd been part of Marseille society for decades that didn't apply to anyone else.

Many of the soldiers Simone met had flown in several missions, and she learned that England was undergoing night after night of bombing. It wasn't clear if they could keep the Germans from invading. Simone didn't know what to tell them, but she rededicated herself to the work.

One morning as she set up her materials for a day of forging, César came up from behind and kissed her neck. "I'm headed out," he said. "Meeting some people who source passport covers."

She turned to look at him. "Be very careful out there."

"Always, my love."

She stood and hugged him, then stepped back and said, "I'll be working all day on papers for our friends in the RAF."

His face grew serious. "I've been thinking about Barry. It's rough, not knowing how the guys fared. Especially Barry."

Simone touched his cheek. "I think we'd hear if he was arrested. Let's imagine he made it over the border and back home to his shepherd's pie—or whatever rationing allows."

César smiled and pulled her in for a long, warm hug then headed out the door.

Simone performed her usual warmup of drawing circles and letters, then pulled from a pile of papers a chart she'd created listing the names of the next Englishmen on her list. In one column she'd listed their English names, and to the right of each, their new French names.

Robert	→	Pierre
Colin	→	Gaston
Gavin	→	Simon
Bernard	→	Jacques
Thomas	→	Antoine

Then she added the surnames. Robert became Pierre Barbier. Colin—Gaston DeRose; Gavin—Simon Roche; there was Jacques Travers and Antoine Gautier. Place of birth had to be added—still using the method they'd used in Paris—choosing faraway places in France, preferably small villages or towns that had been bombed, which would make it difficult for officials to check records.

Now that she'd matched the names, she began to fill out their papers. René had snapped the photographs after the men had arrived at their safe house, and a few of the men had been in César's "hospital" at Jules's place while they mended enough to get to Caskie's to prepare for their journey up the mountain. Simone and César kept the photo setup so it could be used as needed. Some of the men had to recover for a month at a safe house, either with the nannies or in a *maison de rendezvous*, which was without a doubt the men's favorite location. Simone had not yet met the women at one establishment, Chantal and Marguerite, but she was told they were charming ladies who were full of fun, warmth, and nurturing. They fed the men well, getting food from whatever back-alley deals they could manage. They even danced with the men, if their injuries allowed. There was a rumor that the coffee served there, Italian coffee, was a heavenly brew, the only place in Marseille that served real coffee. How Chantal and Marguerite managed that was anyone's guess.

That September morning her Mr. Lieb came downstairs carrying his violin case, dressed in his only suit. He carried his hat and a warm overcoat that Émilie had found for him.

"Bonjour, Mademoiselle. You're at work early today." He bent down and kissed Simone's forehead. He smelled of tobacco, coffee, and old wool.

"So many men—but we're saving them. Look—aren't they handsome young men?" The documents were nearly complete—the forged signatures and stamps, the small photographs attached. They just needed to be signed.

Together they flipped through the documents and gazed into the faces in the small square photographs. "That Thomas, he's quite the handsome devil," he said.

"How about Gavin? Those eyes!" Simone laughed.

He kissed her head again and laid his face against her cheek. "You're so brave, my dear Simone. Look at what you're doing."

"They'll be our emissaries in England. The English will know that someone in France cares about them." Simone scuffed the leather covers of the passports so they appeared well used.

"With de Gaulle in London, he holds the hope of a new France. A resistance movement idea, but not much can be done from England."

"René and Gabrielle assure me that it's developing here. The underground, the network in Vichy. We're part of it."

Her dear Mr. Lieb put his arms around her. His signature tobacco and linseed oil scent always made her feel calm, at home. Safe, even in this faraway place where every day brought something new and potentially dangerous. She squeezed him hard in return, then broke away and looked into his eyes. "You be careful out there. Don't let those Vichy police harass you."

"Yes, Mademoiselle Forger. I'll see you later at dinner. We'll have a glass of wine."

"Where are you going?"

"Violin lessons. Two new students! I'm so happy to give lessons again. Chuffed to bits, as the English boys would say." He lifted his violin high like a banner and turned to go out the door. "Au revoir."

As Simone watched him leave, an uneasiness surrounded her like a shawl. She should have said, "Â bientôt."

Underground Passages

His face flushed hot despite the dank conditions in the deep caverns under Marseille. César could hardly contain his anger at the men standing before him in the dark, cave-like passage near the port.

"These, how could you try to pass these off to me?" He flung down the documents. "They're obvious fakes. The printing isn't registered properly, and the paper, it's crap. Where did you get these materials, the bottom of a ship?"

The men hung their heads. They were unshaven with greasy hair and dirty clothes. "It's not our fault," one of them protested.

César tried not to breathe too deeply. The cellar under a deserted old structure by the port stank of urine, ink, sweat, and something rotten. People in the clandestine underground often met each other in underground tunnels and cramped, dark cellars. Marseille was built on layers of ancient rocks and foundations all the way back to thousands of years BC, and the stone tunnels and passageways had been used for centuries by those needing to do business in the dark, hiding from the law. From their enemies.

César cursed himself for following a string of referrals for printing passports instead of vetting everyone himself. But

René didn't personally know everyone either—he had to count on decent referrals too. A guy knows a guy and so on down the line—it was part of the risk of this kind of work, which was one reason René was so cynical and cautious. The desperate need for false papers led to great risks, but there was no other way.

"You have to leave. I'll be sure to tell René never to hire you again." He gestured at the sorry-looking men in front of him, their heads hanging. He could see they were hungry, for food and for the money they expected from him for a job badly done. He turned his back and slicked off bills—a third of the promised fee—from a roll of cash René had given him. He handed it to them and said, "Here, consider yourself lucky. Go!"

The men remained standing, mouths hanging open. They were the worst example César had seen of dealing with the underground element of Marseille, but the leader of the group, Draco, was dressed in a somewhat clean suit. He at least had the grace to look embarrassed at César's confrontation. He nodded at the other fellows, and they shuffled out.

Draco stood with his feet apart, shaking his head. "We were told they were legitimate workers with experience. People pass jobs and materials along to us—you know how it is."

"You're supposed to check everything. It's life and death here."

"Yes, we know. The noose, we're all facing it."

"Not *you*! The soldiers, the refugees. This is their last chance. If they don't escape from Marseille, they'll be shot or at the very least arrested. The Gestapo is combing the borders to catch people, and they're examining papers more closely now. They know about the rescues over the mountains."

Draco held onto his hat and swayed back and forth on his feet, his expression dour but not fully repentant. He'd hold out to get his money, as much as he could. Now César would have to find new people to work with.

César waved him away. "Just go. Good that I caught this before . . ."

Draco remained where he was. "I should probably tell you. . ."

"What is it?" César felt a pinch in his gut. More bad news.

Draco's face screwed up in distress. "We made two deliveries before yours."

César felt a chill come over him. Bad documents spreading through Marseille—this could spell disaster. "Who. *Where*? You must get the papers back before the forgers use them."

"I can't."

"Why not?"

"Because my bosses will kill me if they find out. You can't tell them."

César was almost too disgusted to speak. "Just *go*."

César had no idea who the bosses were, which was probably good. Then he couldn't be tortured to give up names. Then a terrible thought came to him as Draco was leaving. "It wasn't for the Mission, was it? The delivery?"

The man's eyes shifted back and forth. "I don't know anything. Nothing." He looked miserably down at his shoes.

Sick to his stomach, César waved him on. Caskie's Mission was one place where the documents could have been delivered, but there were other safe houses functioning on the same razor's edge between life and death. Could he find out who'd received them—likely not. These things were done in secret. Perhaps Caskie would let him look at the blank documents he'd received. Then César would have to give René the bad news that would send him sky high with rage. He needed to think this through.

He washed his hands at the sink. With the shortage of soap, it was always hard to get the ink stains off his fingers. As he ran his hands under the water, his memories of scrubbing up as a doctor came back to him, and it seemed a dream, the life of another man.

He'd never imagined he'd find himself in the sewers of Marseille dealing with criminals and gangs. And now here he was, a criminal himself.

He ran his fingers through his hair and brushed his chin along his hand to test the roughness of his beard. In the two months since arriving in Marseille, shaving had become a luxury. If he shaved without soap, his face burned. It's okay, he thought. Simone liked the feel of his beard on her skin.

He carefully made his way through the lower chamber and climbed the roughly hewn stone steps upwards. Rats squealed and scampered around him. Water from the sea dripped down the old stones, etching them away inch by inch. His torch revealed stones that might have been walls built by the Greeks or Romans. Or in some other century. They reeked of the passage of time.

Intrigue and secrets—these were not new to modern Marseille. He climbed another set of uneven steps toward the surface and emerged, his face slapped by wind and stinging rain. That wasn't good. The weather made for dangerous conditions for the lads who had to climb the mountain and for the Brits trying to get to Gibraltar by boat.

He turned toward Rue Forbin. He had to see if blank documents had been delivered and he wanted to find out if Caskie had heard how Barry—André that is—had fared. *Did he and the other lads get across the border?* Dear Barry—and the other lads. Twenty years old, and already their lives were dominated by war. He knew what that was like. But no one could know how the war would go. It looked bad right now with the Luftwaffe pounding London. He shook his head, rain dripping into his eyes. *No, Hitler couldn't engulf all of Europe*, he hoped. The lads, the resistance in France—so many were fighting to try to preserve a way of life. But he also knew about defeat. Spain had lost everything. Everyone.

The Rafle

By a café near the port, a violinist played soulful folk music for a gathering crowd. Mathieu tapped his foot to the rhythm as he sipped his coffee. The setting sun glittering on the water lifted his heart. If he didn't know about the dark dangers rumbling behind the scenes, Marseille would have felt like any seaside town on a sunny afternoon.

People swayed to the music, then stopped themselves and stood still, obediently listening. Dancing was prohibited in Vichy France. Caught up in the music, Mathieu didn't notice the blue-clad police who began to circle the café.

The violinist missed a few notes and then went silent. Footsteps clattered on the cobblestones as people ran away.

The gendarmes closed in until they formed a circle around everyone who remained.

"Come with us, vite, vite," shouted the police.

Mathieu felt panic in his throat. He grabbed his coat and violin case. *Should he run?* No, he thought better of it. A few women captured in the *rafle* were weeping while others stood frozen like statues. The gendarmes lined everyone up and demanded papers. Shaking, Mathieu tried to appear calm as he handed his to a guy with a big moustache and fierce eyes.

"What is your name?"

Mathieu stood tall and looked the policeman in the eye. "Mathieu DuBois."

"Your profession?"

His papers stated his profession as cabinetmaker, an *ébéniste*, and that he worked with Jules Martel. He hoped the reference to a longtime resident would speed his release. He told himself it was all right, that they were double-checking everyone, those who looked like refugees, layered in clothing, and those who looked like locals who had simply stopped to hear the music.

Despite the terror coursing through his body, he tried to stay calm. Jules had warned him about *rafles*, emphasizing that once a person was caught in the net, it was unlikely he'd be released.

The officials finished looking at papers on the street and told the group to follow them to the police station. He tucked his violin case under his coat and walked, mentally berating himself for going to the café after teaching his violin student. *Why hadn't he gone straight back to Jules's? Why had he tried to pretend that Marseille was just a normal seaside town where he could go to a café and enjoy a peaceful coffee?*

At the station, the group was led down a long hallway of shuttered windows. They reached an office where bright lights illuminated three dour-looking officials dressed in wrinkled uniforms. In the office were dozens of shelves stuffed with files, and the desks were piled high with papers. An official ordered the prisoners to put their belongings into sacks and hand over their money. They would get it back when they were released. The new prisoners looked at each other. *Released?* That sounded hopeful.

Mathieu sheltered his violin between his legs, trying to keep it covered with his long overcoat as he pulled money from his pocket. He didn't think he could survive losing his family treasure. A pale-faced official behind a paneled divider typed slowly with one finger, filling out paperwork in triplicate.

Mathieu watched as another official with beady eyes was handed a piece of paper. He called out the names of several prisoners from the list, including Mathieu's. His heart pounding, Mathieu approached the desk.

"You!" barked Beady Eyes, pointing at Mathieu and waving his identity papers. "These papers, they're forgeries!"

Sweat burst out on Mathieu's forehead. *Was this a test?* He pulled his shoulders back. "That's a mistake. I am Mathieu DuBois. See, there is my residence and ration cards."

"I don't know who you are, but you're not French. The officer at the port caught your accent."

"Probably a Jew," said one of the officials.

A sour-faced official holding a cigarette smirked. "We can find that out easily enough, can't we?"

Mathieu's face flushed hot as he realized how they planned to check.

"I'm Mathieu DuBois. I'm a luthier."

"Says here *cabinetmaker*." The man squinted at him over his wire-rimmed glasses.

"Yes, luthier *and* cabinetmaker."

The official leaned forward, his beady eyes triumphant. "I'm from Alsace, and you are German. Born in Germany. I'd bet on it."

"No, no, I'm . . ." Mathieu was left speechless. When César had created the papers, he'd been wise to designate Alsace as Mathieu's birthplace. But now what? Sweat dripped down his ribs.

"Take off your coat."

Mathieu hesitated, but these men looked deathly serious. He carefully removed his coat and covered his violin with it.

"Pull down your pants."

Mathieu froze. He glanced across the room and saw another man suffering the same humiliation, pants around the ankles, police jeering. He didn't move, hoping the degradation of one man might be enough for them.

"Give us the coat." The official gestured toward Mathieu's feet. Mathieu didn't move.

The official pursed his lips and slammed his fist on the counter. "Now!" When Mathieu remained still, the official peered beyond the end of his desk to the floor. "What do you have? What are you hiding?"

Very slowly, Mathieu picked up his coat and revealed the violin case.

The official's face lit up as if he'd just discovered a diamond. "What do we have here? You aren't allowed to keep valuables."

"But I, I made this violin." He had to convince them it was special, that he couldn't live without it.

"Is it any good?" the official asked, looking down at the case, gesturing for Mathieu to hand him the violin.

"Of course, we made violins of the finest quality." Mathieu could hardly breathe as he clicked open the case, carefully lifted the instrument out and laid it into the official's meaty hands.

Then he realized that if the official looked inside the violin, he'd see the *LiebViol* label. The official grinned as he turned the violin over and over. "My cousin always wanted a violin," he said and tossed it to an officer standing a few feet away.

Mathieu shouted, "No! I made it, it's mine. Don't . . ." Mathieu leaped forward to catch it, but the other official grabbed it in midair, fingers twanging the strings. Mathieu lost his footing and fell to the floor, landing on his right knee. Pain shot up his right side, and with an effort he stood up and saw the gleeful look in the eyes of the official.

"This is now the property of Vichy. Maybe soon we'll have enough instruments for a concert." The cackling of the official's laughter sliced the thick air.

Tears burned Mathieu's cheeks. "It's my very own violin. I made it from old wood from the forest. It's very precious to me." He reached out for his beautiful violin, its inlaid ivory design glistening in the harsh office light, but the beady-eyed man stepped back.

The official said, "My father was a violinist, and I know about violins." Then he lifted the instrument and peered inside the f-hole.

"*LiebViol* it says. Would that be *Lieb violin*? *A Jew* name?"

Another official looked at his clipboard. "His papers say he's French. DuBois."

"That's a forgery," Beady Eyes replied to his underling. Then he turned back to Mathieu. "I'd bet my father's gold watch that we have a Herr Lieb before us and that he is a Jew. A Jew who makes violins."

"No, it's a German name, but . . . my father. I mean, it was a company I worked for." Mathieu's thoughts scrambled as he tried to say something, anything that would help. "In England I'm known for my violin business. Perhaps with their sponsorship . . . perhaps I could apply through the consul and . . ."

Two officials laughed and one of them said, "Ha! England is the enemy!"

"You're a Jew!"

"I *am* Mathieu DuBois." His voice was thin and unconvincing, and the officials stopped talking to him. He gazed at the cracks in the ceiling while men laughed and joked. He heard the echo of his instrument as they shoved the violin back into its case and snapped it shut.

The paperwork went on for at least an hour as the arrested men stood in front of the officials. Mathieu's back hurt and his heart ached. Would they let him call Jules? No such offer was made to the men, and then they were told they were going for a ride. It was only then Mathieu accepted that he wasn't going home.

As the lorry rattled and bumped down the road, dread crept through Mathieu's body. *Where were they being taken?* In the darkness he heard what sounded like an old man struggling to breathe. Then women began to weep. It all felt like a dream, but the night air slashed at his face, assuring him he was wide awake in a living nightmare.

All at once, it hit him: Dear Simone—she'd be devastated when he didn't come home. His friends would hold dinner for him and wonder what could have made him late. They'd wait for him as they enjoyed a glass of wine, expecting him at any time. They'd reluctantly start eating, trying to stave off worry. Then they'd speculate about a *rafle*. Simone would try not to cry, and Jules would promise to investigate in the morning. César would become angrier and angrier.

The lorry finally stopped, the back doors were flung open, and uniformed guards told them to jump down. They'd been driven to a sand-colored building that filled a city block and was ringed with barbed wire and bright lights. What was it—a prison of some kind? Was this an internment camp? Mathieu and the other men were ordered to walk through the guard station where they stood for another hour or more of paperwork.

Lighting the way with a torch, a dull-eyed man dressed in rumpled civilian clothes led them up four flights of stairs to a dark cavernous space. Mathieu could tell the area was large because of the coughing and moaning sounds that rose from a distance. There must have been hundreds of men on that floor alone. As his eyes adjusted to the darkness, he could make out pallets of straw, each the width of a man's body, occupied by what looked like filthy-looking fabric, but there were actually people lying there. The stink of unwashed bodies and urine made his eyes water.

The man nodded at him and pointed to one of the pallets. "This is yours. The latrine is down those stairs. What's your name?"

"Lieb here. Joshua Lieb." Those words of truth lifted his heart. He *was* the Lieb of LiebViol. Joshua the luthier.

Into the darkness, he said, "What is this place?"

A voice replied, "Camp des Milles. Make yourself comfortable because nobody gets out."

$\mathcal{L}\!ost$

$\mathcal{T}$he dim light of morning crept into Simone's window. She peeled open her eyes, gritty from a restless night of fragmented dreams. In her sleeping mind, Mr. Lieb was with her. Strains of his violin music filled the room, easing the ache in her stomach. But now she was awake, and waves of torment washed over her. *Mr. Lieb, my dear Mr. Lieb, where are you? Are you scared? Cold? Where are you?*

Simone jumped at a tap on her bedroom door. "Is he home?" she cried out as she threw open the door to see Jules standing there. She realized she was wearing only her thin nightgown, so she shut the door and grabbed her robe. Last night, they'd all waited up until two in the morning, but he hadn't come home.

She opened the door again and saw César and Jules. Jules said, "No, my dear, he isn't, but César is heading off to talk to the police in Marseille. We'll start with the station near the port and visit the other stations. René and Gabrielle will help, as they have decent connections with the flics. We'll be back as soon as we can with news."

Simone took a breath, trying to control her tears. "I should have seen him in the afternoon, but I was so busy with the passports. I wanted to see him after his violin lessons, but he said he'd be home for dinner and we'd have a glass of wine."

Émilie put her arms around Simone and held her close, whispering, "You can't blame yourself. This is how the Vichy government works. You never know when they'll strike."

"But I should have felt the danger. And we should have looked for him last night. I can't bear not knowing what's happened to him."

"Don't let guilt take hold. We'll find him. And we'll get him out. Trust me. We won't stop until we do."

César wrapped his arms around her and held her close. He whispered, "We'll find him. We'll find him and bring him home."

As he woke up, Joshua coughed from the brick dust that filled the air in the camp. Bricks were everywhere, forming tables, walls, and chairs as inmates arranged things for some semblance of civilization. He lay there listening to the sounds of prayers being sung, throats clearing, and the incessant murmur of voices. It had been three weeks since the Vichy police had abducted Mathieu and thrown him into this hell hole where he'd become Joshua Lieb, a Jew, again and where there was no respite from the din of a thousand men shouting, complaining, crying. Endlessly talking. About everything, about nothing. In every direction he saw blighted men gathered in groups or walking, pacing, weeping. The rank air was thick with the coughs of the men and the great stink of wet straw, unwashed bodies, and despair.

Each day in this place was the same. He arose from a straw bed only two inches from the next man on either side after a night spent jagged with snores and men calling out from their nightmares. Roll call was at seven every morning. Shivering, he stood in a queue while names were read, answered or not answered, and then he went on through the routine of the day, shuffling ankle deep in shit at the latrines along with a hundred other men, waiting, some unable to wait. He could almost feel the shivers of dread surging across the camp. All the men feared being sent to a camp in Germany. Or never getting out of Les Milles.

But there were other moments that reminded him of humanity at its best. Artists etched pictures on the walls, sharing ink and paper and paint. He heard that the artist Max Ernst had been there and the novelist Lion Feuchtwanger, and though he never encountered them, knowing they'd walked the same floors made him feel connected to the artist in himself. He'd pass time listening to beautiful music played by string quartets, quiet, dignified musicians who soothed souls for hours at a time. His heart ached for his violin, as he discovered that some prisoners had been allowed to keep their instruments. Luckily, one day, a young man named Mordecai offered his violin to Joshua. He accepted graciously, with tears in his eyes and the ache in his heart still strong. That afternoon, he sat on a pile of bricks playing Beethoven for men who desperately needed to hear it. Then a cellist joined him, and together they played out of tune and in broken rhythms, but when they played, they were transported somewhere else, performing as seriously as if they were on a grand stage, dressed in black tie. Each man reunited with his soul after a few bars. Lifted from hell up to heaven. Only to fall back into hell again.

In the weeks following Mathieu's disappearance, Simone's rosy color and vibrant smile had faded. César grew worried about her state of mind. Everyone—Jules, Émilie, Gabrielle, and René were working hard to find out what had happened to Mathieu DuBois. Their search took them to police stations throughout the city where the same phrases were repeated: "There is no record of a man by that name." It was as if he'd disappeared from the earth.

Despite her sorrow, or perhaps because of it, every day after breakfast Simone sat at the big table with her pens, inks, photographs, and a stack of documents to create false papers for Caskie's soldiers. The rest of the time, she stayed in her room. She said she was sketching and writing in her journal, but César often heard her weeping. When he knocked, she told him to let her be.

Four weeks after Mathieu's disappearance, René arrived at Jules's house with news. They all gathered at the table in the dining room, each with a glass of Jules's homemade wine. René slicked back his wet hair and took off his coat. He pulled out a chair and shook a piece of paper, damp from the rain. "The good news is that he is not listed as dead or deported to Germany. That's what we know so far."

"So far?! That's all?" Simone cried, covering her face with her hands. César patted her back to comfort her, but she jerked away from him.

René frowned and said, "There's more. You won't like it."

César let out quick breath. "Go on . . ."

René sighed. "Vichy is beginning to move people out—to camps, to Germany—using them as a government workforce to build the Atlantic wall and bunkers along the coast."

Simone wiped tears from her cheek.

René's eyes narrowed. "I know, it seems bad. But we're looking into the internment camps now. He might have been sent to one directly, though that isn't typical, and there will be a record. There are several camps in the Free Zone."

Simone's face grew even more pale.

René continued, "We're starting with the one close to Marseille, Camp des Milles. It's a transit camp, but people are sent there in roundups and sorted out later. There's also Vernet, a god-awful hell hole. They say it's worse than Dachau."

"Stop talking about camps! Just find him!" Simone sobbed. César pulled her close to him and put his arms around her. She let herself sink into him, her mind going in all directions. The very thing Mr. Lieb was afraid of: a camp.

René got up from his chair and put on his coat. For once he seemed genuinely regretful. "We don't mean to upset you, but. . ."

Jules said, "Just get the word out to our people. We need to find out where he is, as fast as possible."

César pounded the door with his fist. "Damn Nazis. *God-damned* Vichy!"

Burning with rage, he turned to see Jules and Émilie quietly looking at him, fists in the air. Solidarity.

October 1940

In October 1940, a chill wind blew through Vichy France, a biting wind that would place France in the crosshairs of history. The Vichy government was a collaborationist state willing to fiercely target Jews and "enemy aliens," taking positions even more anti-Semitic than those in Germany: In early October, Vichy passed laws called "Statut des Juifs," which created a special underclass for Jewish citizens and excluded them from joining the armed forces, practicing the arts, or working as doctors, nurses, lawyers, or teachers.

Simone felt the stab of those laws as she and César walked arm-in-arm near the Vieux Port on the way to René and Gabrielle's and saw, painted across the windows of a Jewish-owned shop, *Juden Raus—Jews out.* It was just like those grim days in Berlin when she'd walked past crowds of frothing Nazis with their arms thrust upwards in the Hitler salute, shouting "Death to the Jews!"

Just behind them now, another angry mob pounded through the streets of Marseille shouting *"Juden Raus! Juden Raus!"* Her ears filled with the boom of drums, the tramp of boots. Were *Germans* marching in Marseille? César pushed her into a doorway and stood tall against her to block the sight of her from the men who stomped by. Her body vibrated with the thunder of drumbeats, the impassioned shouting, the rhythm of the boots on cobblestones.

"French. They're French," César said, as if he knew the torment in her mind. But Nazis, Vichy. They all shared the same twisted beliefs.

She buried her face in César's shoulder, her body shaking with sobs. Mr. Lieb was missing, and now Marseille seethed with the same threatening hatred she thought she'd escaped. César squeezed her close, so tight she could feel his heart beating against her. His breath was hot against her neck as he whispered, "René's house is a block that way. Let's go."

The roar of the crowd had passed on, but Simone could still hear the crystalline sound of glass breaking as storefronts were destroyed. César grabbed her hand, and they ran as the biting wind struck her face and her tears landed like shards on her cheeks. Would these people soon come for her and César?

César's feet pounded beside hers as they streaked through narrow passageways. In the apartments high above them, people shouted from windows, "Death to the Jews!" Others were silent, drawing back, closing their windows and doors.

Out of breath, Simone and César pounded up the stairs and banged on the door. "René! Gabrielle, open up!" Simone's head whipped all around as she kept thinking she heard footsteps headed their way.

René threw open the door and waved them in. "Come in quick. Those fools!"

Gabrielle rushed into the living room from one of the bedrooms. "Shhh. One of the lads is asleep in the bedroom. We were going to take him to Caskie today but . . ." She lit the stove to heat water.

"We must stay off the streets today." René mopped his sweaty brow. "We can sneak him out at night."

César said, "They're smashing windows, and the police just stand around." They all looked out the upstairs window toward the fracas below.

Gabrielle went back to the kitchen and poured barley coffee into cups. "These new laws—I hope they don't affect Émilie and Jules," she said, handing a cup to Simone.

"What do you mean? Aren't they *French* Jews?" César asked.

"According to the new laws, if you have three Jewish grandparents, or only two if your spouse is also Jewish or you belong to the Jewish religion, you're a Jew, which means that today a lot more people in Marseille are Jewish than yesterday. I'm worried."

Simone caught her breath. "This is bad. In Germany, to be Jewish meant having three Jewish grandparents." Her head hurt. She tried to force the coffee down, but she'd hardly been able to eat or drink since her Papa had been picked up. "This can't be happening."

René said, "This is only the beginning." Then he smiled, just a slight hint of a smile. How could he be smiling at a time like this? "But not all the news is bad," he said. "Last night, we found what happened to Mathieu, and he's all right."

Simone cried out, "He's alive! He's . . ."

César said, "*Where* is he?"

René sat back, palms resting on the table, smile fading. "You aren't going to like this. He's interned at Les Milles, the camp outside of Aix en Provence."

Simone covered her face in her hands. *He's alive. He's safe. But he's in a camp.* She sagged against the chair. César patted her shoulder in comfort.

Simone wiped her eyes. "How did you find him?"

Gabrielle laughed. "We had fun bribing one of those idiot gendarmes at the police station where they brought him in.

Got the guy a little tipsy with help from our flask of brandy. He remembered a man who made a fuss about keeping a violin. But when he checked his register, there was no Mathieu DuBois."

René added, "But their records, as it turns out, listed a Joshua Lieb."

"No!" said Simone. "His *real* name? Now they know about his false papers. Now they know he's a Jew!"

Gabrielle said, "Yes, they mentioned his false papers."

Simone gasped, "How is that possible? Those papers were good."

"His accent? The violin? Who knows? The guy told us his superior is Alsatian and has a keen ear," Gabrielle said. "Remember, a town in the Alsace area was listed as his birthplace because it's close to the German border. But each region has its own accent."

Silence fell across the table. Then César said, "My God, now he's a German Jew in that camp."

They were all silent for several seconds, then René stood up and grabbed a bottle of whiskey, poured the brown liquid into four glasses, and passed them around the table. "I think we need this." They all reached for their glasses and tossed back the alcohol.

Simone coughed and tried to calm her thundering heart. "Can we send a note or visit?" She had to see Mr. Lieb with her own eyes. Was he hurt? Was he eating?

"No visitors." René shook his head.

Gabrielle explained, "Even the prisoners' wives have to stand by the barbed wire and watch their husbands from outside the fenced yard. It's terrible. Their children hang onto their mothers' skirts, crying."

Simone asked, "*What* can we do? How can we get him out of there?"

René growled, "It's about money, connections, and plain luck. We're digging into it."

Gabrielle poured another drink. "Focus on the good news. He's alive."

Simone pressed on, "René, you must know the right people."

"With the proper connections?" César added.

René stood up and poured another glass of whiskey. "We'll contact people in the underground. It's very difficult to get someone out of the camps. Nearly impossible, but there are ways. That Varian Fry, the American who's helping the artists—his group got someone out."

Gabrielle said, "Yes, the novelist Lion Feuchtwanger. He was famous, as are many of the refugees Fry is saving, so perhaps there was extra help for political reasons. But of course, not all rescue attempts are successful. Perhaps you've heard of Walter Benjamin, the German philosopher and writer. The guides managed to get him up the Pyrenees—it took two days. He was in bad health, and he barely made the climb up the mountain. He got over the border, but when he arrived in Portbou in Spain, he learned that the Spanish government had cancelled all transit visas, so Benjamin was going to be sent back to France. He must have been terrified at the idea of being captured by the Nazis." Gabrielle paused to take a long drink of whiskey. "He took an overdose of morphine."

Simone sighed. "This happened in Germany too. Some refugees kept drugs with them so they could choose how to die. They thought it was the only way out."

René explained that refugees on the *surrender on demand* list—anti-Fascists, writers, teachers, and artists—were Fry's priorities, though he did get involved with helping British soldiers escape to Gibraltar.

"This surrender list—what's that about?" César asked.

René's face twisted in anger. "It's in the Armistice that France has to hand over anyone the Germans want to take into custody."

Simone stood up, disgusted by all this talk of France collaborating with Nazis. "We need to get to people who can negotiate a release for Mr. Lieb."

"Perhaps people at the consular level, those who have the power to get things done," Gabrielle suggested.

René lit a cigarette and blew smoke into the air. A gray cloud settled over the room. "The officials want nothing to do with any of this rescue business. We've heard that the Americans don't approve of Fry's under-the-table activities and want him to leave."

Simone sat with the stories, letting the whiskey burn through the ache in her stomach.

César gently turned her toward him and looked into her eyes. "What *we* can do is make new papers for him. When we get him out, he'll need papers to get him over the border."

The idea of Mr. Lieb's escape began to take root in Simone's mind, along with the reality of her papa living in some other country, far from where she could depend on him, help him, learn from him. She would miss him terribly, but if he could be saved from arrest, from deportation, he'd have his life back. Then he'd start a new life in England where he had people, connections through his violin business. Even if London was being bombed, music was needed more than ever. Getting him out of France was the only way. She shuddered at the thought of the condition he might be in—trapped in a cold prison where he was enduring mental and physical abuse. *Was the place infested with rats? Was he sick with worry? Was he being beaten? Starved? Tortured?*

Then, surely without realizing it, César made her feel even worse. He said, "Over the Pyrenees with the lads he will go."

Les Milles

$\mathcal{T}$ ime seemed to remain very still in the dark caverns of the camp even as late autumn began to whistle through the cracks in the crumbling walls. Some windows had no glass, and makeshift screens that had been crafted to block the cold quickly blew away in the freezing winds. At night, prisoners shivered beneath thin blankets. There were outbreaks of typhoid, and many of those who went to the infirmary were never seen again.

Joshua stared up and watched the wind stir the masterful silk webbing of spiderwebs that hung between the rafters. He sank deeper into his straw bed, his spine feeling every inch of the wooden floor underneath. It had come upon him quickly, the weakness—his legs and arms like jelly. Diarrhea. He'd adjusted to painful, itchy rashes from lice but not to the cold, bitter wind, or soup served with maggots floating on the surface. Max, his mate on the next straw pallet, lugged him to the latrine and to help Joshua break into the queue, bartered with pieces of chocolate he told Joshua he'd bought in the makeshift café on the lower level of the camp.

For several days, he leaned on Max as they stumbled back and forth from pallet to toilet. And as he lay trembling with cold and sickness, Joshua felt a deep sense of gratitude. Even if he were to die now, he'd been cared for by men whose hearts still beat in their chests: dear, patient Max, who did all he could to nurse Joshua's frail health; Frederick, the cellist who soothed souls with his music; and Mordecai, who so generously loaned his violin.

His thoughts drifted to Simone, her shining eyes—she looked so much like her mother. Was there such a thing as prayer? Was God listening? Surely God wouldn't allow this war to proceed or for the Nazis to take over France. Joshua sensed that everyone in Les Milles felt deep grief that God had still not intervened.

He turned on his side and faced a row of bricks. Staring at him from only a few inches away was an enormous black spider with thick, fuzzy legs. The creature didn't move as Joshua pondered what could be on the mind of a spider as it stayed frozen in place during their staring match. They remained like that for several minutes, just looking at each other, and then Joshua closed his eyes. The insect would either bite him or leave him alone. He'd let the spider decide.

Le Petit Poucet

As Marseille slipped into a cold, rainy winter, the work to help British soldiers continued. César tended to their wounds and escorted them to Caskie's or other safe houses where they were prepared for escape. Simone, pen in hand for hours each day, forged their new papers. René, Gabrielle, and other members of the underground pursued leads for a rescue, but that didn't stop Simone from fretting about Mr. Lieb day and night. *What were the conditions in that camp? Was he being brutalized because he was a Jew with false papers? Were the rumors true, that almost no one ever escaped?* she agonized.

One morning during the first week of November, René and Gabrielle stopped by Jules's to talk about Mr. Lieb. "We're looking into several methods of rescuing him—laundry truck, ambulance. We don't know who yet, but . . ." René rubbed his fingers together, "money talks. Money's scarce these days, and food is getting even harder to find."

Simone asked, "How do we know whom we can trust?"

No one answered. They shook their heads, as if words were dangerous. Finally, Jules said, "We must keep our faith in the good nature of people. Sometimes you don't know whom to trust, but still you have to trust."

Gabrielle said, "You're a faithful soul, Jules. Some of us have become cynical."

Simone thought about how quiet César had been when she'd kissed him goodbye that morning before he left for Marseille. "Do you think César has grown cynical?" she asked.

Gabrielle's eyes softened. "He's grieving that some of his lads were killed at the border. That kind of grief can lead to hate."

Simone thought about how often César returned from Caskie's in a pensive mood looking sorrowful. But sometimes he still reached for her in the night with intense passion and looked into her eyes and told her he loved her. Those deep, dreamy eyes—they could melt her any time of night or day. But she remembered his dramatic mood change after the *stuka* attacks and worried that anger and hate might again dim the light in those beautiful eyes.

The clock chimed ten. It was time to stop worrying and focus on what needed to be done. She smiled at Gabrielle. "If you're going into Marseille, may I go with you? I told Émilie I would go into town and bring back thread and yarn."

"Of course—we'll take you. Get your coat. You can meet the lads first. They'll get a thrill seeing a lovely young woman like you."

Every few days, René and Gabrielle would gather the next group of lost British soldiers—"parcels," they were called—at le Petit Poucet café on Rue Dugommier. Messages of what to do and where to go were relayed to them by way of the refugee telegraph. Along their dangerous journey to Marseille, most of the soldiers would swap their uniforms for whatever civilian clothes they found discarded along the way. It didn't matter how mismatched—they'd do anything to avoid being arrested by Vichy or the Nazis.

At the café in Marseille, the hopeful Brits would wait for their contact while nursing a drink alongside countless other refugees who waited for papers and prayed for good luck. For these encounters, René wore a green beret and Gabrielle a green plaid jacket so the soldiers could recognize them as their rescuers. Today Simone was being allowed to watch it all happen in front of her eyes. Following René and Gabrielle into the café, she found it amusing to see her friends dressed like characters in a Scottish play, but she knew that even those small hints of Britishness probably offered comfort to the weary Englishmen.

When they entered the café, three young men waved at them and stood up. By their height and broad smiles, she could tell they were British soldiers. Also seated at their table was a charming-looking woman dressed in a fancy black hat and coat. The way she held her cigarette holder aloft seemed familiar. The woman looked up, and Simone's heart leapt at the sight of the artist who had so captivated her in Paris.

"Sophia! I can't believe it!" gasped Simone.

"Rosemarie—what a surprise!" Sophia stood, and they kissed each other's cheeks. Sophia smelled sweet, like roses. She took a step back to get a fuller look at Simone.

"Lovely Rosemarie! I suppose everyone ends up in Marseille these days." Then she gestured to the young men. "These are my new friends."

They greeted her with a very English sounding, "Bonjour."

"We didn't exchange names," Sophia said with a smile.

After a brief mention that she now went by Simone, she introduced Sophia to René and Gabrielle.

"I think we've met," René said with a smile.

Gabrielle added, "Everyone knows everyone in Marseille."

Simone was confused. How could they know Sophia? But at that moment, René told the lads to hurry, adding, "You'll be happy to know that food is waiting for you."

The men gathered themselves to leave with René and Gabrielle. "Ma'am," they said, nodding at Sophia. She smiled and gave them a thumbs up.

Gabrielle kissed Simone's cheeks, "See you at Jules's tomorrow. I'll leave you to reconnect with your talented artist friend."

Simone slipped into a chair beside Sophia. "I can't believe you know my friends."

Sophia smiled and flipped open her cigarette case. "The complex world of Marseille. Cigarette?"

"No thank you. And yes, there are many secrets in this place."

Sophia squeezed her hand. "My dear, you're looking well. Of course, a little thinner, as we all are." She gestured to the café patrons who were nursing cups of ersatz coffee. "They sit here all day and into the night. Everyone is waiting for something, for someone to save them."

Simone looked at the bleak expressions all around her and wondered, *What are these people going through? What must it be like to have no sense of control over where your life is headed?*

"Most have no place to sleep," said Sophia. "Fortunately for me, I don't have that problem." She didn't say any more about it, and Simone didn't ask.

Being with Sophia reminded Simone of Paris, the Café de Flore. The bells of Notre-Dame in the afternoon. Art galleries and museums. Now they were all exiles living in a world of nightmares. This café felt nothing like the glorious cafés of Paris where the air was full of music and laughter and the chatter of dynamic people energized about the future. Here, the air was filled with the scents of stale cigarettes, unwashed bodies, and desperation.

Simone leaned forward and spoke softly, "I'm here with Mr. Lieb and his friends—but he's . . . he's . . ." Simone hesitated. "He's away right now." She didn't want to name the internment camp with so many people listening. "How long have you been here? What are you doing here?"

Sophia nodded, looking curious. "Ears are everywhere. Eyes too. Let's walk."

Sophia headed toward the exit, and as Simone gathered her things, she noticed several men watching them. She noticed one man's furtive glances at them. *What did that mean?* She tried to shrug off the worry as she hurried to catch up with Sophia.

As they blended into the bustle of the city, Simone nearly froze at the sight of several German officers walking directly toward them. Sophia tucked her arm into Simone's elbow and pulled her close, "Just keep walking. Look happy. Don't react." The two women kept strolling down the street arm in arm, chatting brightly as if they were talking about nothing more serious than the discovery of a new artist. Sophia was masterful at this game. With a smile in her voice, she said, "Those Germans are probably from the Kundt Commission. They're looking for people who are wanted under the surrender on demand article of the Armistice. Jews, anti-Fascists, artists. I also heard that they're hunting people in the internment camps."

Hearing about Germans on the hunt shot a stab of pain into Simone's stomach. "Terrifying. Those poor people—there's no escape."

"It's heartbreaking," replied Sophia. "Did you have any idea that artists are so dangerous? We promote free thinking! Mustn't have that in a Fascist state. Just keep walking, my friend. Don't look in their eyes."

Several gray-green officers strolled by, and the two women looked straight ahead. "Just show them deference and then ignore them," Sophia told her. When they were several steps beyond the

Germans, she said, "So you want to know what brings me to Marseille? I'm here hoping to get papers for America. I might be on that surrender list. My activities in Vienna were, shall we say, controversial to the regime. But that American, Fry, might be my savior."

"Fry," said Simone. "I've heard of him." She thought back to the day when she'd seen all those refugees desperately hovering outside his hotel, the haunted looks on their faces.

Out of the corner of her eye, Simone saw a man who she thought looked like the terrifying Captain Schmidt from Berlin. A bolt of fear shot through her body. *Could it be?* She gasped. "It can't be him," Simone mumbled and tripped on a cobblestone.

Sophia steadied her. "What is it?" she asked, slowing her pace. "Tell me."

"Someone, I'm not sure. From the past." She was shaking so hard her voice trembled. "It must be my imagination. There's no way . . ."

Sophia pulled her aside. "Stop here and look in the store windows. If someone is following, we'll see them behind us."

In the window's reflection, patches of umber and black, indigo blue and gray-green rushed by. Then a shape caught Simone's attention. It appeared to be one of the Germans stopping to peer into a shop window across the street. His image was blurry—could it be *him*? She was desperate to turn around and look but stared at the store window before her, trying to see if it was . . . him.

Sophia pretended to primp in the window's reflection. "Who's following us?" she asked.

"I'm not sure but . . ." Simone whispered.

"You're shaking. Let's keep walking." They continued quickly down the street. Now the man who'd been looking in the window was nowhere in sight. Was it *that* Nazi? She tugged at Sophia's arm. "Where are we going?"

"My residence. It's safe there. It's a special *maison*."

"A hotel?" Simone rushed to keep up, looking back over her shoulder every few seconds.

Sophia's shoes tip-tapped the cobblestones. "Not exactly."

She remembered what René had told her about the *maisons de rendez-vous*. "Chantal and Marguerite?" she asked.

"You know them too. What a small world, this Marseille." Sophia hustled them even faster down the quiet street and then let go of Simone's arm and walked just ahead of her. They seemed to be getting farther from the public eye, which made Simone even more nervous. Then, as if reading her mind, Sophia said, "This is a safe place—they even have bodyguards! And the police don't check who the residents are—they might run into a colleague—you understand. Quickly, now!" Simone marveled at how fast Sophia moved, despite her fine dress and fancy heels.

Sophia called over her shoulder, "We're almost there. Who are we running from?"

"A Nazi," Simone half-whispered, almost out of breath. "He knows I'm Jewish. But he wanted me to . . . he . . . tried to . . . he . . ."

"I see. Just down the next passageway here. We're almost there . . ."

Simone looked back as she ran but saw no one following. Maybe he'd given up. Maybe she'd imagined the whole thing.

Sophia turned down a narrow passageway that looked like the entrance to a nightmare. Dark. Desolate. Enclosed. Simone stopped. "We can't go down there . . ."

Sophia said, "Just ahead, there's a shortcut to the *maison*—you can't see it, but . . . come on." She tugged Simone's arm.

"We can't." Simone tried to catch her breath, but it caught in her throat.

Sophia hissed, "Come down this alley. We *must* hurry."

Simone felt adrenaline shoot through her system and propel her forward as she stumbled with Sophia down the dark passage that smelled of urine and rotting fish. A cat, or was it a rat, scampered in front of them. Sophia pulled her toward a bend in the alley where a sliver of light intersected the darkness. "Just to the end there," Sophia said, but before they could take another step, the silhouette of a large man stepped just at the edge of the light.

Simone could see only the outline of a fedora and a long coat.

The two women froze in place, and Sophia grabbed Simone's hand and squeezed it.

"Sarah?" a deep voice called, slow and sinister.

Dark Passage

Simone gasped. It had to be Captain Schmidt. It *was* him. No one here knew her as Sarah. Terror shot through her as she realized they were trapped. No more than ten feet ahead, he stood between them and the opening to the street.

"Sarah," the menacing voice said, "we meet again."

Simone stood rigid. She opened her mouth, but all she could utter was, "I . . ." Sophia stood silent at her side, the squeeze of her hand growing tighter.

The Nazi took one step forward and stopped. Now he was standing in the beam of light, and she could see clearly the face of the officer who'd terrified her in Berlin, the reason she and Mr. Lieb had fled in such haste. The reason she'd had to leave her mother behind.

"Sarah, you don't seem happy to see me. Did our intimacies that night mean nothing to you?" His smile was malignant. "But this time you won't be able to get away . . ."

Simone's heart nearly shattered with fear and shame. She yanked her hand from Sophia's, then turned and began to run back down the dark alley.

"Jew bitch!" the Nazi screamed, and Simone heard the clunk of his heels on the stones as he dashed after her.

Then in an instant, she heard both Captain Schmidt and Sophia screaming. He let out a yelp of pain and shouted, "I'll get you!" Still running, Simone glanced over her shoulder and saw him on the ground, his hands clutching his knee. *What* was happening?

"Help! Rape! Help!" Sophia screamed as Captain Schmidt reached out and grabbed her ankle, which sent her crashing to the ground next to him. Sophia's screams pierced the air, "Help! Let me go! *Rape! Help!*"

Simone sprinted back toward them. As the Nazi tried to scramble to his feet, she charged forward and kicked his kneecap as hard as she could. He yelped again in pain, screeching obscenities, then bent over and let out a growl that could only be described as raw fury.

He struggled to rise to his feet, and tried to reach his hat. The look of rage on his face was the most horrifying thing Simone had ever seen. This man was going to kill them.

As fast as she could move, she slipped her hands under Sophia's arms and struggled to help her get back on her feet. Then suddenly, Simone heard a terrible crunch that sounded like the smashing of bones. She looked up to see Schmidt tumbling to the ground, his head making a horrific thud as it bashed against the cobblestones. An enormous man was leaning over him, punching his head again and again until the Nazi lay completely still as a pool of blood formed on the ground. For several seconds, she stared at the ghastly sight, and before she looked away, the stranger pulled some kind of hood from—from where? It was as if he'd pulled it out of the air—and shoved it over the Nazi's head.

Sophia stumbled to her feet and with Simone's help began to limp toward the *maison* several yards away. A woman with flaming red hair had bolted from the open doorway and wrapped her arm around Sophia's waist, and the three women rushed toward the building. What had just happened?

The woman pulled them inside and slammed the door behind them. "Sophia!" she said, "Can you walk?" Without waiting for an answer, she said, "Follow me!" then dashed ahead of them down a carpeted hallway.

Simone and Sophia lumbered behind her down a warren, and finally the red-haired woman opened the door to a large bedroom furnished with a luxurious-looking bed, plush carpets, and long, thick drapes. She ushered them in and said, "Rest here. We'll bring coffee, real coffee, and some wraps for your injuries. You're safe here."

Sophia flopped heavily onto the chair in front of the dressing table and said, "Chantal, we owe you . . . we owe you . . ."

"Our lives," Simone managed to croak as she tried to calm her breathing.

Sophia waited a moment for Simone to catch her breath, then gestured to Chantal and said, "Simone, please meet my very good friend, Chantal, also the proprietor of this lifesaving establishment."

"*Enchantée,*" said Chantal with a smile. Then she curtsied and dashed out of the room before Simone could say another word.

Dabbing a tissue to her eyes, Simone asked, "Sophia, are you okay? Are you badly hurt? You saved my life!"

Sophia slid her dress above her knee to inspect her injuries and said coolly, "I won't be dancing tonight, but I'll live." She fluffed her dress back down her legs. "Are *you* okay?"

Simone felt her face flame with embarrassment. "What the German said. What he said about that night in Berlin . . ."

Sophia interrupted, "My dear, you needn't say another word about that vile Nazi. It's understood what the problem was, is. You need to forget it."

Sinking into the sofa, Simone nodded. She'd never forget it.

Sophia removed a flask from her purse and unscrewed the top. "Here, this will help."

The alcohol burned its way down Simone's throat. She sat back against a pillow and closed her eyes for a moment, picturing Schmidt's threatening silhouette, feeling his rough hands.

She handed the flask back to Sophia, who drank a long pull and then screwed the cap back on. "Whiskey. It's like liquid gold." Sophia looked at Simone. "You're okay now. Chantal's right— you're safe here. That man isn't going to be able to get to you here. In fact, *if* he survives, he'll have no idea where you've gone."

Simone tried to hold back another surge of tears. "I wonder what he's doing here—and out of uniform."

Sophia plucked a cigarette from a Gauloise Blue package, fitted it into her long holder, and clicked the lighter. "Some Germans are undercover here, you know. There's also the Kundt Commission looking for people on their hit lists. You have good reason to be terrified of him."

Hesitating, Simone said, "He's the main reason I had to flee my own country . . ." She thought she might say more, but the words didn't come.

Sophia said, "You've had your share of escapes, like many of us." She inhaled slowly and blew out the smoke in graceful circles. "It means you're a survivor."

Simone nodded, grateful for the warmth of the alcohol. Then she jumped at the sound of a knock on the door. A curvaceous middle-aged woman with jet black hair and a gracious smile entered with a tray holding a white China coffee pot, cups and saucers, and a big round pastry on a plate.

"This is Marguerite," Sophia said as the woman set the tray on the dressing table.

Marguerite smiled and said, "I must tell you that we make these pastries using real butter, well half at least, and wheat flour, mostly. Don't ask us how."

"You have a café?" Simone asked. "I thought you were a . . . I mean, I . . ." She stumbled over her words, trying not to say *brothel* or *maison de rendez-vous*, and the two women laughed.

Simone's face flushed hot. "A safe house, that's what I was trying to say." She laughed too, astonished she could laugh about anything. "René and Gabrielle told me about it."

Marguerite poured coffee into cups. "Oh, René. Yes, he brings the Brits here from time to time to hide. But that man in the alley, he won't recover from this event very soon. And it's unlikely he'll completely remember what happened." She handed the cups to Sophia and Simone.

Simone sighed. "But . . . how can you know that?"

"I didn't see much of it, but I'm familiar with Arnoldo's work."

Simone paused a moment, trying to make sense of Marguerite's implication. "What will he do . . . with the man in the alley?" Simone almost didn't want to know, but with dread she imagined what her life would feel like from now on, always watching over her shoulder.

"If you strike the head hard enough," Marguerite said, "well . . . maybe that man is no longer the man he once was." Simone didn't take her eyes off Marguerite, who so casually explained the aftermath of violence as she wiped the surface of the coffee table. "Don't you worry, dear. Arnoldo doesn't care much for men who attack women. You shouldn't be hearing from that one again."

"But . . ." started Simone.

Marguerite interrupted, "It's probably best to know nothing more. Let's all be grateful that you and our Sophia are well and here with us now."

"Marguerite," said Sophia, "can you get word to René that our friend Simone is here? He can give her a ride back to where she stays."

"I'll do it now," she said, "and I'll be back with wraps." And then just as Chantal had done, Marguerite made a slight curtsying gesture and left without another word.

Simone shuddered at the thought of that Nazi lurking in the shadows of Marseille. *But had Marguerite just told her that he was dead? Or worse than dead?* Then she shuddered at the memory of the sound his skull made smashing against stone. *Did she hope he was dead?* She shook her head and tried to clear her thoughts, feeling deep gratitude for Sophia and her friends.

Sophia sat before the mirror and tucked in loose strands of her hair while Simone sat on a sofa behind her and savored another sip of coffee. Simone asked, "What if the German comes back here looking for the woman who attacked him?"

"I'm not concerned," Sophia said, speaking while still looking in the mirror and dabbing a tissue around her lips. "Even if he survives, after tonight I won't be here. I'll be staying at Varian Fry's safe house—they call it a villa—in Cassis. I'm taking the tram down in a couple of hours."

"Cassis? Fry has a place there?"

"It's toward Nice, on the coast. The villa houses refugees on the surrender on demand list. They wait there for papers. André Breton and his wife and Max Ernst. Some political people. Writers—you know how dangerous we all are. And a poet. I heard he was helping Wanda Landowska."

"The harpsichordist?"

"The very one. But some people don't want to leave. Matisse refused. Can you imagine? Fry offers him a ticket to freedom and he declines it. But Fry's not only helping famous people, you know. He's helping as many as he can to escape France."

"How heroic. We're lucky to have the Americans."

"Hardly!" Sophia blurted as she turned away from the mirror to face Simone. "The American government wants Fry stopped. The America First movement is rabidly anti-Semitic, and they're influencing politicians and diplomats.

"But so many people think America is where they'll be safe."

"Americans have quotas and even laws against accepting refugees—remember the ship the St. Louis? Cuba and the United States wouldn't even let the ship dock. Nearly a thousand Jewish people and families sent back to Europe." Sophia turned back to the mirror and patted powder on her nose, sorrow in her dark eyes.

Simone swirled what was left of her coffee and examined the patterns in the bottom of the cup, wishing she could read the future. Everything felt so unsteady and dangerous now. Mr. Lieb in Les Milles, the group still with no plan for getting him out. Even a walk down a street could mean violence.

"Perhaps it's my Vienna escapades that qualify me to join the people at this villa. Who knows?" Then she sighed heavily. "When I think about my old life, my artist friends in Vienna, it crushes me. I think of Ella and Friedl and Rosa. Greta. Helene von Taussig, a great talent. All in danger, some already dragged off to torture camps. I think about them every day. Are they dead? It's almost unthinkable. The vile Nazi government. Monsters." Sophia bowed her head.

Simone felt herself sink into despair at hearing about these women sent off to camps, tortured and dying. Her hands began to shake. *What if Mr. Lieb was being tortured? Did they do that here in Vichy camps? What about the hundreds of thousands of people already in camps or being hunted, even here in the Free Zone. Would her efforts to forge documents for a few people make even a dent?* She said, "I . . . don't know what to say. It's so much to take in. Even here, René and his wife and my friend César and I—we're trying to help save people. I'm forging documents, and César and René are helping British soldiers get to Spain. But I know it's not enough." Simone felt her tears well up.

Sophia rose slowly from the dressing table and sat next to Simone on the sofa. "Forging documents? Excellent—using your talent to save lives. That's quite a secret. You should be very proud," she said, smoothing Simone's hair. "Good people will always fight evil. We *must* not give up. Your work is so very important, Simone. You're lighting a candle rather than cursing the darkness."

"Yes, I suppose," said Simone with a sigh.

"And never, never forget the power of art. Fascists fear us because our work makes people think and feel. It gives people hope, reveals the human soul. Artists and writers and musicians— we must march on. Never stop creating art, Simone."

Sophia touched Simone's shoulder and kissed her forehead. And for a moment, Simone felt warm and safe, as if enveloped by a magic veil of tenderness in a private room in a small corner of Marseille. Then Sophia said, "Nice touch—that kick to the knee."

Simone managed a little smile. "Nice screaming and . . . and why did he fall? Did you do that?"

Extending her uninjured leg, Sophia twisted her foot this way and that. "I know how to stop a man in his tracks."

Simone laughed and felt herself flush. "You tripped him! I can't imagine what might have happened to me if you hadn't been there."

Sophia brushed a strand of Simone's hair from her face and said, "In such situations, a woman finds out what she's made of. Has it sunk in yet, what happened here today? Today, you fought a Nazi. We physically fought against a Nazi. And still here we are."

Shaking her head, Simone covered her face with her hands. *I still can't believe it,* she thought. *We fought a Nazi, part of the Reich, the greedy beast that has tentacles everywhere.*

She thought through what she would tell Jules and César and the others about why she was at the *maison*. No one but Mr. Lieb knew about Schmidt, and she wanted to keep it that way. But he haunted her now. She kept hearing his chilling voice, "Sarah. *Sarah, we meet again . . .*"

She would tell them about Sophia's extraordinary bravery and how they were rescued by Arnoldo and the fast-thinking women at the *maison*. But how much of the rest of it would she share? How much would she tell César?

It was a decision she'd worry about later.

She turned to Sophia and said, "My friend, how about that flask?" Sophia smiled and reached into her purse.

A few minutes later, there was a knock on the door. Marguerite peeked her head in and said, "René is here. And he's in quite a hurry."

Simone looked into Sophia's soulful eyes. "Oh Sophia, I can't bear to say goodbye."

Sophia hugged her tightly, then leaned back and said, "You must go right now. René isn't a man to be kept waiting. I do hope we'll meet again someday. Until then, my lovely artist friend, don't lose faith." She kissed both of Simone's cheeks.

Marguerite said, "Here we go now," and with that, Simone was hustled back down the long hallway toward the alley of shadows.

Simone followed Marguerite to the end of the hallway where Chantal was waiting with the door held open. Simone stepped into the alley, then looked right and left, then right and left again. René's truck idled a few feet away, and he motioned for her to get in.

She hopped into the truck, and René slammed it into gear. His lips were clamped shut, his jaw firm, his face rough with stubble.

She took a breath and plunged in, "René, what would you do if a very bad German from the past discovered you were in Marseille? And then he was beaten up, and he might not even survive. Or maybe he's been hit in the head and maybe that means . . ."

"Eh? What kind of craziness are you rambling about? Get to the point."

As she spoke, she looked out the window of the truck. "In Berlin, a German officer helped me get away from some Hitler Youth, but afterward he . . . he wanted . . . well, he found out I was Jewish and he . . . he offered . . . well actually made clear that he was going to . . ."

"I see. Go on . . ."

"My name was Sarah then. I told Mr. Lieb about the Nazi, and he found a way to get us out the very next day. Then today, there were so many Germans on the streets and . . ."

René slammed his hand on the steering wheel. "Damned Boche! Already they infiltrate Marseille!"

Simone paused for René to say more. She waited to hear a question. But he only stared ahead and drove with a hard grimace on his face, so she continued, "And then I . . . I thought one of them looked just like that German I met, so Sophia and I rushed through the streets to get to the *maison*. Then he stepped into the alley and called my name. My heart stopped!"

René said, "He was alone?"

"I think so. I mean, yes, it was only him in the alley. Sophia screamed for the *maison* bodyguard, who attacked him and then . . ."

René was all business as he asked, "Is he dead?"

"I don't think so. Oh, I just don't know! Do you think he could come after us?"

René stuck his neck forward, brows furrowed as he maneuvered the truck through the Marseille streets. "Have you ever seen him outside of Berlin?"

"No, I would have said something."

"Do you know his name?"

"Kurt Schmidt. He's a captain."

"We can try to look into this. Tell Jules and César everything the minute you get home."

Simone sat back against the truck seat and looked out the window, burning with shame as she thought about Berlin again. *How did that man find her so far away? Was it coincidence? Did he want revenge for the way she'd humiliated him?* She started shaking again.

The truck bumped along. René lit a cigarette, and the smoke filled the cab. He seemed tense and agitated, even more than usual. Simone asked, "Is something wrong? Did something happen?"

Eyes fixed on the road, he said between clenched teeth, "Damned collaborationist Vichy."

"What is it?"

"Some men we saved were turned back at the border—something about a problem with their visas. The idiots in Spain won't let them in. And of course, the welcome arms of Vichy were right there to catch them," he slammed the steering wheel again as he added, "and deliver them straight to the Germans!"

This was terrible news. She wanted to ask if anyone knew whether Barry had been one of those caught by Vichy, but she was afraid to ask. They drove the rest of the way in silence. Finally, the truck pulled up at Jules's. René's rage seemed to have burned off, and he sat slumped against his seat. "I'll see what I can find out about the German. Just tell them all to be on the alert."

She said goodbye and thank you, and then René sped off in a torrent of dust. Simone rushed into the house, and everyone welcomed her to the dinner table where they were all enjoying a special treat—real potatoes from the garden instead of the usual tasteless swedes. She sat with them and tried to appear as if nothing was wrong, slowly chewing and swallowing, her heart pounding. Then she drank a sip of wine and said, "I ran into Sophia today, my friend from Paris. Remember her, César, the artist from Vienna? She's going to live in the house that Varian Fry set up for refugees in Cassis—most of them are artists and writers, people on the surrender on demand list."

Everyone nodded, focusing on their food. Trying to keep her voice even, she continued, "A German officer was following us, and the bodyguard at the *maison* where Sophia stays stepped in and protected us."

"A *German*?" Jules looked up, his fork suspended in the air. "What are you talking about?"

"He was someone I recognized . . . from Berlin."

"*What*?" César slammed his hand on the table, sending all the dishes rattling and clanking.

Simone kept talking. "This German . . . in Berlin he found out I was Jewish, and . . . well, it was clear that he intended to harm my mother and me. That's when Mr. Lieb and I quickly got out of Germany. But today—there he was, right here in Marseille." She looked around the table at her astonished friends, their faces locked in expressions of shock, and then pushed on, "He recognized me and . . ."

"Wait, *wait*," César interrupted. He slid his chair closer to Simone's. "This German who was after you in Berlin is in *Marseille*? And he followed you and Sophia today?"

Jules rubbed his chin. "Could he have followed you here tonight?"

"No, no. Definitely not," Simone answered. "We were just outside Sophia's *maison*, and we shouted for help. The bodyguard showed up and hit him hard."

They all began to interrupt with questions, so she raised her voice and said, "Hold on, please. Let me finish. I'll tell you everything." Then they all listened as she described the dark alley, the Germans all over the streets, how the Nazi had called out "Sarah," how Sophia tripped him and was knocked to the ground. Then the bodyguard, the violence, and the quickness with which Chantal pulled them inside to safety, Sophia's plans to go to Fry's villa, and then what René said about his people looking into it.

After she finished her story, she looked down at her lap where she nervously rubbed her hands together. She didn't want to look up. She was afraid of what she might see in their eyes. Would they be angry that she had jeopardized their safety? Would they think less of her to have known this German soldier and to have kept it secret? Would César no longer want her? Would he think her damaged now?

After a long, quiet moment, César held her hand with both of his. "You're okay? He didn't hurt you?" The softness of his voice nearly brought tears to her eyes.

"I'm not hurt," she answered. "Sophia injured her leg, but she says it's not bad."

"What an ordeal," said Jules, leaning back in his chair. "We're lucky this wasn't much worse. How fortunate we are to have the people of the *maison*." His use of *we* filled Simone with warmth. She really was part of something here.

Émilie said gently, "You need to stay home for a while—you cannot go into the city."

"Yes," Simone said. "I understand. If you don't mind, I'd like to go to sleep now." The events of the day pressed heavily on her body.

Émilie jumped up from her chair. "Of course, my dear! You must be completely exhausted. Let me prepare a bath for you."

"No, thank you," Simone replied. "I really just need sleep."

Jules and Émilie wished her a good night as César helped her from her chair and reached his arm around her to walk her up the stairs. Inside her, feelings clashed with each other—the comfort of his warm, strong touch battled the shame of the secret she'd kept from the man she loved. César could never know what had happened on that shocking day.

As they climbed the stairs, he murmured that she was brave, that she was safe. Then he tucked her into bed and kissed her forehead, his dark eyes looking deep into hers. She held her breath to keep the tears away, so grateful that he loved her.

As César left and closed the door behind him, Simone pressed her face onto her pillow and sobbed.

For the next two weeks, Simone didn't leave Jules and Émilie's property. The others came and went as usual, but she stayed busy forging documents and making herself useful around the house. On one rainy evening as she sat sewing with Émilie in front of a blazing fire and César talked to Jules about rescue strategies and safe houses, René burst through the door dripping wet and erupting with news. At the sound of the door crashing open, Mozart leapt from his cozy curl by the fire and stood at attention but then wagged his tail at the sight of the familiar face.

"Lots of news—the lads, Barry, crossed into Spain!" René was even smiling.

"Such wonderful news!" César exclaimed.

Simone took César's hand and squeezed. Beaming at him with pride, she said, "You saved him."

"No, René here, Gabrielle, all of us. Caskie too. The guides who got him to safety. It takes all of us."

René nodded, rain dripping off the ends of his hair. Then his expression shifted to a dour grimace.

"What else, René. What is it?" said Jules.

"I've been to the *maison*," René told them as he peeled off his jacket. "I spoke with Arnoldo."

Simone sat up straight. Jules asked if René wanted a whiskey.

Jules handed him the whiskey, and he downed it in one gulp. He shook out his wet hat and coat and sat down.

"So about that Nazi. He was taken care of by various . . . well, characters—you wouldn't want to know. Of course, nobody's really talking, but I've been given the impression that we don't need to worry about him."

Simone gasped. "But the Germans—won't there be a search? Retaliation."

Jules shook his head. "The Germans will try to find out what happened to one of their men, but if he was on his own conducting some revenge hunt for Simone, that's going to cloud everything."

"That's right," said René. "The Germans might not know what to make of his disappearance. It's possible he didn't tell anyone what he was doing, so they probably don't know where to start."

César nodded. "We'll keep our ears and eyes open. But Simone, you still can't go to any more cafés in Marseille."

Downing the rest of his drink, René said, "There's another big reason I'm here. Simone, you've been summoned."

"What do you mean, summoned?" César demanded.

"By Varian Fry himself," René said, looking at Simone. "Says he needs you at his villa, tonight."

Simone stared at René. "Fry needs *me*? Why?"

René tipped his head back to get the last drops of whiskey from the glass. He seemed uncharacteristically nervous, slapping his hat on his leg, his eyes darting around a room he'd been in countless times.

"His forger was arrested. I don't need to tell you what that means for the guy." All around the room there was silence. Jules shook his head.

"Why is he calling upon Simone?" César asked. "He can't just demand her service, just like that. In the middle of the night?"

Simone got up and stood by the fire. This wasn't up to César. She spoke directly to René, "Why does he want me right now?"

René said, "There are papers that must be done, and very quickly, it appears. He's been told that you're a skilled forger," then he cleared his throat and added, "and I confirmed it."

Simone felt a rush of heat climb up her neck toward her face.

René continued, "The situation is desperate. His guests at a safe house in Cassis have a deadline—their steamship and train tickets and visas. Many of these people are well-known artists and political people—anti-Fascists. Without papers to get them out, they're stuck here and likely to be arrested."

Simone said, "I'll get my coat."

In a loud voice César said, "You can't take this risk. The police could be watching them. I can do the papers. It's safer for me."

"Safer, why? Because you're a man?"

Jules poured a glass of whiskey and handed it to César. "César, if he asked for Simone, then . . ."

Émilie spoke up, "I agree. Let Simone do what she's good at. And Fry makes a powerful ally. Keep that in mind."

René jumped in, "He *did* ask for Simone. He's made clear who he wants."

Simone drew in a long breath and said, "I'll get my things."

"I forbid this!" César roared.

For a moment, the room went silent except for the sounds of rain slashing against the house. Everyone's eyes were on Simone. She looked at César, and in a gentle but firm voice said, "I work for the cause. We all do. Each of us must decide what we're willing to do." Then she started for the stairs.

César wasn't giving up yet. "Your Mr. Lieb would want you to be safe. I'm sure he'd urge caution. And what about him? We're doing everything we can to get him out of there. And if we do, he'll need papers at once."

Simone stopped at the foot of the stairs and said, "Fry is only asking that I help tonight. I'll go now and do these urgent papers—then we'll see what else he has to say. You know there's nothing I would put ahead of Mr. Lieb."

Jules said, "René, you'll take Simone in the beast, yes? And perhaps you'll stay for a moment or two and see how things look. If anything seems amiss, she can turn right around and come back with you." He glanced over at César, whose dour expression remained unchanged.

Simone dashed upstairs and grabbed her coat, hat, and an umbrella, then dashed back down to the living room. César had barely moved from where he stood near the fire. She went straight to him and kissed him on the cheek. "I'll see you tomorrow. I'm sure this will take all night."

He let out a gasp and wrapped her in a tight embrace, murmuring into her neck, "I need you to be careful, *mi amor.*"

She pressed her forehead against his. "I *will* be careful. Very careful. I promise. Always." Then she whispered, "*Je t'aime.*"

René slapped his hat onto his head, then Simone said her goodbyes and followed him out into the slicing rain.

Villa-Air-Bel

The gazogene truck careened across dark, muddy roads as the rain in the truck's headlights flashed like electrified droplets. Simone clutched her coat and steadied herself with a hand pressed against the passenger door. Now that she was actually on the way, her stomach spiked with sharp pains. What if the police were keeping an eye on Fry's residence? It would make sense. And then she might be arrested as soon as she entered the house. *Don't think about such things,* she told herself. *Focus on the cause. Think about Fry. Think about refugees.*

Headlights appeared behind them, and René kept glancing in the rearview mirror, shaking his head. "There should be no traffic around here this time of night."

The truck bumped up and down the back roads to Cassis, pitching the beams from the headlights up and down into the fog.

René took care to drive the speed limit and even slower around the dangerous curves. After several miles, the vehicle that had been behind them turned onto a side road, and they both heaved a sigh of relief. After nearly an hour on the road, they passed through arched stone portals etched with the sign *Villa-Air-Bel.* In the dark, Simone could see a rambling three-story house surrounded by enormous trees. A single candle flickered in a window.

René grabbed her arm as she reached for the door handle. "Look, it's too soon to be certain, but we might have someone who can help with the Les Milles problem. I knew you'd want to know, but don't bother Fry about it. He's trying to save a lot of people with more importance attached to their names than our luthier. You're here to forge papers. For now, focus only on that."

She nodded, secretly vowing that if she had a chance to talk to Fry about Mr. Lieb, she'd grab it.

At the door, René rapped a coded knock—three, pause, two. They stood and waited. The only sounds she heard were the tapping and splashing of rain, and then someone unlocked the door. A young blonde woman with a sleepy little girl clinging to her neck opened it.

Pushing Simone toward the door, René said, "This is Simone, at Fry's request." Then he turned toward his truck. "I'll wait here until you send word about how long you need to stay."

Shivering, the young woman greeted her and closed the door behind them. She had strikingly beautiful eyes. Simone had no idea if she was one of the artists staying at the villa, but she looked like a tired mother. The woman picked up a candle, and Simone followed the flickering light through the ghostly darkness of the mansion's hallways.

The woman knocked on a door off the hallway and a frazzled looking man opened it. His hair stuck out in curls around his head, and he needed a shave, but he nodded pleasantly as he told them to come in and then thanked the young woman, who shuffled out quickly.

Even in the dim, moody lighting of the villa, there was no mistaking that this was Varian Fry. Simone noted his intent gaze that emanated from his dark brown eyes behind black-framed glasses. The room was like a library straight out of a Balzac novel—large dark shelves, sturdy but ornate wooden desks, leather chairs, and wallpaper that featured classical Greek images.

He nodded and said, "Mademoiselle Simone, I am, *we* are, deeply grateful for this emergency visit. We're rather frantic."

Fry pulled out an overstuffed chair for her and then sat near her in a chair just like it. "That young woman is the wife of the writer, André Breton," he said. "All kinds of people—the famous, the unknown, the old, the young—they're all looking for asylum." He dug out a cigarette and clicked the lighter, offering her one. Simone shook her head.

"As you've surely surmised by now, we desperately need your help. You know the nature of my work? And you know I lost my forger?"

"Yes, and I'm very sorry about that. I hope I can help you."

"And we're sure the police are watching us. That doesn't frighten you?"

"It does."

"Even more impressive that you came right over in the dark of a rainy night. I'll get to the point: I need flawless papers drawn for some very important people wanted by the Gestapo. The stakes are very high, and I was told you're the best." He picked up a large folder stuffed with papers. "Here are those who need emergency papers. And they all have to be ready for these people to leave by tomorrow."

Simone stared at the stack of files. "You want papers done for *all* those people. Tonight?"

He gestured to his desk. "It's asking a lot, I know. I was able to buy blank passports from the Lithuanians and Czechoslovakians, and we have the usual blank identification cards. In this stack," he set his palm on a pile of papers about a foot high, "are the original documents from the various districts in France where the applicant is supposed to have been born. A few people need forged birth certificates. Most just need identity documents and passports with the proper stamps and signatures."

"I understand," she said. This was going to take hours and hours. She'd probably be up all night. "Would you mind sending someone to let René know he's free to go?"

Fry smiled. "Ah, your ride awaits a signal. Smart. But before you accept, I must let you know that we're Vichy targets. At any time, they might raid us, shut us down, haul us all in. You could be arrested for this, you know."

Simone said only, "I know." She thought that if she spoke little, maybe he wouldn't hear the rattle of her nerves echoing throughout her body.

"Because of the raids, we have systems in place. If you're sure you can do this, you'll work upstairs in a room with thick blackout curtains. If there's any kind of disturbance, anything that alerts your instincts, turn off the light and wait for the signal rapped on your door: three knocks, two, then three again."

"All right," she answered. She knew she sounded calm, but she had to knit her fingers together to hide her trembling hands.

Fry went on, "The Germans are crawling all over this town—it's not just Vichy police. It's kept hush hush, but the Germans are here already." Was he trying to talk her out of this?

Simone tensed but said coolly, "I know. Go ahead, let René know he's free to go."

Fry stepped out of the room for a few minutes and then returned with two glasses of whiskey. He set one before her and sat back down in the leather chair.

She took a sip of the liquid gold and said, "You should know that I'm illegal too."

He shook his head. "Makes your work even more meaningful, I suspect. But I guess at this point we're all illegal in some way."

Simone looked at him. Then at the stack of folders.

"It's a lot of work, I know. But we're desperate. Frankly, if you hadn't accepted, I might have begged. Simone, if these people don't get out tomorrow, there's a good chance they're never getting out. They'd have to wait months, and by then it might be too late."

Simone met his eyes, and her shivering fear began to wane. She pressed her shoulders back and said, "I should get to work."

Fry exhaled relief, then stood and said, "Let's get you set up in your studio."

This Must be Hell

*I*t was unbearable to Joshua, the gossip that had spread like wildfire through the straw beds and colonies of refugees that morning. Seven suicides. One of them his cellist friend, Frederick. *Why, Frederick? And why now? Your beautiful music kept many of us going. What were the secrets in your heart? What happened to your promise to see your family who smiled from the photographs fastened to the bricks around your straw bed?*

Joshua curled himself under his thin blanket, but the incessant bites and itching and angry red rash forced him to scratch his legs. It was impossible to ignore the burning, even though the doctors in the infirmary had warned him not to scratch, that he might create an infection and die from it.

There were so many ways to die. Frederick had chosen to die by rope. He had hanged himself from one of the rafters. Another man had hidden enough morphine to kill himself and then ingested it all. Another stabbed himself with a knife from the kitchen. Anyone could die of dysentery or typhus, pneumonia or cancer. And those in charge had almost no reaction to any of it; each death simply meant one less mouth to feed.

Hundreds of new residents were herded in every week. Hundreds of unwashed bodies, lungs that gurgled and coughed, stomachs that growled, and intestines that spewed more shit into the latrines. Every day they stood for hours ankle deep in the muck of human waste, waiting or just letting it all go on the ground.

The stench was impossible to remove from clothing or shoes, but now and then Joshua bargained a few francs to wash himself and his clothes. There was no soap, but one had to try to clean up for the sake of decency. Joshua felt that if he stopped trying to hold onto his self-respect, it could be a very quick downhill slide to the end. Without the desire to still grasp for dignity, it could be easy to give up.

Many in the camp played music, painted, or wrote, and the sounds and sights of these people continuing to create art sometimes saved Joshua from sliding into the darkest chasms of despair. Those who used their minds to create beauty seemed to have some light left in their eyes, some purpose, some hope. But still, day after day, they had to survive what felt like endless hours of breathing in brick dust and hearing bad news about Vichy in its collaboration with Germany. He knew from experience that the Germans—and now the French—placed older male Jews at the top of deportation lists. His life was coming full circle. From the Reich to freedom in Paris and back to the Reich.

The reality inside the camp was grim in every conceivable way. Each demoralizing day was followed by another dreadful, ominous day. He'd heard about Hell. This must be what they meant.

Forger of Marseille

Varian Fry picked up his drink and the stack of folders. He lit a candle and said, "Follow me." Then they climbed the stairs to the third floor. The house creaked and moaned in the wind, and water pinged into pots as rain found its away in through holes in the roof of the shabby nineteenth-century structure. The building was charming and oozed history, but it looked like it had been deserted before this group took over. Fry opened the door to a room with thick curtains and a lamp, desk, and chair. There was dust everywhere, and the wallpaper was peeling in strips.

In the large box on the desk, Simone saw supplies left behind by the previous forger—handmade stamps, rubber carefully carved and glued on top of empty spools of thread. Ink pots, black, blue, red, and green, were lined up on one side of the desk and pens on the other. She felt strangely linked to the man who'd used these tools before her, as if united with a comrade in resistance, a connection to the man who at this moment might be paying the ultimate price for his courage. His arrest made her even more determined to stay bright and focused, to pick up where he'd left off, to serve the cause with her most extraordinary effort.

Fry motioned for her to sit and then set the stack of folders on the table, his glasses slipping down his nose. "Here are those who need papers immediately."

She watched as he flipped through each file. She said, "You have seven files there?" She counted how many hours it would take—all night and part of the next day. "Two to three documents per person?"

Fry opened a folder and spoke quickly and brightly, as if afraid he was going to lose her. "This person was a well-known politician in Germany, and the Gestapo is eager to arrest him." He opened another file. "And here, a poet who has spoken against the regime. As you can see, words are dangerous."

"Yes, I know. I'm from Berlin."

Fry looked up from the folders, "I was in Berlin in '35. I saw the SS stab a man in the hand at a café—for no reason. People were beaten in the streets. I never could get it out of my mind. That's why I volunteered for the Emergency Rescue Committee in New York. I came here with a list of two hundred names I hoped to help save. But there are truly thousands who need help, and they aren't on any list. Sometimes we must make impossible choices."

Simone could see his pain. How agonizing it must be, deciding who would live and who might die.

He tapped various stacks of papers on the desk. "Here are the identities we created. Then in this stack are blank birth certificates and a list of parents' names, occupations. You'd be surprised how many electricians, bricklayers, and car mechanics we've had to create." He set down the box of papers and turned toward her with a tight smile. "I'll let you get to it. Let me know if you have questions or if you need anything at all." Then he left the room and closed the door behind him.

Her mind began to whir. *I know how to do this*, she told herself as she surveyed the documents.

One by one, she read through the folders, as if introducing herself to each person within. Men. Women. Old. Young. People with talent, deep intelligence, and infinite promise. They'd used their voices, spoken out, and taken risks for their beliefs in democracy, the right to speak freely. Some of these people weren't famous—they were simply stateless and Jewish. Fry was saving ordinary people as well. She looked deep into the eyes of every one of them—safe for now in their little square of the identity photograph—and she could feel them looking back at her. *I'm here,* she thought. *I see you. Tonight, we'll shape-shift each one of you into a new person with the new name and background and occupation. You'll no longer be Jewish or German. No longer stateless and wanted by the Gestapo. Fresh start, every one of you. A chance.*

Simone began. Slowly and carefully, she filled in the documents with names and birthdates, professions, and other necessary details. The ink seeped up her fingers in a rainbow of colors. She carefully copied the signatures from prefects in different *départements* in France and found the stamps needed for each one, pressing them precisely into the ink pads, trying to imitate the registration of the printing on the stamp, using her brush to feather in corrections.

The night wore on, and she shifted in the chair and took long, deep breaths to stay awake as she created identities for seven people who didn't exist until the moment she endowed them with a birthplace and new parents. The pounding of the rain, her extreme weariness, and the fantastical nature of the work made her head begin to swim. Eventually, she began to feel she was floating through some surreal painting.

As she finished each passport, she looked into the subject's eyes and wished them all good things—the soundest of decisions, the kindest of encounters, the greatest of luck—as they took their next precarious steps into the unknown. "Good luck to you, Georges. And you, Marie. Phillippe. Françoise. Celeste. Lucien. Yves."

With each stroke of the pen, a past was erased and a chance for a future born.

Simone awoke to the feeling of a hand on her shoulder. Her eyes felt dry as a desert as she opened them and tried to orient herself to the unfamiliar room around her. She felt like a rumpled mess, shoulders aching, stickiness on her tongue. She'd fallen asleep, face down on the desk.

She pulled herself upright and saw Fry smiling down at her, coffee cup in hand. "Oh dear," she said, sitting up straight and trying to suppress a yawn. "My hand cramped, and I thought I'd shut my eyes for just a moment." That must have been at least a couple of hours ago. Blue light now hinted at the windows.

He placed the cup on the desk along with a slice of bread and a pale jelly-like substance on the plate. "Sorry, this is all we have. Coffee nationale and a grape concoction that almost tastes like jam."

"Thank you," she said, welcoming the hot liquid at the back of her throat. She glanced across the large wooden desk. Thank goodness the documents were stacked neatly. "Almost everything is finished. I have only two more left to sign."

He sat back and sorted through the documents, his fingers tracing the stamps and signatures. "These are magnificent, truly professional," he marveled. "Thank you. I know we didn't give you much choice. I can hardly express our gratitude. You've saved lives here."

She watched him in silence, trying to wake up, hoping he might tell her something about the people she'd been bonding with all night, and as if on cue, he granted her wish as he leafed through the folders. "Lipschitz. Modigliani, the brother of the well-known artist. Considered degenerates. Very dangerous." He shook his head.

She shivered at the memory of the Degenerate Exhibit in Berlin, the Hitler Youth marching through the gallery singing the Horst Wessel song about cutting Jewish throats. But the art—it had so lifted her that day. "I saw that exhibit," she said. "I saw a Picasso and a Chagall and so many other great works."

"Funny you mention Picasso. He announced that he's staying in occupied Paris. And Chagall—there's a stubborn man. I just got back from Gordes. Tried to persuade him to emigrate to no avail."

"He refuses?"

"He can't bear the thought of leaving France. The same for Pablo Casals, the Spanish cellist. When he escaped Franco, he ended up in Prades just over the border in France, but he doesn't want to emigrate. At least Chagall seemed to consider it, even asking if there were cows in America. You know how he loves to paint cows." Fry opened another file. "This woman, Hannah Arendt, is a philosopher with dangerous ideas, according to the Reich. There are artists on our list, writers, political people. Big thinkers. Visionaries. People considered very dangerous to Hitler—too influential in making people see through Fascist lies."

Fry seemed wide awake and rested, and Simone sat fascinated in an exhausted haze as she sipped her coffee and listened to him speak of the nature of his work and the people he was risking everything for. He said that Thomas Mann's brother and son were on the lists, waiting for papers. He spoke of journalists who wrote fiery rebuttals to the policies of Hitler and novelists who satirized the rising class of Hitler's Reich. On the lists were those who challenged the anti-Semitic policies and the oppression against free speech. "They advocated for the rights of all people to have a voice, an opinion. To express themselves."

Now Fry looked up from the papers and into her eyes. "When did you leave Berlin?"

"After the Anschluss. Mr. Lieb, a father to me and a good friend to my mother after my own father died, was convinced that if we didn't leave then, it would be impossible to escape." She looked down into her coffee cup. "My mother stayed behind with her parents, but we haven't heard from her in some time." Simone paused, wondering how much to tell him. Finally, she said, "Mr. Lieb and I and César, my . . . friend, we all arrived here after the exodus from Paris. But then Mr. Lieb got swept up in a *rafle* and now he's imprisoned in Les Milles."

"Oh, Simone, I'm so sorry," said Fry. "That must be agony for you."

She decided it was now or never. "This man, Mr. Lieb, stepped in and raised me after my father died in the first war. He's extraordinary, a luthier and a musician. And . . ." she took another sip of coffee, "my friends, René and others, we're trying to find a way to get him out of the camp. It's difficult, as you know."

He crossed his arms and said, "Yes, I know all too well."

He didn't appear to be catching her hint. "I couldn't forgive myself if I didn't ask—is there anything you can do for my Mr. Lieb? Joshua Lieb, a violinist incarcerated at Les Milles? He's in his fifties, and I just know that . . ."

Fry interrupted, "I'm afraid it's very difficult to work that particular miracle."

"But you work miracles every day, Mr. Fry. Many people have escaped certain death because of you."

"This work is much different. Vichy runs those camps. I have no sway with them. No strings to pull." He seemed to be getting uncomfortable with the conversation and stood up. "If you'll excuse me, I have more refugees awaiting my help." He started toward the door.

Simone wasn't giving up. "The word is that you helped Lion Feuchtwanger escape Les Milles. He even spoke of it in his interview in New York."

Fry stopped at the door and turned back. "Damned man, spilling secrets. His big mouth cost lives, I can tell you that!" He crossed the room to the window that looked out over the property and watched the black branches of naked trees swaying wildly in the wind.

Simone said, "I hope I haven't offended you. But we're desperate—"

He spoke without moving his gaze from the trees. "They're trying to throw me out of this country. And the US state department is trying to stop me from sending more refugees to America. There are so many forces against us, trying to shut this down. At least I'm not in this alone—the Unitarians, the Quakers, the Jewish organizations, the YMCA—even Peggy Guggenheim is doing what she can to get artists out of the country . . . and their paintings. There are others fighting the fight, but there's so much need, just so many desperate people . . ." He hung his head, looking miserable.

Simone forced herself to blink back tears. Then, as Fry stood silently looking out the window, she felt a surge of anger. She picked up a stack of blank documents and flung them down on the desk. He whipped his head around at the sound of the folders landing with a slap. "Mr. Fry, you summoned me on a cold, rainy night, and I came running, at tremendous risk, as we both know. Because of me, there are seven names now added to the list of the lucky ones. Forgive me if I now appear brash, but this speech of yours sounds defeatist to me."

He turned toward her, eyebrows raised. Was that almost a smile on his lips? "I see. You're a fighter too."

Exhaustion crept into Simone's bones, and she sank back into her chair. The floors creaked as people all around the house were starting to wake up.

"I thank you profoundly for your work here tonight. It was remarkable." Then Fry pulled an envelope from his pocket and placed it on the desk. Simone could see it contained several French notes. "A small token of our thanks. Au revoir, Mademoiselle. You have been heroic. There's a car waiting for you outside." Then he turned and left the room.

Simone sighed. At least she hadn't let Mr. Lieb down completely. She had tried.

She drank the coffee and took small bites of bread. After wiping her hands dry on a rag, she picked up her pen and with the steady hand of an expert, signed the remaining two documents. Then she checked and rechecked every piece of paper she'd forged throughout the night. In her final ritual, she again wished each person safe passage as she tried to visualize the new lives awaiting these refugees in America or wherever they were going. Wherever that was, at least now there was hope.

Just then there was a knock on the door, and a woman's voice whispered, "Simone?"

It must be someone letting me know it's time to leave, she thought. Gathering her coat, she rushed across the room and opened the door. There, looking like a brunette Greta Garbo with her soft eyes and dark hair, stood Sophia. They embraced in a long, silent hug. She'd been in this woman's presence only a few times, but every encounter had been deeply meaningful, laden with intensity. The essence of Sophia always seemed to flow straight to her soul.

"Bless you dear, and bonne chance," Sophia said. Then she kissed Simone on both cheeks. Simone returned the gesture, wondering if she'd ever see her friend again.

Walking down the hallway in a fog of fatigue, Simone saw what appeared to be shadows of people darting in and out of the villa's rooms.

"Au revoir," voices called out. "Merci, Merci!" Were they real? Were they talking to her? Could these people ever understand how connected she felt to them?

She wove her way to the house's entryway, pulled open the heavy front door, and ran out into the rain.

Architecture of Escape

That cold morning in November, César, René, Émilie, and Jules sat by the fire discussing the matter of rescuing Joshua. He'd been incarcerated for ten weeks, and César knew that if they could get him out, he'd be weak. Undernourished. Hopefully he wouldn't be ill, but typhoid and dysentery were common in all the camps.

Jules poured coffee into their cups, and Émilie cut pieces of an apple pastry she'd made of potato flour. Jules said, "Rumors are growing about the impending move of men at Les Milles to another camp. If they do this, we've lost him. We need to secure that guard. Today. And the plan—what is it?"

Just then the front door opened, the rain blew in, and there stood Simone, drenched but with a big smile on her face. The men stood to greet her, and she waved an envelope. "Look what Fry gave me!" Then she opened it and poured a bundle of notes onto the dining room table. René's eyes popped open wide. Jules swore, "*Mon dieu.*"

César rushed to the dining room and threw his arms around her. Ah, to see her face again—what blessed relief. He buried his face in her wet hair. "I'm so glad to see you." She squeezed him tight, and he stood back to look at her. "Tell us everything."

Her face was alight with excitement. "I did papers for seven people. Two or three documents for each of them." She pulled off her gloves. "Look at my fingers." They were stained a rainbow of colors, red, blue, green, and black.

César helped her off with her dripping coat then embraced her again. Jules poured her a cup of coffee. "Welcome back, Simone! Tell us about Fry."

She kissed César then let go of him and stepped toward the fire. "A man intensely dedicated to his work. We were able to talk both before and after my marathon of ink—mostly about the kinds of people he's saving."

"For someone who's been up all night, you look very alert." Jules pulled out a chair for her, and Émilie kissed her on the cheek and presented her with an extra-large serving of pastry.

"Well, there was that time I fell asleep on the desk!" she laughed. "But by then I had all but wrapped up the work."

She looked like she was still buzzing with adrenaline when she told them about the beautiful, creaky house, the room on the third floor, Fry's work with so many interesting people. Then her voice quieted as she described those whose papers she had so carefully forged. "By the end of the night I felt I knew them. It was as if they'd watched me work."

"Yes," César agreed, "I know this feeling."

"René," Simone said, "Please don't be angry, but I asked him about helping us free Mr. Lieb."

"Why would I be angry?" René snarled. "You only dismissed the *one* request I made of you!"

Jules ignored René and said, "And?"

"I must have been lightheaded from exhaustion, but I implied that he owed me. I might have been a bit too assertive now that I think about it."

"Bravo!" Jules clapped his hands. "Why not, I say. What have you to lose? In the room with the man himself and not to make such a request? You must seize every opportunity you can."

René sat silently sneering into the fire.

César kissed her forehead and said, "This is not a woman who backs away from a challenge."

Simone looked at René. "I'm sorry, René, but he's Varian Fry, and it's my father we're talking about. But he kept telling me that he has no connections at Les Milles. I pushed, but he seemed in a hurry to get back to his work. He thanked me sincerely, dropped the money on the desk, and had one of his people drive me home. And here I am."

César said, "At least you asked. Do you think he'll ask for your help again? The man is without a forger."

Simone appeared to ponder the question when Jules said, "I suspect he will. People tend to return to those whose work they trust."

César turned the focus to René. "Let's talk about the plan for Joshua. What can your people do?"

René lowered his voice as if the enemy could be listening. He told them he was using his connections to find someone who could bribe a guard or two at Les Milles—this seemed to be the best way in, as those men always needed money, and their loyalty to Vichy was wavering at best.

As René spoke, César gazed at Simone. His heart swelled with pride for her courage and skill. And for being so bold with the powerful Varian Fry. He caught her eye and blew her a silent kiss, and she sent back a proud smile.

René leaped from his chair and pulled on his coat. "We know of a couple of guards who might be easily persuaded. We're calling in favors. We're doing everything we can. Jules, you have the safe house list. Choose a couple of places nearby, and César, where else? How about another safe house near the mountain? We need to be prepared for different outcomes."

"You think we can act on all this quickly?" Jules asked.

René said, "Something could happen tonight for all we know. When opportunity presents itself, you strike. At *all* times be ready."

Simone was quiet. César knew it was painful for her to hear about rescue plans—so much could go wrong.

César said, "He gets out, we hide him, and then get him to the guides to go over the mountains and out of France." What he didn't say was how much he worried about Joshua on the mountain. After living through prison conditions, who knew how weak he might be?

René said he was headed "back out into the battle" and left, and Jules got busy making calls. All César wanted to do was hold Simone in his arms. He pulled her to the sofa and wrapped himself around her.

"I really should have a bath," she laughed.

Émilie offered to draw it for her. Simone thanked her and turned to kiss César.

César buried his face in her hair. "But you smell so good to me," he said and kissed her again on her cheeks, her lips, her forehead. She sighed then laid her head on his shoulder and together they stared into the fire.

Simone was back safely and she'd been successful. For now, he would keep his dark thoughts to himself. He wouldn't share that his mind had been filled with everything that could go wrong with a scheme to bust a man from a prison camp. He wouldn't speak of his immense fears that a broken man would find it nearly impossible to scale the Pyrenees. He wouldn't tell Simone that her Mr. Lieb might be forever changed. He simply pulled her closer and rested his cheek upon her head.

Joshua was almost grateful that the only thing left to do anymore was to lie on his straw pallet feeling the silent hum of his body as it grew lighter, as the invisible strands that tethered him to the earth began to loosen. The usual sounds of the camp came and went: the music, the arguments as they unfolded day to day, the backdrop of life in Les Milles. He mused about a man's ability to get used to anything, even dying. It seemed like a natural unfolding of time, just like a musical phrase or the movements of a symphony. Sometimes he would get lost in the existential questions, like what difference will his life have made, really? What had he accomplished?

In other moments, he found himself walking the old forests, the trees whispering their wisdom. He'd be with his grandfather listening to him weave stories of creatures that lived in the trees, the heartbeat that each tree possessed, how the trees listened to each other. And he'd stand beside his father who taught him how to tune into the songs of the trees and their wisdom . . . to know as he worked with the bare wood, trimming, smoothing, and shaping a new violin, that all this wisdom was just waiting for the violin to express it.

But then his mind returned to this life, the one he was leaving behind. His heart anguished that his beloved violins were gone forever. It was the loss of his family, the theft of his history. The tears ran out of the corners of his eyes and fell upon the coat he used for a pillow. After weeping, he returned to a cottony, peaceful feeling, knowing that Simone would not forget him, that

Lucien would keep making violins as would Thomas Banks in London who had worked with him in LiebViol through the years. These thoughts comforted him and allowed him to disappear back into the fog of fantasy.

Tonight, he would dream of water. He closed his eyes and pictured himself on the deck of a ship with billowing white sails and built of strong, glossy oak, soaring free across a clear blue sea.

One night—he didn't know when exactly—he sensed a disturbance. Low, tight voices hovered around him, murmuring. The sounds of decisions and instructions disturbed the cottony softness he'd grown used to. Then he heard, "We've got you," and he stiffened and tried to call out, but his voice was weak, and his protests whispered into a void. In his fog he sensed he was being deported. It was happening. He was being sent to a camp in Germany! He raised his arms to fight back, but they fell back to his side. He looked up and tried to focus on the faces of two men. Were they dressed in white? He couldn't make out features—were they wearing masks? Then a prick in his arm and a gauzy feeling. Peace and surrender.

Another feverish dream. The blurred men, gloved hands, white masks, muffled voices. And then the sky. The sky! What was happening? His mind couldn't follow. Silvery clouds, stars. A moon. Was this heaven? No, think . . . he didn't believe in heaven, but sometimes he tried to believe in such a place, a beautiful world without pain. He'd meet Bach there and they'd play fugues together.

Why was he hearing the sounds of a motor and smelling cigarette smoke? And he was moving—somewhere in a vehicle. Men's voices. Who were they? Where were they taking him? Everything was fuzzy. He couldn't hold a clear thought long enough to think anything through.

"Who are you? Where are we going?" he called to the air. Or did he? Were his words clear? No answer. There was pressure again on his arm, a sting, then the fuzzy feeling.

Then he was a boy again, and there was his father. What a comforting sound, his father's boots breaking underbrush in the snow, snapping twigs. His heart leaped toward the beauty of the snow-covered trees. The aroma of the forest signaled it was time. The smell of cut wood, earth, walnut tobacco. He was where he belonged. There would be a roast waiting when they got home, his mother's beautiful smile. The sun burst through the thick branches of the tall spruce trees after one was felled. It was sad and happy at once, this ritual. He could smell spruce on the ground, in the air, everywhere. His father was smiling, his cheeks rosy. Now, in an instant, the boy was grown. He began to cry, but Lili rested her hand on his chest, her eyes filled with love. *Lili?* But Lili was dead, Lili and their child. *Where is this?* "Where?" he cried out. Did he say that or did he think it? The gauzy blur calmed him, and he returned to the forest.

Ever since she'd been a child, Simone had thought snow was some kind of magic. Blanketing the earth in a layer of mystical sparkles, snow delighted her more than any other natural event. But now as she looked out the window of the safe house within sight of the Pyrenees, the sight of the landscape covered in snow filled her with dread. It was an early snow, but it might be a deadly one.

For two days now she'd been a tangled wreck of emotions. Joshua had been rescued from prison! But had he? She saw no evidence of it. There were only words, words of men she knew nothing about, men who were involved because money had changed hands. And where were they now? *Where* was he? What was going on? Had Joshua and the mystery men been arrested? Was he even alive? The waiting churned Simone's stomach.

César smiled at her warmly as he sipped the watery soup they'd made for lunch and dinner, conserving their supplies. René had shown up with warm clothes and a thick stew, and they saved the hearty stew for Joshua. He would need as much nutrition as he could take in. In prison he'd probably survived on old beans or a piece of vegetable floating in putrid water. Maybe a rotten potato.

Then the sound of car doors slamming sent a jolt through her body. César and Simone nearly tripped over each other rushing to the window where they gasped at what they saw.

Two men wearing dark work clothes emerged and lifted a thin man with a sickly gray beard from the car. The old man wore a long coat and furry hat and swayed back and forth as the men steadied him.

"Papa?" Simone said aloud.

She lost control of her emotions, not sure if she was laughing or sobbing. César drew her close to him, the warmth of his body helping to steady her.

"Shh," René whispered from his spot by another window. "We mustn't make a scene. Let him get to the door, then we'll welcome him. Remember, we're an ordinary family, and our grandfather is visiting."

Simone clung to the door jamb to keep herself from running down the stairs. Tears came to her eyes as she watched the old man shuffle along, so unsteady on his feet as the men held him upright. What had those Vichy animals done to him? She gritted her teeth in fury.

The men guided him to the foot of the stairs that led to the front door. "Grandfather, we're so happy you could visit us today," René called out.

Simone could hardly bear watching him clamber his way up one slow stair at a time. This fragile old man, pale and sickly, struggling to breathe. He stopped three times to catch his breath. How could he possibly climb a mountain? In snow!

"The snow. It's so beautiful," a frail voice said.

At the top of the stairs, René helped him over the threshold. At first his eyes darted around as if he was confused. Then he found Simone, and cried, "My dear, Sarah. My sweet Sarah." His thin blue-veined hands shook as he reached for her. He smelled of disinfectant and urine, and the only parts of him she recognized were his blue eyes, clouded and red as they were.

"Oh, my papa," she whispered and gently folded her arms around his fragile body. His bones and angles felt sharp. He was shaking, and a soft moan escaped his lips.

"My Sarah." His head rested against her shoulder.

He seemed so fragile, and it felt strange but also very sweet to hear him calling her by her given name. She fought back tears and squeezed him softly, feeling him relax into her embrace, his body trembling. Holding him like this brought back memories of her mother's embrace. Oh, the constant ache of worry she felt about her mother. When would she see her again?

For now she'd concentrate on how grateful she was to have Mr. Lieb back. Simone didn't want to let him go, but she wanted to look at him. They slowly moved apart and she looked into his eyes, so full of pain and wisdom. His smile broadened, and she saw that he was missing a tooth. Their tentative smiles then eased into the edge of a laugh, and they kissed each other's cheeks in the French way. His cheek was all grime and grizzled whiskers, but he was here. Alive.

César wrapped his arms around Mr. Lieb. "Joshua, Joshua." Tears ran into Joshua's gray beard.

"And you, César. Oh my, how very good to see you."

With a faint sparkle in his eye, Mr. Lieb slowly turned toward René. "Even you, René."

Laughter filled the room.

Sniffing the air at the aroma of stew bubbling on the stove, he licked his lips. "What's cooking?" he asked before slumping to the floor.

Simone stifled a scream. René and César gathered him up like a rag doll and tucked him in between blankets on the sofa. Then César took over. He checked Mr. Lieb's pulse, listened to his heart, and told René to get water. After he'd rested for several minutes and had sipped water, René brought him a small bowl of stew. Simone held the warm bowl and spooned the stew gently into his mouth. As he slowly chewed, his face lit up. He took his time, carefully swallowing after each spoonful and each time asking for another.

César said, "You mustn't eat too much at first—it could make you sick. You can have more in an hour. Let's give you a bath."

Mr. Lieb shook his head. "I know. It's disgusting how I am now."

They all reassured him that he was perfect. César said that a bath would refresh him, and then guided him into the bathroom. All Simone heard for some time was running water and a few wrenching sobs.

An hour later, César walked Mr. Lieb, now dressed in clean clothes, to the parlor and settled him on the sofa. He looked exhausted but alert, taking in everything around the room and eventually settling his gaze on Simone. She sat next to him and squeezed his hand, waiting for the right moment to present him with the surprise she'd barely been able to hold back since the moment he'd arrived. After he seemed comfortable, she reached around behind the couch and ceremoniously placed the violin on his thin lap.

His sharp cry stabbed her heart, the sound of longing and sorrow as he openly wept. He hugged the instrument to his chest and plinked the strings, and they all wept together. Even René wiped his eyes on his sleeve.

"My grandfather's very own," he whispered.

Simone and César cradled him on the couch as he held his violin to his chest, gasping, "Thank you, what a blessing," as quiet sobs rippled through his frail body.

Junction of
Present and Future

Two days later, Joshua sat by the parlor window and watched snowflakes fall across the gentle rolling hills of France. His eyes tracked from the foothills of the Pyrenees up to the rising peaks that disappeared into clouds. The soft-falling flakes created a silence that was profound and beautiful.

He sighed and turned over, pulling the wool blankets tight around him on the sofa. Finally, real warmth. He burrowed deeper into the cocoon of blankets and warm clothes that covered his arms, now reduced to mere bones covered by a thin layer of pale flesh.

After two days of César's careful regime of a small bowl of soup—a few tablespoons every two hours—and gentle walking exercises across the parlor floor, Joshua began to reconnect with his body, and his mind began to piece together his life. He asked Simone and César to tell him what they were planning next—he'd overheard them talking about "the plan."

They said, "After your nap," and before he could protest, he was asleep.

"Mr. Lieb. Joshua, Joshua?" Voices he remembered from another life called to him.

The aroma of fresh bread stirred him to wakefulness, and he sat up. Simone stood before him, warm bread on a plate, and César kneeled before him, spoon in hand.

"Ah, give me that. I can feed myself," he said.

He opened his mouth and leaned forward with his spoon in hand, and most of it landed in his mouth. Warm. Delicious. Careful chewing allowed it to travel down his throat with a wonderful sensation. A smile spread across his face, and everyone broke into laughter.

"Papa, you're going to be fine! We have so much to tell you," Simone said with a smile.

He found the second bite easier to manage, and soon he was scooping one spoon after another until César slowed him down. "Remember, not too fast. Your body needs time to adjust."

César guided him to the lavatory, a miracle in itself—a toilet, not a hole. No standing in shit for hours, never able to escape the revolting stench. He reached for a small sliver of soap on the sink. Simone had said that soap was one of the few luxuries people had these days. This lovely little slice that smelled like roses must have been Émilie's gift to him. He smoothed it on his skin and breathed it in.

After he returned, they all sat down in the parlor. Simone said, "Papa, we want to talk to you about the plan."

He thought it a bit strange that a plan for his life was already in place without his being part of its creation. But he said only, "I'm interested."

"We have it all charted out—how you can escape France." César showed him a map drawn in ink by hand.

Jumping in quickly, Simone sounded nervous. "You must get out of France, and we know how to help you escape. I already did the paperwork." She waved several sets of papers in front of him. "And the guides expect us in a few days."

Joshua felt the air leave his lungs. "Guides? Guides to where? And what do you mean, a few days? Haven't I only just arrived back in civilization, with you, the people I love?"

Holding his hand in hers, she said, "You're not safe here anymore. You're an escaped man who was found to have false papers. There is no scenario where you're safe in France. You must realize that, no?"

He had no argument for that point, so he only looked back and forth from Simone to César.

César sat next to him, his tone earnest. "Thomas Banks has that shop in England as part of LiebViol. You could live there and return to a normal life."

"Normal life? Aren't they bombing London? And Simone, what about you?" He felt lightheaded.

Simone said, "Papa, please understand. We can't leave here right now, and London will be safer for you than here with the Fascists roaming the streets looking for you."

He slumped against her. Everything was being taken from him again. When he caught his breath again, he asked, "Why can't we all go to England?" He could see from the looks on their faces that this was an argument he wasn't going to win.

No one spoke as René banged around in the kitchen, then within seconds he marched into the living room, and while wiping a dish announced, "We need to get you over the border into Spain. You're going over the Pyrenees, and then there's a course charted for you to make your way to England where you'll be safe. That's the plan." Then he walked back into the kitchen.

The three of them sat quietly in the wake of René. Then Joshua asked Simone, "You want to stay here? In Vichy France?"

"I've found great purpose here, Papa. I'm doing some of the

most important work a person could ever do. I am a forger in collaborationist France. I am a forger in Marseille."

He smiled at her. "I know you're tremendously talented at this forging business, but . . ."

Interrupting, César said, "So talented that Varian Fry himself called on her in the night to prepare some emergency documents. Simone is very important to the cause."

What could he say to that? But how could he leave his Jewish daughter behind? Here? Now?

René charged into the room with a tray of bread and small cups of ersatz coffee. "You need to talk about the plan before he gets too tired."

Simone kissed him on the cheek. "Papa, listen to the plan to walk you over the Pyrenees and . . ."

"I'm going to climb a mountain? You must be joking."

César said, "We have ten days to prepare, and every day you'll eat well and exercise. People in bad shape, ordinary citizens who have never hiked in their lives, are getting up that mountain, with a little help, of course. I will be your cane, your support. You can lean on me. I can carry you, if necessary."

"Simone? Will you be there?"

She draped her arm around him. "I won't leave your side until you cross the border."

"The border? Surely it's not that easy—just to walk across."

Once again, the room went silent. What were they keeping from him? "Tell me the truth. What are the dangers?"

César and Simone didn't reply.

René plunged in, "He's a grown man, for god's sake. He's been in war. He's been in prison." He turned to Joshua. "Simone has done your papers. We get you to the border with the help of guides. At the border you present your papers to the Spanish guards to be officially stamped. Then, a train to Madrid and on to Lisbon. But first you have to get out of France, and there are rumors that the Germans are patrolling the border, not just the Vichy police. We've heard that people have been arrested and killed on this kind of venture."

"René!" cried Simone.

Joshua lifted his hand. "My dear, it's fine. He's not scaring me. I've been through so much already. Of course, it's dangerous. I just didn't think that . . ."

She said, "We will get you ready. We'll make sure you're ready."

Did she really believe that? Joshua smiled, but he didn't for a minute believe that any of them thought he'd make it up and over that mountain.

For the next few days, Joshua followed César's every instruction and worked hard to rebuild his strength. They all laughed when he lifted his legs high like a soldier and marched across the parlor. He was winded after five steps, but he still took three more. And more after that. César gave him a bag of potatoes to lift, three sets of five lifts. The bags got heavier every day. He strained and grunted and sweat broke out on his forehead, but he did it.

When it was clear that Joshua was worn out, Simone led him back to the sofa and settled him in while César unfolded the map and explained, "The day of departure, we'll take the train to the village at the foot of the mountain, at Banyuls-sur-Mer. We're to meet a woman in a red dress, and she'll take us to a safe house. The next morning, very early, we'll meet guides for the climb. You must wear special shoes, espadrilles, which will help keep your balance on the rocks. We'll all climb together."

Simone continued, "We can tell you all the details over the next few days. We'll have had ten days, Papa, to get you strong." Then she showed him his new identity card. "You're now François

Joubert. Your profession is cabinetmaker. That will explain the wood curls you always carry around in your cuffs!"

Everyone laughed, but Joshua quickly went quiet again. London. So far away. His daughter so very far away. The people he loved most in the world would be so far from him—Marseille, Paris, Germany. But, no, today he would look to the future. In London, he would at least have his work. The aroma of linseed oil and the gracious curves of violins all around him. The chance to create beauty again.

Simone watched him closely—she was always so sensitive to his state of mind. He sat up tall and said brightly, "Joshua! Lieb! DuBois. François! Who am I anyway?"

She laughed and gently kissed his forehead. "I know you. And it's my dream that one day I will arrive in a train station— maybe in Paris or London—and I'll be greeted again by Mr. Joshua Lieb."

Woman in the Red Dress

he train rolled toward the village of Banyuls-sur-Mer as Simone watched out the window and marveled at the shoulders of the great Pyrenees rising over the plains. What a miraculous thing, a mountain range. For how many millions of years had the Pyrenees stood mighty and steadfast?

She looked over at the man who was now "François" sitting next to her, his lap covered with a blanket and his violin tucked between his knees. Mr. Lieb and his beloved violins . . . their enduring connection filled her heart with joy and pride. His blue eyes were sharp, and his face had lost much of the gauntness that three months in the camp had sculpted. He was thin, but he'd been a determined patient, lifting weights and walking as he built back his strength. César, René, and Simone had given him most of their rations, and René's family donated food they'd grown on their farm. Eventually he gave up protesting their sacrifice and ate whatever was set before him. Many times Simone had lamented, *if only they had more time*. But they simply did not. Tomorrow he'd have to climb a mountain, and he was as ready as they could make him.

Steam flowed by the windows as the train chugged and wheezed up through the village of Elne. The next stop was Argelès-sur-Mer, the village where César had lost his family and had then been dumped into an internment camp. She glanced over at him and saw a gleam of tears in his eyes as he looked out the window and then quickly back toward the floor of the train. He pulled his cap over his face and crossed his arms, pretending to sleep.

The train made quick stops in beach towns where people disembarked, others boarded quickly, and then the train puffed on to Port-Vendres and through several tunnels carved into the heart of the mountain.

His eyes still closed, César murmured, "Banyuls-sur-Mer is next."

Simone took deep breaths. It was time to meet the woman in the red dress, which meant they'd be that much closer to the climb. So many things could go wrong. Simone was no mountain climber, and what about Mr. Lieb so recently healed? Was this François up to a climb that would challenge even a young, healthy man? Even from forty miles away, the Pyrenees looked every bit as fierce as César had described. But the mountain was often spoken of in whispers, as if it were a god, a presence greater than any human. It had claimed victims, but it also offered protection, a natural boundary. Many of Caskie's soldiers and Fry's refugees were alive because the mountain had let them pass.

The train pulled into a small adobe station with a red-tiled roof, and the conductor called out "Banyuls-sur-Mer!" Simone helped François up from his seat, and César reached out to guide him, but he marched toward the exit with surprising energy. They climbed down to the platform, and she breathed in the aroma of trees and earth. There was a gentle dampness in the cool air, but this was November in the Pyrenees. In a moment, the weather could shift from mild to deadly.

In the station, a blue-suited gendarme tapped his leg with a baton, squinting at the disembarking passengers. Simone, César, and François stood quietly in line as the gendarme examined the papers of the couple ahead of them. While they waited their turn, the train shrieked and spewed steam, and the stationmaster waved it on to Cerbère, the last village in France before it crossed the border into Spain.

Simone stiffened as they approached the gendarme. César whispered, "Act natural." He leaned over and kissed the top of her head. "I look forward to seeing Auntie Charlotte, don't you, François?" he said in a loud voice, uttering the network's assigned reason for the trip.

"Papers please," the gendarme said to Simone. His eyes ran up and down the length of her, and she smiled, recreating her flirtation with the agent the day they'd arrived in Marseille.

"Of course. Here they are." She let her hand linger after she placed the papers in his palm.

Frowning, he opened her documents and examined them slowly.

Behind her, César made small talk with François about fictional Aunt Charlotte. "Perhaps she'll make that bouillabaisse we love."

The official handed back the identity card and asked Simone for her travel pass. Now his dark eyes seemed to look through her. She smiled and handed it to him, then turned toward César, her skirt whirling around her legs. "I think we can fix something simple," she said. "The turnip pie is a reliable dish."

The gendarme looked from Simone to César and back, then

surprised her by saying, "Good thinking—you'll preserve your coupons," as he handed back her pass and told her to move on.

Her stomach was a nervous jumble as she stepped just beyond the checkpoint and scanned the station. No sight of a red dress. She looked back at the line of passengers waiting to make it through document check. François appeared pale, shifting from one foot to another and pressing one arm against the violin that hid beneath the folds of his coat. He loosened the scarf they'd wrapped around his neck to signify his inability to speak. This time they weren't going to risk anyone detecting the German in his accent.

After a few minutes, the gendarme let César move ahead. Then it was François's turn. Simone could barely breathe as the official conducted another measured examination of papers. She'd created his documents a few days earlier and had scuffed and dirtied them for a weathered look, but did they still appear too new?

The official looked at the papers and asked, "So François, how did you enjoy your train ride up?"

Simone froze. He wasn't supposed to speak. Would he blurt something out of nervousness?

César threaded his arm into François's and squeezed. "As you see, Sir, he has a war wound and can't speak. We're very proud of his courage."

Simone noticed François gather himself and stand taller as if he was a proud veteran. He looked directly into the official's eyes.

Just then a man behind them took off running past the gendarme, his footsteps slapping the pavement. The gendarme shouted, "Stop!" then shoved François's papers back into his hands and ran after the man. He blew his whistle and another official joined him in the chase. César grabbed Simone's hand and signaled to François to walk slowly and deliberately, eyes ahead.

"I wonder how Aunt Charlotte is doing. I certainly hope the house will be warm," César prattled on as they entered the station.

They stopped and looked around. No red dresses. François looked very confused—or was it worried?—as they crossed to the other side of the building. A path led from the station to a road, and César tipped his head for them to follow him. Maybe their contact had already been in the station and sensed danger. Maybe something didn't feel right, and she'd left, abandoning the plan. Simone began to sweat despite the cold.

François's eyes darted back and forth, but he kept pace with them. Simone locked her arm in his and said, "François, I'm sure you're looking forward to having a nice meal when we get to Aunt Charlotte's."

"Yes, of course," he managed to say, looking behind him. "It will be . . . so . . . so very good."

"Don't look back just . . ."

Just then a young woman with long chestnut hair and dark eyes appeared beside them—Simone had no idea where she came from. Her coat was open, and the red dress showed off her curvaceous body. "Aunt Charlotte is expecting you," she said with a smile. César and François's eyes lit up as men's do at the sight of a strikingly beautiful woman.

"Let's walk," the woman said. "It's only a mile to the house."

In silence, they walked briskly through streets flanked by small houses dimly lit in the dusk and then entered a wide-open landscape of foothills where trees cast deep indigo shadows. Then without slowing the pace, the woman said, "My name is Dina." François introduced the three of them. César added, "This is my old homeland, except a bit further south."

"So, you're Catalan. That's good for making conversation with the workers. Some vignerons will walk along with you on the first part of the climb." César began to ask a question, and Dina raised her hand to stop him. "I'll explain more once we're inside the house."

For another half hour or so, they plodded along a rocky pathway that Dina kept lit with a small torch. Finally, she stopped and shined the light on a set of steep stairs that led down to a small house tucked into the hill. A gentle amber glow shone behind the windows, and Simone could smell smoke from the chimney. They made their way slowly down the stairs to the house, and Dina opened the door to a kitchen where a pot of delicious-smelling soup bubbled on an old stove. On the walls of the small room just beyond the kitchen Simone saw paintings of a voluptuous young woman who looked very much like Dina.

"As you can see, I'm the model for the paintings by the artist Maillol," said Dina. "He's lived here for many years and doesn't approve of the current government, so he set up this safe house to help people escape over the mountain. And of course, I help."

César bowed and thanked her, and François kissed her cheeks. "We are deeply grateful," César said.

She smiled. "The soup is ready. After you eat, you should bed down on the pallets laid out in the back room. We're up at three in the morning."

Simone said, "I've heard of Maillol—he's also a sculptor, isn't he?"

"Yes, he's well-known for his sculptures of the female form."

François said, "How very kind of him to open his home to us. And of you to show us the way."

Dina smiled. "We believe very much in justice." Then she began to dish soup into bowls. "You'll leave well before dawn to reach a plateau a few hours away by daylight. You'll blend in with the vignerons for a while, then continue up the trail for a few hours to the border."

César said, "I imagine it's the Catalans who still work the vines here."

Dina nodded. "The old traditions still hold. It's French Catalonia on this side of the border. The split of Spanish and French Catalonia doesn't mean much to the people who live here."

César added, "History shapes us, but we're still part of the land that made us." Then he wrapped his arm around François. "But right now, my job is to make certain this fellow gets all the way to the top."

"That's a true friend! And will François be crossing the border on his own?" Dina set the bowls on the table and invited them all to sit down.

As they sat, Simone said, "Yes, do you think there will be German agents up there?"

"It's hard to predict what will happen on the trail. Keep your eyes open and speak as little as possible—and always in a hushed voice. Your guide will be Lisa. She'll arrive early in the morning and can give us a report of the latest sightings of police or agents up here. Sometimes there are none. Other times . . ." She didn't finish her sentence, only cleared her throat and said, "Let's hope it will be an uneventful climb."

They finished their soup in silence.

They set up their pallets, and François lay down. Simone tucked him in and kissed his forehead. It had been such a long day of travel and worry and tension, they were all exhausted. As they all lay side by side, she sensed that they each had things to say, but within minutes, François and César were snoring, and soon afterward Simone fell asleep.

The Mountain

Simone bolted awake and looked around, trying to get her bearings. César was already putting on his shoes. "The guide is here."

Today was the day.

She looked at Mr. Lieb's empty pallet. Her Mr. Lieb was leaving that day. She'd remember to call him "François" but in her heart he would always be Mr. Lieb. And today Mr. Lieb was going to climb a mountain and then cross international borders on his own. She caught her breath. "Where is he?"

"He's having coffee and flirting with the young women," César said with a sly smile.

Simone laughed. "That's a good sign. We need him feeling youthful."

They finished dressing and made their way toward the sound of voices and the aroma of coffee.

Dina was talking to a woman with an angular face and dark circles under her eyes. Her black hair was pulled back in a tight bun. Dina said, "Meet Lisa, your guide."

Mr. Lieb smiled. "Lisa knows the trail well."

Simone nodded at Lisa who was lacing up a pair of shoes with rope soles. "Nice to meet you. We're a bit nervous, to be honest."

Lisa finished tying her shoes and looked directly at Simone. "My husband and I have been guiding people up the mountain for months. Old, young—we've gotten dozens up and over."

Mr. Lieb took Simone's hand and held it up, showing off her inky fingers. "This young lady is one of the bravest people I know. She and César here forged papers for refugees in Paris, and now they continue their work in Marseille."

"Ah, then we are comrades," Lisa said and smiled at them.

Dina opened a chest by the doorway and produced several pairs of shoes like Lisa's. "Espadrilles. The workers in the vineyard wear them—keeps them steady on the slippery rocks. Put them on now."

They all pulled on the espadrilles for the climb, and Mr. Lieb tucked his own shoes into the pocket of his coat. His violin case hung by his side, attached to a shoulder strap, and when he put on his coat the instrument was hidden.

"They might let you through with that, they might not. Keep it hidden," Lisa warned. "Are we ready?"

They gathered at the door and finished pulling on coats, hats, and gloves. Dina handed them small bundles of bread and cheese, which they tucked into their pockets. Then the four of them walked out into the dark and headed toward the path that led to the base of the mountain. Dina waved as they went. "Bonne chance et bon voyage."

Simone waved and hoped her smile looked less forced than it felt. Lisa pointed ahead to the trail. The ground was damp, and the rocks glistened in the light of her torch. "We'll be on this trail for a long time, climbing gradually. We should meet up with the vignerons in about an hour, then we'll keep climbing and there will be a clearing. After that, seven pine trees. That's where the climb begins in earnest. You need to know that there will be less oxygen as we go higher. Keep your breathing even. We'll stop for water and rest. It needs to be a slow and steady climb."

Mr. Lieb walked behind Lisa, then César, and Simone brought up the rear. She looked back at the little house as they turned a curve and realized that in a few hours she and César would be back here, but without her Mr. Lieb. Her heart ached at the thought, but she repeated silently, *he will be free. He will be free.*

The foothills grew slightly steeper as they walked, and before long a dozen workers wearing heavy coats and carrying tools over their shoulders walked along with them. César spoke to them in Catalan. They responded briefly, and then the only sounds Simone could hear were the steady plodding of feet, the clanking of tools, and deep breathing as they all continued up the Pyrenees.

The sky was peppered with millions of stars and a tiny sliver of moon. Simone's eyes adjusted to the darkness as she inhaled the crispy cold air and the scent of earth and shrubs and trees. Dogs howled in the distance.

After what felt like a couple of hours, the sky began to lighten, and the wind picked up and whipped through the oak and maple trees that creaked and whined as they swayed back and forth. She guessed they were no more than a couple thousand feet up. If the wind was already pushing trees around at this elevation, what would they find once they reached four thousand feet? Even higher? Would a winter storm whip up and try to blow them off the side of the mountain?

She distracted herself by thinking about resilience—hers, Mr. Lieb's, César's. Between them, they'd been through countless storms, and still they were climbing. And then she remembered what Mr. Lieb had told her about his childhood walks through forests. He said the trees that survived the storms made the best violins.

The power of the mountain seemed to flow up through Joshua Lieb's feet and into his body. Strangely, after an hour of steady climbing, his legs moved more easily, as if his body was growing stronger. He was grateful for the vigorous routine René and César had put him through at the safe house. Perhaps his body was like a violin refurbished after an accident, rebuilt with tenderness and patience. He thought about how he'd repaired his violin after it was damaged at the book burning. He thought about the many times he'd brought wounded instruments back from the edge of ruin by attending to the seams, healing cracks in the wood, fitting a new bridge and strings. But he knew that the real cure for a broken violin was found in the arms of a musician. He wraps his body around it and warms the wood. The vibration of the strings resonates through the instrument, and the wood comes to life again. It is the meeting of the music's heart and the musician that makes the wood sing.

The mountain and the scent of the trees and earth and rain and rocks seemed to be giving him his health back. He pulled ahead to walk on his own, and with a raised eyebrow César let him go.

He was a survivor of the First World War, Nazi Germany, a grueling exodus from Paris, and was now an escapee from Les Milles. And here he was—less than two weeks after being broken out of what he thought might be the site of his grim deterioration and a grisly death—walking to the top of the world.

Hours passed as they strained and stretched for each rock and foothold, each next plateau where they could catch their breath. The muscles of Joshua's legs ached and burned, and he distracted himself from the pain by thinking about Simone and César. What a team they had become. He wanted to say so many things to them—fatherly things, words of advice and appreciation, warnings—but as they paused on an outcrop of rocks overlooking a valley, he stopped, waited for César, and simply said, "Thank you for saving us in Paris."

César patted his shoulder. "How could I not?"

"And the way you are with Simone—your skills, your inspiration. Your love . . ." He couldn't find words for all he felt César had given her, so his sentence trailed off. César wrapped his arms around him and held on for a long time. Simone joined them and they both squeezed him with loving hugs from both sides, holding him tight. He closed his eyes and tried to capture the moment, embedding it into his sense memory so he'd never forget it.

A boom of thunder made Joshua jump and Simone yelp, then she clapped her hand over her mouth. Seconds later, a bolt of lightning struck a tree on a nearby peak, sending sparks flying. Then came the torrents of rain and a wild wind that whipped icy shards of rain into their faces. Despite starting to feel numb with cold, Joshua felt gloriously alive. He took deep, greedy breaths of the magnificently clean mountain air and turned his face to the sky, welcoming the wash of rain.

Lisa rushed them to an overhang where they huddled together, steam from their breath circling in clouds around their heads. Joshua took off his glasses and tucked them in his pocket, resting as he looked out at the now blurry pine trees and teeming rain. But the longer he stood immobile, the heavier he began to feel, as if by stopping he'd allowed the strength to drain from him. He bent over, taking even breaths with his eyes closed, imagining propelling himself up the mountain by sheer willpower. Then he remembered his youth, when climbing had been so easy and the thrill of seeing the world from on high was always exhilarating.

He stood up straight again and shook out his legs. César rested a hand on his shoulder and squeezed. It was like a message to keep going—one rock, one foothold at a time.

In the rain and wind, César heard the mountain sing an old Catalan song, repeating verses like the switchbacks that circled round and round the craggy earth. In rhythms of timeless time, it sang to César of his people who'd inhabited this place, ancestors joined by land and food and customs and the cycles of birth and death. It sang to him of ancestors who had fought for freedom, even as it was stripped from them again and again.

While the others were resting, César stepped away and bent down to scoop a handful of gritty dirt into his mouth, tasting the soil, the minerals—swirling the earth in his mouth before spitting it to the ground. He stood up and inhaled the sharp wind, welcoming the way it cut his lungs. He was part of the mountain. He wanted to feel everything. Taste everything. He was home.

Simone slipped on the slick rocks and panicked as her feet skidded out from under her. Suddenly she was on all fours, sharp pebbles grinding into her knees and palms. César reached for her and hauled her up then let go after she regained her balance. She brushed herself off and took a few tentative steps forward, with each stride willing the pain away.

Lisa stopped and referred to the map. "We carefully pick our way up now, rock by rock. It's steeper through here," she said, pointing out a jagged line that looked to Simone like every other jagged line on the map. Then she led them through switchbacks and over slippery stones to a wider part of the trail. Along the way, each of them slipped once or twice, and they all stopped to offer the other a hand. Rivulets of water and mud flowed into rock crevices, and miniature waterfalls splashed from above. The journey was as beautiful as it was dangerous.

The rain eventually stopped, and they continued the climb through a thick mist topped by a blanket of clouds. Then for a moment, the clouds parted, and as if by magic, an expanse of landscape appeared below them—an endless mural of greens and browns and slate gray. Mr. Lieb, Simone, and César let out cries of pleasure as they took in the majesty of the landscape below. Then as quickly as the clouds had parted, they folded back into a gray mist.

After a few minutes, the wind calmed, and Lisa stood up. "We must press on—it's getting late."

For another two hours, they moved in single file, hands on each other's shoulders and heads down as they carefully chose each step up the trail. Then Lisa pointed toward a misty area just beyond a stretch of steep incline. "The border is just up there."

At the sound of that announcement, Simone and César shared a glance that at once seemed warm, frightened, and excited. The trail straightened, and Lisa pressed a finger to her lips, then signaled for them to stop. Simone could hear men's voices not far away. Lisa sniffed the air, and Simone copied her. The smell of tobacco. Was a border patrol just ahead? Germans? Had they been spotted?

Mr. Lieb's eyes grew large behind his glasses. Lisa held up a hand to make clear that no one should move, and with her other hand, she cupped her ear. Simone's heart thundered. Was a patrol waiting just above them?

After a few minutes frozen in place, they heard footsteps on the rocks above them and the sound of laughter. A cigarette stub fell to the ground near them.

They all stood motionless and silent. Simone could hear the creak of her knees. She held her breath. Then she heard the sound of boots moving away, men's voices growing fainter. Lisa kept her hand up—wait. A few more minutes ticked by.

Finally, Lisa waved for them to continue, and for several minutes, Simone vibrated with alertness, tilting her head right and left to listen for voices, shifting her eyes in all directions to watch for movement in the trees, sniffing for cigarette smoke.

Lisa stopped and gestured to a trail below them, whispering, "The old Lister route is just below us. It's the smuggler's route—an ancient pathway. French patrols monitor it. And the Spanish. We mustn't speak. The border isn't far now."

The border. The end. The idea of it pressed like a knife against Simone's ribs.

Gusting winds kicked up again like live creatures, making it nearly impossible to stand upright, so they huddled together in a cave that seemed to have been carved into the rocks by eons of rain and snow and wind. Pine branches sang and creaked. Mr. Lieb laughed. "It's like a symphony up here."

Lisa guided them out of the cave, and for a few more minutes they all continued to climb. Then Simone heard César gasp. She lifted her head and saw that they'd reached the top of the mountain. Far below through the mist she could see the wild Mediterranean Sea on one side, its swells surging in the winter storm. On the other, an endless blue-gray blur. Somewhere across that expanse was England. Simone stood between César and Mr. Lieb as they marveled at their success. No one spoke. The victory of the climb hung in the air.

But this was it. It was time. This was where they would part. This was goodbye to her Papa, her Mr. Lieb, here, on the top of this mountain. How could she say goodbye to him? How could she let him go?

Her throat clenched as she watched César and Mr. Lieb shake hands, then clap their arms around each other in a long, tight embrace. Then Mr. Lieb turned to Simone, tears in his eyes, his face pinched in pain as he shook his head slowly from side to side. She couldn't speak, so she threw her arms around him and cried into the rough fabric of his coat.

He said, "Remember where you came from. Remember who we are. Au revoir, dear Sarah."

"Oh, Mr. Lieb. You're *my* Mr. Lieb."

He pressed a kiss on her forehead.

Lisa cleared her throat. "You need to go. Here are your papers . . ."

Mr. Lieb gently lifted Simone's arms from around his neck then stood beside her with a strong arm wrapped around her shoulders as Lisa continued to give instructions. "These are your Portuguese and Spanish transit papers. Your passport. Now, look ahead. Take that flat path there, and where it forks, go right. *Don't* go left. Then in a few moments beyond, you'll be in Spain. At the border crossing show the guards your transit visa and all your papers and get your entrada stamp. Then it's a short hike down to Portbou." She patted him on the shoulder. "Take the train to Madrid, then on to Lisbon. Your ship from Lisbon to England sails in two days. Be there!" She kissed both his cheeks.

The wind blew a ragged opening in the clouds. Mr. Lieb turned to face Simone just as a stream of sunshine illuminated the silver in his hair and the sparkle in his blue eyes. He smiled and winked as he opened his coat to flash her a view of the violin case. She let out a quick breath of a laugh. It was deeply comforting that he would continue the journey with his wonderful violin by his side.

They all stood together, then César broke the silence. "Au revoir. Take care."

Simone could summon only fragmented thoughts for this last moment with the man she'd known all her life. Why hadn't she prepared better for this farewell?

"Au revoir," she finally said with a broad smile, flicking a strand of hair from her face. "À bientôt. Be safe. Send news. And play your violin for me."

Then her dear Mr. Lieb flashed a smile and began to walk down the path to Spain. And just when he was almost out of sight, he held his hand high with a thumbs up.

Lisa said, "He's stronger than I thought." Then she clapped her gloved hands together. "Come now—the train from Banyuls to Marseille leaves in four hours." And she turned to head back down the mountain.

Icy wind blew Simone's hair around her face as she and César stood at the border between France and Spain. She looked up at his strong profile as he surveyed the view below them. He looked so natural up here, so much a part of the Pyrenees with his weathered skin and the dark eyes of his ancestors. Simone let the moment seep into her soul, leaning against him as they stood and watched the trees sway to the rhythm of the mountain's ancient song.

After several quiet minutes, César took her hand in his, and they began their descent.

December in Marseille

Christmas carols were playing in the distance at the cafés by the port, but the sounds at 60 Rue Grignon were frantic as ever as Simone shuffled through her documents. Members of Fry's team hustled from room to room, and typewriters clacked as people who'd lined up for interviews whispered and murmured to each other, their eyes wild with anticipation and fear and hope. Some would get out over the Pyrenees, others would sail to Cuba or Casablanca or South America. The lucky ones boarded ships bound for America.

The hallway smelled like cigarettes and unwashed bodies, but Simone breathed freely in this place, knowing how much her work mattered. She'd spent the morning interviewing new clients, writing down information for their papers, choosing names and birthplaces for their new lives. She and her coworkers did their work fast against the equally determined Vichy officials who were quick to arrest, detain, and imprison. It was *us against them*, and every day she suited up, a steely-eyed warrior in the battle against evil.

She pushed back from her desk and straightened the documents she'd completed that morning, then lined up her pens in a row and placed all the stamps back in their box.

There was a knock on her door, and Varian Fry burst in. He was always quick, always scurrying from somewhere to somewhere else. With a crooked smile he waved a sheaf of documents. "These need to be done today."

Simone let out a heavy sigh.

Fry smiled. "It's not as if I'm asking in the middle of the night." Then with theatrical flourish, he dropped a manila envelope on her desk. "Correspondence through official channels."

She grabbed the envelope and tore it open, her hands shaking as she held a thin piece of paper in her hands and read the single sentence written in a script she knew so very well.

The violins are playing in London.

She burst into tears and clapped her hand over her mouth.

Fry winked and closed the door.

"Thank you!" she managed to shout after him. She couldn't wait to tell César about Mr. Lieb's message.

Simone never did find out if Fry had been at the heart of the rescue from Les Milles, but her intuition told her he'd been involved. When she returned from the Pyrenees, he'd asked her to continue to help him as a forger. His focus on saving people was absolute, and she vowed to be one of his tireless soldiers.

Flipping through the documents on her desk she took a moment to study each photograph. So many hopeful people. So many desperate, innocent, terrified people whose lives might be determined by the quality of their papers. When she reached the end of the pile, she felt a burst of adrenaline as she paused on the photo of a beautiful dark-eyed woman. Her name was Marguerite

Nelson, but Simone would know that face anywhere. It was only a photo, but it was as if this smiling Sophia could see right back into her own eyes.

Holding her pen steady and with firm strokes, Simone began to fill in the documents.

As she wrote, she remembered Sophia's words about the power of art, that art offers hope. *Yes*, she thought, *art itself is hope*. Like the violins in London.

Epilogue

Sophia's art graced the walls of Peggy Guggenheim's new museum in New York City, as would the works of other artists Varian Fry and his team helped save from Hitler's malignant stampede across Europe. André Breton, Jacqueline Lamba, Jacques Lipchitz, Marc Chagall, and Max Ernst were only some of the of brave visionaries whose light the dark forces of Vichy France and the German Reich tried but failed to extinguish. In August 1941, Varian Fry was arrested by the French police and escorted to the Spanish border. This event marked the end of his rescue efforts in France, but by then he'd saved between two and four thousand people.

Acknowledgments

I owe a big thank you to my travel partner Daniella Hoffman who four years ago in France helped me get the feel of the story in my bones. In Marseille and at the border between France and Spain, we walked in the steps of those who lived this story.

All writers deserve a tribe, and I've been blessed to be part of a magical one for over twenty years. We call ourselves "the Bellas," and—both in person and on Zoom—we hold each other accountable, offer encouragement, and celebrate our writing successes, great and small. Thank you Christie Nelson, Amy Peele, Hollye Dexter, and Betsy Fasbinder for your love, support, nudging, and belief in this book and in me for all these years.

I couldn't be where I am without the tremendous support of my mentors Brooke Warner and Sands Hall who have taught me about everything from writing beautiful sentences to creating stories that matter. Sands was by my side during this story's rough, raw beginnings, and she helped me to find my way to new drafts. Brand new to fiction writing, I kept asking her, "How do you know what to make up?" She assured me that it would all evolve. To keep writing into my imagination. As a memoir writer, I was accustomed to sticking to truths I'd lived, and I thank Sands for helping me see how to stay true to history while creating a living fictional world.

A special thank you goes to my amazing editor Jodi Fodor. She taught me about the "fiction" part of historical fiction and pushed me to create tension and not let my characters (or my readers) off the hook. As a therapist for forty years, I kept wanting to soothe them! I feel as if I've just taken a master class in fiction writing, and I'm more than grateful. She put in the footwork too, editing my book on planes, trains, and automobiles to meet the deadline!

I'm particularly grateful to my final editor, Anne Durette. She brought her expertise about France and the French language to the project and helped to create an accurate portrait of the era. I appreciate how she caught any loose ends that would distract the reader from being fully immersed in the story and the era. Merci beaucoup!

During my most recent trip to France, I was lucky and blessed to meet Hanna Diamond, author of *Fleeing Hitler: France 1940*. The new Resistance and Liberation Museum had just opened in Paris, and she curated its special exhibit on the exodus. Over a cappuccino, we geeked out over the stories and histories that fascinate us both. Hanna, thank you for being so generous with tips and corrections as I worked on this novel. Most of all, thank you for believing my story would come to life! Also, that October in Paris, readers at The Red Wheelbarrow bookstore heard my research story and cheered me on to write it.

At She Writes Press, publisher Brooke Warner has created a community that invites and encourages women of any age to flower into the creativity that exists in their souls. For over fifteen years, Brooke has been cheering me on, and I'm deeply grateful for her support of my ideas and my books. Brooke and her staff at She Writes Press all have helped me to create a book I can champion. Julie Metz—Thank you for your fantastic cover!

And there's the whole She Writes Press community—we show up for each other and celebrate the creativity of women of all ages!

Much gratitude to my early readers—Peter Verburgh, Gabrielle Robinson, Hollye Dexter, and Betsy Fasbinder. You helped me to see the book through new eyes. I also want to thank James Fry, Varian Fry's son, for allowing me to quote from his father's book, and Neil Kaplan for giving me permission to use an image from his website ourpassports.com.

Finally, I want to thank Marlina, the proprietor of The Grape Nest in Point Richmond, California, who for over a year has introduced me to wonderful wines from all over the world as she's listened to the day-to-day saga of my researching, writing, and revising of the novel. Thank you for being a tireless champion of creativity and for making me your "Grape Nest Author." Let's raise a glass to all the arts you support!

About the Author

*L*inda Joy Myers has always been fascinated by the power of the past to affect people in the stream of time. She learned about World War II thanks to her grandmother, a passionate Anglophile who would rhapsodize about the unfairness of war, and when Linda Joy was thirteen, she and her grandmother watched stark black and white war documentaries together. This shared interest became the seed of a passion for history that Linda Joy went on to integrate into her own struggles with intergenerational trauma and work as a therapist and a writer.

The Forger of Marseille is inspired by Varian Fry's memoir *Surrender on Demand* and Donald Caskie's *The Tartan Pimpernel*, two books Myers discovered as she researched the history of Vichy France and its role in WWII. These and other memoirs inspired her to call deserved attention to the daunting courage of the many people who risked everything to save the lives of thousands of refugees, British soldiers, and other lost souls during the chaotic and cruel outbreak of the war in France.

Founder of the National Association of Memoir Writers, Linda Joy is the author of four books on memoir writing. *The Power of Memoir* and *Journey of Memoir* help writers to write their healing stories and publish their books. Her two memoirs *Don't Call Me Mother* and *Song of the Plains* won the Bay Area Publishing Association Gold Medal award and the 2018 Next Generation Indie Book award, respectively.

When Linda Joy isn't writing or editing, she travels, tends thirty rose bushes, and develops her extensive garden. When she is, her two kitties, Harvey, a Maine Coon, and Charlie, a Norwegian Forest cat, like to sit on her desk and dangle their paws over the keys. Her children and grandchildren have learned more WWII history than most, and she writes about history with future generations in mind.

You can find Linda Joy's memoir classes at www.namw.org and www.writeyourmemoirinsixmonths.com More information about *The Forger of Marseille* and the history surrounding the book is here: https://theforgerofmarseille.com.

Author photo © Reenie Raschke

$\mathscr{A}$uthor's $\mathscr{N}$ote

$\mathcal{J}$ he spark to write this book began when I was introduced to Varian Fry in the book *Villa Air-Bel: World War II, Escape, and a House in Marseille* by Rosemary Sullivan, but it was Fry's memoir *Surrender on Demand* that grabbed my heart and never let go.

Fry was a journalist in New York who represented the Emergency Rescue Committee that wanted to help writers, Jews, artists, and anti-Nazis whose lives were in danger when France fell. Fry arrived in Marseille with a list and three thousand dollars taped to his leg. The story of camps, thousands of people lost and desperate in Marseille, and the brutality of the collaborationist regime gripped me from the beginning, but it took several years to find my way to *The Forger of Marseille*.

A voice held me back: *I'm a memoirist. What do I know of making things up? Besides, French history and the resistance are so complicated, it would be difficult to get them right.* But I kept reading, and the history of that era haunted my dreams.

Piles of history books and memoirs stacked up in my living room as I dived into what a friend called "research rapture." France in that era *was* complicated, and eighty years later the loyalties and betrayals hadn't been resolved. Who was to blame for the fall of France? Or for the exodus in June of 1940 of millions who tried to escape the German blitz? Who was to blame for the fate of the immigrants and the Jews who had to try to escape the Vichy police and Gestapo in the unoccupied zone, also known as Vichy. Vichy was a collaborationist government set up by Pétain, a World War I hero, and his henchmen. Within three months after the war's end, Vichy had created laws and traps for innocent people that perfectly mirrored Germany.

I'd been reading about WWII for the last sixty years. I grew up with a grandmother who was passionate about English history and the history of the war. When it came to Churchill and the Brits after the fall of France, she'd pace the room, crying, "England stood alone! We should have helped them!" Years later I discovered that she'd traveled by ship five times by herself to visit England and Scotland. Her love of England gave her a personal view of Great Britain, and her emotions fed my interest in the history of WWII.

My research about the war began in earnest when I found a *Time* magazine with Hitler's picture on the cover as 1938 Man of the Year written in the "now" of 1938. I had to know how he had become the Führer and why people believed in him and did his bidding. William L. Shirer's *The Rise and Fall of the Third Reich: A History of Nazi Germany* began to answer those questions and led me on a quest to read everything I could. So much background reading about the Reich, World War I, and the Spanish Civil War gave me a decent foundation from which to imagine and create characters who found their way to my story. Two characters were German Jews who lived in the shadowed, dangerous world of the Reich. A third character came to me on top of the Pyrenees and whispered in my ear. That story you will find on my website.

While most of my characters are fictional—yes, I'm a memoirist who had to learn how to make things up!—there were several significant people who risked their lives to save people besides Varian Fry. As I did with Varian Fry, I learned about them through their memoirs. Donald Caskie was a Scottish pastor who risked his life to set up a mission in Marseille to save soldiers—becoming part of the early resistance against Vichy and the Germans. And Lisa Fittko. As a Jew and anti-Nazi, she and her husband had fled for safety to Paris, but in 1939 when the war began, the French police rounded them up with other Germans, Czechs, and Austrians and sent them to an internment camp in the south. After escaping, she became one of the guides who led people over the Pyrenees into Spain.

Dina Vierny: I discovered her when I visited the village of Banyuls-sur-Mer where the French sculptor and painter Aristide Maillol's safe house is now a museum. She was his favorite model and they both engaged in offering help to the refugees. Later she was arrested for her resistance activities, as was Donald Caskie.

I wanted to bring into real life the extreme courage and bravery it took for people to decide to resist the government, the police, and the Nazi rulers to save people's lives. It was a death sentence if caught; a noose image posted on trees in Marseille warned of the likely fate for those who tried to help.

The theme of identity—who am I, how do I know who I am, even if my name is changed, is a thread in the book. Who am I without a home, a family, a country? These questions haunted millions of refugees during that era.

George Santayana's quote, "Those who cannot remember the past are condemned to repeat it," has always whispered in my ear. As a memoirist and therapist for forty years, I have seen transformation as the past is revealed and healed. Literature invites us to live through the experience of others and find in their story the wisdom that enlarges our own lives.

The story of war, refugees, and how to survive as normal life is upended is much larger and more complex than one novel can encompass. Each character in my book became a guide for me to imagine how it would be to find enough courage. They pressed their hearts toward compassion for others at great risk to themselves. My hope is that people will become curious about this history and want to read more.

Please visit my website: http://theforgerofmarseille.com. A bibliography and links to information about the era and the people offer more insights into the significant history that inspired this book.

Selected Titles From She Writes Press

She Writes Press is an independent publishing
company founded to serve women writers everywhere.
Visit us at www.shewritespress.com.

A Ritchie Boy by Linda Kass. $16.95, 978-1-63152-739-5. The true, inspiring World War II tale of Eli Stoff, a Jewish Austrian immigrant who triumphs over adversity and becomes a US Army intelligence officer, told as a cohesive linked collection of stories narrated by a variety of characters.

Don't Put the Boats Away by Ames Sheldon. $16.95, 978-1-63152-602-2. In the aftermath of World War II, the members of the Sutton family are reeling from the death of their "golden boy," Eddie. Over the next twenty-five years, they all struggle with loss, grief, and mourning—and pay high prices, including divorce and alcoholism.

Shanghai Love by Layne Wong. $16.95, 978-1-93831-418-6. The enthralling story of an unlikely romance between a Chinese herbalist and a Jewish refugee in Shanghai during World War II.

When It's Over by Barbara Ridley. $16.95, 978-1-63152-296-3. When World War II envelopes Europe, Lena Kulkova flees Czechoslovakia for the relative safety of England, leaving her Jewish family behind in Prague.

This Is How It Begins by Joan Dempsey. $16.95, 978-1-63152-308-3. When eighty-five-year-old art professor Ludka Zeilonka's gay grandson, Tommy, is fired over concerns that he's silencing Christian kids in the classroom, she is drawn into the political firestorm—and as both sides battle to preserve their respective rights to free speech, the hatred on display raises the specter of her WWII past.

Portrait of a Woman in White by Susan Winkler. $16.95, 978-1-93831-483-4. When the Nazis steal a Matisse portrait from the eccentric, art-loving Rosenswigs, the Parisian family is thrust into the tumult of war and separation, their fates intertwined with that of their beloved portrait.